Montana Homecoming

Montana Homecoming

Kathleen O'Brien
Dani Collins
Eve Gaddy
Terri Reed
Roxanne Snopek

TULE
PUBLISHING

Contents

Long Way Home

A Montana Homecoming Story

Kathleen O'Brien

Dedication

To Nancy and Lori, who never let me down

Dear Reader,

Home means so many different things to different people, doesn't it? It can be the place you come from, or the brand new sanctuary you bravely carve for yourself out in the big, bad world. Sometimes it's not a place at all, but a person—the one broke your heart-, or the one who pieces it together again.

For Abby Foster, home used to mean Marietta, Montana. It used to mean her father, and their beautiful family ranch. Most of all, it meant Joe Carlyle, the wild, sweet boy who was her first and only love.

Then Abby made a terrible mistake, and as a result she ended up exiled from everything that ever mattered. Eight long years later, she returns for Marietta High's Homecoming Weekend, though she's not sure why. Her father's gone. The ranch is sold. And Joe will probably never forgive her for what she did to him back then.

But the pull is too strong to resist.

And that's the miracle of Home. It's the place that calls to our soul, and when we answer, it accepts us as we are. It's the people who love us, warts and all, and always stand ready to rescue us from ourselves.

I hope you enjoy reading Abby and Joe's story as much as I loved writing it. And I hope that, wherever you find yourself today, it feels a lot like Home.

Warmly,
Kathleen

Chapter One

ℰᏜᏟᎡ

"I DIDN'T CHOOSE to fall in love with Joe, Charlie. And if I knew how, I'd stop loving him right this minute. I swear I would." Abby Foster sat slumped inside a jumble of blankets on the floor of her darkened bedroom. She rubbed her small horseshoe charm necklace with one hand and with the other she squeezed a pillow against her stomach.

From her perch across the room on the window seat, Charlie didn't answer. But Abby imagined she heard skepticism in her friend's stony silence.

"It's true, Charlie! I *want* to stop. I know it's the right thing. For my dad, for me...and probably even for Joe. *He* doesn't love *me* anymore He made it clear he wouldn't take me back now, even if I asked him to."

She squeezed her eyes shut and bowed her head, remembering how furious Joe had been, the last time she saw him. The names he had called her...

She whimpered softly, lifting the pillow to muffle the sound. "But how do you stop loving someone, Charlie? *How?*"

Still no response. Abby wasn't surprised. There was nothing to say that hadn't already been said a hundred times. No one had the answer, not even wise Charlotte Morgan, Abby's best friend, and the most sensible person she knew.

Because there *was* no answer. There was no hope. Abby was trapped. She couldn't stop loving Joe, and, when the morning came, she couldn't escape marrying Blaine Watts.

Just a few hours left…

She glanced at her wedding dress, hung over her closet door to "fluff out," as the maid called it. In the daylight, it had seemed beautiful, even to Abby, whose emotions were so mixed. But tonight its pearls and sequins played tricks with the moonlight and shadows. It might have been a ghost pinned there, restlessly glimmering.

Was it really possible that, in the morning, she'd put on that dress, walk out onto the lawn, and in front of two hundred strangers become Mrs. Blaine Watts? If she did, happy Abby Foster, the spoiled little rich girl who had fallen in love with wild Joe Carlyle, would disappear forever.

Happy Abby Foster would become the ghost.

But the ghost of Abby's happiness wouldn't haunt this bedroom. More likely, people would report seeing her floating around the old swayback Carlyle outbuilding, where she and Joe made love the very first time.

And the very last time.

Despair washed over her again, like storm waves pummeling the shore. She felt bruised on the inside, wet and eroded.

"*How?*" she repeated in a whisper. Then she cried for a little while. Softly. The loud, hiccupping sobs had worn themselves out at least an hour ago, when the effects of the Kahlua, which she'd smuggled upstairs to help numb the pain, had kicked in.

Time drifted, marked only by an occasional sniffle, or a fresh seeping of tears. Eventually, though, the unnatural silence from the other side of the room began to register. She let go of her necklace, and she lifted her head.

"Charlie?" She squinted toward the arched windows, where Charlie sat in a beam of blue moonlight. No response. Suddenly, Abby couldn't even remember when Charlie had last murmured so much as an "um-humh" to anything she'd said.

"Charlie, are you awake?"

Nothing. Abby dropped her pillow, unwound herself from the blankets, and walked across the room, her bare feet making no noise on the thick carpet.

When she got close enough, she had her answer. Charlie was dead asleep, her face pale, with shadows under her eyes. She was still propped upright, with her willowy, beauty-queen legs stretched along the cushioned seat, but her mouth was open, her head tilted awkwardly toward her shoulder.

Her notepad had tumbled to the carpet, and her right hand dangled beside it. Somehow, the ballpoint pen still rested in the limp crook of her fingers.

Aw...poor Charlie.

Abby glanced toward the fireplace, where her mother's gilt-and-white Limoges clock had stood as long as Abby had been alive. Stephanie Foster hadn't needed it...she'd died while Abby was being born.

To Abby's surprise, it was already two a.m.

A sliver of shame pierced her fog of self-pity. Charlie was such a good friend. She'd agreed to spend this awful night here, though she must have guessed Abby wouldn't sleep. She'd shared the Kahlua, though she didn't like it much. She'd listened without judging...and she'd even agreed to help make this list of the arguments for and against the wedding.

Abby bent down and scooped up the notebook. Across the top, in her firm handwriting, Charlie had written *Marrying Blaine Watts.* Below that, she'd created two columns, labeled *Pros* and *Cons.*

Even from a distance, you could see how lopsided the debate was. Charlie had taken faithful dictation, copying down every word Abby said, without even changing the pronouns.

The *Pros* side was long.

1. *Blaine's a real grown-up. And successful. I'd be secure for life.*

2. *He loves me.*

3. *He's very attractive.*

4. *Dad says this is the kind of marriage my mother dreamed of for me.*

5. *Dad needs to know I'm taken care of, especially since the cancer.*

6. *I've spent so much money on the wedding.*

7. *All those people are coming from everywhere, all his bigwig friends. How embarrassing for him if I called it off.*

8. *I gave my word to Dad.*

9. *I gave my word to Blaine.*

Abby frowned at it. The list was pretty compelling, here in black and white. All those great reasons to go through with it.

And on the *Cons* side, just one entry.

1. *I still love Joe.*

She stared at those four words a long time. The sentence looked so small. Insignificant …maybe even selfish…next to the nine big, righteous reasons in the other column.

But so what? She had a sudden urge to rip the notebook to shreds. The list had been a stupid, stupid idea. No one could make a decision this important with a *list*. Love wasn't measured in words and ink. Happiness couldn't be predicted by its weight on a scale, like fish at the grocery store.

But then, in this tug of war between her heart and her brain, the brain side of the argument gave a sharp yank.

Be honest with yourself, Abby. The decision's already made.

She'd come too far to turn back—and where would she go, anyhow? Joe had said he never wanted to see her again. And her father was dying, so the perfect harbor she'd known all her life was smashed. She was in the middle of the ocean, with no land in sight. She didn't have the courage to overturn the boat now.

As someone once said, *when you're going through hell, keep going.*

She glanced through the window at the white party tents below, already erected in the backyard, waiting for the ten thousand white Dutch roses that would arrive by jet at dawn.

Number Six. She'd spent so much money…

When she'd finally said yes to Blaine—after weeks of ugly scenes with Joe that always ended with him calling her a snob, or a spoiled coward—she'd started planning the wedding. In spite of the rush, she'd insisted on the best of everything. She'd felt like she deserved it, if only for being the obedient daughter and choosing the "sensible" life path.

So she'd asked for the dream dress, which cost more than most people made in a year. The diamond the size of a boat anchor. The cake that rose nine tiers, the bridal march played by a string quartet, the honeymoon in Greece, the trousseau fit for a queen.

Her father had paid even the most outrageous bills without complaint, just as Blaine had done with the solitaire and the cruise. Both men had actually seemed amused, as if her extravagance proved her excellent taste, and her worth as a trophy wife and daughter.

Joe, however, had recognized the reckless spending for exactly what it was—a bribe from the men. A bribe Abby had accepted out of a deadly mix of despair, anger, and maybe a little revenge.

He hadn't cared whether calling it a bribe insulted her. Joe had always been a straight talker, and he didn't mince words about this, either.

Just three days ago, when Abby and Blaine were picking out chocolates from Sage Carrigan's store to add to the dessert buffet, Joe had spotted them. Impulsively, he'd stormed into the shop and barreled right up to Blaine. Two of his brothers raced in after him, but they were too late. Joe already had shoved the heels of his hands into Blaine's broad chest.

"You pathetic pile of horse manure," Joe said in a hard voice, so loud everyone in the store could hear. "Do you think she's a *whore*? Do you think you can *buy* her?"

Devlin, four years older than Joe, caught Joe's right arm. Rafe, who was only ten, caught the other arm, but Devlin obviously was doing all the work.

"Shut up, Joe," Devlin said, his voice low and steady, though the glare he shot toward Blaine was every bit as poisonous as Joe's. "Let's just get out of here."

Joe didn't even seem to notice he'd been pinned. He was still lunging forward. "I asked you a question, you useless stuffed shirt. You think you can *buy* her?"

Blaine's answering smile was contemptuous, as if Joe were just a gnat at his picnic, easily disposed of with one carefully placed thumb.

He chuckled. "I don't have to buy my women, son. But apparently you do. And this one, unfortunately, has just been priced out of your reach."

Joe surged forward on such a powerful fury that even Devlin could hardly control him. But somehow he held on and kept Joe from launching himself at Blaine like a torpedo. Abby recoiled, honestly believing, in that moment, that the boy she loved, who was so gentle with his family's horses, his over-worked mother, his pesky little brother, could have done real violence.

Even then, Blaine remained unfazed. Still smiling, he watched Joe wrestling against Devlin's hold the same way he might watch a bug squirming on a pin.

Abby's cheeks grew hot, embarrassed for Joe, and for herself. It was such a hopeless mismatch.

On one side, there was Blaine. A muscular former athlete, a millionaire at almost thirty, he was sublimely confident—of his money, his physical power, his two-hundred-dollar haircut, and, most of all, his claim on Abby. Joe might still be fighting this war, but for Blaine it was already over. He'd already won, and he'd chained his gaudy rock around Abby's finger to prove it.

On the other side, there was Joe. Only seventeen—a full year younger even than Abby, who had turned eighteen last week. Skinny, eternally underfed and wiry from working long hours with the horses.

He was dressed in the same black t-shirt and faded blue jeans he wore every day, the little rips stitched in irregular lumps by his own clumsy hands so he wouldn't add to his mother's burden. His glossy dark hair, already a month or two past needing a trim, tumbled over his forehead in messy waves. It stuck to his neck with bits of grass and mud.

Of course Joe had already lost. He'd never had a chance. The minute it became clear Blaine wanted Abby, everybody had advised Joe to back off gracefully. His mom, all three of his brothers, Abby's father, Principal Stern, and even Reverend Davis from St. James. *Everybody.*

They told him he wasn't ready to get serious about any girl. He was still a minor, still in high school, still flunking history. Why, just this past summer, he and his brothers had been arrested for letting cows loose in the computer lab at the high school.

He was a fool to imagine he could take on a wife. And he was a *selfish* fool if he asked Abby to wait for him, especially if it meant she'd have to give up a catch like Blaine Watts.

Behind her, Abby heard one of the chocolate store's customers snicker. And then a woman said, in a stage whisper, "One of the crazy Carlyle boys, I assume?"

The crazy Carlyle boys....

At that moment, Abby had hated Joe. Hated him for being so young, so poor. For being so hot-tempered and easily provoked. For not being able to beat Blaine without beating him up.

She'd hated him for having inherited the wild streak everyone in Marietta called "the Carlyle crazies." All the boys had gone through it, people said, though luckily the oldest two had seemed to have come out the other side okay.

Most of all, she hated him for proving everyone right—for proving that he wasn't ready to be trusted with her future.

Pushing the memory aside now, she let the notebook fall back to the carpet and pressed her fist against her heart, which pounded painfully. Hated him? Yes. She had. But even in that moment, she'd loved him, too.

She'd loved him then, and she loved him now. Her dad could call it "a hormonal haze," but she knew she'd still love Joe tomorrow morning, when she put on that white lace gown.

And she'd still love him tomorrow night, when she was alone with her new husband, when Blaine started unbuttoning those pearls, and peeling away the lace, and putting his hands on her bare flesh.

Goose bumps ran across her shoulders. The Kahlua rose in her throat. *No. No.* She couldn't let Blaine....she just couldn't...

"*Oh, God, Charlie,*" she whispered through her raw throat. "What am I going to—"

But then she closed her lips, forcing back any more sounds. How selfish was she willing to be? Charlie was exhausted and needed sleep.

Besides, the only person who could end this nightmare was Abby herself.

It wasn't too late. In the war between her brain and her heart, there was still time for her heart to pull off a surprise victory. She still had more than eight hours. She caught a glimpse of herself in her cheval glass. All she needed was courage. Surely somewhere underneath this pampered princess froth, she had a little of that?

Time to find out.

She touched her horseshoe necklace again, as if for luck. She would go to her father right now, and she would kneel beside him, and she'd make him understand. Surely, surely, he could see the truth. He loved her. Everyone called Markham Foster ruthless, and cold, and a beast of a businessman. But no one ever said he didn't love his only daughter.

She dragged on her robe and made her way to the door, careful not to step on any of the debris she and Charlie had scattered around the room through the long night.

She flew down the hall. She rapped softly on his door and whispered. "Daddy?"

No answer. She cracked the door. Her father wasn't in his room.

Her heart sank. Was he still downstairs, talking to his friends? Four other guests were bunking at the ranch tonight, people who had arrived from other states on early planes. A congressman from California, a hot-shot cattleman from Colorado, a woman who owned a meat processing plant in Texas, and Abby's mother's only living relative, an elderly distant cousin named Gerty.

Except for Gerty, Abby didn't know any of them. In fact, of the two hundred people expected for the wedding, she'd met only twenty-five or so.

Oddly, that thought gave her an extra shot of courage. She didn't know them, so why should she care what they thought? Sure, they'd gossip, but her dumb little soap opera couldn't hold the interest of a California congressman for long.

She descended the central staircase slowly, still careful to make no sound. When she reached the first floor, everything was in darkness, except for the moonlight coming through the fanlight over the door, and a bronze glow emanating from the library.

Maybe her father had fallen asleep in there, reading. Since he got sick, he seemed to drop off in odd places. He slept in chairs as often as he slept in bed. Still, she approached the room quietly, in case he wasn't alone.

The door stood ajar. Just as she put her hand on the knob, her father spoke. She let go, startled.

"You know, Gerty, sometimes I still talk to Stephanie," he said in an odd voice. Was he just tired? Or had he been drinking? The *s*'s were a bit slurred. But, as far as Abby knew, he hadn't had a single drink since the diagnosis six months ago.

"Well, of course you talk to her, Mark." The old woman's crisp, no-nonsense tones didn't seem changed by either drinking or exhaustion. "You miss her."

"I do. God, Gerty, you'll never know how much I miss that woman."

Abby pulled back, bewildered. If she didn't know better, she'd say her father had been crying. Was still crying.

But her father *never* cried.

"Mostly, I talk to her about Abby. I say…I say…" The slurring continued, even worse. "I tell her how beautiful our baby girl is. How sweet, and smart, and good. I tell her she'd be proud."

In those few sentences, her father's voice had shifted through an agony of registers, through the wetness of tears, the high pitch of a tightened throat, the chest-deep bass of pain. Only half-conscious of moving, Abby sank to her knees, bracing herself against the wall. She clutched the doorframe.

"She never even saw the baby. Did you know that, Gerty? They'd put her under, and she never woke up. Stephie never saw how perfect our little girl was."

"Yes," Gerty said quietly. "I knew."

"But before that, when we saw how bad things were…she made me promise the baby would be fine, no matter what. She made me promise I'd always protect her, and love her…and…"

"Which you have, Mark." Gerty broke in quickly, her voice crustier than ever, as if she were eager to prevent a total breakdown. "God knows you've given that girl everything. The only thing you can be accused of is spoiling her. You might have said no, once or twice. Might have been good for her."

A silence greeted that, as if her father were thinking it over. It gave Abby time to think, too. She knew Gerty was probably right. Joe certainly thought so. *Spoiled, superficial, weak.* Those had been the least horrible of the labels he'd thrown at her.

Weak. Too weak to fight for him. For *them.*

"You know what the hardest part was, Gerty, when I found out about the cancer?"

Abby shot a glance toward the door, surprised by the sudden change of subject. Apparently her father had not been thinking about Gerty's comment. He'd been following his own tragic thoughts. His voice was clearer, as if the tears were finished, but the grief in the sound was bottomless, and Abby felt a sudden rush of vertigo, as if she might faint.

"No, Mark," Gerty said steadily. "What was the hardest part?"

"It wasn't the idea of dying. Hell, no. I don't care about that. It was knowing I'd see Stephie on the other side. And I'd have to explain why I didn't keep my promise, why I left Abby all alone."

"Mark—"

"No, don't tell me it's ridiculous. It's how I felt. But it's over. I'm not afraid anymore."

Gerty made another small noise, but he kept talking, apparently oblivious to anything but his own thoughts.

"Blaine Watts is a good man, a strong man," he said. "Strong enough to protect Abby when I'm…when I'm gone."

"Mark, don't. It might be a long time before you—"

"No, it won't. But that's all right. It's so much easier now, because when I get there, I can say…" His voice broke one last time. "When I get there, I can say, *it's all right, Stephie. I left her in good hands.*"

ෂාෂ

TEN MINUTES LATER, Abby was once again sitting on her bedroom floor. She was propped against the wall beside the window seat, finishing the bottle of Jack Daniels she'd filched from the dining room as she fled upstairs.

She was down to the last quarter inch when she heard Charlie mumble, shift, and finally wake up.

"What was that?" Charlie blinked, rubbed her face sleepily. "Oh, darn. Sorry. I guess I dozed off. But I'm good now. Where were we?"

Yawning, she fumbled in her lap, then leaned over and picked up the notebook. "Oh, yeah. We were working on the list. The *cons*. Let's see… we'd just put down…*I'm still in love with Joe.*"

"*I'm still in love with Joe,*" Abby repeated, and then she laughed. Or at least she meant it to be a laugh, but it didn't quite come out right.

She should have brought two bottles. Ignoring Charlie's anxious gaze, she lifted the whiskey to her lips and sucked out the last few drops. Then, tossing it onto the carpet, she smiled down at her toes cryptically. It felt like a cat smile, all tight, curling lips and half-closed eyelids.

"Abby?" Charlotte's voice was pitched low. She sounded worried.

"Hmmm?" Abby wiggled her toes, wondering why people even had legs if they weren't allowed to use them. These two healthy legs should have been able to run her straight out of this house. They should've been able to take her far, far away. But look at them! They were absolutely useless.

"Abby, listen. I shouldn't say this, probably, but…" Charlie hesitated, then started again somberly. "If you really still love Joe…"

"Ah, Charlie, my sweet, clueless, innocent Charlie." Still staring at her toes, Abby shook her head and waved her hand airily, dismissing all that. "I'm getting married in three hours, honey. What on earth has *love* got to do with it?"

Chapter Two

ဆဝ

Eight years later

"JOE, HAVE YOU seen Rafe?" Mary Carlyle appeared at the stable door, a saddle in one hand and a rolled-up lead line in the other. "The little devil has disappeared without starting the stew. I've half a mind to let him starve. He can pass out on the field tonight, right in the middle of the homecoming game. See if I care!"

Joe smiled. His beautiful, acerbic mom hated cooking, and with four sons her only hope had been to teach them to prepare the mountains of food they constantly required. Through the years, they'd all become pretty good cooks—better than she was, anyhow. She always got bored and wandered off to check on the horses, letting everything burn.

But none of them, not even Joe, would ever be as good at horse-training as Mary Carlyle. She might be caustic and impatient with her sons, but never with her animals.

"*Nobody* will care if he passes out, Mom," Joe said, giving one last pat to the paint he'd been brushing and closing the stall door behind him. "He's not exactly the star of the team, and the homecoming game is a big deal. Rafe's runty butt will probably spend most of the night on the bench."

"*Runty butt?*" His mother's blue eyes flashed dangerously, as they always did when anyone dared to insult her boys. "Joseph Carlyle, don't you talk about your little brother that way."

Joe smiled. She could call them every name in the book, but no one else had better dare to, even her other sons.

"You were runty, too, when you were his age," she went on. "Carlyle males never come into their own until—"

Joe had heard this mantra often enough that he could finish the sentence with her. "—until they pass through the crazy phase, which burns a tremendous amount of calories."

His mom scowled, aware that he was teasing her, but the frown quickly turned to a light laugh.

"Well, it's true," she said tartly. "And you found it a comfort, once upon a time. The bottom line is, you'd better plan to get your own dinner before the game. And if you see Rafe, tell him he's in a heap of trouble!"

"Yes, ma'am." Joe had already glimpsed Rafe coming around the side of the house, but the boy had ducked behind the fat trunk of an oak as soon as he saw his mom, gesturing dramatically that Joe mustn't give him away.

"Come on out, squirt," Joe said when the coast was clear. "Hurry up and spill your news, whatever it is. I've got work to do."

Rafe sidled out from the tree's shelter, refusing to be hurried, every inch of him slouchy and out of sorts. Sighing, Joe put his foot on a nearby three-legged stool and got comfortable while he waited.

Watching his little brother walk toward him was like looking in a time-warped mirror. Six-feet of lanky bones topped by a shaggy black mop and marble blue eyes—Rafe could have been Joe or Devlin at that age, right down to the sulky, emo mouth, hunched shoulders and belligerent chin. Their oldest brother,

Brian, was the only oddball, with his blonde hair and sweet smile.

Rafe looked seriously down in the dumps. What now, Joe wondered? He hoped the kid just wanted to borrow money or something simple. He didn't have time for one of the eternal melodramas with Wendy the Rich Witch. He needed to turnout the boarders and check on his own mare before he could shower, and it was already three o'clock.

"What's up, Stormcloud? You look like you lost your last friend."

"I need to talk," Rafe said. His head still ducked low, he glanced left, then right, as if a spy might be hiding behind every tree.

Yeah. Like everyone in Marietta was dying to eavesdrop on Rafe's monotonous whining about Wendy.

"So talk." Joe moved into the small stable office. He'd discovered that one of the boarders knew how to unlatch the stall door, and he needed to write it down in the chart before he forgot. "I can update the records while I listen."

Rafe followed, his boots dragging, scuffing up the stone dust that lay over the grid flooring. For a couple of seconds, he watched as Joe flicked on the monitor and searched for the horse's file.

Finally, Rafe sighed. "Okay, the thing is…it's Wendy."

"*Wendy?*" Joe looked up from the charts, widening his eyes in fake shock. "And here I thought you wanted to debate the geopolitical implications of transatlantic trade."

Rafe's brows lowered over his blue eyes. "Damn it, Joe, knock it off. This is serious."

No, it isn't, Rafe. You're seventeen. *Nothing's serious at* seventeen.

Joe knew that was what he ought to say, what his mother would have said, what Brian and Devlin would have said. *Girls like Wendy are a dime a dozen. It's just hormones, you'd better shop around, plenty more fish in the sea...*

But Rafe had come here because he knew Joe was the one person who wouldn't spout garbage like that. Joe was the one person who knew, first-hand, that a seventeen-year-old heart was perfectly capable of falling in love. *Real* love. And it was perfectly capable of breaking. *Really* breaking.

"Sorry," Joe said. "Just trying to lighten the mood. What's happened? Is it the homecoming dance?"

Wendy had been named to the homecoming court, whereas Rafe, naturally, had not. Joe hoped the selfish little twit hadn't decided to go to the dance with somebody else, somebody "cooler." She'd persuaded Rafe to man the photo booth for two hours, an activity he wouldn't have touched with a ten-foot pole, except that her service club was sponsoring it.

Rafe shook his head. "No, not homecoming. That's all good. I just...I just want to know what you think about something." He shoved his hands in his jeans pockets, took a breath so deep his shoulders almost bumped his ears, then blurted out, "I wondered if you think there's any chance in hell Mom would give me permission to get a marriage license. I only need it because I'm not quite eighteen yet."

Oh, boy.

Joe finished typing his notes onto the entry carefully before answering. *ALWAYS double-lock Misty, as apparently she's learned to unlatch the stall door. NOTE: Check for environmental or social triggers— insects, leaks, loose roof boards, territorial neighbors?*

He didn't really need to list possibilities. Everyone who worked here knew what to watch for. But he needed a minute to calm down.

A marriage license?

Finally, he looked up. "No," he said, flatly. "There's no chance in hell. You know that, buddy."

Rafe's scowl grew even darker. "Why not? Just because mom wasn't willing to let you marry Abby Foster doesn't mean she wouldn't—"

"This has nothing to do with me and Abby Foster." Joe closed the spreadsheet, then clicked off the monitor. Point of fact, their mom hadn't refused to let Joe get a marriage license, because Joe hadn't ever asked. No need to, given that Abby already had a marriage license...to wed another man.

"Is it because she doesn't like Wendy? I know she seems snooty, but she's not, not when we're alone. We're in love, Joe. And don't try to persuade me I'm not, don't start talking about hormones, because—"

"Did I say that?" Joe shook his head. "I don't doubt for a minute that you're in love, buddy. I guess what I'm not so sure about...is whether Wendy is in the same place." He paused to let that sink in. "You know?"

"No. What are you saying? You think she's just...just...*pretending?*"

"Not exactly." If Rafe didn't look so young, so pale and stricken, Joe might have smiled at what he was about to say. It was an ironic twist of the classic "He just wants one thing from you, honey" lecture dads had given their daughters since the dawn of sex. "I'm just wondering if she's quite as serious about the whole thing as you are."

"Of course she is. She's given me...she let me take—" Rafe broke off, his cheeks coloring as if he were ten years old. "I mean, I was her first...we've...*you know.*"

Yeah. Joe knew. He'd known the day it happened, when Rafe's angular slouch had abruptly taken on a pantherish grace, as if he'd suddenly discovered how all his parts worked. At the exact same moment, Wendy had gone all sloe-eyed and Lauren Bacall.

The two of them might as well have taken out a display ad in the Courier.

The inevitable family dramas had ensued—Mary Carlyle wasn't the hand-wringing, worry-in-silence type. She was more the scream the rafters down, break all the dinner dishes, threaten to boil the boy in oil if he kept being so stupid type.

But they all knew nothing was likely to stop Rafe now. Wendy was going to be his version of the Carlyle Crazies.

Brian, their oldest brother, had been home that week, and after he'd talked Mom down from her banshee fury, he'd run downtown, bought a crate of condoms, and left them in Rafe's room with a note that said, "I still think you're an idiot, and if Mom doesn't kill you Wendy's dad probably will. But till then, at least be careful."

"*Given* you? *Let* you?" Joe shook his head irritably. "That's outdated patriarchal terminology, little brother. If you have sex with a virgin, that doesn't make you a stud-god, and it doesn't *take* anything from her. She's no more diminished or *ruined* by having had sex than you are. And believe me, the fact that you were her first doesn't mean you'll be her last."

Rafe's hands fisted in his pockets, as if he'd like to hit someone. Probably Joe. "Don't insult her, god damn it."

"I'm not insulting her. Don't you hear me? Would I be insulting *you* if I said you'd probably have more than one lover in your lifetime? Of course not. So why are the rules different for Wendy?"

"They're not." Rafe bunched up his mouth, obviously tangled on the logic. "I mean, I'm *not* going to ever have more than one lover, so…"

Right.

"Look, Rafe, the thing is…for most—" Joe hesitated. He'd almost said "for most girls like Wendy," but that would just trigger a reflexive "there aren't any girls like Wendy." And besides, that was sexist, too. This didn't apply just to girls, so he rephrased it.

"For most *people*, being wildly attracted to someone isn't always the same thing as wanting to marry them. Marriage is about more than sex. It's about paying bills, and having kids, sharing similar backgrounds and values, working toward common goals—"

Rafe's shoulders twitched with repressed fury. "Hell, Joe, now who's being old-fashioned? *Similar backgrounds?* That's just code for pointing out she's loaded, and I'm not. You're saying I'm just her temporary boy toy, good for a roll in the hay, but when it comes time to settle down, she'll marry some rich dude instead."

Actually, Joe had been trying pretty hard *not* to say that, in so many words. But maybe he was being too subtle. Why was he lecturing a seventeen-year-old on modern sexual politics and socio-economic realities, anyhow? He knew how hopeless that was.

"Okay, yeah, basically, that's what I'm saying." He gave up and chose tough love. "I'm saying the odds are you're probably her boy toy. Or maybe you're a good way to rebel against Dad, or Mom, or the system, or whatever makes her feel cramped right now."

For a minute, as Rafe's fists came out of his pockets, Joe thought his brother really might hit him. But for so many years Mom had drilled into them that only stupid people solved their problems with violence—and his training held true. He killed Joe hard with his blazing eyes, but he didn't touch him.

"You know what, Joe?" He stabbed the air with an angry finger. "If you ask me, it's pretty pathetic that you still think every girl in the world is just as superficial and materialistic as that awful Abby Foster."

"Hey. Hold on. I don't—"

"Sure you do. And it's not fair to the other girls, you know?

I mean, Abby was a wretched bitch, nobody's denying that, and I'm sorry she sold you out. But for God's sake, it was eight years ago, and it doesn't have anything to do with me and Wendy. So just *get over it*, why don't you?"

Again, Joe started to protest…he *was* over it, he wasn't judging Wendy by Abby standards…

But oh, well. *Whatever.* The kid was mad, and he needed to let off steam, so Joe just shrugged.

Rafe glared at him, chest heaving, for a few seconds, then, obviously realizing he should have stalked off ten seconds ago, he turned on his heels to make his exit.

And ran right into a woman standing at the office door.

Rafe inhaled, a low, surprised sound, and jerked his head back as if he'd been scalded. He stumbled, mumbled oddly, then darted around the woman without managing anything that sounded remotely like a word.

Joe looked at the newcomer curiously, wondering who could have reduced Rafe to such an inarticulate mess.

Wait…what? For a split second, his eyes and his brain simply couldn't process what he saw. What he *thought* he saw. *No.* No. *No way.*

It looked like…

The long, silky, chestnut hair with wine-red highlights. The lively green eyes under dark, arched brows. The bowed pink lips that, even at rest, always seemed to be on the verge of a smile or a kiss.

And the body. Five-five, damn near perfect, all the way from the wide, pale forehead to the butt, rounded and firm as an apple. The tiny waist and the luscious breasts that could make a teenager crazy…

Or a grown man.

Instinctively, his palms warmed, and his fingers twitched. His groin tightened. And then his brain kicked in. *Aw, hell.* How much of that crap with Rafe had she heard?

"Enough," Abby Foster said, as if he'd spoken the question aloud. She tossed a glance over her shoulder at Rafe's hurried retreat. "Yikes…can you say *awkward*?"

Then she turned back to Joe, who had an unpleasant feeling his mouth was hanging open, catching flies.

"Yep," she said with a smile. "It's me. The wretched bitch herself."

Chapter Three

ഇരു

H E CERTAINLY HOPED he didn't look as disoriented as he felt. He closed his mouth, a good first step, but if he didn't start talking in the next couple of seconds, she'd know how much power she still had over him. Enough power to render him mute.

Frantically, he felt around in his mind for some clever comment, just as he might feel around in the dark for his keys if the house were on fire. But he didn't have anything ready. He had honest to God believed he'd never see her again.

His first impulse was to try to get cute. "Of all the gin joints in all the towns in all the world…"

But no… *Casablanca*? He might as well burst into tears, or fling himself into the sawdust and kiss her feet. Nothing said "you broke my heart, you faithless harlot" like quoting Casablanca.

But he had to say *something*, damn it. He picked up the pencil on the desk, though he didn't need it, just to have something in his hands.

"Abby Watts," he said. Not exactly diamond-sharp repartee, but at least she couldn't read much into that. Simple was better than clever. Safer.

She shook her head. "No, not Abby Watts. Abby *Foster*."

"Oh? You didn't take your husband's name?"

"I took it." That small smile still curved her lips. "But I gave it back."

Gave it back? He hesitated, reluctant to jump to conclusions. "How is that done?"

"The normal way. We got divorced a couple of years ago." She lifted one shoulder. "I legally went back to Foster, and he found someone else to be Mrs. Blaine Watts."

She sounded so matter of fact, as if divorce, and losing Blaine to another woman, didn't bother her very much. He wondered whether her calm was an act. Abby Foster hadn't been very good at acting, or lying, back in the old days. But who knew what skills she might have picked up in her years as Mrs. Blaine Watts of New York City?

Just because she looked heart-stoppingly the same didn't mean she really *was* the same. She'd been living on the other side of the country, as another man's wife, for nearly a decade. That would change a person.

Heck, he'd stayed right here in Marietta, in the family business, even in the family home—and look how different he was.

"Really," he said stupidly. "He remarried, huh?"

He drummed the pencil on the desk blotter, wondering why he had to fight for every line in this conversation. Once, they'd been able to talk all night long.

Problem was, the news truly shocked him. If she divorced two years ago, that meant their marriage had lasted only six. It hardly seemed possible that she'd broken his heart—both their hearts—for something that lasted only six years.

But, again, the silence had stretched too long. He needed to say something.

"How about that." He dropped the pencil and scooted his

chair back, as if to rise. "Divorced already. That didn't take long."

Something tightened in her face. "I guess time is relative," she said. "It seemed like an eternity to me."

A fist of discomfort got hold of his chest for a split second and twisted. Of course, her calm was just an act. Divorce was always painful—and whatever had caused the divorce had obviously left scars, too.

He needed to be a better person than this. He'd forgiven her long ago. He'd moved on. He had no interest in punishing her for those choices now, or being insensitive to what she might have endured.

"I'm sorry," he said, finally rising. In this small office, the move brought them so close he could smell the sandalwood and cinnamon of her perfume. "I didn't mean to sound flip."

"It's okay," she said. "You have the right to sound however you want."

He shook his head. "Look, Abby, I'm trying to get this right. But the truth is I'm darned surprised to see you. I haven't a clue what the right thing to say is. I'm sorry if you were unhappy, but—"

"But I asked for it?" She attempted a smile, but she didn't quite make it. "Don't try to think of the *right* thing to say, Joe. Just say the real thing."

"The *real* thing?" He laughed softly. "What on earth would that be?"

"Surely you're dying to say 'I told you so.'"

He hesitated. Was he? Maybe. But...the words wouldn't come. It wasn't as simple as that.

"I don't blame you," she assured him. "You *did* tell me so. You warned me I'd be miserable. You predicted my marriage would be a living hell."

"Yeah, but you know I didn't—"

She tilted her head, frowning slightly. "*Joe.*"

The way she spoke his name made it a soft reproach, and it stopped him. She was right. He couldn't honestly claim he hadn't meant it. After she left, for several months he'd prayed, with every fiber in his bitter heart, that she'd never know a moment's true happiness. He'd told himself he wanted the pleasure of revenge, but the truth had been that he wanted her to be so miserable she'd come running back to Marietta—and to him.

He shrugged. "You know why I said those things. I meant them, I guess, but later, when I grew up a little, I understood more. I came to understand why you chose Blaine. The two of you had so much in common, and not just money. I figured you'd thrive as a New York socialite."

Culture, luxury, social ties and position could form a strong bond, even in the absence of true love and true passion. It was the basis of many a long, stable marriage, not just in big cities, but in small towns like Marietta, too. Even if she didn't adore Blaine, she'd probably adore being Mrs. Watts.

And Joe couldn't seriously imagine Blaine getting bored with his trophy wife. So he had to accept that the steely trap had closed, and it wasn't going to just voluntarily open and set her free. Unless…unless…

One day, about a year after her wedding, he realized he had started to calculate the odds that eventually she might be a widow. Blaine was twelve years older than she was, so in the normal course of things, someday…

Whoa. Sinking that low had scared the hell out of him. Was he going to live his life—or even worse, put his life on hold— waiting for another man to *die?*

That was when he'd started compulsively dating every half-intelligent, half-attractive female in Montana.

"Abby, look, I don't mean to be rude, but…why are you

here?" He looked closely into her face, wishing he could read her mind. "Why have you come back?"

She met his searching gaze squarely. "Don't you know?"

"No, I don't. With your dad gone…" He caught himself. He'd never had the chance to offer his sympathy about her father. Not that Joe, or anyone in Marietta, missed the hard-hearted old buzzard, but he knew how much Abby had loved him. "I'm sorry. It must have been tough for you when he died."

"Yes," she said simply. "Thank you."

"But the truth is, you don't have any family here anymore. And since your dad sold the ranch almost immediately after the wedding…" He smiled wryly. "Don't tell me you came all the way across the country because you wanted to see the home-coming game."

"Of course not," she said, matching his smile, but still meeting his eyes with a sober, unwavering gaze. "I came because—"

"Joe, are you still in here?" His mother's voice sounded breathless, as if she'd been running. "Tricia called, and she said she can't—"

As Mary Carlyle poked her head into the office, she spotted Abby, and she stopped mid-sentence. Her face went very still.

"Oh, you're busy. I'm sorry. I'll come back later."

"Mrs. Carlyle." Abby was smiling, and for a minute Joe thought she might intend to reach out and hug his mother. He knew, from an instantaneous reading of his mother's eyes, that a hug would not be welcome.

Almost as quickly, Abby seemed to sense the same thing. Her body returned to a passive posture, and she didn't try to close the space between them.

"Hello," Mary said coolly. "I'm sorry…it's…oh, my heavens, is it Abby? Abby…" She pretended to be searching for the last name. "Oh, of course, Abby *Foster*. Except, you changed your name, didn't you? I'm sorry, but I can't remember your husband's name at the moment. How have you been, dear? My goodness, it's been a long time, hasn't it, Joe? Isn't it nice to see Abby looking so well?"

Joe almost laughed. The performance was terrible, but he understood what his mother was trying to do and loved her for it. If she displayed the least hostility, if she came across as an angry mama tiger, it would be proof that Abby had hurt Joe deeply. So she tried to pretend Abby had been so insignificant they'd all forgotten her name.

"It's good to see you, too, Mrs. Carlyle," Abby said politely. "But there's no need to worry. I'm divorced now, and I'm back to being just Abby Foster."

If she'd thought the news of her divorce would help his mom to relax, she'd badly miscalculated. Divorced? Free to come after Joe again? Every muscle in Mary Carlyle's body began to hum with tension, as if she were a wild animal that sensed a threat lurking in some dark part of the forest.

"*Divorced?* That's too bad. Too much of that these days, if you ask me. When people take a vow, they can't just give up the minute things get difficult." She gave Abby a bright smile. "Till death do you part should mean exactly that, don't you think? So I'm sure you two will patch things up soon."

"Thanks, Mrs. Carlyle, but unfortunately that's unlikely." Abby's voice was pleasant, too. "Considering Blaine is already remarried."

His mother's mouth fell open. In the momentary silence, Abby turned to Joe. "I should be going. Any chance you've got time to walk me to my car?"

"Sure." He nodded, flicked off the computer, and without hesitation followed her toward the stable doors.

Abby went through first, saying a polite goodbye to Mary, who stood frozen in place, just outside the office doorway. As he passed his mother, Joe teasingly nudged her shoulder. She glared at him, but he simply smiled.

"Lighten up," he murmured. "I can handle this."

"Oh, I'm sure you can *handle* her," Mary said irritably, putting her hands on her hips and transferring the glare to the back of Abby's head. "That's exactly what I'm afraid of."

Chuckling, Joe caught up with Abby just as she reached her car. To his surprise, it wasn't a Mercedes or a BMW. It was a sensible Ford, late model but decidedly unglamorous.

She beeped the lock and put her fingers around the handle. But before she opened the door, she turned back to Joe, her face somber but stunning in the afternoon sunlight.

"I came back," she said, as if their conversation hadn't been interrupted, "because I've spent the past eight years dreaming about you, and it's nearly driven me crazy. I came back because I wanted…no, I *needed* to see you again."

She'd been *dreaming* about him? He wondered, for a second, whether he might be the one having a dream. He'd had a hundred that went just like this, but he always woke up annoyed with himself, well aware that flirtatious Abby Foster didn't ever lay her emotions out like that, exposed and unguarded.

"Abby, I—" His heart did a trip-over-itself thing, but somehow he kept his face still. "I have to say I'm surprised. That's quite the declaration. What happened to the princess who used to love to keep us all guessing, and always played hard to get?"

"She grew up, I guess. I don't play games anymore. I tried that. And I tried doing what other people said I should do. None of that works. So now I tell the truth. *My truth*, whether anyone likes it or not."

"Your truth…"

"I want you, Joe. I know it's over between us, what we used to have. I know I ruined that. I'm not asking to go back to where we were before. I'm not even asking you to forgive me. I'm only here for three days, but I thought that maybe those three days could…we could…"

"*Three days?*"

"Yes. I leave Monday. So I'm not here to mess up your life, no matter what your mother thinks. I'm not looking for anyone to lean on, to replace Blaine—I won't ever sign my life over to any man again. I'm just here because I've never stopped wanting you. I've never stopped thinking about you, about us, about how it was when we were lovers. And if you think about that, too—if you still want me—"

"Wait." He put his hand on the hood of her car. "Let me be sure what you're saying. When you say you want me. You mean you want to *make love* to me?"

She nodded. "I can't help it. I can't stop remembering…" She reached up and touched his face. "It was good, wasn't it? It was so good that nothing…no one…"

He felt everything inside him harden, like liquid metal cooling. "I see. In a nutshell, your rich, suave husband never satisfied you in bed. You've been sexually frustrated, and you need someone to fix that."

Though her cheeks colored, she lifted her chin. "This has nothing to do with Blaine. I'm not going to argue with you, Joe. You have every right to be angry with me, even to hate me. So if you don't feel the way I do, if you don't still think about me…about us…"

She bit her lower lip, a habit that used to drive him insane. "If you don't have any interest in spending this weekend with me, then just say so. I'm being completely honest, and I hope you will be, too."

For a long minute, he didn't say anything. He had so many emotions moving through him, careening into each other like bumper cars, that he couldn't sort them well enough to give any of them a voice.

Behind him, he knew, his mother was still watching, anger

and fear radiating out from her, all directed at Abby. Off to the side, toward the ranch house, Rafe was watching, too, waiting to see whether Joe would seize this chance for a little payback.

Abby obviously was aware of the others, too. And yet she stood there, exposed and vulnerable, her shoulders squared and her feet planted, ready for whatever he said.

And suddenly, as he studied her face, he saw the changes he'd been looking for—the subtle differences created by the eight years apart.

Yes, at twenty-six she was still sexier than any female should be. But some of that high-spirited arrogance was missing. Her green eyes no longer had that flinty touch of self-absorption, the easy certainty that she was the cutest thing for miles around, and that every dream she had was standing in line, waiting to come true.

Instead, he saw something new in them, something even more powerful. He saw depth, strength, passion. He saw an awareness that she'd have to make her own joy, just as she must endure her own pain.

She clearly understood things now that she hadn't even glimpsed at eighteen. She'd learned that she could be hurt. She'd learned that she could lose.

In short, she was a woman, not a girl. Making love to her would be richer. Sweeter. And infinitely more dangerous.

"All right. I've heard your truth. Now here's mine." He stepped back. Just one movement with one foot, but it spoke volumes. "I'm sorry, Abby. But I have exactly *zero* interest in being your weekend lover."

ℰℭ

IT TOOK ABBY almost an hour to find Charlotte. She went first to the Chamber of Commerce, where Charlie worked, but she wasn't in her office. No one seemed quite sure where she'd gone, and they couldn't raise her on her cell.

Finally, though, the secretary remembered that Charlie was in charge of the Chamber's homecoming float, which meant she'd be downtown, putting the finishing touches on their papier-mâché replica of Copper Mountain.

When Abby arrived at the parade's staging area, the elementary school parking lot, she understood instantly why Charlie wasn't answering her phone. She couldn't possibly hear it ringing over this deafening din.

The scene was pure chaos. At least ten or twelve colorful floats lined the lot, the flatbeds bouncing as students dressed as scarecrows and pumpkins and everything remotely connected to this year's theme, *Harvest Moon*, jumped on and off, tweaking the decorations.

On the ground, what looked like a thousand football players, cheerleaders, baton twirlers, band members, service club reps, and members of the homecoming court swarmed around like red-and-white bees, trying to find their friends, their instruments, their places in the lineup.

Adding to the chaos, dozens more adults—alumni, business people, drivers, carpenters and photographers—raced about barking orders, trying to get everyone to "calm down, people! *Focus!*"

It was as if every single citizen of Marietta was here, and they'd all hit the panic button at the exact same time.

Abby looked at her watch. Four-forty. Well, no wonder. The parade was scheduled to start at five, leaving from the elementary school, winding around the perimeter of downtown, and ending up at the high school stadium by six.

"Get over here, you dunderheads!" To Abby's right, a good-looking, muscular man blew a whistle. "The game's at eight! You want to forfeit to Livingston because you're still tossing plastic footballs to toddlers on Main Street?"

An outraged roar went up from a cluster of boys in football uniforms. "No, sir!" they shouted collectively. "Crush the Pumas!"

The man turned to Abby with an apologetic smile.

"Sorry, didn't mean to break your eardrums. But I swear, it's like herding cats."

"No problem," she said, smiling back. She didn't recognize him. A new coach, maybe? As the players came jogging over, she felt an odd, dislocated sensation. So much had changed. So many faces she didn't know...

Maybe she was just tired. The past few weeks had been stressful, and she'd been on the road since dawn. After the cold reception she'd received at Joe's ranch, this sea of unfamiliar faces, this crowd of people working together on something she had no part of...it felt like a door slammed in her face.

Why had she come back? Had she imagined that, on some level, Marietta was still home?

She was about to turn around and head back to the hotel when, miraculously, she spotted Charlie, squatting beside a float that clearly was designed to represent the beloved Marietta landmark, the peak of Copper Mountain. At least Abby hoped it was Charlie. From this angle, she could see only her long, shining brown hair.

Relief swamped her, as if she'd been drowning and the sight of a friend was a life raft.

"Charlie!" She pushed past a cluster of kids practicing a barbershop quartet version of "Shine on, Harvest Moon." A couple of floats over, she spotted Rafe Carlyle, huddled in intense conversation with a blonde cheerleader, but luckily he didn't see Abby. For a minute, he looked so much like a seventeen-year-old Joe that she froze in her tracks.

"Hey! Lady, you need brake lights!"

"Sorry," she said, pulling herself together enough to smile at the kid who had crashed into her from behind. The boy had already moved on, making a beeline for the senior float—a giant papier-mâché hand that rose up out of an artificial gridiron turf. *!!!!Crush the Pumas!!!!*, the float's sign screamed.

Suddenly, the woman squatting beside the Chamber float stood, turning around quickly.

"We've got a flat here," Charlie said crisply. "We need someone who can—"

And then she froze, her eyes widening. "*Abby?* Oh, you've got to be kidding me. Abs, is it really you?"

Abby didn't have time to do anything more than nod—and then plant her feet firmly on the asphalt so Charlie's onrushing hug didn't knock her over.

"It's so great to see you!" Charlie's embrace lasted so long, and squeezed her so tightly, that Abby almost couldn't breathe. But it was worth it. For the first time since she got here, Abby almost felt... saying she felt "at home" would still be a stretch, but at least she no longer felt like an unwanted interloper.

When Abby squeaked softly, Charlie let go with a laugh.

"Sorry!" She kept her hands on Abby's shoulders, holding her just far enough out to give her the once over. "Wow, you look tired."

Abby raised her eyebrows. "Well, thanks. I love you, too."

"No, you look terrific, you know that. You just look tired. Did you drive all the way from New York? And why on earth didn't you tell me you were coming? I told you we'd find a place for you to sleep, if you did."

She had promised that. But Charlotte was a newlywed, and Abby had no intention of intruding on their privacy. "I didn't want you making a fuss. I'm staying at the Graff, so there's no need to put me up."

"But I *wanted* to." Charlie looked genuinely disappointed—

but Abby was willing to bet her new husband, Jesse Guthrie, would appreciate the reprieve.

"Heck, I would have been glad just to hear from you at all," Charlie went on. "You haven't responded to any of my emails in a month. Maybe six weeks. I was starting to worry. So seriously, Abs. Why didn't you tell me you were coming?"

"I just…" Abby hesitated. "Honestly, Charlie, I wasn't sure I could really do this. Right up to the county line, I was still thinking I might turn around."

Charlie nodded slowly. "Okay. That I believe. But you *didn't* turn around."

"No." Abby bit her lower lip, glancing one more time toward Rafe and his cheerleader, who now seemed to be arguing hotly. "But maybe I should have."

Charlie's brows drove together, and Abby knew she understood. Even after all these years, Charlie still knew her so well. She could read her tone, or her eyes, or something between the lines.

"You've seen Joe," Charlie said.

For a second or two, Abby couldn't trust herself to speak, so she just nodded. As she'd driven away from the Carlyle ranch today, she'd locked her disappointment deep, refusing to dwell on it. He would either reconsider, or he wouldn't. She'd done all she could. Brooding wouldn't help.

But suddenly the sinking, lost feeling was back, double.

She wasn't sure why it hurt so much. All the way from New York to Marietta, a three-day trip, she'd lectured herself about facing reality. Joe undoubtedly would still be hostile, and he would probably reject her offer—once he was finished giving her a piece of his mind.

But somehow the lectures hadn't prepared her for the kicked-in-the-gut feeling when he actually did it.

"Okay. You saw him." Charlie lowered her voice. "And it

didn't go well?"

"Yeah, that's one way of putting it." Abby kept her voice down, too. Rafe seemed absorbed in his own drama, but you never knew where ears were hiding in a small town. "His brother called me a wretched bitch. His mother acted as if she didn't remember my name at first, and then tried to poison me with her eyes."

"Okay, but…" Charlie *tssked*, dismissing Rafe and Mrs. Carlyle. "What did *Joe* say?"

Abby tried to smile. "He said *thanks but no thanks*, don't let the stable door bump your butt as you leave."

"*Ouch*." Charlie put her hand on Abby's arm. "Hey, don't let it get to you. It's an act—you must know that. The fool man has been holding his breath for eight years, just waiting for you to walk back into his life."

"Sure didn't look that way. And, frankly, that's not what you've been telling me in your emails." Abby spoke brusquely, trying to cover the stupid flare of hope. "Remember, you said he'd dated every female in three counties? And he actually got engaged to two of them."

"Rebound romances," Charlie said. Then she grinned. "Okay, it was *five years* of rebound romances, and I'll admit getting engaged twice was overkill. But I told you…he's probably only had a handful of dates in the past three years. He's practically a workaholic now. Hardly ever leaves the stables."

Abby knew it was unfair, but she hoped it was true. She still got a chill every time she thought about the two engagements. What if one of them had stuck? What if she'd opened one of Charlie's weekly emails and found news like that?

Hey, Abs. Sorry to be the bearer of bad tidings, but Joe got married last Saturday. :(

"Ms. Guthrie!" A good-looking boy in football uniform

came dashing up to them, his eyes wide and panicked. "I've been looking everywhere for you! We've got a huge problem." He glanced at Abby briefly. "I'm sorry, but it's like an emergency."

"What is it, Flynn?" Charlie sounded studiously patient.

Abby glanced harder at the boy. Could this be Flynn Goodwin, Chase Goodwin's younger brother? She would never, ever have recognized him.

Of course, it had been eight years, and she'd never known either Chase or his younger brother, Flynn, all that well. Flynn had been only about ten when she left. And the difference between ten and eighteen was huge.

She had to stop kidding herself that eight years wasn't very long. It was. It was, obviously, *too* long.

"It's an *epic* fail, Ms. Guthrie! You know Billy, who's playing the Livingston quarterback on our float? He keeps falling out of the hand. Like every single time the car stops or starts." Flynn groaned. "We're going to look like such losers if our sign says *Crush the Pumas*, but we can't hang onto him for thirty seconds."

"Okay, Flynn, let's go see what we can do." Charlie turned to Abby. "I've got to put out a few brushfires, but we'll talk later, okay? See if you can find Jesse. He should be around here somewhere, and he'll take care of you till I'm—"

"No need for that." A deep baritone spoke suddenly, just inches from Abby's left shoulder. "Abby can go to the parade with me."

Startled, Abby wheeled around and found herself looking into Joe's sunlit blue eyes. Her heart pumped a hot spurt of painful joy. His eyes weren't exactly smiling, but maybe, just maybe, they weren't as cold as they'd been back at the stables, either.

"I'm not sure I understand," she began. "You said—"

Charlie laid her hand heavily on Abby's shoulder, sending a clear signal to *shut up*. "What's not to understand, Abs? Joe just said you'd go to the parade with him." She beamed. "So I'll leave you guys alone, then. I'm sure you have lots of catching up to do."

Abby frowned. "But—"

But nothing. Charlie was out of earshot before Abby could finish her sentence, waving breezy fingers over her shoulder in a merry goodbye.

Thanks a lot, old buddy. Though two hundred people churned around them, Abby felt suddenly as if she'd been abandoned, alone in a desert, or in the middle of the ocean. Alone with Joe.

A trembling began in the pit of her stomach. It was part fear, part excitement. Hauntingly reminiscent of how she used to feel when she heard Joe's car sputtering up the long drive to her father's ranch.

She squared her shoulders and turned back to face him.

"Charlie may understand you," she said as calmly as she could, "but I don't. Why would you want to watch the parade with me? Just an hour ago, you explicitly said you had no interest in ever seeing me again."

Joe tilted his head, and he almost smiled. *Almost.*

"Nope. I think if you go back over our conversation very carefully, you'll realize that isn't at all what I said."

She frowned. What had his words been, exactly? He'd said he had zero percent interest in...in...

In being her *weekend lover.*

But... that didn't really clear anything up, did it? She didn't want to try to read tea leaves, parse sentences, unearth hidden meanings. She didn't play emotional games anymore. She said what she meant. *Always.* And she was clear about what she wanted. *Always.*

She didn't do coy, or cagey-cute or manipulative. And she didn't allow anyone to manipulate her, either. Not even Joe. She'd made a vow never again to do anything that her heart told her was wrong.

"I don't want to play a guessing game about this," she said. "I remember what you said. You said you didn't want to be my weekend lover. But what does that mean? That you don't want to be my lover at all, even for seventy-two hours? That you'd rather be enemies? Or that you just want to mend fences and part as friends?"

She swallowed hard. "Or does it mean you want *more* than a weekend?"

She started to add that, if he'd meant he wanted more, they had a problem. She wasn't in Marietta to stay. She'd also vowed she wouldn't let herself run straight into another man's arms, relying on another big strong shoulder to help her face her scary new world. She was going to stand on her own two feet, for once.

But how could she say that? It seemed presumptuous to start warning him she wouldn't be his permanent girlfriend when he hadn't admitted he wanted her at all.

"I just need to be sure I understand," she finished lamely. "It seems better to go into this with both of us clear about what we're asking for."

He stared at her for a long moment, his gaze darkening, as if a cloud passed over the bright blue of his eyes. Around the still center of that stare, the parade chaos continued to swirl, but she couldn't hear it very well anymore. The voices, the laughter, the barked orders...they all seemed to come to her through the hollow of a tunnel.

She suddenly wished she had something to lean on. She felt shaky, the way she might feel if she hadn't eaten in a long time. Which, she realized, she hadn't. Not since yesterday.

Yes, she was hungry, and tired, too. She wasn't nervous, or afraid. Or if she was, she would overcome it. Another thing she'd decided two years ago was that she'd never be afraid of any man again.

If only he felt more like the old Joe. If only he didn't seem so...different. Somehow she hadn't expected him to look so...so...

She couldn't think of the word. She kept wanting to say "big," but that wasn't right. Big sounded like overweight, and there wasn't a spare ounce on Joe Carlyle. Big sounded awkward, and he was anything but that.

It was just that she'd walked away from a boy. And she'd come home to a *man*.

"You don't have to sugarcoat it," she said, needing the uncomfortable silence to end. "Just tell me the truth."

"The truth," he said slowly, "is complicated."

"And I'm fairly bright," she countered. "Try me."

"Darn it, Abby." He dragged his hand through his hair. "The truth is that I don't *know* which of those two things I meant. I've tried to hate you for so long I don't have a clue what I *really* feel. Hell, I don't even know who you are anymore—and you don't know who I am."

I do, she wanted to cry out. *I know exactly who you are. And I can't have changed so much that...*

But she knew she had.

"All right." She took a breath. "If you don't know who I am, and you don't know what you want from me, the question remains. Why are you here?"

"Because I thought..." Finally, he smiled. "I thought we could use these seventy-two hours to find out."

Chapter Four

ଐଔ

A BBY HADN'T INTENDED to stay for the parade—or the football game. Even if Joe had said yes to her original proposition, back at his ranch, she'd planned to go back to the hotel. She could shower, and rest a little, while he performed whatever alum, volunteer, chaperone or big brother duties he had accepted for homecoming.

Even now, she assumed Joe would probably want to meet her at the Graff after the game. If the point really was to get to know each other again, several hours of making small talk in loud crowds was hardly going to help.

But Joe clearly had other ideas. "We've got little enough time as it is," he'd said when she proposed that plan. "Why waste any of it sleeping?"

The electric sizzle that went through her at those words was ridiculous, really. She tried to act normal, but from that moment on she felt as if her veins were filled with carbonation, and she'd been shaken so thoroughly she might explode.

The parade was sweet, but silly, lots of cars carrying the homecoming royalty, lots of nature clubs and ranches and businesses promoting themselves with placards held by smiling kids. One or two of the floats were fancy, professional-quality, but most were homemade affairs with Drama Club or Student Council scarecrows waving from pumpkin patches.

But the parade was merely a prelude. The real excitement didn't build to its crescendo until the sky darkened to wavy banners of purple, gray and black, and the parade drew up to the high school. Instantly, the crowds dispersed, the floats unloaded quickly. And suddenly hundreds of people were pouring into the stadium, which was bright with klieg lights and humming with anticipation.

The evening was going to be frosty enough that Abby was glad she'd worn a heavy, turtleneck sweater and good boots. But the cold apparently hadn't kept anyone at home. By kick-off time, the stands were packed under the clear, starry black sky. The band was in place and had begun the classic spirit song, urging everyone to stomp their feet until the bleachers thundered.

With the opening notes, Abby caught the old, familiar thrill. It felt like all those other nights, when she'd arrived at the football games with her friends. Heart in her throat, she'd scanned the bleachers, looking for Joe...

He'd always found her. And then they would ditch their friends and walk around together, sometimes saying nothing at all, content to let their shoulders brush, turned on by the simplest touch of their hands.

It was the same now, as they walked along the sidelines, looking for a good seat. Their shoulders grazed, setting off fireworks inside her.

Joe knew everyone, of course. They couldn't move ten feet without having to stop and say hello. He always introduced her, though the noise was often too loud for either side to catch names. When they ran into someone from the old days, a few jaws dropped, but most of his newer friends obviously had no idea who Abby Foster was.

As the crowds grew, Joe reflexively reached back for her hand, so that they wouldn't lose each other. As she took it, her breath momentarily froze. She was so hyper-aware of him, of his body, and her body. *Seventeen again, and so much in love.*

She smiled at strangers and tried to act normal, though her entire body felt lit from within by their secret—the secret that, under their clothes and their smiles, their bodies were already on fire. The secret that hummed between them invisibly. Soon they would sneak away. They'd find some shadow dark enough to hide in, and they would kiss, and press together, until he was groaning, and she was dizzy.

He would ask for more...beg for it. And maybe...probably...she would say yes.

And no one knew any of that. Just as he had back then, he held her hand casually. He hadn't even turned around when he took it. But everything thrilled inside her. She couldn't remember feeling this edgy—or this alive—in years.

Eventually, some people hollered out his name, pointing and indicating they'd saved seats for him. Great seats, on the fifty-yard line, just a couple of rows up, so close they could hear the coach barking at the players.

Joe let Abby slip in first. She settled next to the young couple who had called them over, smiling an apology for crowding them.

As he sat, Joe let go of her hand, but he had to shove close to fit his whole body on the bleacher. His hip pressed against hers, hard and warm beneath his jeans, and the muscles flexed as he reached up to remove his jacket.

From half-lowered lids, she watched him shrug those amazing shoulders free. Suddenly the chilly air was filled with the masculine scent of soap and amber...and something mulled and sweet that was pure Joe.

She shivered, and he glanced down at her. "Cold?"

She nodded…though that was a lie. As she'd hoped, he draped his jacket over her shoulders, and she gathered the collar tightly around her throat to capture the intoxicating scent.

"The game probably won't start for another few minutes," he said, his gaze skimming the field, obviously searching for Rafe. "Are you hungry? Want a hot dog? Some popcorn?"

"Not till the guy comes around," she said. She was starving, but she didn't want Joe to get up and leave her. She didn't want anything to break the spell.

A man sitting behind Joe slapped him on the shoulder, and Joe turned with a smile. "Ryan!" The two started an easy chat, discussing Marietta High's new coach, and what apparently had been a very good season for the Grizzlies.

Knowing little about all that, Abby watched the green field, now streaming with boys in red and white. Across the grass, like a mirror image, another set of boys, except these were dressed in green and yellow. The Marietta players looked especially eager, Abby thought. All of them were in motion—bouncing, sprinting, fidgeting, throwing invisible footballs to test their arms.

One of the fidgeting players, she realized suddenly, was Rafe. His helmet under his elbow, the boy turned, obviously looking for Joe. When he found his big brother, he grinned, and waved eagerly, too excited to play it cool. He must not have seen Abby sitting there, because his smile never faded.

His face looked almost impossibly young, his body scrawny and child-like inside his immense, lumpy padding.

A tight heat formed in her throat. So this was what seventeen looked like from the other side. The boys out there didn't just *seem* like children. They *were* children.

Which meant Joe and Abby had been children at seventeen, too. Poor, doomed children, in so far over their heads they'd never really had a chance.

As if he sensed a change in her mood, Joe bent toward her. "Everything okay?"

"Yes. It's just…I can't believe I was planning to skip this," she said. Her words came out on a small puff of misty white. "They're so young. So innocent, and—" She couldn't quite find the words to complete the thought, so she just smiled. "So touching. Homecoming really is magic, isn't it?"

He didn't answer for several seconds. He just gazed down at her, as if he were trying to understand words that had been spoken in a foreign language. Then he smiled.

"I don't remember your being a big football fan," he said. "I don't remember us making it to halftime, even once, before we ditched the game for something more interesting."

Her cheeks flushed slightly. She tried to think of a clever answer, but her mind was suddenly flooded with memories…

…Her back pressed against the cold wall of a concrete storage building …the smell of dank cement everywhere… the muffled show tunes of the marching band barely audible in the distance….

Joe's hands had been so hot, and his mouth hard. He unzipped her jeans, pushed them down. Cold air raised goose flesh on her thighs. When he touched between her legs, she'd cried out, unable to stop herself. Then the bright beam of the security guard's flashlight, and the smell of his cigar…

"We were pretty reckless, weren't we?" He was smiling, as if the memories playing in his mind were amusing, instead of overwhelming. "If that security guy hadn't been a friend of Brian's, we probably would have been suspended, maybe even expelled."

That security guy. The cigar-smoking guy with the flashlight was the only one who ever caught them. So Joe *had* been remembering the exact same night. With her jeans near her knees, and her blouse half-unbuttoned, she'd definitely been in violation of about a zillion school rules, but suspension would have been the least of her worries. If the guard had called her father...

"Plus, your dad would have flogged me in the town square," Joe said, and she blinked, startled at how easily he seemed able to read her thoughts.

He grinned. "Of course, he would have had to catch me first. I was an idiot at seventeen, but I knew enough to run."

Abby chuckled, but before she could respond, an elegant blonde woman in a lush suede coat reached in from the stairs and tapped Joe on the shoulder.

"Hey, cowboy. Did your mom give you my message?"

Smiling, the woman flicked a quick glance at Abby, obviously trying to place her—or at least decide whether she was Joe's date or just a stranger on the same bench. Abby straightened her back and loosened her grip on the collar of his jacket, suddenly wondering if her recent X-rated thoughts were written all over her face.

"Yeah, she told me you couldn't make it to see Dancer tonight." Joe didn't seem to find the encounter awkward, so Abby relaxed a bit. "No problem. I took care of her before I headed out."

He put his hand on Abby's knee. "Tricia, you never knew Abby Foster, did you? Abby, this is Tricia Landers. She and I have gone in together on a little venture at the stables."

Tricia raised her eyebrows. The glance she shot Joe was cryptic. "A little venture. I guess that's one way to put it." She held her hand out across Joe's chest. "Hey, Abby. Nice to meet you."

Abby agreed, though she couldn't help wondering what these undercurrents meant. Nuances floated all over this exchange, but she couldn't tell if they were romantic or something else entirely.

At least Tricia hadn't said, "I've heard a lot about you." That classic line could be insult or compliment...except that, when you said it to your boyfriend's ex, it was *always* an insult. You knew the unspoken ending was, "And none of it was good."

"So are you staying for the game, Trish?" Joe eyed the crowded bleacher dubiously. "I'd say you should sit with us, but—"

Suddenly, something on the field distracted him. He leaned forward, shaking his head incredulously. "Good lord. They're putting Rafe in!"

"No kidding?" Tricia looked just as stunned as Joe, but she smiled toward the field, obviously pleased. "I told you Coach Holden was a nice guy."

Abby assumed all this flustered shock meant Rafe wasn't exactly a star player, which of course made sense, as he was still in that wiry string bean phase the Carlyle boys had to endure. She tried to identify him on the field, but helmets were on now, obscuring that familiar black hair. The players were all huddled together and she couldn't remember what his number had been.

Tricia, Joe and Abby were suddenly intently quiet, all three of them leaning forward, as if they could will Rafe to use this moment to shine. Abby crossed her fingers, though she honestly didn't know what to hope for, exactly. Joe was right—she hadn't learned much about forward passes or quarterback draws from the shadows of the concrete supply shed.

The huddle broke up with a brisk, unison handclap. The players ranged themselves along some invisible line. The boy with the ball dropped back. The other boys ran around, and suddenly, there was Rafe, running all by himself, down toward the goal posts.

"Catch it, catch it...keep your eye on the ball." Joe was muttering under his breath, as if Rafe could hear him.

So now Abby knew what to hope for. *Catch the ball, Rafe. You can do it.*

In a beautiful, arcing swoop, the ball sailed through the air, and for a split second, Rafe did seem to catch it. A cheer went up. It was in his hands, between his fingers…

And then, just as suddenly, it wasn't. It squirted out like an oiled pig…and then it hopped and bobbled across the turf, with green-and-yellow players diving all around it, trying to smother it and make it be still.

The crowd groaned. As a whistle blew shrilly, the boys came loping off the field. Rafe came in last, just as the clock ticked away the final seconds before halftime.

The coach met him as he reached the sideline and grabbed his shoulders.

"Dang it, Rafe. That pass was catchable!" The coach was yelling, but only to make himself audible, probably. He didn't sound out of control. "If you'd kept your eye on it, we'd be going into the locker room with a lead."

Joe sat very still, watching the moment unfold. Abby glanced at his face, wondering whether he thought the coach was being unkind, but his expression didn't reveal much.

"He *did* take his eye off the ball, you know," Tricia observed with a smile. She, too, was gazing at Joe, but she must have been able to read his features better than Abby. "So there's no point going all papa-bear on poor Coach Holden."

Joe laughed. "God, you really do have a crush on the guy, don't you? But don't worry. If anything, I think he's too easy on the kid." He shrugged, and turned to Abby. "You want to watch the halftime show? Or are you hungry yet?"

"Definitely hungry," she said. It was true—she'd been famished for hours. But it was also true that she was starting to wonder whether Tricia Landers intended to stand there leaning on the railing all night, preventing Abby and Joe from being alone. Maybe if they walked around a little, they could shake her...

"Tricia?" Joe posed the question to the newcomer politely as he stood, stretching out his shoulders and bending his neck to loosen up after the tight fit. "How about you?"

Tricia shook her head. "I'm fine. I thought I saw Matt Locke over there. Joelle's with him tonight, so if I'm going to ask him about..." She slipped another odd glance toward Abby, then blinked at Joe. "About that *thing* we discussed, I should probably do it now, when the whole Winslow voting block is present."

"Good idea." Joe nodded his approval without further comment.

Yes, very *good idea, Tricia,* Abby thought, though she had no idea what they wanted from Winslow Farms. She had to laugh a little at the familiar fussy feeling. Joe was no longer hers in any sense of the word, and yet seeing him with other females made her as waspy and jealous as ever.

Odd, wasn't it? Especially since she could remember times when, as she'd watched Blaine flirt with other women, she'd felt nothing but a half-hearted hope.

Maybe, she'd often thought wistfully, this is the one he'll leave me for.

She felt like an idiot, now. A doormat. Why hadn't it ever occurred to *her* to leave *him*?

Finally, Tricia left. Joe held out his hand, and Abby took it. They descended the two or three steps and started the slow trek toward the concession stand, still stopping every few feet to accept condolences about Rafe's conspicuous muffing of the pass.

Mostly, sympathy was expressed by a back slap or a mournful headshake, not words. If conversation had been difficult before, it was impossible now. The band had marched on field, and had struck up a jazzy rendition of "Shine On, Harvest Moon." The drums weren't completely in sync, and the horn soloist struggled to hit a few of the higher notes, but what they lacked in finesse they made up for in sheer volume.

Throughout the stadium, homecoming spirit was clearly sky high, even though Marietta trailed on the scoreboard. Every now and then someone in the stands would randomly scream "Go Grizzlies," while on field the band formed and reformed intricate patterns, and sequined dancers tossed sparkling silver batons in the air, then magically caught them in white-gloved hands.

Even the football players were still out on the sidelines, laughing and whistling at the dancers. They traditionally didn't go into the locker room until the homecoming court was announced. It was a rare year that the king wasn't a quarterback, anyhow.

Eventually, as they inched through the crowd, Abby fell back a pace, soaking in the moment, letting Joe lead. As she trailed in his sociable wake, her gaze fell time and time again on his beautifully tapered back...mesmerized by the way his jeans rode low on those narrow hips, fascinated by the new breadth of his shoulders.

Not that the nitty-gritty of real life was about cute butts and strong shoulders...

She'd learned that much, at least, in the past eight years. On Monday, she'd go to Billings, where she had three job interviews lined up. She'd spent the past two years getting her paralegal certificate, and she was ready to start supporting herself. She'd have to get serious about a lot of things then, and she wouldn't have much time for staring at sexy shoulders and trim hips.

But this weekend wasn't "real life." With any luck, this would be a seventy-two-hour fantasy idyll, a gift to herself. It was a time capsule, in which she'd transported herself back to her youth. Before Blaine. Before New York. Before life turned sad or scary. Before she made such a mess of everything.

Suddenly, a solemn voice over the loudspeakers began introducing the homecoming court. Abby turned, watching as pretty girls who must have been freezing in their strapless gowns walked slowly out, escorted by nervous boys in suits they probably bought yesterday.

She couldn't help smiling at their innocent joy. She'd felt so important the night she'd been named queen. When they put the tiara on her head, it had seemed like a message from Destiny. Fate's promise that she was special, destined for some perfect and glorious future.

She'd been hearing that all her life, from her father. And she'd liked the idea too much to question it very deeply. She never asked herself whether beating five other small-town girls for the right to wear a gaudy paste tiara at a three-hour dance in the local high school gym really made her immune to sorrow, failure, and pain.

Suddenly, she noticed that Joe was watching, too. With Abby's hand still tightly wrapped in his, he was staring at the field, his mouth tight as the voice on the loudspeaker announced, "Wendy Wysocki, escorted by Boomer Duchamp."

Abby was surprised by the intensity of his focus. Joe wasn't the homecoming court type and never had been. But then she saw. Wendy Wysocki was the lovely blonde cheerleader who'd been arguing with Rafe at the parade.

The petite beauty looked about five years older now, in her red mini-dress with crystals winking all over the bodice, and her silky blonde hair piled in crazy curls on top of her head. Five years older than she'd looked just hours ago—and definitely five years older than Rafe.

Clearly the mini-dress was a big hit. Several players on the sidelines whistled roguishly, followed by a brazen male voice that called out with a lazy insolence, "Go for it, Boomer! I'd Wysocki that myself!"

"Shut up, asshat!" A voice that sounded more like a growl rose out of the cluster of players. For a second, the girl on the field froze, her brilliant smile dropping as if it had been held in place by suddenly cut strings.

"Why don't you *make* me, Carlyle?"

And then, out of nowhere, all hell broke loose on the sidelines. Scuffling, yelling, windmilling bodies in red and white...

Abby had no idea what had happened, but Joe seemed to get the picture instantly. He cursed once, low, under his breath, and then let go of her hand.

He moved so fast she couldn't have stopped him if she tried. In two seconds, he was reaching into the knot of angry boys and pulling his brother out by the scruff of the neck, like a magician performing an emergency rabbit trick.

"Damn it, Rafe." Joe's voice was gruff. "Get a grip. Don't be such an idiot."

"Did you *hear* him?" His chest heaving, Rafe turned on his brother with eyes of fury. "Did you hear what he said about Wendy?"

Joe nodded. "Yeah, but don't—"

He didn't get a chance to finish the sentence. The coach's reflexes were good, too—and he arrived two seconds later. But he hadn't come to calm things down. He had come to yank the weeds out by the roots.

"Carlyle! Didrikson!" His index finger stabbed the air. "Hit the showers. You two are *done*."

Chapter Five

෨෬

"BUT YOU'RE JUST taking Abby back to her car, right?" Mary Carlyle frowned. "It's late, Joe."

Joe tried not to react to his mother's bossy tone. Between hearing that her youngest son had been ejected from the football game and seeing Abby Foster in her kitchen, Mary Carlyle was having a bad night. Her jaw was so tightly clenched the words could hardly get through.

"And it's cold," she added. "Very cold."

Joe didn't want to embarrass his mother in front of Abby, but she knew better than to try that tone on him anymore. He raised his eyebrows, silently reminding her of reality. Then he bent over and kissed the top of her head.

"We'll survive," he assured her. "Just promise me Rafe will, too. I don't want to get back here in the morning and discover you've skinned the poor kid in his sleep."

"In the *morning*?" His mother's spine was as stiff as a steel rod. "You plan to be gone *all night*?"

He met her angry gaze calmly. What exactly was she pulling here? Was she trying to make Abby think he still lived in the main house, with a curfew and an allowance he earned by doing chores? His mother hadn't known anything about where he slept, or with whom, since the day he turned twenty-one and decided to renovate the interior of the old outbuilding as his personal quarters.

The structure was ancient and ugly, with its rotten roof and its scarred log walls, but it had the prettiest views on the whole Carlyle spread. The front porch looked out on a horizon of hills that in silhouette might have been the peaked surface of a choppy sea. The back porch opened onto a twisting silver creek.

Best of all, the building was separated from the Carlyle main house by five acres of rolling land and trees that guaranteed privacy. Joe knew his mother needed his help with Rafe, and with the training business, and that was fine. Just not at the expense of his personal life.

"Good night, Mom," he said. She didn't answer, but he moved toward the door anyhow. He motioned for Abby to join him.

"Good night, Mrs. Carlyle," Abby said, her voice carefully neutral, her pace measured, as if she were skirting around an only-partially domesticated bobcat.

His mother opened her mouth, but Joe fixed her with another meaningful glare, and she slowly shut it without speaking. Good. Better silence than disrespect. He hadn't brought Abby along to drop Rafe off just to let her get roughed up.

In fact, he almost hadn't brought her at all. She hadn't wanted to come. She'd assured him she could walk back to the Graff from the stadium. Joe had protested. He'd explained that sometimes, after the games, the kids could get rowdy. Two homecomings ago, an alum who had started celebrating the big win early actually drove three blocks on the sidewalk before running into a light pole.

"*God.* Just let her walk back alone already," Rafe had muttered from the back seat, his words surprisingly clear, given that he was folded into a resentful knot in the corner, his forehead against the window. "She'll be *fine*."

"*Button it, moron.*" Joe had tightened his hand on the steering wheel and flicked a hard glance in the rearview mirror. "You don't get a vote."

Bottom line was, Joe hadn't intended to let Rafe's shenanigans cut this evening with Abby in half.

After they shut the door on Mary Carlyle's glowering face and walked to Joe's truck, he waited until they were both settled and the engine was on, with the heater sending out waves of soft air. Then he turned to Abby.

"What now? We could go back to the game, if you want. Or I could take you back to the Graff." He rubbed the palm of his hand over his kneecap. "Or we could go to my place."

"Your place?" She glanced toward the ranch house, where the light had already flicked off in the kitchen window. "I thought…"

He nodded. "That's what she wanted you to think. But I'm living out in the Swayback now."

Her eyes widened, catching the moonlight. *Swayback* had been their name for the ratty old place, back when it had been their secret meeting spot. Abandoned for years even then, it had been a mess, inside and out. The roof had sagged so dramatically in the center that it had looked like a swayback horse.

"Impossible," she said, shaking her head. "You *live* there? Even the mice wouldn't live there."

He smiled. "I spruced it up a little, put on a new roof, added a couple of rooms. It's nothing grand, but it's still got those views. Want to take a look?"

She hesitated a second or two, which surprised him. He would have thought she'd jump at the chance. When it came to seducing Joe Carlyle, her success rate in that old building was one hundred percent.

Or maybe it had been the other way around. Maybe he'd been the one doing the seducing. *Whatever.* They hadn't used words like "seduction" back then. Back then, sex had felt more primal, more natural and inevitable. They took each other the way they would have taken food if they were starving, the way they'd have slept if they were tired.

Either way, he would have figured she'd consider the invitation as his surrender. It wasn't. Or at least he hoped it wouldn't be. He didn't intend to make love to her tonight, but even he could see that returning to Swayback with Abby Foster was pushing his luck, flapping his wings way, way too close to the flame.

"I'd love to see it," she said suddenly. She took a breath, then turned to face forward, her hands laced casually in her lap.

"Good," he said, equally casual. But as he put the truck in reverse and began to back out, he glanced down at her braided fingers. The knuckles were as white as the moonlight.

It took less than five minutes to get to the house. He parked the truck and led her up the back porch stairs. The moonlight was bright enough that she could tell the outline of the structure had completely changed, and he heard a little murmur of surprise.

"Oh," she said. "The roof." She sounded disappointed.

He nodded. "I actually thought about leaving it the way it was," he said as he twisted his key in the back door lock. "But I couldn't get a construction permit without replacing it. They said it was unsafe. It undoubtedly was, of course. I guess we're lucky it never caved in on top of us."

He'd thought about that sometimes, especially while the crews had been removing the rotted boards and all the nasty debris from inside. He'd taken so many foolish risks, back then, with his own safety, and with hers.

Sneaking out here in the middle of the night, to this abandoned shack full of rotting ranch equipment, broken antlers, half-empty paint cans and bugs the size of his fist, the two teenagers could have fallen prey to anything.

Poachers, wild animals, snowstorms, creek floods, rusty nails, snakebite, roof collapse. Joe hadn't actually been prepared for any of those emergencies. No knife, no gun, no cell phone, no tourniquet, no emergency thermal blanket. Heck, he hadn't always even brought enough condoms, and he hadn't let that stop him, either.

It shamed him, now, to think back on what a selfish, hormone-driven kid he'd been. Her father had been right—Joe really had not been man enough to take care of her.

When he held the door open, she moved into the warm, dimly lit interior slowly. She moved from the kitchen to the one long room, and stood in the center of that space while he walked around switching on lamps to brighten things up.

"I'd offer to give you the tour," he said, "but other than the bathroom this is it."

It wasn't a tiny room—the original outbuilding had been about twenty by fourteen, and he'd added the bathroom and kitchen to that. The main area was arranged simply and sensibly, with two distinct living spaces, one for sleeping and one for working. He hadn't bothered to put up walls between the two. Not even a curtain. It would have been extra expense, which he hadn't been able to afford at the time.

Besides, living alone as he did, what was the point?

He'd brought a lot of women here, especially in the couple of years right after he finished the place. But this was the first time it made him mildly uncomfortable to have his bedroom in plain sight.

He wondered why. He had made up the four-poster bed this morning, as he did every morning, his early training too entrenched to let go just because his mom wasn't checking. He never left clothes lying around, or beer bottles on the nightstand, and he didn't even own any girly magazines.

But even so the bed looked self-conscious, as if it had been caught naked, with no privacy shield to hide behind. And he suddenly wondered whether bringing her here looked crude, as if he were a two-bit Romeo-cowboy, showing off his hand-made love nest.

"It's beautiful, Joe," Abby said. "I love that you didn't change the basic structure, but you made it a real home."

He looked at her dubiously, wondering for a second whether she'd sensed his self-consciousness and was trying to reassure him. But no...that was her genuine smile—it dimpled her cheeks, and it sent light all the way to her green eyes.

She moved through the room, stroking everything lightly, as if to learn it. Her touch was respectful, almost affectionate. She really did like the choices he'd made. She liked the corduroy armchairs, and the craftsman-simple wooden tables. She liked the hearth rug and the river-rock fireplace. Maybe she even liked the bed.

"Thanks," he said, trying not to think about those slim fingers grazing the warm skin of lampshades, the nubby buttons of chairs. "I'm comfortable here."

She had made her way all around the living area, and she'd come back to center again. She looked at him for a long minute, and then she walked over to him slowly, never taking her gaze from his.

When she reached him, she put the palm of her hand against his cheek.

"I love it," she said softly, and he reacted before he could think...the word "love" moving into him like an arrow. *Stop that,* he ordered his body, like a fool. It was too late. She hadn't said she loved *him*, this had nothing to do with that kind of love, and yet heat fell like fiery rain through every vein. He felt his breath start to grow shallow.

After a long moment, she stood on tiptoe and slowly brought her lips to his. She grazed his mouth lightly, brushing from left to right, then back again. Delicate…almost no pressure…just a hint of sweet, heated breath, just a suggestion of moisture below…

Somehow, through it all, he held himself perfectly still. The groan that rose from deep inside him never made it out into the air, and the burning in his groin remained his own, tormenting secret.

After a few seconds, she stopped. Dropping down from tiptoe, she looked up at him, her eyes shadowed.

"Nothing?" she said, and the open vulnerability in her voice nearly undid him. "Nothing at all?"

He stepped away while he still could.

"I think we need to eat," he said. He glanced toward the kitchen. "We never got dinner."

She bit her lips, as if wounded by the abrupt change of subject—which had been a rejection, no matter how you sliced it. Then she nodded.

"Good idea," she said. He had a feeling she'd have said the same thing if he'd suggested watching cartoons on TV, or painting the floors green.

But eating really was, in fact, a good idea. They needed to lower the temperature, before they did something they'd regret. Plus, he knew her face, even now, and he knew she was exhausted, and half-starved. He wondered how long it had been since she'd eaten or slept.

He probably should have taken her straight back to the Graff, but he'd been too selfish for that. He'd wanted her here, where he could talk to her. Where he could try to find out who she was now and why she was really back in Marietta—and whether they had any common ground left to meet on.

And so, pretending to be just a normal pair of old friends, they sat on his nubby sofa and shared what was left of last night's cold pizza. She suggested they have coffee, too, but he knew she was trying to stay awake, and he had other plans, so he said he was out of coffee right now.

At first they talked about safe, impersonal things. The weather. The new stores in town. The expansion of the high school. His renovations to Swayback.

Then they risked getting a little more personal. They discussed some of the people they'd seen at the game. Then the game itself, which inevitably led to Rafe and Wendy, and the romance that caused the ruckus at halftime.

From there, it was inevitable they'd come to his mother.

"Could she really think I'd believe she forgot who I was?" Abby didn't meet his eyes when she asked the question. Instead she concentrated on moving a piece of pepperoni around on her pizza slice awkwardly, as if she couldn't find the perfect position for it. "I mean, she and I were friends long before you and I—"

She broke off. He knew what she meant. His mother had given Abby riding lessons from the time she was eight years old. That was how someone like Joe had stood a chance of dating someone like Abby in the first place. They'd been children together, in a place that didn't recognize income—a stable. He'd been a more accomplished rider, even then, which gave him a status he didn't possess anywhere else in Marietta.

He'd helped Abby overcome her fear of horses.

"But I guess that just made it worse," Abby said, finally leaving the pepperoni alone. "That we'd been friends, I mean. She probably felt I'd betrayed her, just as much as I'd betrayed you."

"It's not about her own feelings—it never is with her. You know how she is." Joe dropped his last bit of crust into the empty pizza box on the coffee table, then grabbed a paper napkin to wipe his hands. "The woman could give mother tigers lessons in defending their young."

She nodded slowly. She knew, of course. Everyone in Marietta knew how fierce Mary Carlyle could be. Eighteen years ago, her husband had been kicked by a horse they were boarding, and after a terrible two-week lingering he'd died, leaving her a young widow with three little boys and a fourth on the way. From that moment until today, she hadn't looked right or left—she'd focused only on her sons, and the horse-training business that put food on their table.

All these years, she'd been both father and mother to them. She'd always stood by with the toughest discipline and the most unconditional support. Even when they went through their teenaged crazy spells, she never panicked, never gave up. She just tossed a rope of clear-eyed love around them, and dragged them, kicking and screaming, to the other side.

Thinking back on it now, Joe realized it was a wonder his mother hadn't been even less civil to Abby than she was. She knew, though she'd never forced him to talk about it, exactly how bad it had been.

An awkward silence hung in the room for a few seconds. They both knew they'd run out of small talk.

"So...I guess we've let the elephant sit on the table long enough." Joe mustered a half-smile. "Maybe we should just go ahead and talk about it."

She didn't ask what "it" was. She seemed to be holding her breath for a long minute. Then she placed her own unfinished slice into the pizza box, as well. She extended her hand just far enough to let her fingers rest on his knee.

"We could. If you think there's anything good that could come of rehashing all that unhappiness." She watched him with shadowed eyes. "Or we could just...stop talking."

For a minute, with her fingers touching him in that way that was both achingly familiar and electrifyingly new, he thought he'd give in. *Of course* he wanted to make love to her—he'd dreamed about it, awake and asleep, for eight years now. Memories of her had driven him into other women's arms, and then had driven him back to celibacy and frustration.

But if he did give in...then what? Would he wave goodbye to her on Monday with a smile on his face, pleased to have scratched an itch that had tormented him too long? Or would he be back where he'd been eight years ago?

He had no idea—as he'd explained to her, he didn't know how he felt. And he didn't know who she was, why she was here, or what she really wanted. He'd been a fool for her once. He didn't intend to do that again.

"I think we should talk," he said calmly, ignoring the warmth of her fingers, and how it had begun to course out, through his legs and toward his core.

She bit her lower lip, as if she had to stop herself from arguing. She took her hand away from his knee and rested it in her lap.

"All right," she said. "What do you want to know?"

"Everything—or, I guess I mean *anything*." He put his right arm over the back of the sofa, angling himself to get a better look at her face. "Your dad sold the ranch right after the wedding, and from then on it's just a blank. No one had news from you, or if they did they didn't share it with me. I pictured you living the high life out there in New York, dripping with diamonds, and loving every minute of being Mrs. Blaine Watts. Obviously it wasn't quite like that."

"No." She smiled, and he noticed that she rubbed her left hand, where Blaine's gigantic engagement ring used to be. "Not quite."

"Okay." He tried not to be impatient. "So what *was* it like? What went wrong?"

Turning her head, she looked out the window for a few seconds, but there wasn't much to see except a wavy, indistinct reflection of the two of them, and the amber coronas of lamplight on the end tables. It was midnight, and the creek was black in the shadows of the pines, untouched by moonlight.

"It's difficult to explain," she said, turning back to face him. "I don't want to sit here and disparage Blaine. Nothing *went* wrong. It already *was* wrong. It was wrong of me to marry him in the first place. I knew I didn't love him, and I should have been strong enough to say no."

He kept his face impassive, somehow. But this proved what an idiot he was. He *really* liked hearing that sentence: "I knew I didn't love him."

Truth was, he'd never been entirely sure. The minute Blaine had come to visit at the Foster ranch, Abby had seemed so impressed by the older man. She'd spent the first month of Blaine's visit repeating every clever thing he said at dinner. Every sentence she uttered began with "Blaine says…"

Joe had felt so inferior to the world-traveled rich man who chatted about skiing in the Alps, his conversation punctuated with French phrases. He'd felt so young, so uneducated, so boring.

So *poor*.

"I won't take anything you say as badmouthing Blaine," he said now. "I'm just trying to understand what happened."

She nodded. "In some ways, I'm still trying to understand it, myself. It was such a mess. The basic problem was that we'd all had private reasons for wanting the marriage—and our reasons were all at cross-purposes."

"What reasons?"

"Well…my father knew he was dying, so he wanted to hand me off to someone who had the money to take care of me. Dad was obviously the only one who realized our own finances were such a mess that he'd have to sell the ranch soon. Certainly, Blaine had no idea. Poor Blaine believed that, by marrying me, he was marrying a fat bank account that could shore up his own sinking ship."

"Sinking ship?" Joe had promised himself he wouldn't interrupt, but the grunt of surprise escaped before he could stop it. "Blaine was in financial trouble?"

"Always." She smiled, but she'd begun to toy with the edge of her sweater, folding and refolding a piece of wool between her thumb and forefinger. "He was a risk taker. He'd lose a fortune before lunch and find someone to bankroll a new investment before dinner. Making it rain, he called it. Except he started having dry spells that went on longer and longer. By the end of our marriage, it was like the Sahara."

"He was broke?"

"Almost. He had enough to keep up appearances. And he had a very wealthy 'friend' who wanted to be the new Mrs. Blaine Watts. So I suspect he landed on his feet."

Joe's mind felt confused, as if he were a little drunk, unable to thoroughly process the implications of all this. He had assumed, when she first said Blaine hadn't been as rich or as secure as he pretended, that Abby had wanted out. But now it sounded as if Blaine himself had decided to trade Abby in on a wealthier model.

"So...you two broke up because...I mean...whose idea was the divorce?"

"His." Abby frowned. "I had this ridiculous idea that I owed it to him to try to make it work. When I found out that my father had misled Blaine about the money, I felt so guilty."

"*Guilty?* The bastard was marrying you for your money, and you felt guilty because you didn't have *enough* to bail out his reckless investments?"

She raised her eyebrows gently. "I married him for money,

too, didn't I?"

He hesitated, his mind stumbling over the inconvenient fact. Even now, he was so eager to make someone else the villain. "I—I guess so. Hell, I don't know."

"Of course you do. You said so often enough, in no uncertain terms. Remember?"

Of course he remembered. He'd said so many terrible things, maddened by impotence and fury. He'd dimly understood that every time he insulted her, every time he yelled that he never wanted to see her again, it was as if he shot a flaming arrow onto the fragile ribbon that connected their lives.

He'd sensed it, but he hadn't been able to stop himself. One accusation after another, he'd set the thread ablaze, and then he'd watched it burn. When it was all over, they had stood on opposite sides of an unbridgeable gulf.

"I said a lot of things I wish I hadn't said." He shook his head. If only he could go back in time, gag that angry young man, and make him shut up. "I meant them—but that doesn't necessarily make them true. I wasn't quite sane at the time."

Her gaze softened, as if she appreciated his attempt to shoulder some of the blame. "The Carlyle Crazies?"

He nodded. "In spades."

"Still…you weren't wrong. Not really. I married Blaine because my father wanted me to. He knew he was dying, and it felt almost like a sacred last wish. But that's not the only reason I accepted Blaine. It's not even the main reason."

He waited, but she was silent a long time, as if she was searching inward, probing for the right words to express something so complex and murky.

She looked tired, he realized suddenly. Her eyes were shadowed, her face pale. He'd noticed the pallor back at the ball game, but he'd hoped getting a little food might help. If anything, though, she looked more exhausted than ever.

He wondered whether it was the ordeal of talking about her

marriage that was really draining her.

A gentleman would let her off the hook. But he wasn't a gentleman. He was a rough Montana cowboy with a crudely stitched-up broken heart, and he wanted to hear her explain. Why had she married a man she didn't love—when she knew it meant giving up forever the cowboy she did love?

Funny. Now that she was here, in front of him, close enough to touch, he no longer doubted for a minute that she had loved him. While she'd been gone, it had been easy to construct an imaginary Abby, a heartless snob who wore too much mascara and hair spray, and presided over bitchy New York intellectual parties.

But that was just a cliché, just a paper-doll Abby. This was the real woman. And suddenly he remembered everything about her. He remembered how she threw up the one time she tried to smoke a cigarette, how she cried whenever she heard "Auld Lang Syne," the way she used to dangle a French fry over his mouth, as he lay with his head in her lap, and then eat it herself to torment him.

He remembered how she'd sparkled in the moonlight, the night he made love to her while she wore her homecoming queen tiara, and nothing else. In this very room. He remembered the purring sound she made after sex, when she turned her face into his chest and rubbed her cheek against his skin. He remembered…

He remembered *everything.* It was as simple, and as overwhelming, as that.

And he needed to hear her explain. Even if she was so tired she could hardly speak. So he just waited.

"The main reason I married Blaine," she said finally, "is that I was a coward. I was faced with losing my protector, the father who had handled every detail of my life, from the moment I was born. The idea of being without him terrified me. I think, subconsciously at least, I was looking for another father figure, someone to take over as my protector."

"And you didn't have any faith that I could do it." He tried not to sound bitter. "You didn't trust me."

"No," she admitted, speaking slowly. "I guess not. Or not enough, anyhow." She blinked, and her lips pressed together for a second, as if they might be threatening to tremble. "But you know what the worst part is? The worst part is that I didn't trust *myself*. I wasn't a child. I should have had the courage to take responsibility for my own life—plenty of eighteen-year-olds do. But I didn't. I just...didn't."

The last word cracked. She put the back of her hand against her mouth, as if the sound shocked her.

Suddenly, out of nowhere, a tear slid down each of her cheeks, shining amber in reflected lamplight. She made a choking sound and hurried to wipe the wetness away, but the sight had already pierced him deeply, and he couldn't bear it.

"Abby," he murmured. He reached out and grabbed her hands. Her fingertips were damp against his wrists, and she was subtly trembling, as if even the movement of blood through her veins was too rough for her, in this fragile state.

He pulled her up against him. As if ashamed of her tears, she twisted in his arms, so that when she reached his chest, her face was turned away from him. But he didn't need to see her face. He folded his arms around her and held tightly.

At first she was stiff, embarrassed or nervous or confused. But he held on. And gradually, as she breathed against his shirt, warming the cotton, and then the flesh beneath, she seemed to breathe in the comfort she needed.

Slowly, her shoulders softened. Her breasts pressed into him. Her hand crept up to his shoulder, then to his neck. Finally her fingers nestled in the hair that curled against his collar.

"I'm sorry," she said, her voice muffled. "I'm so sorry."

With the sensitized nerve-endings under his collarbone, he could feel her lips forming every syllable.

"I'm not," he answered softly. He moved his hands into her hair. Her long, silken hair that his fingers had stroked a thousand times. She liked that. He'd always lulled her to sleep, after they'd made love, by running his hands through her hair.

She made the purring sound, and burrowed her nose toward his shoulder, as if she wanted to breathe nothing but the scent of him.

Her scent drifted up to him, as well. Sandalwood. Cinnamon. The perfume of young dreams he thought he'd given up years ago....but clearly had only covered over with a façade of indifference.

He shut his eyes and tried to ignore the rising heat between his legs. He would not make love to her tonight. No matter what she said, she didn't really want that. Not if she still had tears to cry over those two reckless children they had once been. Tears that had been bottled up for the past eight years.

She might have told herself she'd come home to Marietta for a fling. But apparently even after all this time he knew her better than she knew herself. The lovemaking she offered to him was penance, not joy. Guilt, not love.

What she really needed was forgiveness—from him, and from herself.

He didn't know whether he could find the strength to offer her forgiveness. That was a lot to ask. But he could at least find the strength to stop himself from taking her body as payment for the past.

Without speaking, he stroked the smooth, auburn silk that ran down her back. A steady rhythm. Her fingers still twined in the edges of his hair, but were barely stirring now. She breathed deeply. Then more deeply still...

Finally, her fingers stopped moving. Her body grew light and soft against his. He could have picked her up like a child.

Abby Foster had fallen asleep.

Chapter Six

೮ಎ೧ಚ

FOR A SECOND, when she woke, she had no idea where she was. She was comfortable, warm, stretched out on something soft, her nostrils filled with a faintly masculine, tweedy scent. A warm light beat against her closed lids, and she knew it was day.

But which day? And where?

Then, as her mind cleared, it came flooding back. Marietta. Homecoming. *Joe.*

Their beloved Swayback, cleaned and tamed and turned into his bachelor quarters. Opening her eyes, she rose on one elbow, his cushy sofa yielding under her weight. She pushed her hair back from her face with her other hand.

"Joe?"

The apartment was silent. She threw back a soft blue blanket he must have spread over her during the night, swung her feet to the floor, and stood.

"Joe?"

Still no answer. One sweep of the open-plan room showed her he wasn't there. She went into the kitchen. With half a dozen windows letting in the bright morning sunlight, it was charming.

And sparkling clean. Except for a mug in the sink, and a few papers on the counter, everything was tidy, the obviously new appliances as spotless as if he'd never used them.

But he'd left a note for her on the refrigerator door.

Seeing to horses. Back by 8.
—J

She opened the jaws of the small navy blue plastic clip that held the paper and pulled it down. She ran her fingers over the jagged black letters. His handwriting was so familiar. That thick, slanted slash of his *J*... she'd always thought there was something almost unbearably sexy about it.

She'd received a thousand notes from him through the years...not impersonal like this one, but wonderful, hot, fevered things. He would put them in her locker, wedge them through her car window, slip them in her purse as they passed in the hall between classes. He'd leave them here, in Swayback, under an old paint can, in case he had to miss a meeting they'd arranged.

Always short, to the point, yet rich with the sound of his voice. Immediate and intense. Never flowery, of course—he was a cowboy, not a poet. But they'd made her heart flutter just the same.

I love you.
You're sexy as hell, Abby Foster.
Swayback Friday after school? Ditch cheerleading practice.
Come this afternoon. I need you bad, Abs.

But those notes were all gone now, most of them wadded up and tossed as soon as they were read. There had been so many—and she'd believed there would always be more. The remaining few had been left behind when she married, and then discarded with the other "junk" when the ranch was sold, no doubt.

She folded this one carefully and put it in her jeans pocket.

She found the small bathroom, used it, and then washed her hands and face in the sink. She put some of his toothpaste on her finger and did her best without a toothbrush. She returned to the great room and retrieved her purse, where at least she had a hairbrush and some gum.

She'd just pulled herself together when she heard his footsteps on the back porch. With one last tug at her rumpled sweater, she met him at the kitchen door.

"Hi," she said as he came in on a gust of brisk, clean air. It must be a very cold morning. He wore a black, fur-lined windbreaker, and he carried his hat and work gloves in his hand. His dark hair was tousled and his high cheekbones were burnished red-gold by the October wind. His blue eyes shone from exercise and reflected morning light.

He was so beautiful she had to put one hand against the countertop to make sure she didn't go weak in the knees.

"Hi," he said with a smile. He stamped his feet on the mat just outside the door, then stepped in. He dropped the gloves on the counter and hung his hat on a hooked rack by the window. "Sleep well?"

"I did," she said, suddenly self-conscious, remembering how emotional she'd been last night, and how thoroughly her dream of a fun, no-strings fling had gone awry.

"Your sofa is surprisingly comfortable. Thank you for the blanket. I'm sorry I was so..." She put her hands in her back pockets awkwardly, hating this stilted sound. "I don't know what got into me. I had been driving all day, and—"

"Hey." He put a finger up to her lips. "There's nothing to apologize for. You were tired. You slept. Nothing could be more natural."

Before she could argue the point, he removed his finger and

picked up a small orange flyer from the kitchen table.

"And now, it seems to me, the natural thing would be to have some breakfast." He held out the flyer. "I've got a gig flipping pancakes in half an hour. Want to come along?"

She took the piece of paper and scanned it quickly, skipping the clip art of grinning harvest moons and stacks of what probably were meant to be pancakes and bacon.

The football team pancake breakfast fundraiser. This morning, in the high school cafeteria.

"I don't know…" She handed it back to him. "Right now?"

"Yeah. Why? You're not hungry? Impossible! I know we had a gourmet meal last night, all that wonderful, cold, stale pizza and all. But surely you've got room for a couple of pancakes."

She laughed. "It's not that. It's just…why don't we stay here? I haven't showered, or…"

"You look fine." He smiled. "Better than fine. You look so good, in fact, that I suspect we'd be safer out in public."

Blushing, she plucked at the sleeve of her sweater. It was a lovely compliment, but still…she felt a sting of disappointment. She had hoped he was past the "must resist" phase.

"Even if that were true, which it isn't—I just looked in the mirror, so you can't kid me—these are the same clothes I wore yesterday. I can't show up at breakfast in the same clothes I wore to the game last night."

He tilted his head, shoving his hands into the pockets of his windbreaker. "Why not?"

"Because—" She frowned, well aware he was teasing her. "Joe, don't be silly."

"What's silly about it? So you show up in the same clothes. You're afraid people will talk? So what? You're only in town for another…what, forty-eight hours? What do you care what they say?"

"I don't. It's not that. It's just…" She suddenly felt ridiculous. Why *did* she care? Hadn't she vowed to listen only to her own instincts? Besides, she and Joe weren't bad little high school kids sneaking around anymore. Neither one of them was married, or committed elsewhere. Her father was dead, and even tiger-mother Mary Carlyle no longer had any power here.

"Awwww," he said, his eyes twinkling in the sunlight that danced through the kitchen. "This is so sweet, Abs. Are you afraid you'll ruin *my* reputation?" He pulled his truck keys from his pocket and jingled them lightly. "Come on. Let's go."

An hour later, she'd eaten so many pancakes her stomach hurt. The cafeteria was jam-packed, the bare-floored, bare-walled space ringing with chatter and laughter just as it she remembered it.

The rows of folding tables along the walls, laden with electric griddles and pancake-makers, were always busy. Long lines of high schoolers and their supportive families, not to mention half the population of Marietta, stood, plates in hand, waiting for freshly flipped short stacks filled with blueberries or pecans or chocolate chips.

The air was heavy with the scents of bacon and maple syrup, and even though Abby was full to aching, she was contemplating getting just one more. Chocolate chips this time, she thought.

Joe had been busy cooking since they arrived, but she hadn't been lonely. She'd found half a dozen people she knew from the old days, and she'd made half a dozen new friends, just because they were sitting near enough to smile at. Around here, smiling led to talking, and talking led to friendship…straight line, no detours.

She'd almost forgotten how different Marietta, Montana, was from Manhattan. In this small town, there was no such thing as a stranger.

For the first few minutes, she'd shared a table with Tricia

Landers, the lushly groomed blonde she'd met at the game last night. Tricia's cool glance flickered knowingly over Abby's green sweater, but she didn't mention that it looked familiar. Tricia didn't seem at all tense about it. Abby had to assume that, whatever the woman's connection to Joe might be, it wasn't sexual and never had been.

Tricia left early, after picking politely at a pancake. But her place at Abby's table was quickly scarfed up by another slickly polished professional. It turned out to be someone Abby knew casually—Josh Butterworth. A lawyer here in town, though not one her dad had ever used, he'd given a few career-day speeches at the high school.

She was glad to see him again. She had high hopes of getting something in Billings next week, but it never hurt to have another friend in the legal community. When she told him about her career plans, he'd playfully offered her a job, and though she knew he didn't really mean it, it still felt encouraging to hear the words.

"Dang," Josh said with a grin when she mentioned the Billings interviews. "You're serious, aren't you? I wouldn't ever have taken you for the worker-bee type, Abigail Foster. I sure do wish I'd represented you in your divorce. I could have gotten you enough to guarantee you never had to work a day in your life."

Abby just smiled. She wasn't in the mood to get into a discussion about the difficulties of getting blood from a turnip.

"I'm excited to start working as a paralegal," she said, nibbling on her third piece of bacon. Tricia Landers might be counting calories, but Abby wasn't. Not this weekend. This weekend was all about joy, and this bacon was to die for.

"I loved my classes—I'm even thinking about continuing on to law school." She pointed her fork at Butterworth lightheartedly. "If I do, I might just come back here and hang out my shingle in Marietta. Some competition might be good for you."

"Do it," Butterworth said, slapping the table. "And speaking of competition, if you come back maybe I could give Carlyle over there a little competition, too. I go by Josh, but I was christened a Joseph, you know…in case you're fond of the name."

He was just teasing again, of course. Josh Butterworth was a well-known flirt. But Abby liked him, in spite of that. And she liked the way Joe kept flicking glances over at her table, frowning at Butterworth as if he wished the man would get lost. It wasn't a "just friends" look, no matter what he told himself.

She excused herself to Josh and returned to Joe's line for another pancake. When she reached the front, she held out her plate. "Chocolate chips this time, I think," she said, unashamed.

He laughed as he poured some oil into his griddle with a flourish. "They're going to have to roll you out of here in a wheelbarrow if you keep this up," he said. "And you better watch out. Butterworth doesn't flirt with women who actually *eat.*"

"He's not flirting," she said, batting her eyes innocently. "He offered me a job. He's looking to hire a new paralegal."

"I bet he is." But Joe was smiling, and Abby grinned back. "Look," he began. "After I'm done here—"

His sentence was interrupted by the sound of music. The griddle next to Joe's was manned by Bentley Larkspur, an old fisherman everyone called "Fly," and the old man had suddenly burst into song.

"Shine on, Shine on, Harvest Moon!"

Another older man, on the other side of Fly, picked up the melody. Fly elbowed Joe, who shook his head in annoyance, but started singing obediently. Pretty soon, the whole room was crooning along.

Without warning, Abby's eyes suddenly stung with tears.

Harvest Moon wasn't a song she had ever been particularly fond of, and frankly she'd already heard it enough this weekend to last a lifetime. But there was something about the wistful tune. There was something about the easy camaraderie of this little town…the way they came together to raise money, to break bread, and to sing songs…

Marietta had been her home, once. It was still the only place she'd ever felt a sense of belonging. She wondered whether Billings would ever come to feel like home. Even after eight years, Manhattan never had.

The song ended as abruptly as it began. Fly waved his pancake turner toward Joe, like a wizard brandishing a wand.

"Carry on," the old man said. "You were about to say something to the beautiful lady." He winked at Abby. "Sorry to interrupt. It's just what I do. I sing. I spread joy. You're welcome."

She laughed. "Thanks," she said. And she meant it.

Then she turned back to Joe, who had her chocolate chip pancake ready to slide straight from the pan onto her plate.

"I was *about* to say…" Joe shot a quick glare toward Fly, who wriggled his eyebrows to show how little he cared. "When I'm done here, let's go to the stables."

Again, disappointment stung at her. The stables? She'd hoped he was going to suggest returning to the Swayback, or maybe to her room at the Graff.

"I've got a new horse," he continued. "He's pretty special and—"

But once again a noise broke into the sentence. With an annoyed growl, Joe glanced down at the folding table, where his cell phone was buzzing angrily, setting up a waspy vibration against the plastic surface.

"Damn it." He picked up the phone and read a message written there. It wasn't long, but it must have been troubling.

His brows drove together, and his mouth hardened. When he looked up at Abby, the playful light had disappeared from his eyes. "Scratch that. Listen…your car's still here in the school lot from last night, isn't it?"

She nodded.

"Good. Because I'm going to have to head straight home." He reached down and dialed his griddle to the "off" setting. "My cell's the same. Text me your number. I'll call you when I can."

She was still holding her empty plate out, too surprised to set it down. "All right." In the back of her mind, she wondered how he knew she'd still remember a cell phone number from eight years ago. "But…what's wrong?"

"It's Rafe, of course." His voice was scratchy with irritation, and under that she heard real anxiety. "My mother can't find him. Apparently the idiot went and stole her car."

སྠིལྩ

"WELL, UM, I don't know that we actually *have* any dresses like that." The pretty little salesgirl at the boutique on Main Street frowned, obviously perplexed. She'd clearly been taught that she must always, always find something to please every customer. But Abby's requirements were just too outrageous. "I mean, the dress you've described…."

"Exists only in her dreams?" Charlie sighed and cut a frustrated look in Abby's direction. "I've tried to tell her that."

Abby ignored them both, wandering off to check a far rack, where used consignment dresses hung. She never spent money on clothes anymore. Between being Markham Foster's daughter and Blaine Watts' wife, she had a wardrobe that ought to last any woman a lifetime. Problem was, she hadn't brought any of the dresses with her to Marietta. Everything like that was still in a storage unit in Manhattan. No point moving any of it until she knew where she'd be working.

But Charlie had recruited her to help handle the dessert tables at the dance tonight. Joe would be there, chaperoning, and Charlie knew that Abby would want to be wherever Joe was.

And that meant Abby needed something nicer than her jeans to wear. It had to be perfect. Sexy enough to tempt Joe beyond his willpower, but not so sexy she'd set tongues wagging. Not too young, as if she were trying to upstage the teenagers, but not too old, either. Warm enough to be comfortable outside, but cool enough to dance in. Dressy, but practical. Preferably red or white, the school colors, or maybe black, but definitely no green or yellow, Livingston's colors.

And, above all, *cheap*.

She had planned her post-Blaine finances carefully, and she knew exactly how frugal she had to be to make her bank account last until she got a regular paycheck. Mess with that plan, and she'd have to eat scrambled eggs for a month to catch up.

Not that eating was high on her list right now. She pressed her hand to her stomach as she fingered through a series of heavy satin mother-of-the-bride type dresses. Even now, four hours after the pancake breakfast, she was still carrying around a lump of batter as heavy as a bowling ball. She might not ever eat again.

"No, no, not those!" Charlie sounded horrified, and she tugged Abby's elbow, pulling her away from the rack. "Do you want to show up looking like his *mother*?"

"Good grief." Abby laughed. "That definitely wouldn't help with the campaign."

That was what they'd started to call it. The Campaign. The war to get past Joe Carlyle's surprising new barrier of cool, impregnable self-control.

Surprising might be an understatement. When she'd decided to come to Marietta and look up her old love, she'd expected to find either a guy who hated her guts or one who lusted after her memory as much as she lusted after his.

What she had *not* expected to find was a cautious man who fell somewhere in the middle, and who apparently believed his smartest move was to talk and talk and talk...and end the weekend as friends.

If she couldn't find a way to awaken his old feelings, and convince him that they'd both feel better if they got some real closure, she'd probably drive to Billings on Monday morning with nothing more than a new LinkedIn contact...and the same old hunger gnawing at her heart.

"How about this one?" Charlie held up a gorgeous, sparkling red sweetheart dress, with lots of tulle and crystals. It was a hair on the sexy side, but Abby was drawn to it, anyhow. Maybe better to be a little too tempting than not tempting enough?

She ran her fingers over the softly draped bodice, feeling the cool nubs of crystals. Then she let her hand fall to the sleeve, where the price tag dangled. She turned it over.

"Nope." She shook her head firmly. "That's three times as much as I can afford."

"Darn." Wrinkling her nose, Charlie slid the dress back onto the rack with a sigh. "Too bad you're not about five inches taller. I have some dresses that are exactly what you're looking for."

Abby laughed. "I've spent my life wishing I had your beauty queen figure, Charlie. I'm pretty sure it's not going to happen now."

"Well, I guess that's only fair." Charlie shrugged. "Considering how much of my life I spent envying your house, your clothes, your horses..."

Abby almost reached over and hugged Charlie for the kindness of that fib. Charlie's family hadn't had a lot of money, but they'd had each other, and their warm, humble house had been Abby's favorite place in the world to visit.

And now Charlie had a wonderful, perfect marriage to a man who was both lover and friend, partner and passion. While Abby had...

A divorce, a tight budget, and a move to a city where she didn't have a single friend in the world. And an old ghost she couldn't bury, no matter how hard she tried.

The salesgirl drifted away to help other customers, clearly writing Abby off as a lost cause. Seizing their moment of privacy, there in the mother-of-the-bride nook, Abby blindly pulled out a dress. Squeezing it up against her chest, she turned impulsively to Charlie.

"Why did I do it, Charlie? You remember that night. You knew I was making a mistake, and so did I. Why did I go through with it? Was it really just the money?"

Charlie didn't answer immediately. That was one of the things Abby loved best about her. She took every question like this seriously. She cared.

"No. I don't honestly think it was the money," Charlie said finally. "You had plenty of that...or thought you did. It had more to do with your father, probably. He wanted it for you. Think of all the beauty pageants I entered, even though it was my mother's dream, not my own."

"Yes, but...a beauty pageant isn't a lifetime commitment. And you won college scholarships, so you *did* want to enter them, just not for the reasons everyone thought. Marrying someone—that's so much more..."

She couldn't think of the right word. *Stupid?*

"I know." Charlie's eyes were sad. "But look. No one was pushing me, not like your dad was pushing you, and even so I almost married the wrong man, too. Even after I'd seen what it did to you, I almost made the same mistake."

"But you didn't."

"Only because Tom fell for someone else. If he hadn't, who

knows what I might have done?"

Abby knew. In her gut, she was convinced Charlie never would have married Tom. She remembered the way Charlie's email had described the engagement ring Tom had wanted to buy her. Every time she'd tried it on, it had bit into her finger, she'd said, and even Abby had understood the "bite" was a warning blast from her subconscious.

Abby's subconscious had sent out the same kind of siren screams. But she had closed her ears and ignored them. That was a special kind of self-destructive. No wonder Joe wouldn't forgive her, or agree to renew their relationship, even for a weekend.

She wondered now whether maybe he hadn't ever mourned her loss at all. Maybe he'd been relieved to be rid of any girl as messed up as crazy Abby Foster…

"Oh, my gosh!" Suddenly, Charlie's eyes grew wide. She reached over, grabbed the dress Abby held, and plucked it right out of her hands. She held the garment at arm's length, so that she could study it with her expert eye, honed by all those years of competing in evening gowns.

Suddenly Abby saw why Charlie sounded so excited. How had this lovely design ended up back here with the stuffy dowager frocks? It was the most lightweight, supple black velvet, the kind a person's fingers itched to reach out and feel. A simple, knee-length sheath, with three-quarter sleeves…but those modest touches were balanced by the tight, curve-hugging shape, and a surprisingly sensual heart-shaped bodice of sequined satin.

Abby was stunned by how beautiful the dress was, now that she really looked. She'd yanked it out mindlessly, just to keep up the pretense of shopping while she talked to Charlie about more important things.

For a few seconds, Charlie murmured approvingly as she ran her hands over the velvet. Finally satisfied with the quality, she bit her lower lip and seemed to hold her breath as she checked the price tag.

She turned to Abby, her eyes glowing. "You're a genius, Abby! This is the one!" She held the black velvet up to Abby's neck and squinted so that she could imagine it on.

"Yes. This is the secret weapon the campaign has been searching for, Abs! Now if only Joe's annoying little brother will behave himself, so that Joe can get there in time to see you wearing it."

Chapter Seven

෨ﻌ෬

JOE ARRIVED AT the dance an hour late and in fairly foul humor. It had taken him hours to track Rafe down, and then hours more to persuade his mom not to tie the kid up and lock him in the barn for the rest of his life.

But the hardest part of all was convincing Rafe he still had to attend the homecoming dance, even without Wendy. "You promised to work the photo booth," he'd reminded the boy. "Carlyles keep their promises."

He'd practically had to drag Rafe to the high school by the scruff of his neck, much the way he used to drag him into the dentist's office when he was a little kid. And, just for the record, the dead weight of a seven-year-old brat was a lot easier to maneuver than the dead weight of the same brat at seventeen.

He dumped Rafe off at the photo booth, set up at the far end of the gym, where the cheerleaders were raising money by taking photos of couples posed in front of a huge, round, yellow Harvest Moon the art department had affixed to the back wall. Singles could opt for posing with a scarecrow, played by one of the drama students dressed in straw-stuffed overalls and a squashed stove-pipe hat.

Rafe's stint was scheduled for nine to eleven, so he wasn't more than a minute or two late. But the cheerleaders on duty gave his arrival such a snooty cold shoulder even Joe felt a twinge of pity for his obnoxious little brother.

"It's only two hours," he said. He tried to put his hand on Rafe's shoulder, but the boy twitched away, turning to stare at the wall.

Yeah, that's right, Prince Charming. That'll help.

He shook his head internally, then headed over to the punch table on the other side of the gym. Unlike Rafe, Joe *was* late. His shift should have begun at eight. Whichever PTA mom he'd been supposed to relieve was undoubtedly going to be ticked.

He hoped it wasn't Ginger Baker. Ginger was Super Mom, and she seemed to think that, if the punch bowl weren't guarded every single second, four-hundred-proof whiskey would magically find its way into the fruity sugar water and then the whole evening would devolve into a shameful, drunken orgy.

He prepared his apology as he made his way across the gym floor, dodging strands of fall leaves in orange, gold and red. The prom committee had gone to a lot of trouble to hang them from the web of ceiling beams and ductwork that held the gym's lighting and sound system. Brushing strands from his shoulder, Joe remembered guiltily that he'd promised to help, but he hadn't made it back from Bozeman in time.

He'd missed the alumni dinner, too.

So much for the Carlyles always keeping their promises.

As he neared the refreshment tables, which had been set out along the sidelines, once the bleachers had been retracted, he was relieved to see that the punch lady was too short and shapely to be Ginger. It looked more like...

Oh, man. It was Abby.

He hadn't even known she planned to be here. Someone must have recruited her. Charlie, maybe...

He froze for a second, beside a display of fall flowers and tree trunks and pumpkins, and let himself drink in the sight of her. Waves of girls in red lace and while silk, with boys in white tuxedos with red cummerbunds, washed past him, heading for the dance floor, or to the round tables decorated with jewel-colored fall flowers.

But he didn't really see any of them. The only spot in the whole gymnasium that was in focus was the spot where Abby Foster stood.

God, she was beautiful. Her sweet, heart-shaped face was pale and lovely, framed by a loose upsweep of heavy, shining hair that gave her an old-fashioned look, like a painting of a Gibson Girl. She wore a simple black dress, but on her it wasn't simple at all. The damn dress almost seemed to be making love to her body. Across her breasts, tiny sparkling flares exploded, like kisses of light, whenever she moved. And everywhere else the black fabric clung to each of her curves with a darkly silent, almost animal sensuality.

She turned, bending over to pick up a bottle of Seven Up. The velvet molded itself hungrily to the curve of her rear, slid down her thigh and licked the inside of her knees. As he inhaled raggedly, his body turned on like a light switch, and he was instantly filled with heat and power and a terrible, yearning pain.

Somehow he tamped it down enough to walk again, and made his way over to her. She looked up with a happy smile, obviously unaware of how she affected him.

"Joe! You made it!"

He nodded, not trusting his voice just yet.

"Did you find Rafe?"

He nodded again, cleared his throat, and slipped his hands in his pants pockets. "Yeah. He was almost in Bozeman, though. Apparently Wendy's father decided his daughter would be safer in another town."

Abby's smile slipped away. Her green eyes clouded. "I'm sorry." She shook her head. "*Fathers.*"

He smiled. "To be fair to Mr. Wysocki, he's absolutely right about that. Rafe has the common sense of a maggot right now, especially where Wendy is concerned."

"How did you find him? Did you have to call the police about the car?"

Joe laughed. He was starting to feel slightly more in charge of his body, as his temperature returned to normal. Everything on him still buzzed slightly, as if he were only one touch away from another savage surge of desire, but he could actually breathe without pain.

"No police. Rafe's not slick enough to make tracking him very hard. The housekeeper at the Wysocki house told me Wendy and her dad were on their way to Bozeman to visit relatives. From there, I just followed the trail of purchases on the debit card Rafe and Mom use. She puts his allowance on it, so he has a copy of the card. The online site showed that he bought gas west of town, then fast food just west of that. I found him there, still sulking over a burger and fries, still at least ten miles east of Bozeman."

A burger and fries, and nothing but water to drink. That had given Joe hope for the kid. Rafe hadn't bought any soda because he'd used up every penny in the bank that was legitimately his.

Abby frowned. "Poor kid."

"Yeah, well, don't feel too sorry for him. Right now he's probably sitting over there planning to murder me in my sleep."

"I doubt it," Abby said. "He obviously adores you. He was probably waiting at that burger place, praying you'd find him and stop him before he did something really dumb."

He had thought the same thing himself, actually. Rafe's Carlyle Crazies were probably the least treacherous of all the brothers. Though he'd never admit it out loud, Rafe did seem to want guidance. He seemed to *want* to be saved from himself. Joe, Devlin and Brian hadn't. Not even a little. They'd all bought their one-way tickets to perdition gleefully, without a backward glance.

Maybe the crazy genes had been watered down by the time they reached the fourth Carlyle son. If so, lucky Rafe. Because fighting your way back up out of Hell wasn't easy.

"Abby, if Joe's finally here, can you come back over and handle the dessert table?" Ginger Baker, who held a clipboard with a pen poised officiously above it, called over from her station by the gym doors. "Heather needs to take a break."

"Sure!" Abby waved her agreement to the other woman, then gave Joe a rueful smile. "Better go. Ginger isn't fooling around about that schedule. But maybe...maybe I'll see you later?"

He should say no. He *wanted* to say no. He'd thought about it all afternoon, while he listened to Rafe rage and weep about Wendy. Loving the wrong person, at any age, brought you nothing but misery.

Saying no to this one-night stand would be hard...but not as hard as it would be if he said yes. He'd made it through last night, working through the past like an adult, getting answers to the questions that had tormented him so long, finding a way to make peace...all without giving in to temptation.

But he knew that he'd achieved that victory mostly because she'd fallen asleep before his resolve could weaken. He knew damn well that if he went to her room at the Graff tonight, they would make love.

And then it would kill him to let her go tomorrow.

Maybe he was a coward. But he didn't want to go back to square one. Looking at Rafe had brought every moment of agony back, full force.

He couldn't face having to get over her all over again.

"I don't know," he said. "It depends on Rafe, to some extent. And it depends—"

He broke off, but she waited, her gaze sweeping his face, as if she wished she could read there the words he refused to say out loud.

"*And?*" Her eyes were somber. "What else does it depend on?"

"On how strong I am," he said, opting for the truth. "Look, Abby, we want this, of course we do. Because…"

He shook his head. "I don't know why, exactly. You're here. You're beautiful. You're offering. And, hell, maybe we're conditioned to want each other, after all those years. It's habit. It's like…an animal instinct. But we both know it would be a mistake. We can do this right, if we try. We can make peace…make friends…put the past to rest…without taking advantage of each other. Without doing anything we'd regret. In fact, that's the *only* way we can make peace."

"Abby!" Ginger was frowning hard, tapping her pen on the clipboard. She took a step toward them.

"Coming," Abby said. She looked one last time at Joe. "I can't argue with your logic," she said. "This isn't a matter of reason and common sense. All I can say is…I really think you're wrong, and I hope you'll change your mind."

୫୬

BY ELEVEN, THE dance was winding down. The dessert table was almost empty. The DJ had been playing nothing but slow songs for the past twenty minutes, and half the tables were abandoned, littered with discarded punch glasses and plates of half-eaten cake, and bruised petals from wrist corsages.

Abby was tired. The strobe lighting and the loud music had made her head ache, and these "sexy" shoes she'd borrowed from Charlie had become instruments of torture.

She glanced around the gym. Dozens of couples were still dancing under the twinkling lights, but the chaperones seemed to have thinned out even more than the students. Ginger and Charlie and even Joe were nowhere to be seen.

Wiggling her toes inside her shoes, and leaning against a fake tree trunk for support, Abby finally decided her need for fresh air outweighed her responsibility to protect the dregs of the dessert offerings.

She left the table untended and exited through the gym's front double doors.

The night was cold and clear, its blackness so full of spiky stars it looked like shattered glass. She stood just under the front portico of the school, inhaling the clean air gratefully. She hadn't realized how stuffy the gymnasium had grown with the scent of flowers, and two hundred different brands of perfume and aftershave.

Behind her, the wistful strains of Eric Clapton's "Wonderful Tonight" just barely were audible. They'd played that at her homecoming dance, too. They probably played it at every homecoming, every year, in every city on the planet—and every girl there felt as if the song had been written for her.

Abby certainly had.

What a tragedy that only now, when it was too late, did she realize the truth. Her sparkling tiara had made her the queen of the homecoming dance. Her red dress, custom made to drive boys wild, had made her queen of the flirts.

But it was Joe's skinny, protective arms around her, Joe's warm cheek against hers, and Joe's loyal heart beating firmly in time with her own, that had made her queen of the whole world.

What a fool she had been! A small, pained sound rose from her bruised heart. She put her hand up to her mouth instinctively, though there was no one around to hear.

"If you're going to puke, the hedge over there is your best bet."

She whirled at the sound, shocked that she wasn't alone. She searched the shadows, until she found the source of the voice. In the corner formed where two wings met, Rafe Carlyle sat on the grass, his black suit blending into the darkness so completely that he looked like a pale, skinny face floating disembodied in the air.

"Sorry. Didn't mean to scare you."

"You didn't. You just startled me." She moved a little closer and smiled tentatively toward the dark shadows of him. "You okay, Rafe? It's pretty cold out here."

"You bet, Abby." The boy's voice was laced with exaggerated sarcasm. "I'm just *dandy*. How about you?"

She didn't answer that, well aware he didn't give a damn about how she was. And why should he? But she cared about him, whether he believed it or not. She wanted so much to think of something to say that might make him feel better. She wanted so much to be able to keep history from repeating itself with these two unhappy children.

"I know you've had a tough day," she said carefully. "Joe told me your girlfriend's dad took her out of town."

"Wendy's not my *girlfriend*," he said. His voice was harder than the glassy black sky. "She's my *fiancée*."

Abby digested this without responding. Something in the defiance of his tone told her he wasn't so sure about that fact. He wanted it to be true...he wanted Wendy to be his fiancée, but he didn't quite believe it, did he?

"You know...sometimes what seems like the end of the world really isn't." She bit her lip, aware that she wasn't quite hitting the right note. She could hear how patronizing she sounded, though she didn't intend to.

She tried again. "I mean, her father has the power to take

her away now, but he won't always be in charge. When she's able to make her own decisions, when she's really grown up...she might come home. And, if you are still here, and you still want her, it might be the right time to make those dreams come true."

He looked at her a minute, his blue eyes black in the shadows, but glittering coldly. Then he laughed. "You mean like you just came back to Joe?"

She wasn't sure what to say. She knew that no young person in love wanted to believe their heartbreak was like any other heartbreak the world had ever known. And yet...

"Not exactly," she said, cautiously. "But in some ways, maybe—"

"No." His voice was as sharp as the lash of a whip. "Not in *any* way. Wendy's not one bit like you. She'd never wait to come back until the day she ends up broke, and she discovers I'm rich. She'd never wait until the day she discovers there's some *money* in it for her."

She shook her head, confused—and strangely hurt by the personal, pointed savagery of his attack. "I don't know what you mean, Rafe."

"The hell you don't. Everybody knows you're poor now. Your dad lost all his money, and your rich husband threw you away. So when you heard Joe and Tricia struck it big with the new horse, well, wow, what a coincidence. You suddenly also discover how much you miss him. You suddenly can't wait to come home to see if you can land yourself a brand new sugar daddy."

She felt a little as if he'd stunned her with a physical blow. She knew she wasn't thinking clearly, but all she could do was echo the most bewildering part of the whole, bewildering diatribe. "Joe struck it big? What do you mean?"

The boy unfolded himself from the shadows, making a nasty, dismissive sound between his teeth. "*Brother*. Save your innocent act for Joe. I don't think he even wants you anymore. And I damn sure don't think he's dumb enough to believe you, but hey. You never know."

The rumbling sound of an old pickup's engine suddenly filled the air. Rafe waved his hand, and a rusty white truck stopped in front of the nook where he'd been sitting. The boy started to walk toward it.

"Wait...Rafe..." She held out one hand. "I honestly don't know what—"

"Yeah, right," he said. "Why don't you ask *him*, then? See what he says."

His walk quickened, and turned into a lope. Within seconds, he reached the truck and yanked open the door. She heard the sound of laughter, which was abruptly cut off when he slammed the door shut again. Then the truck's tires squealed on the frosty pavement, and the vehicle peeled away.

She stood there a long time, trying to make sense of what he'd said.

Tricia and Joe struck it big with the new horse...

Could it be true? Was that what all those cryptic remarks had been about? If so, why hadn't he just told her, outright? Why hadn't he shared the happy news with her? Why hadn't Tricia felt free to talk about it, either?

Because he didn't want Abby to know. That was the obvious answer. Because Rafe was right. Joe did believe that, if she knew he had money, it might change the way she felt about him.

Because he still believed she was nothing but a spoiled little girl who cared only about herself. A professional trophy wife, who sold her affections to the highest bidder.

Suddenly, in spite of the crisp, beautiful night, she found it difficult to breathe. Her lungs felt crushed, as if something heavy had been piled on her chest.

Her legs felt weak. She had left her purse inside, and her car keys were in it…but suddenly the gymnasium seemed a million miles away. She didn't see how she could walk all that way back inside. Not in these shoes, not carrying this heavy weight on her heart.

And then, out of nowhere, the slow, romantic drowsiness of the party's final stages erupted into utter chaos. People began to yell. Girls screamed. The music screeched to a halt, with a strange, grating scrape on the loudspeakers.

And, mixed in with all that, the sound of something squealing…something that sounded like frightened animals…

She turned, her own misery forgotten. As she pushed back inside, she had to fight a tide of humanity moving in the other direction, rushing out of the gym.

"What happened?" She caught a girl's arm. The girl looked both alarmed and excited. She was laughing, but she was also running, clearly eager to escape into the open air. "What is it? What happened?"

"Pigs!" the girl exclaimed in a high, overwrought voice. She shook off Abby's restraining hand and kept moving, calling back over her shoulder. "It's Rafe and Cody and the rest. They let some pigs loose in the gym!"

Chapter Eight

೫০ᏣᎡ

J OE WAS GOING to kill him.

Yep. No more futzing around. The kid had really done it now. Two hours after the incident began, the cops still had Rafe over in the corner of the gym, and they showed no signs of calming down. Instead, they were getting madder by the minute, grilling him about the goddamn pigs.

And Rafe was grimly enjoying every minute.

Actually, once the cops arrived, it hadn't taken long to find the first three animals. Pretty quickly, the chaperones and the cops together had managed to corral three huge, muscular hogs with pink punch on their hooves and cake icing on their snouts.

The panicked animals had left about a thousand dollars of damage in their wake, along with some aromatic manure, a dozen overturned tables and punchbowls, and a trampled sound system.

But Rafe and his moron friends hadn't been satisfied with normal mischief. *Of course not.* They had to elevate their prank to the downright diabolical level. First, they'd stolen the hogs from somebody…one of the nearby livestock show breeders. The Garrisons, probably. Then they'd spray-painted huge, garish red numbers on the sides of the animals.

And here's where they got too clever for their own good. They'd numbered the pigs "1," "2," and "4."

The furious, frustrated cops had spent the next hour searching the school and the grounds and the parking lot, crawling under hedges, edging behind dumpsters, creeping beneath bleachers and poking inside every classroom…looking in vain for the one marked "3."

Observing his little brother's mulish, self-satisfied expression, Joe had realized right away that there was no number "3." That was, of course, the punch line.

He'd even tried to tell the cops, but they were too bull-headed and pissed off to listen. Most of them had been on the force for years, and remembered the time he and Dev and Brian had set the cows loose in the computer lab. They even had the audacity to suggest that Joe might have encouraged his little brother to follow in the family footsteps.

You couldn't reason with people who held grudges that many years. So, with a deadpan glance at Rafe, who raised his eyebrows, Joe held up his hands and withdrew. He retrieved a folding chair from the wreckage, scraped it upright, checked that it didn't have any punch stains on the seat, and made himself comfortable until it was time to pay bail.

Luckily, it didn't come to that. The Garrisons had a teenager of their own, and apparently the boy was one of the gang, so the hog-nabbing didn't quite qualify as theft.

Once Joe reminded the cops that Rafe was still a minor, and once he wrote a generous check that more than covered the damages to the school and promised to hire a crew to clean things up, they agreed to release Rafe into his custody.

Which was fine with him. Made it that much easier to strangle the brat.

Or, on second thought, he might just take Rafe home to

their mother, who had been alerted and was undoubtedly waiting up to have her say. By the time she was finished with Rafe, the kid would wish Joe had killed him first.

They drove most of the way home in silence. Joe wasn't sure he should say anything, for fear he might start laughing, which wasn't a suitably paternal attitude to take. And Rafe was too smart to broach the subject on his own.

As they skimmed along the empty streets, his headlights occasionally catching the dusting of frost just barely visible on the right of way and making it glimmer, Joe's thoughts turned to Abby. It was almost three in the morning. Obviously she must have given up any hope that he might come tonight.

No big deal, right? It wasn't as if he'd stood her up. He'd more or less told her he wouldn't. Maybe he'd convinced her better than he'd convinced himself. Maybe she'd believed he meant it and had gone comfortably to sleep.

But suddenly he needed to talk to her. Right now. He couldn't wait till they got home, and he finished the endless melodrama of explaining to his mother what the hell had happened at the homecoming dance.

He couldn't stand the thought that Abby might be still awake, alone in that impersonal room, waiting…hoping he'd knock on the door.

He took out his cell phone, its glow weirdly green in the darkness, and dialed the Graff, which he'd put on his speed dial earlier, just in case.

Oh, yeah, sure. He hadn't intended to meet her there tonight. *Right…*

"I thought you told me never to use the phone while I'm driving," Rafe commented petulantly.

Joe shot him a quelling look. "I also told you never to smear the gym in hog manure, but did that stop you?"

Rafe rolled his eyes and returned to staring out the window.

When the Graff's front desk answered—it sounded like Mary Ann, who had taken riding lessons from his mom last year—Joe asked to be put through to Abby Foster's room.

"I'm sorry, Joe." Mary Ann's voice was professional, but it had an oddly sympathetic undertone. "Ms. Foster checked out about an hour ago."

"She checked out?" Joe couldn't make any sense of that. Who checked out at three in the morning? His chest tightened. Was she all right? Had there been some kind of emergency?

Then he noticed that Rafe's head whipped back toward him, and the boy stiffened nervously in his seat. He frowned. "Did she leave me any messages?"

"No." He heard the sound of Mary Ann shuffling papers, double-checking. "No, she didn't leave any messages for anyone."

"Thanks." He clicked the phone off and tossed it on the seat beside him. The green glow faded and disappeared.

"She's gone?" Rafe's voice was studiously casual, as if he didn't really care, no big deal, he was just asking to be polite.

"Yeah." Joe impaled his brother with a sharp, no-nonsense glare before transferring his gaze back to the road. "She's gone. And you, buster, have got exactly three seconds to tell me what you know about that."

80)03

JOE STOOD AT the kitchen window, watching the dawn rise pale gray and lemon yellow over the stables. Behind him, Rafe and their mother sat, side by side on the sofa, with the boy's head on her shoulder.

Both of them were wiped out, too exhausted to get up and go to bed.

The past few hours hadn't been pretty. His mom had hollered so much the rooster started crowing as if he'd been awakened by the trumpet of the apocalypse. And Rafe would undoubtedly have to replaster the wall where the silver salt shaker had left a dent. Their mom said it was Rafe's fault, because she'd been aiming the shaker at his head, and he ducked.

Both boys knew that if Mary Carlyle had intended to hit her son, she would have. But neither of them argued.

They were all so relieved to have weathered this storm—the details didn't matter. All that mattered was that the Rafe crisis was over. Really over. The Carlyle Crazies always ended with a bang, when the Carlyle in question hit rock bottom. But after that, they started to grow up. Their mom always called it their Wizard of Oz day, meaning it was the day they finally got a brain.

"You boys hungry?" Mary yawned, patting Rafe's knee as she propelled herself to a standing position. "You ought to have something to eat before you go back to the high school and start the cleanup."

"What?" Rafe widened his eyes. "No, Joe said he'd hire someone to—"

"You'll do it yourself." She scowled at her two sons, first one, then the other. "I'll be darned if I'm paying good money to—"

"*I'll* pay for it," Joe put in firmly. He had things to do today, things that did not involve mopping up hog manure.

"Oh, you're so rich now, with your fancy racehorse, that you don't clean up your own messes anymore?" His mother had her hands on her hips.

"It's not my mess," Joe said reasonably. "It's Rafe's."

"It's yours, too. You were supposed to be watching him. That's what *chaperone* means. And don't give me that look, young man. If you didn't feel guilty, you wouldn't be offering to pay in the first place."

Joe shook his head, chuckling helplessly. "Whatever. I'm still paying for a cleanup crew. I've got things to do today."

She frowned. "Like what?"

"Well, for starters I've got horses to tend to. A ranch to run. And after that, I'm going to find out where Abby Foster went."

His mother opened her mouth, but he kept talking, not loudly, but with a firmness she couldn't mistake, so she closed it again without saying anything.

"Yes, Mom. I'm going to find Abby. And, if I can, I'm going to bring her back here. That could take an hour, or it could take a week. So I better get started."

"Naw, I don't think it'll take that long," Rafe said, stretching out along the sofa with a big yawn. "What would you give me if I told you I could find her for you in two minutes flat?"

I'd give you a good shaking, Joe thought, suddenly mad as hell. "Damn it, Rafe. You said you had no idea—"

"Whoa. Calm down. I said I had no idea where she was, and that was the truth."

Stuffing a cushion under his neck, Rafe propped his head against the arm of the sofa. He shut his eyes and folded his hands under his armpits, obviously preparing to take a nap right where he lay.

Joe felt like throwing a salt shaker, himself. "Then how—"

Rafe smiled, both mischievous and sleepy, and cracked his eyelids a half-inch to peek at Joe. "Easy. I just now saw her car pull up beside the stables."

Joe and Mary both turned toward the door. At the same instant, a knock sounded there. Polite, but firm. They both started toward the noise, but Joe got there first.

He yanked the door open so hard that the rod holding his mother's little yellow-and-white checked café curtains rattled in its bracket.

He'd half-suspected Rafe was messing with him. But there

she was. She wore jeans and a gold sweater, and her hair hung loose around her shoulders, the auburn tips lifting in the cool morning breeze.

"Abby." He sounded oddly hoarse, as if he'd been yelling for hours…or as if he hadn't talked at all in a week. "I thought you were gone. They said you'd checked out of the hotel—"

"I did." Her expression didn't tell him much. She looked neither happy nor upset…just calm. "I went to Charlie's house for a few hours. Right now, I'm on my way to Billings. But before I left town I wanted to…"

She hesitated. She glanced into the kitchen. "Well, the truth is…I was hoping to talk to your mother."

Chapter Nine

ഇൗരു

J OE ALWAYS TOOK care of all the other horses, the ones the Carlyles owned and the boarders, before he went in to see Dancer. Before he had any employees to look after her, before he knew she was going to be a moneymaker, even before she'd run her first race, much less *won* anything, he'd felt a powerful connection to the, feisty filly.

Sometimes he thought it was because she reminded him of Abby. She was petite, but filled with so much grit and energy she seemed twice her size. Her coat was golden, and her mane had flashes of auburn that caught the light when she ran. On a sunny day, she seemed to be on fire.

But she also had a sweet side. And a sweet spot for Joe. She was his special girl, long, long before she gave birth to champions.

Sunday was the only day he had her to himself anymore. Tricia came by often, to protect her investment, of course. She was the one with the racing experience, and the upfront money to get the breeding business started in the first place. But he also had new hands just for the breeding, a secretary for the scheduling, and a second trainer. Add the regular vet visits and the constant construction crew presence as they built a heated indoor arena and three new turnout pastures, and he rarely got a day in here alone.

Still, the bond never broke. Today, Dancer seemed to recognize immediately that he was agitated. She made a soft whinnying sound when she saw him, and trotted over without hesitation. Watching him intently with those big, bright eyes, she extended her head over the stall door and nuzzled his shoulder.

She wasn't looking for treats. Her diet was too strictly regulated, now that she was the key part of his breeding program. She was just trying to show her support, trying to express that she was his ally in whatever trouble he was facing.

"Nothing to do but wait and see, kiddo," he said, reaching up to stroke the side of her head. She flicked her ears, listening not for words but for tone. "God only knows what's going on out there, but at least nobody's yelling, so that's gotta be a good sign, right?"

She stepped once, making a small noise with her hoof on the floor of her stall. It wasn't agreement in a human sense, but Joe chuckled, deciding it was close enough.

At least an hour passed. He'd finished feeding and watering everyone before he heard human voices approaching the stables. It was Abby and his mother, and though they spoke too quietly for him to make out words, it was as easy to read their tone as it had been to read Dancer's nuzzle. It was the sound of two friends, comfortably chatting.

Trying to wrap his mind around that, Joe turned toward the stable doors just in time to see Abby hugging his mother. The two embraced for several seconds and then, without so much as a glance at Joe, his mother turned and walked back toward the house.

Abby stayed. She hesitated in the doorway, just a silhouette against the rising morning sun, but still able to send a jolt of electricity to his system. Dancer whinnied again, and he touched her face automatically, soothing without saying anything.

He watched the doorway, waiting to see if Abby would come in.

Finally, she did. Like an apparition materializing into a physical form, she developed into full color and focus as she moved out of the backdrop of bright light. By the time she reached his side, he had read every nuance of her beautiful face.

She was nervous. But, in spite of that, she was oddly at peace with herself. A paradox, but unmistakable nonetheless.

"Is this the magical racehorse you discovered?" She turned her attention to the horse. "Is this Dancer?"

When she said the horse's name, Dancer turned her gaze to investigate. Abby held out her hand carefully. Dancer blinked, then chirred softly, clearly indicating a pat would be welcome. Abby understood and stroked her neck.

"She's beautiful, Joe. And I hear she's an incredible racer."

"Yes. She's very special. I wouldn't have realized her racing potential, though, without Tricia pointing it out. Her father used to own racehorses. She's the one who suggested we go in together and set up a breeding operation."

Abby nodded. "And Charlie tells me it's starting to be very successful."

"Yes. The first couple of years were rough, but we've had some great foals. Breeding's always a gamble, but so far we're winning."

She continued to stroke Dancer's glossy neck, and the horse continued to love it. Whenever Abby's hand slowed, Dancer would nudge her, reminding her to keep going.

"I didn't know about her," Abby said quietly. "Maybe you'll find that difficult to believe, but I didn't know. No one told me, not even Charlie, until I went to see her last night and demanded the truth. I had no idea you were…" She seemed to stumble as she searched for the right word. "That you were…that you had money."

He smiled wryly. "Well, I don't. Not the kind of money you're accustomed to. I'm just not broke anymore, that's all. I might do well, and I might end up broke again. As I said, breeding is a gamble, these days more than ever. It's a dying occupation, for the most part."

"Unless you get lucky and find a special horse. Like Dancer."

"Yes. But even then, sometimes you lose." He needed to be very clear about this. Luckily, he'd been rehearsing this speech in his mind all night, and he at least had some idea where to start.

"I'm not rich, and I may never be. I want you to understand that part, Abby."

"Why?" Her gaze raked his face. "Was Rafe right? Do you really believe I came back to Marietta because I had heard about Dancer, and I wanted to make a play for your money?"

"No." He had to smile, hearing his suspicions confirmed. He'd known Rafe had something to do with Abby's quick departure last night. "I think you came back to Marietta because you wanted me to forgive you for marrying Blaine, and you didn't know what to offer in return except sex."

She flushed, ducking her head slightly, as if she hoped to hide the burn. While she stared at the stable floor, she took two deep breaths. And then she lifted her chin.

"You may be right. I did want your forgiveness. And I did think perhaps making love would help…would soften you toward me and make forgiveness easier. But forgiveness isn't all I want."

He tilted his head. "No?"

"No." She swallowed roughly, bit her lower lip, and went on. "I want *you*, Joe. Not just for this weekend, and not just in my bed. I want you in my life."

He wasn't breathing. Once again, he had the oddest sensation that he might be dreaming.

"I love you," she said, the words tumbling out quickly now, as if she feared that even a pause would cause her to lose her nerve. "I've never stopped loving you, no matter what else I did. I can understand if you don't believe me. I know I haven't given you much reason to trust me, through the years. I almost ran away last night, when I heard you had made good, because I was so afraid you'd think I had only been after your money. But, when I got to the edge of town, I realized I couldn't do it."

She'd gone as far as the edge of town. She'd almost left Marietta…and him. *Again.*

"Why not?"

"Because I'm through running, Joe. It's time—way *past* time—for me to stand my ground. It's time for me to fight for what matters."

He should say something. He shouldn't let her just stand there, her slim shoulders squared with such touching courage, wondering what he thought of her declaration. Her hand trembled on Dancer's neck, and he should speak. He should end the embarrassment, the fear…

But everything she said was like a soothing balm on an old wound that had always refused to heal. Every word she spoke was one he'd waited so long to hear.

"I wanted to talk to your mother first," she said. "She loves you so much, and she was clearly so threatened when I showed up here after all these years. I wanted her to understand my intentions. I wanted to set her mind at ease that I haven't come to break your heart again."

As if just seeing Abby Foster hadn't cracked his heart, and his soul, wide open. How could she *not* break his heart? It dissolved him to even look at her, to hear her voice. His mother knew that.

"Joe, I don't know what to say to repair the damage I've done. I'm so sorry I wasn't brave enough to fight for us, back then. If I could go back and change the past, I would. But I can't."

"No," he said gravely. "I tried that, myself. A hundred times."

She nodded. "All I can do is try to be braver and more honest from now on. If you don't think you can ever forgive me, I understand. I know you don't want to be enemies—I saw that in your kindness last night. If all you'll accept from me is friendship, I'll be your friend. But I won't run away from Marietta again, and there will never be any other man for me."

There will never be any other man...

A slow smile spread, from one corner of his mouth to the other. He hadn't intended to grin...he'd intended to be serious, to show her how deadly earnest he was about this decision. But suddenly the stupid joy was just there, written on his face.

"There darn well better *not* be," he said.

She blinked. Her hand stilled on Dancer's mane. "What do you mean?"

"I mean...I've learned a few things through the years, too, and I won't be letting another man take you away without a fight, not ever again."

"Joe..."

"We've both learned a lot from these years, I know. But the most important thing I learned is that it wasn't all your fault. I was too young, too angry, too jealous...too *everything*. It's no wonder you wouldn't put your life in my hands. I would have dropped it, smashed it carelessly, the way I smashed everything else back then."

"Joe, you were—"

"I was a kid. I know. I was in my crazy phase. I couldn't help being young, but I could have stopped myself from being cruel. I could have stopped myself from blaming you, demonizing you, just because that was easier than facing the truth about myself."

She didn't speak. Her eyes glistened and seemed very large and round.

"But I'm not a kid anymore, Abby. I'm a man, and I've learned how to be honest with myself. And I've also learned to fight for what I want. I've learned how to fight for the woman I love."

She opened her lips, but only a soft, wordless sound escaped.

"Yes. *I love you*," he said, answering the question she hadn't been able to ask. "I knew it the minute I saw you again, though I couldn't admit it, even to myself. My love is as strong and wild and painful as it was when I was seventeen. And it always will be. If you hadn't come here this morning, I was going to Billings to find you. Or to New York, or California, or wherever you were. I was going to ask Charlie, interrogate Rafe…I was even going to call that insufferable Josh Butterworth, who offered you a job, to see if he had any idea where you were going."

She shook her head, as if she couldn't quite believe what she heard.

"Joe, I—" Her voice broke. When she started again, the sound was still ragged, even though she tried to smile. "You might not want to get in the habit of calling him 'that insufferable Josh Butterworth.' I might be working for him. I'll go to the interviews in Billings, because I promised I would. But I'll be coming back in two days, and I'll probably be his new paralegal come Monday."

"Fine. I don't care about Butterworth. Be whatever you want to be. Work for him, go back to school, don't work at all. Just as long as, whatever you do, you do it as my wife."

"Your wife…" She repeated the word as if it were a magical

incantation, as if it were a big, beautiful, but very dangerous word. "I've been a wife...but I've never...never felt like one."

A tear slid down her cheek. He reached out to touch it...to wipe it away with a gentle thumb. "Stop that, sweetheart. Haven't we cried enough for one lifetime? If you'll have me, if you'll finally be my wife, I promise I'll never make you cry again."

With a low murmur, and eyes so bright they must have been half-blinded with the rest of the unshed tears, she moved urgently into his arms.

Dancer tossed her head back, out of the way, just in time. Abby laughed, and reached back to give the horse an apologetic caress.

"I'm sorry, girl," she said. And then she turned to Joe. "Yes," she said. "Yes, yes, yes."

Yes. She would be his wife.

Relief flooded his veins. *Finally.* Finally the nightmare was over. She had come home to him.

Homecoming...

He'd never hear the word again without thinking of how much more it could mean. She was home, and she was going to be his. The church bells, the little gold rings, the white picket fence...this time, the fairy tale would belong to *him.*

He had no intention of waiting for church bells, though. He had to make love to her now. Eight years of hunger roared through his veins, and he suddenly felt as much animal as man.

He had just lowered his head to claim her lips when a shadow fell across the stable doors.

"Go away," he growled, not caring who it was.

"Well, great. Make *me* the bad guy," Rafe complained. "Like I want to see this mushy crap, anyhow. Mom said I had to. She wants to know if Abby is staying for lunch."

Joe growled again. Who cared about lunch? He wanted to be

alone to rediscover the dream he thought he'd lost forever. He wanted to sweep Abby into his arms, carry her to the Swayback, and make love to her until neither of them could move.

He grinned down at her. "Are you hungry, my love?"

Her tearful smile lifted toward him was all the answer he would ever need. "Only for you," she whispered.

"So?" Rafe scuffed his feet, obviously both embarrassed and impatient. "What do I tell Mom? Is Abby staying for lunch or not?"

"*Not*. But tell her…"

Without so much as glancing at his brother, he kissed Abby's tear-stained chin, and then her neck, then lowered his head even further, where he could sense the rapid beat of her heart against his lips.

"Tell her Abby is staying *forever*," he said, though his voice was muffled, and half-strangled with the swelling passion inside him. "Tell her….we might have taken the long way, but we've finally found our way home."

The End

Hometown Hero

A Montana Homecoming Story

Dani Collins

Dedication

This book simply must be dedicated to the amazing Megan Crane (aka Caitlin Crews) who has been an incredibly supportive friend since before we properly met.

When I finally sold after a million years of trying, I quickly learned that my first book was not going to come out in North America. I was devastated and put out a call for 'pictures in the wild.' My first came in from Megan, who happened to be in the UK, bought it and sent me her photo, reading my book, along with a lovely note that she'd read it and loved it.

About six months later, I met her at an RWA conference. I had pretty much dropped out of the RWA world in the previous decade, convinced by all my rejections that everyone in publishing hated me. I felt like The New Kid Who Doesn't Know Where To Sit. Megan introduced herself and told me again that she liked my book. I was astonished that she remembered me or my book. I must have looked like a deer in headlights. I'm pretty sure she thinks that's my signature look.

Along with being incredibly savvy about the publishing business, she is funny and smart and introduced me to Jane and Tule. (And told me how to pronounce Tule. 'Jane' I figured out on my own.)

So this book really wouldn't exist without Megan (and Jane and the amazing team at Tule.) So a big hug of thanks to all of them, but particularly you, Ms. Crane. I've got your back should we ever venture into the dark alleys of the French Quarter again.

Dear Reader,

What drew me in most about writing for the Montana Born series was the setting of Marietta.

I live in BC, not Montana. I come from farm stock, not horse people, but small town is small town. It has its own mindset and I love it. You wait in the line at the grocery store because the person ahead of you has to chat with the cashier. (Sometimes that's me!) When friends and family come to visit, they see me waving at people and ask, "Who was that?" "I don't know," I say. "We just do that here." My sister came back from running out for milk one time and said excitedly, "A stranger waved at me while I was out!" See? It makes you feel good.

So I knew that genuine love and connection to the town would be a cornerstone of my story. Skye Wolcott's ancestors pioneered a ranch in the area. She's the school secretary. She knows young and old alike in Marietta. It's her home.

Chase Goodwin suffers the other side of small town life. His father was the town drunk and everyone knew it. He worked his butt off to get out of town via a baseball scholarship and now plays in the big leagues. His worst nightmare is returning to Marietta.

They always had a thing for each other, though. When Chase is forced back to town to help his younger brother, and he discovers Skye is recently divorced, they have a chance to see where things might have gone. But Chase can't give up his career and Skye doesn't want to leave Marietta. Where does that leave them?

I hope you enjoy learning how they answer that question.

Chapter One

C HASE GOODWIN WAS in the one place he had never
wanted to come back to, especially in September: Marietta
Senior Secondary.

At least he was in the gymnasium, the part of the school he
could tolerate if he wasn't on the field. Watching a basketball
game would have been his preference, but it was a school dance
complete with the kind of club music he hated. Not that he'd
minded the dances so much ten years ago. The girls were as
giddy and nubile as he remembered, but so *young*. They nearly
leapt out of their skin to land on a boy. The boys were all limbs
and pimples. Had he overflowed with that much fascination
coupled with terror back then?

"It's like watching kittens and puppies," he said to Max
beside him, one time catcher to his pitch when it wasn't football
season. Max was a good four inches taller than his own six two
and was twice as wide. He'd taken over Mr. Kelton's job running
the P.E. department and watched the poorly lit, gamboling
teenagers like he was watching the progress of a game, ready to
shout orders to pass.

Max flashed a grin. "You said you wanted to know what

your brother was up to."

No, what he'd said was, *If you want some help with the teams, I'd love to keep busy while I keep an eye on my brother.* Max had put in a good word for him with the new football coach, Mitch Holden. In exchange, Max had roped Chase into chaperone duty. So here he was, suckered into reffing body contact at a dance to raise money for the homecoming float.

Another slender, ripening body swished across his field of vision. *Don't look*, he reminded himself, but—*hold the phone.* He recognized that ass.

Deep in the back of his brain, where a crew was supposed to be working to retrieve her name, every single cell dropped his tools to take a long drink of the female that had paused about ten feet away to talk to his old classmate, Chelsea Collier.

The woman was a knockout, athletic and tight beneath a red plaid shirt knotted at her waist. Faded blue jeans hugged her firm round ass and were painted against long thighs before they disappeared into sassy red cowboy boots. Her shiny brown hair cut a precise line across her shoulder blades, held off her face by a headband like Alice in Wonderland's—exactly the way she'd always worn it and it was still too innocent a look for a body like that.

He couldn't hear her over the music, but the way she leaned close to Chelsea and gestured gave an impression of animation and humor. From her profile, he could see pale, clear skin without so much as a freckle to mar it. Her cheek rounded and he glimpsed perfect teeth, braces gone. She smiled and nodded.

Brown eyes, he recalled, even though he couldn't see them. She had melty brown eyes like a baby animal. The kind that made you want to cuddle her to your chest so she wouldn't get stepped on. She used to look at him like that when he came up to his locker and she was already at hers. She'd hide behind her door and watch him like she didn't quite trust him.

Maybe she'd known she made him hard.

Skye Wolcott.

God, he hadn't thought about her in years. He'd made a concerted effort to forget everything about this town except to send money home and check in with his brother as often as possible. His reaction to Skye was as strong as he remembered, though. He tried to turn it off, exactly the way he had intentionally resisted the lure of her then. She'd been taken and so had he. She'd also been a lifer, obviously intending to die here in Marietta. He'd been determined to get a scholarship, preferably baseball, and leave. He'd set her on the out-of-bounds shelf and barely chucked her a *Hey* when he saw her.

He was ready to talk now. *Hey girl.* Damn.

"You're staring, dude," Max said, keeping his own eyes forward.

"That Skye Wolcott?" he asked, pretending he wasn't sure. Pretending that was the only reason he was asking. Pretending he wasn't blindsided by old lust that threatened his well-developed, *no distractions*, determination.

A blank pause before Max gave a jerky nod. "Yeah. She goes by her married name, Mrs. Baynard. It took me a sec to remember that's who she used to be."

Married? *Fuck.*

Oops. Where the hell had *that* come from?

Wait, "*Terry* Baynard? She *married* him?" Dusty pieces of history fell together, reminding him of the other reason he'd held off pursuing her.

"Yeah. People are saying she turned him gay." Max rolled his eyes at the small-minded concept. "They're divorced now. He moved to San Francisco, but she still uses his name. I don't get how they're still friends when he lied to her all that time and she was as shocked as anyone when he came out, but I guess they are."

Chase stared at Skye's back, dumbfounded. And a tiny bit uncomfortable. She must have known Terry was gay. Maybe the guy had been deep in the closet, but *he'd* known Terry was gay. He'd honest-to-God believed she was Terry's beard. He had thought she was being nice to a guy who was obviously terrified of being found out, which had made him like her even though he barely knew her. He hadn't totally understood why a girl like Skye Wolcott, with so much to offer, would tie herself up like that, but he hadn't seen the point in going after her, wrecking Terry's setup, when he wasn't sticking around.

"So she's not married," he said, grasping at the most important detail.

"Yeah, but she's not interested," Max said matter-of-factly. He was married with two kids so his dismissive warning wasn't male possessiveness. It was the tone they used to take when out-of-town players thought they could hit on the local girls. Small town wasn't all small minds. There were things about it, people here that were nice. They were a community, a team. They looked out for each other.

Chase knew that and respected it.

"I'm not interested either," he drawled. "Especially if she has the power to turn men gay—"

Oh shit. The music stopped. His voice, pitched to carry over the pulsing beat, came out nice and loud and hit Skye right between the shoulder blades. He saw her back jerk like an arrow had struck the middle of her spine. She turned and her vulnerable brown eyes weren't the least bit soft and helpless.

Her eyes narrowed, dark and ferocious, wounded and angry. They fixed on him like the dark spiral of a tornado seeking its touchdown point.

Oh hell.

ॐ

SKYE WAS TRYING very hard to pretend she wasn't on pins and needles. *Chase Goodwin was back.* Dear God she'd had a crush. Such a deep, terrible crush. One so everlasting that whenever she crossed paths with Flynn, his half-brother, and Flynn smiled his good-natured Goodwin smile, she always wanted to ask, *How's Chase?* Like she and Chase had been friends or something.

Oh how she'd ached to be something with him.

But he'd been a year ahead of her, dating a cheerleader, and focused. So incredibly determined to play ball. And he'd done it. Like everyone in town, she was incredibly proud of the local boy done good, drafted out of high school and playing for the majors, doing stints on talk shows and even cheesy sketches on Saturday Night Live. Chase Goodwin had been a legend in high school. The full package of brains, brawn, and backbone. Now he was epic and even further out of her reach. Well beyond her small-town after-school league.

No, she'd gone after good, solid, comfortable Terry. Who'd had orientation issues he hadn't confronted until she had begged him to start a family. That's when he'd finally admitted he wasn't in her league either. He was playing for the other team.

After a loss that big, she'd quit the game.

But when she'd heard whispers that Chase was back in town, her inner teenager had tingled back to life, hoping to catch a glimpse of him, just like old times. Then she'd walked into the gym, caught an eyeful of his muscled silhouette against the strobing colors of the dancing bodies and a whoosh of excitement had nearly knocked her off her feet.

Nothing wrong with going to the stadium to watch, right? It wasn't like she actually wanted to take the field with him.

Except she couldn't resist getting close to him. It had taken supreme concentration to walk naturally as she crossed to Chelsea and tried to hold a normal conversation, all the while aware she was reverting to high school tactics, using her friend to put herself in a particular male's line of sight. It was juvenile and she felt immature and uncertain, yet so thrilled to be near him again.

Aware. Chase Goodwin had energy so intense it practically gave her a tan, filling her with warmth and making her heart race with excitement.

Not that she expected him to notice her. He'd rarely made eye contact with her back in the day, never mind actually talked to her. She had always frozen like a bunny whenever he had arrived at his locker beside hers. He had usually acted like he didn't even see her.

This moment of regression was silly and she didn't need to look a bigger fool than she already did, given how the last two years had gone, but she stood there aching for him to notice her and—

The music stopped. Chase Goodwin's deep voice stated in his confident way, "—not interested either. Especially if she has the power to turn men gay."

The rest of the world stopped.

Chelsea's face fell in shock before her. She reached out, like she was trying to catch Skye from falling off a cliff.

It was Skye's worst nightmare, the acknowledging of the elephant that had been running amok in this town since Terry had come out. Sure the talk shows could tell people that being gay wasn't a choice, but there were still plenty of folk who believed that Terry had chosen to become a homosexual and Skye must have done something to drive him to it.

Why it had to be Chase Goodwin who brought it all to the surface she didn't know, but it was the final straw. Her wall of *I'm Fine* crumbled. All the whispers, all the suspicions, all the lies Terry had told her over the years as he denied something he didn't want to admit, all the minutes of all the hours she'd spent holding his hand, telling him it was okay while she died a death of a thousand cuts, all of the tears and years empty of the babies he refused to give her... It all detonated under that one flippant comment by Chase Goodwin.

Chase Goodwin, with his perfect life, his money and smarts and stupendously wrong summation of her life, was the final kick from life that made her turn and fight back. She spun and charged toward him.

"What the hell do you know?" she choked.

"Hey—" he started, holding up forestalling hands. "I—"

"You *what?*" she demanded raggedly, fists pounding into the air beside her hips. Distantly she recognized he was a lot bigger than her. She shouldn't pick a fight with a guy this big, but the toxic spew wouldn't stay inside. "You have a tiny dick to match your tiny mind! I didn't turn him gay, okay? He was always gay, but jocks like you kept him in the closet, afraid to tell me or anyone else in case of ignorant statements like that. Terry and I don't blame each other, but I blame you—" She stabbed a finger in his direction, "—and you—" she pointed at Max, ready to condemn every straight man in the room for her pain, "—and every other prejudiced asshat who made him afraid to admit who he is. That kept me in a marriage doomed to fail and all because you enjoy being cruel to someone who can't help being who he is. Go to hell, Chase Goodwin. Go to hell and rot there."

A familiar arm came around her, mashing her into commiserating softness. Chelsea's kindest tone, the one that had been Skye's lifeline through the breakup, murmured, "Okay, Skye. That's enough. Let's go home."

She firmly steered Skye's wilting body out of the gym. They left a silence so profound that the one whispered, "Holy pajamas," was like a shout.

In the office, Chelsea got Skye's purse out of her desk drawer and said, "Give me your keys."

Beginning to shake, Skye protested she could drive herself,

but Chelsea assured her Jasper would help her get her car later. She picked up a bottle of wine on the way to Skye's place even though it was a school night. Then she stuck around to share it with her and, one more time for the cheap seats, fed Skye tissues while Skye cried her eyes out over a dream that had been seared into a pile of ashes.

Chapter Two

ಬಂಬ

S KYE WOKE TO the buzz of her mobile on the bedside. She was just hung over enough to consider calling in sick, but she couldn't. It would be bad enough facing the students and teachers snickering behind her back. She'd learned through the scandal-heavy months of her divorce that the first day after each horrid revelation was always the worst so she ought to just get it over with. Face the music.

But honestly, that tinkling ringtone was more than she could stand at the moment. She didn't want to talk to anyone, wanted to pull the blankets over her head and die. What had possessed her to lose it like that? Wolcotts were good, solid, normal people with manners. If they had a complaint about something, they wrote a polite letter and requested a refund. When they had a disagreement with someone, they were the first to make apologies and amends. They didn't pitch a scene in a public place.

The phone stopped and started again.

Snaking a hand from beneath the quilt, she snagged it and glanced at the face. Her brother's photo glared at her. Sliding her thumb across the strip, she brought it to her ear. "Hey, Stan."

"Why are you on the internet calling a major league pitcher a homophobe?"

"Whaaaat?" Her heart stopped. "That's not funny."

"Some kid posted it last night. It's gone viral."

"Noooo," she cried softly, the sting of humiliation bleeding into her veins as she realized how easily that could have happened. Every second day, there was a new workshop or bulletin about kids and technology and cyber threats.

Still, she tried to will reality from manifesting.

Squinching her eyes shut, she curled deeper under the blankets. "Please tell me you're joking," she whimpered.

"Someone from Channel Nine's news desk just called the house."

"Stan—"

"I'm not kidding. Mom just got off the phone. I looked it up. It's you and Chase Goodwin."

"Oh Ga-awd. Remind Mom I love her, would you? Because I have to go throw myself off the back of Copper Mountain now." She curled tight as a pill bug into the space under her blankets. "I hate my life, Stan. Why does it keep getting *worse?*"

He sighed, both sweetly protective and impatient at the same time. He hadn't wanted her to marry Terry, especially so young. He hadn't wanted her to stand by Terry while he sorted out his life, then keep living in this big, empty house. After their father died, he'd begged her to move back to the ranch. *I'm not squeezing you out of your share*, he had insisted a million times. *This will always be your home, too.*

But this house was her dream home, the one piece she had left of the Happily Ever After pie she'd been baking when she'd married Terry. Terry had felt guilty enough to sign it over to her, so why should she sell it?

"Goodwin's a big deal," Stan said. "You might wind up with quite a bit of attention. Come out here for a week or so until it blows over."

Tempting, but along with everything else, she and his wife lived better apart. And if growing up on a ranch had taught her nothing else, it was that you didn't let a bit of hardship defeat you. When you landed in the dirt, you got on your feet and back in the saddle before fear had a chance to take hold. It sucked. It meant feeling the bruises while you rode out the pain, but it had to be done.

"No, I'll…figure it out," she murmured, not even trying to imagine how. Get out of bed, shower, dress, drive to the school. Pretend everything was normal and fine.

Seriously? The internet? Why did God hate her?

"You know, you're allowed to be angry, Skye, but you should take it out on Terry. He's the one who cut you the raw deal."

She was, but not enough to hurt him. He was her best friend. She loved him. Not as a husband, but as much as she loved Stan. Terry had tried so hard to be what everyone wanted him to be, to give Skye her dream—which hadn't seemed like a big ask at the time, but it had turned out to be impossible.

Which was why she was so angry, she supposed. She came from simple folk and her dream hadn't been far-fetched. All she'd asked for was a steady man who wanted to make a family and a good life. If things hadn't worked out, it should have been due to a normal problem like money or cheating. She didn't understand why her marriage had had to explode in such an extraordinary and public way. Wolcotts weren't flashy. They didn't demand attention. Why did her private business have to wind up in the spotlight?

On social media, for heaven's sake. *Really?*

Her phone buzzed with a second call. Terry.

This was going to be a long, hard day in the saddle.

ෲ

"SHE'S NOT A wing-nut. I won't say that," Chase insisted wearily to the team's publicist.

His phone had exploded last night, about fifteen minutes after they got home. Flynn had elbowed his lanky, teenaged frame into Chase's room and said, *One of the guys got Ms. Baynard's meltdown on his phone. He posted it while we were at the dance. I just told him to take it down, but it's already been shared like a hundred times.*

Chase had just stared at his brother. He was here to keep *Flynn's* life under control, not lose his grasp on his own. The players in the series were the ones under the media microscope right now, not the guy who was out with an injury, leaving his team at the bottom of the standings. He'd been so relieved by the idea of coasting under the radar for the next few months, he'd actually been pissed when he'd learned the town wanted to honor him with Quinn Douglas and a handful of other outstanding local athletes. Quinn deserved it, but not him. He felt like a tool as it was.

Now they were up into the hundred-thousand territory of shares on YouTube. Network news was asking for a statement.

"So you don't want to refute anything she said?" the publicist demanded in a surly voice.

"I don't have a tiny dick! Let's get that straight," he growled.

An hour later he dropped Flynn at school and met up with the physiotherapist he was supposed to visit twice weekly while he was here. The scar from the surgery to repair his torn rotator cuff was healing nicely, but bringing all the muscles back to full strength and range of motion was taking more time. The kind of time that had already been making him antsy when he'd thought Flynn and everything else in Marietta was fine. He hated downtime, preferring the intensity of being caught up in the season: the training, the need to keep his head in the game. Some found the demands exhausting, but he found them a perfect distraction from the mess of real life.

Messes like Flynn taking up drinking and getting kicked off the football team.

All his life, Chase had had one goal: Don't grow up like the old man. That had meant leaning toward baseball over football, which had been his father's first love and ultimate downfall. Not making the cut for a college team had sent his dad into a bottle and he'd never come out.

Chase and Flynn had inherited their father's natural athleticism, but now Chase worried Flynn had inherited the same destructive thirst as well.

He wanted to believe that one Friday night of being a jackass did not a drunkard make, but he'd been out with his injury so he'd flown home to yank his half-brother back onto the straight and narrow. A few heart-to-hearts with Max, Mitch Holden and the other coaches, and he'd earned Flynn a chance to keep up with practice on his various teams. Flynn would bench-warm through the next few games, but sport had been Chase's salvation through high school. Flynn had potential if he would only keep at it. If nothing else, Chase prayed that having a *sober* father-figure show up and act like he gave a damn would carry some influence.

The fact he was a god to some of Flynn's posse was a plus. They wanted to hang with him so Flynn didn't have to make excuses or feel torn between his brother and his friends. He and Flynn got on well, regardless. Flynn's mother—and her pregnancy with Flynn—might have been the reason Chase's mother had left, but he didn't blame his kid brother. At least Flynn's mother had stuck with their dad.

She'd been the main breadwinner until Chase had been old enough to get a real job. That had meant Chase had been the babysitter, dragging Flynn with him if he wanted to go anywhere, balancing him on the handlebars of his bike so he could make practice. Later, Flynn had met him at the feed store after school where Flynn had waited out Chase's four-hour shift, asking Chase for help with his homework between Chase's spurts of loading and unloading trucks.

He hadn't felt good about leaving Flynn when he was drafted, even though his step-mom had had a decent paying job by then. Now he wondered yet again if it had been a mistake, but everything he'd accomplished since leaving Marietta had allowed him to keep a roof over their heads. He and Flynn had talked more than once about Flynn coming to live with him, but Flynn liked his friends here and Marietta was a solid town full of solid people, even if their father wasn't one of them.

Chase really felt he'd done the best he could and he was here now, when Flynn was struggling. That had to count for something. Flynn was a good kid at heart, he reminded himself, just going through the typical strains and growing pains of approaching graduation and adulthood.

He hoped that's all it was. He'd find out while he was here. His entire focus for the rest of the month would be Flynn.

If he could work up the nerve to go into the school and collect the forms that would allow him to hang around students and help with extra-curricular events.

Damned background checks. He'd told Max he would go all-in. Parent driver, chaperone, whatever they needed. *Just get the forms from the office*, Max had said.

It had sounded like a five-minute formality, but that had been before the school secretary had publicly disemboweled him.

Now that formality had become an entry into the Gorgon's cave. He'd texted Max this morning, asking if he could pick up the forms for him. Max's response: *Hell no*. Max had felt bad last night, saying, *I shouldn't have said anything to you about it. I know better. A town like this, you can't move on if everyone keeps bringing up your shit.*

Chase knew something about that, growing up overhearing neighbors talking about his dad, watching people shake their heads with pity and disgust when they heard he was Gary Goodwin's boy. Just thinking about it brought back the sick knot in his belly, the one he used to get before a game, knowing some jerk from a neighboring team would trash talk about his father, trying to get a rise out of him. Trying to get him thrown from the game for fighting.

It's why he'd been so anxious to leave town. Hell, he *liked* Montana. He liked the big sky and the clean air. Sitting in the car in the school parking lot, window open, he took a moment to drink in the sweetly familiar scent of a late summer morning in Marietta. The mower was taking down the grass on the field, the sun was baking dust onto the asphalt, the pines were sweating just enough to tinge the breeze with their faint scent. It smelled like a promise.

Rock music approached with the rumble of an engine. A kid with his mother's car pulled in and slung a backpack over his shoulder. He gave Chase a double-take and a crooked, slightly puzzled grin. He obviously recognized him and wondered what he was doing sitting in the school parking lot.

Procrastinating.

Maybe Skye had called in sick.

Maybe he could apologize and smooth the whole thing over.

Maybe he should just do it.

Leaving the rented SUV, he trailed the kid and entered that unique sound of a school with classes in session, teachers' voices rising indistinctly above the restlessness of students who resented putting their social lives on hold.

They'd painted. He'd noticed that last night. Had a few more trophies in the case.

Quit stalling. He forced his feet to take him to the office.

Ah hell, there she was, turning away to hang up her phone then swing back around in her chair to her computer screen, face pale, expression stoic, gaze lifting as she realized someone was at the open door.

Her eyes widened and he heard her thoughts in the persecution that flashed across her face. *Are you serious right now?*

$$\infty\text{CR}$$

IF HE HAD come to apologize, she was going to tell him where to shove it.

This had been the worst day of her life, worse even than when Terry came out. Then, at least, she'd been the wronged party. Today people were asking, *What were you thinking?* Even Terry had defended stupid Chase Goodwin. *He's not a homophobe, Skye. I, uh, think he always knew I had a bit of a crush on him. He was really decent about it.*

She had *not* needed to know her ex-husband had shared her crush on the town treasure.

"I'm not interested in talking to you," she said to Chase, glancing anxiously toward the open door of the counselor's office, where Brenda had left to fetch a student, then the firmly closed door of the principal's office, where he was meeting with the VP and one of the trustees.

She didn't know which was worse, having witnesses to this confrontation or not.

Chase leaned on the counter exactly the way the students did, like they wanted to order ice cream or a beer. "Maybe you can ask someone else to help me, then," he said without emotion.

He looked insanely attractive, freshly shaved, lightly tanned, his dark brows stern above his intent green eyes, his mouth a sexy male pout that would make any female swoon.

"I need the parent volunteer forms so I can drive students and help with school events," he added.

Take that, Skye. As if he'd come here special to see *you*. Like he owed *you* an apology.

Her throat stung and she feared she might be blushing. Rising, she turned away to open a drawer in the filing cabinet behind her, willing her composure back into place as she took her time fingering through and tugging out the forms. When she turned back, Chase's eyes swiftly lifted to clash into hers.

Had he—?

Her butt tingled and her stomach swooped. *Don't*, she thought. The last thing she needed was to start imagining he'd been checking her out. Hot and hating herself for it, she set the forms on the counter near his elbow.

"I need a copy of your driver's license," she told him.

He reached into his back pocket, the move drawing her eye to the way his T-shirt strained across his shoulders and pecs. Dear Lord, he was beautifully built. Were men allowed to have lean muscles like that without carrying a license for them as deadly weapons?

He offered the card in two fingers. Something in the way he did it made her lift her eyes to his. His brows went up ever so slightly.

He'd noticed her checking him out.

Kill. Me. Now.

She snatched the card from his grip and boiled with self-consciousness as she turned her back on him to make the copy. If he was looking at her backside again—but why would he? She didn't want him to, did she?

What was she doing with her life that she was going off the rails like this? She was basically a happy person. She didn't have self-destructive thoughts so why would she long for a spark between her and someone who would devastate her in all the ways Terry hadn't? It was crazy. Literally not sane or logical.

She took the photocopy to her desk and slapped it into her In tray, refusing to look at his photo even though she was dying to. She'd finish processing this later, after he'd filled out the forms. Sitting down, she set her fingers on her keyboard, determined to carry on with her day and be normal.

He continued to stand at the counter, watching her expectantly.

"What?" she demanded.

"Can I have my driver's license back?"

Oh for God's sake. Blushing hard, she shot to her feet so fast her chair rolled back into the filing cabinet with a crash. Get a grip, Skye. She scooped the card from under the lid of the copier and when she slapped it on the counter, she only dared lift her gaze high enough to see he was biting back a rueful grin.

"Look, I know my being who I am made this worse—"

"Oh, no, my life is great," she snarked, managing to keep her tone a level under shrill. "Isn't it everyone's dream these days to be an internet sensation? Give the forms to Max when you've filled them out. He can leave them in my tray." *Never come back here again,* she willed him.

Then felt inexplicably sad, but honestly. This fixation needed to be carved out of her psyche and cryogenically frozen for a future generation to deal with.

"Hey, I didn't post that clip. And for the record, I was being sarcastic last night. I know you can't turn people gay."

"Sure about that?" she shot back, once again finding herself pushing back for the simple reason that he had the gall to say to her what no one else had. "Wanna put it to the test?"

"I'd love to."

The smoky look in his eyes, the deeply male timbre in his tone, crashed over her like a tropical wave, softening her bones and put a tickling feeling deep in the pit of her belly. A type of yearning.

One that was beyond misguided. Look who he was. He was mocking her. Had to be. Probably because he wasn't any happier than she was about the way she'd embarrassed him.

"That's not funny," she told him. "It's mean." And then, because the backs of her eyes were sizzling, she went into Brenda's office and shut the door.

"Skye!" he called.

She heard a door open and the principal spoke to him, asking if he was looking for her. After a brief exchange, everything went silent, but she continued to hide, bunching a tissue that she dabbed to keep her makeup under control, until Brenda came back and needed her office.

Chapter Three

ℰℭ

S KYE HAD ONE more gauntlet to run before she could feel like her horrible, terrible, no good, very bad day was over. She'd already been to the post office, stopped at the bank, and picked up a handful of items at the grocery store. After she got her workout at the gym finished, she would have faced down the bulk of the stares and tasteless jokes.

Part of her wanted to skip it, but the gym was necessary to her mental health. She'd started going years ago, when Terry had bought his membership. Forever looking for ways to stay connected with her often-reticent husband, she'd started meeting him here. She had run the tread while he pulled weights upstairs. Eventually she'd taken an orientation class and started up here as well. After he left, rather than drink herself into a stupor—which she'd been sorely tempted to do—she'd stepped up her workouts.

She knew there was a passive aggressive motive buried deep inside the action. Rather than wither and crawl away, she was pushing herself more than ever, sculpting herself into the best shape of her life. She was hot, damn it. If anything, gay men ought to be worrying she would turn them straight.

Working on her image was an attempt to keep her confidence up with a side benefit of exhausting her. After a hard workout, she could fall asleep without grinding all her problems through her head into the wee hours. Today she really, really needed that.

First, however, she had to take a ribbing from the regulars. Being the only gym in town, it was as much a community meeting place as church, Grey's Saloon, or the Fall Fair. The gym already had a poster in the window about Homecoming and Jerry, the owner, asked her if she'd drop off the game schedule the next time she was in. Everyone was talking about what a strong football team they had this year, a real chance at the state championship for the first time since the eighties.

Except today they were talking about her and Chase Goodwin.

Her mechanic greeted her with a sardonic, "Killer." Her dental hygienist said in the change room, "I'm not a fan of baseball, either, but I don't know if I'd go as far as you did."

Last mile, Skye thought. Then she'd go home and call this day done.

She did her warm up run and had just started upstairs with the leg press when she heard it.

"Hey, Jerry. What's your drop-in rate?"

※

CHASE HAD ONE hour to get through his routine and get back across town to pick up Flynn. Flynn swore it was a study group for the chem final, but Chase had seen girls walking up from the bus stop. Chemistry all right.

How in hell did you drill into a kid that girls would be in your life forever, but this time of your life could make or break your future?

Maybe the problem was that Flynn knew he had Chase to fall back on. When Chase had been in his situation, he'd had one shot and he'd known it. He hadn't been willing to blow it for anything or anybody—

Skye Wolcott was here.

You've gotta be kidding me. Small freaking towns were a curse.

Skye Wolcott stared daggers at him as she slammed through a set of pulldowns. Not a few girlie disks on the cable either, but a respectable pile of at least ten.

So. Go over and make things worse? Or get on with the routine that would get him back to the life he'd fought for and loved?

He chose the latter because, damn it, he wanted to be ready to play when he got Flynn safely midwived into college and tapped the dust of this town out of his cleats for the last time.

The trouble was, there was no ignoring her. Not only was his male radar tuned to her unique signal, but the place was wall-to-wall mirrors. Even when he was trying to watch his own reflection, the flash of neon pink and lime green kept appearing and disappearing behind his shoulder.

He shouldn't have said what he had this afternoon. He knew that. There were different levels of flirting and he'd gone too deep too soon. But she had sent him all those confusing signals, eying up his chest, blushing and acting all flustered. The sexual awareness had been bouncing around them like these damned reflections, dazzling him into thinking the tide had turned.

Then she'd taken his remark as some kind of jackass taunt.

White hot pain speared through his shoulder and he carefully brought the weight back to rest. *Focus,* he reminded himself. He did *not* want to re-injure.

He didn't like feeling hated, either. This was so freaking high school. She thought he'd insulted her. He'd inadvertently ruined her reputation. They were both acting immature.

And she was so damned hot. Her bright green short shorts hugged her tight round butt to perfection, accentuating the length of her smooth thighs with their light curve of well-toned hamstrings down the back. He imagined kissing his way along those tendons, feeling her flinch under playful bites.

"Rather than stare at other people, you might consider who's staring at you. The reality might not make you very comfortable," she said, switching grips then planting her feet firm for a few more crosspulls.

Did she realize how telling it was that she'd noticed him staring? Biting back a remark about not minding if *she* stared at him, he said with a measure of irony, "People stare at me all the time. I'm famous. And gay men don't threaten me."

"No? That's good because my ex-husband tells me you're quite the object of admiration among his many friends."

Really? She wanted to go there?

"Lady, I'd be careful if I were you, because you're starting to piss me off."

"That would make us even then, wouldn't it?" she said with a frosted-sugar smile.

"You tell me, because I'm getting tired of this."

She sniffed and moved to the leg curls.

He braced his shoulder and used a small weight as he extended through the range of motion his physio had shown him this morning. When he followed his hand to the four o'clock position, there she was, staring at him.

She looked away, but the zing stayed in him, reverberating with sexual attraction.

"Just so we're clear," he told her, voice straining as he moved through the motion again. "If a gay man wants to stare at me, that's his business, but I'm straight. Very, very—" He looked back into her eyes, all the way to the bottoms of those dark chocolate bowls. "—into women. I wasn't joking this morning. Not one bit."

Her weights crashed into the pile and she pushed herself to stand, her body trembling, face flushed and glowing, ponytail crooked and frayed, lips parted as she panted and tried to catch her breath.

"If you want to have a real conversation, we can do that." Code for something else, obviously. "If you're not interested, that's fine too, but let's not do this anymore." He pointed across the adversarial space between them. "We've grown out of it. It's time to move on."

She folded her arms, chin set with indecision, brows bunched together with mistrust. For a moment she looked like she wanted to say something, but then she looked away and glared moodily across the room.

"You done with that?" someone asked beside him. He glanced at the ripped gym monkey who removed an ear bud to hear Chase's answer.

Chase lifted his hand off the weight and stepped away. When he glanced back at Skye, she was gathering her notebook and water bottle. She disappeared into the change rooms without saying anything more, leaving him wondering, *Well? Was she interested or wasn't she?*

๛

IT'S TIME TO *move on.*

Skye had been hearing versions of that advice for months. Chelsea had said it last night. Not in so many words, couching it more gently as, *Sweetie, you're gorgeous. Don't think that losing Terry was the end for you. There are other men out there.*

Even her mother had pulled out the old cliché about fish in the sea when Chelsea had been out to the ranch for a ride and Sunday dinner.

She did need to move on. More importantly, she needed to quit thinking it was all or nothing. One reason she refused to date was a determination not to give up on having a husband and family. If she couldn't see a man as The One From Her Dreams, then she didn't bother seeing any at all.

Not that they'd been lining up to ask her out. No, she was a bit of a pariah with her magical ability to reverse the polarity of a man's compass.

That's why she'd been so sure Chase was having a laugh at her expense this morning. No one really wanted her.

Except maybe…him?

Not for real, obviously. Not forever, but in the way that a famous athlete might want a woman if he was stuck in a small town with little to pick from and she had a decent body and no ring on her finger.

As Skye showered and changed, she tried to sift through how she felt about that. Flattered? Reassured, at least, that she could attract a man. Which only told her how desperate she was for male attention.

Oh, heck, she shouldn't be this tempted. It would be a one-night stand, not her kind of thing at all.

But it was Chase Goodwin. Even back in high school girls had talked about what a good kisser he was. He'd had nothing but practice since then. Quite an opportunity for someone who could really use a better experience than what she'd had.

Give it up, Skye, she chastised herself and zipped her sweat-damp clothes into her duffel. She was probably misreading him again. He hadn't meant anything except that he'd prefer to have a civil conversation rather than acrimonious ones. Which was fair enough. She hated conflict.

She walked out of the change room and there he was, leaving the men's room.

They both stopped.

He jangled his keys, giving her a sardonic look. "I have to get Flynn. I'm not stalking you or anything."

"Okay." She tried not to stare into his eyes, desperate to know whether the attraction he'd alluded to was real. Not that she wanted to do anything about it, mind. She just really wanted, needed, to know.

He waved. "Ladies first."

"Oh." Great. She loved that feeling of his eyes all over her back. Not.

They got to the door and his arm came up next to her, pushing it open so his body heat and the faint smell of manly sweat encompassed her. Earthy, animal scents worked on her. They always had. She was a child of the land.

She hurried ahead of him, disconcerted by a rush of phero-mones that made her even more intrigued and uncertain than ever.

He went past her toward a black SUV with rental plates, cursed, then stopped and came back to her, making her back deeper into the space between her hatchback and the mayor's convertible.

"Can I get a proper apology off my chest?" he blurted with the kind of bulldozer aggression men got when they'd worked up the nerve to talk about feelings and wanted it over with as quickly as possible. "It was a stupid remark and I wish I hadn't said it. I'm sorry that my being a public figure made it worse for you. If I made you uncomfortable by telling you I'm attracted to you, then message received. A friendly wave is all I ever expect from you." He jumbled the keys in his palm. "I'm only in town 'til the end of the month anyway, so I won't be in your face much. Well, except at the school…"

He trailed off as though he expected her to say something, but she didn't know what to say. Her ears were ringing with those bemusing words, *I'm attracted to you*. Something was using her heart as a trampoline, sending flutters through her upper chest while she searched his gaze for duplicity.

"And we're back to the eyes," he muttered, pushing his fists into his pockets. "Apology accepted or not, Skye?"

"What do you mean about the eyes?" She scowled, feeling criticized.

"You always used to look at me like that. Like you thought I was going to eat you alive. I was afraid to say boo in case you flew into a window or something."

"That's not very nice," she said, but chuckled at the image, half-embarrassed and half-elated that he'd noticed her at all back then.

"I'm going for honesty here," Chase said, running with it because he was so delighted she was actually giving him a chance. "You thought I was being the opposite of nice this morning and the truth is, if you hadn't been so shy back at school, if you hadn't been with Terry and me with..." His mind blanked. What was her name? It completely escaped him.

"Candy," Skye provided with a blink of those bottomless brown eyes. "Candace Irvine. She married someone from Tulsa, but they're divorced now."

He so didn't care. "What I'm saying is, if things had been different back then, things would have been different."

"Really." She smirked, mouth working against a twitch of amusement. "Okay."

He realized how stupid he sounded and silently cursed.

But then, as though she couldn't hold it back, the smile came, the one that broke like the sun topping the mountain, spreading warmth across the valley of his heart.

So pretty. He couldn't take his eyes off her clear, smooth skin, dewy fresh from her shower, hair skimmed back in comb rows under her schoolgirl headband. She'd washed all her makeup off and she was more striking than any supermodel he'd ever met and he'd met quite a few.

"Didn't you, um…" Her shoulders wriggled and she caught her bottom lip with her perfect white teeth. "Don't you have to go get Flynn?"

"What?" A blush seared the back of his neck. He cursed. "Right. Yes. Thank you." His turn to forget his brain in the copier. This was bad. What was happening here? Their gazes were tangling like a pair of fishing lines, both flashing with lures. So help him, he couldn't move. They both continued to stand there, staring.

"I'm sorry, too," she said. "For, um, causing a bigger cell phone scandal than the Snowden leaks."

He acknowledged that with a cant of his head, but reassured her, "Someone will take a snap of his junk tonight. We'll be old news by morning."

She laughed freely. Not a simpering giggle like the groupies offered. Not a suck-up *Oh, Chase, you're so funny*. No, her laugh was rich, very appreciative, even bordering on scolding, but totally sincere.

"Do you guys, like, draw straws to see whose turn it is, or…?"

His turn to laugh, caught off guard by her retort. "It's the damned paparazzi that're really behind it."

"In front, apparently."

The banter was silly and lighthearted and he had to work to remember why he was supposed to be walking away from her right now.

Their chuckles petered off to wide smiles of dazzled, mutual admiration. He hooked his elbow on the top of her car and leaned into her space, unable to look away from her. "You're going to let me buy you dinner, aren't you? When?"

She withdrew a little, gaze flickering around self-consciously. "People would talk. They're probably staring as they drive by right now."

"You care?"

"I live here. You might be leaving in a month, but I won't."

Right. He straightened, aware there was a deeper light of warning in what she was saying. She had roots here. He didn't. Wouldn't. That reason, the big reason he'd never pursued anything with her, remained brilliantly relevant.

He still wanted to see her. Bad.

"We could run out to that place." He snapped his fingers, trying to recollect its name. "The one that overlooks the falls. Is it still running?"

"I—Maybe. Probably. I haven't been out there in years, but…"

"We'll check it out. I'd say Friday, but I heard some of Flynn's friends talking about a party this weekend. Flynn swore he doesn't want to go, but I'd rather stick around to keep a lid on him if he changes his mind. Saturday he's working at the pizza place 'til two so I know he won't get into any trouble before I get him. Pick you up at the ranch?"

"No, I'm on Copper Mountain." She told him the address. "In the book under Baynard if you forget."

He wouldn't forget. He schooled an instinctive frown at her continuing to use Terry's name, though. He had a lot of questions about that marriage of hers, but that could wait until Saturday. *Boo-yeah*. Hot date for the weekend.

"Should we get an early start? It's a bit of a drive. Leave at five?" Four, three, two…?

"Okay. Five." It was a squeak, like a kitten's mew. She was practically wobbling she was so wide-eyed yet unsure.

He wanted to gather her up right there and then. Kiss her.

She lifted her hand in, ah hell, was that a friendly wave?

He stomped down hard on his libido, nodded and left to fetch his brother.

Chapter Four

S KYE TOLD NO one.
　　Part of her, the cautious woman who lived alone, said
that keeping her plans a secret was stupid and careless, but her
dented self-esteem was actually the reason she stayed silent. He
wouldn't try anything. He could *say* he was interested, but she
didn't really believe him.

So why go out with him at all?

She didn't want bad feelings between them, she told herself
as her sensible side had words with her inner adolescent. This
date was a step beyond that life she'd told Stan she hated. She
couldn't keep moping. If a gorgeous man wanted to buy her
dinner, maybe even kiss her, she wanted to let him.

Back on the horse, baby.

Even though she was insanely nervous to even have dinner
with him. What would they talk about, coming from completely
different worlds these days? And what should she wear? She
wanted to look her best, but feared her best would never
measure up to what he was used to. Look at the women
inhabiting his sphere.

Not a good idea, she decided, putting down her tablet and

second-guessing the dress she'd chosen, wondering if jeans with a snazzy top would be more appropriate. The restaurant was on the higher end, catering to anniversary celebrations and honeymooning tourists, but this was Montana. Cowboy boots were welcome everywhere. She didn't want to be overdressed if he showed up looking casual.

The dress, she told herself. *Quit being such a chicken liver.*

She shrugged the stretchy fabric over her shoulders then wiggled it down her hips. It was a clingy thing of apricot and peach tones with a low neckline, long sleeves and a hem that went almost to her knees. Not too sexy or formal, but it showed her figure and did nice things for her skin tone.

Her tablet burbled. Terry. Dang. She slid her finger to answer.

"Hey," she greeted. "The girls are coming over, I can't talk," she lied, glancing away. Their marriage might have been founded on one big whopper, but they'd always been pretty honest with each other about everything else. She certainly had.

"Since when do you dress like that for the girls? You look awesome."

"We're going out." She scooped up her shoes as she carried her tablet through the bedroom and down the stairs.

"Group therapy? It's been that bad for you this week?"

"No, my notoriety died down pretty fast. Someone tried to book a rapper for one of the floats in the Homecoming parade." She gave him a goggled can-you-believe-that stare. "They almost had to call up the National Guard to calm the riot."

"Makes me homesick to imagine it. Pour a glass of wine and let's sit on the deck so you can tell me all about it."

She glanced at the clock. Twenty minutes before Chase would arrive and she'd been so excited, she was ready way ahead of schedule. At least talking to Terry would pass the time without her turning into a basket of nerves.

Carrying a glass of California's best Sauv Blanc onto the deck, she set up the tablet to give him the view of the river glittering along the valley floor, put her feet up beside him and gave him the long play version of how some slick-talking promoter had nearly sabotaged the beloved country twang that formed the soundtrack to all of Marietta's community events.

ℯ⌘ℰ

CHASE WAS EARLY. He'd had to drop Flynn at his job at four so rather than zigzag home and back across town, he'd decided to carry on to Skye's. Conserving gas was the ecological thing to do, right?

"Where are you going?" Flynn had asked when they'd climbed into the rental.

"What do you mean?"

"I don't know. You look like you're going somewhere."

"Because I showered?" And shaved. And put on a clean shirt and real pants, not jeans?

"You're not wearing your hat."

Ah. The real tell. He was a ball cap guy, always had been, even in this part of the country. His good one sat on the back seat, but he didn't want hat head. Truth was, he'd come close to putting on a tie.

"Are you going on a *date*?" Flynn had asked, like he couldn't quite believe such a thing was possible.

Chase preferred honesty at all times with his kid brother, even when it wasn't the most palatable thing to do, but he wasn't sure it was the best policy in this case.

"It's just dinner. I'll be home before you are," he sidestepped.

"With who?" Flynn demanded, like he couldn't think of one eligible woman in this town.

"I'll let you know if it gets serious," Chase shot back.

Flynn gave him the guy stare, the one that refused to ask again, but communicated that more information was expected.

Chase pulled into the parking lot behind the restaurant and gave Flynn a smug smile. "Make good choices."

"You too," Flynn snarked back. Damned teenagers and their overdeveloped streaks of sarcasm.

He was still wondering if he should have been more forthcoming with Flynn as he found the top of Skye's driveway and rocked his way down. The drive wasn't too steep, but it was long. What did she do in winter, he wondered?

He reached the bench where her house sat on a nicely landscaped handful of acres. A good-sized lawn tractor stood in a three-sided shed. He didn't doubt for a minute that a girl from a ranch knew how to drive that thing and attach its plow blades herself when the snow flew. If he had to bet between the average jock parking a trailer full of gear and a sixteen-year-old girl moving her horses, he'd put money on the rancher's daughter every time.

This particular one was doing really well for herself. Since when did school secretaries afford a five-thousand-square-foot house with a pool and in-ground irrigation?

Drawn by exceptional masonry down a path along the side of the house, he admired the plexiglass panels that fenced the pool and stepped up to a deck with a hot tub under a small gazebo. A million-dollar view opened before him, the kind of thing he'd aspired to when he'd been the lowly son of the town drunk. The sort of vision he still held in his head to get through a punishing practice or a tricky moment in a game.

Glass clinked onto a stone tabletop and Skye said, "You can imagine what happened at that point. The phones went off at city hall like a five alarm fire. Penny told me—"

"Skye?" Chase took a few steps toward her, expecting her to

turn with a phone to her ear.

She jerked around on her lounger and jumped out of it, looking positively edible, barefoot in a body-hugging dress of sunset colors that matched her blush and glossy lips.

"You're early," she blurted.

"Who are you talking to?"

"What? Oh." She glanced at the tablet set up beside a glass of wine on a small table next to her chair.

"That sounds like one of my kind of girls," a male voice said with mock accusation. "Angel, are you seeing other gay men behind my back?"

"Shut up, Terry. Or I'll throw you off the balcony again."

"Wait. I want to know—" She shut down the tablet and slapped the cover into place, ignoring it when it burbled with a fresh call.

"Again?" Chase prompted, strolling closer to her, but veering to the plexiglass rail and looking down to the terraced rock walls below. A clean fire pit stood on the first level surrounded by more of those well-laid paving stones. A free-standing swing stood on the lowest level, perfect for two to curl up on and watch the sun set.

"The other night at the dance may not have been my first temper tantrum," Skye confided, biting one painted nail. He liked that she'd done that, going all out for their date. Her toes were the same shade of ripening pink. Cute.

"Continue," he prompted, starting to grin, feeling really happy to be here. "This sounds like good information to have."

"I don't blow up often, honestly. I'm a bottler, which is probably the worst kind of temper because I put up with a lot, letting it fester until I reach my limit and then…"

"You throw a man off a balcony. I noticed at the gym you can lift quite a bit."

"I threw my *tablet* off the balcony."

"Ah. But it survived." He glanced at the now silent and sleeping device.

"No, but Terry spoils me. Always has. I came home the next day to a new one on the doorstep. He even had the courier pick up the old one and take it away."

"Is that why you married him? Because he spoils you?" The question came out of him involuntarily, partly because he'd already been wondering, but more because he was so surprised. His spidey-sense for gold-diggers was pretty well honed and she'd never struck him as one. The grandeur of her home took on a new significance.

He came back from glancing at it with new eyes and found her expression had cooled and stiffened.

"No," she said firmly. "I always thought I'd renovate the old homestead at the ranch when I married and raise my kids there, but Terry's father is Rolf Baynard of Baynard and Bradley—"

"Architects, right." He winced at his stupid assumption. "His uncle is Baynard Construction."

"And his mom is in real estate. She'd had her eye on this property for years. It wasn't just my dream home, but a kind of group project we all threw ourselves into."

He took another assessing look at the huge windows and the open floor plan he could glimpse through them. "Terry's an architect too?"

"Interior designer," she said, punctuating that announcement with a pointed look then shrugging and turning away to snort, "The clichés were there like billboards, I just didn't want to see them. You know what I do if I want to get him riled, though?" she confided with a switch of mood to a mischievous grin. "Like seriously get him bent out of shape? I tell him I'm thinking of painting. He starts looking up flights. Won't let me so much as touch up in the laundry room. No joke."

"You really didn't know he was gay?" he asked, latching on

to the one piece of really interesting information she'd revealed.

She sighed, hands resting on the rail as she stared into the vastness over Marietta and beyond. After a brief, indecisive look his direction, she said, "I guess I wondered sometimes. I thought the problem was me, of course. That I wasn't attractive enough."

She splayed a hand on her chest where the top of her dress drew a half circle across breasts that were goddess-like in their perfection.

"That is not a problem you have, Skye. Trust me."

She ducked her chin and laughed shyly. "Thank you. Part of me knew I wasn't hideous, but if I wasn't the issue, then what was? I thought maybe he had an undiagnosed medical condition, because really, things were dismal up there."

She pointed to a balcony he assumed came off the master bedroom.

"I thought that's why he was resisting trying for a family, because he had performance issues, you know?" She blushed bright red, looking at him anxiously, stirring up all his protective feelings. "I can't believe I just told you that. I've never admitted to anyone how bad things were."

"It wasn't your fault, Skye." He sensed that she really needed to hear that.

"I know, but everyone around me seemed to be tearing it up with their guy and it was just too personal and embarrassing to talk about. The worst part was, my real best friend, the one person I always told my problems to, was Terry. And he was the one putting me through it. It was a really confusing time."

"And then you have asshats like me, keeping it alive."

"Fortunately I've lured you to the balcony now and can exact my revenge."

He snorted, silently willing her to make a move. Desperate to reach out and have physical contact with her.

"How did it—he—finally come out?"

"Stan's wife was pregnant with baby number three. I'd always had this dream that our kids would grow up together. I'm really close to him and, you know, cousins. They're the best, right? So I was literally pleading with Terry to try and he just broke down. It was horrible. I had all this pain inside me and his was worse. It really was." Her mouth pulled down at the corners.

He stared at her. "So you didn't kick him out? You had to be angry with him."

"Of course I was, but I couldn't cut him loose. He tried really hard to be straight for so long, really wanted to be for his father's sake, but the lie was killing him. And he was still Terry. Once I got past the shock, I could see that plain as day. His family didn't, though. His parents barely look me in the eye, they're so ashamed of him. They never said a word about me keeping the house. It's super sad."

"Damn, Skye, I used to think you knew he was gay and you were just smoothing things over for him at school, but even after he put you through all that, you're not bitter? I'm impressed."

"Bottler," she said with a point at her collarbone and a fatalistic shrug. "But what do you mean? You knew he was gay when we were in high school?"

Oh shit. Touching his tongue to his bottom lip, he heard himself drone, "Uhhh."

Little shadows edged in behind her soft brown eyes, full of dark suspicions and dying trust.

"Look, I've never told anyone this, but... One time I was showering after gym class, Terry and I were the only ones in there, and I caught him checking me out. There was that weird moment where he wasn't sure if I'd seen him looking and I could tell he was scared that I had. Afraid I'd say or do something. I didn't mean to hold that over him, but I was kind of shocked. Nothing like that had ever happened to me before. We seemed to agree to pretend it hadn't happened. Then you two started going together and I was surprised, but I read it as him really not wanting anyone to know so I left it alone."

She made a noise of finality. "Well, it sounds like you were trying not to judge, despite what I accused you of the other night." She moved to take up her wine and sip, then turned to him with a little start. "Can I get you a glass of wine? Or a beer?"

"I don't drink anything but water."

"Really? Training thing?"

"Child of an alcoholic thing."

Her expression changed, turning somber, taking a moment to decide, then saying earnestly, "Obviously I heard tales when we were kids. It was pretty bad?"

"There's no kind of girl you can date to hide that kind of secret," he said, feeling his mouth twist with old anger and chronic disgust. When he'd come home with Flynn last night, he'd sent Flynn to bed and half carried their father out of the garage himself, filled with the knowledge that he wasn't protecting Flynn from anything the kid hadn't had to do himself, too many times to count. "I think I grew a shell against being stared at before I left kindergarten. That's why the internet thing didn't impact me too much."

"Your dad holds down a job, though, right?"

"If you can call it that. He delivers newspapers to the businesses in town." A nine-year-old could do it. "Cindy works for groceries and whatever incidentals she needs. I pay for the house and all the bills, cover Flynn's gear and school stuff. The only thing Dad needs money for is booze, which we all refuse to buy for him, so he gets himself to work twice a week. I don't know what else to do." He shrugged at the helplessness he'd never been able to shake. "We've all been to meetings. Dad even went into rehab when I threatened to take Flynn. Cindy was okay with it, but I'm on the road so much and Flynn has a lot of good influences here. Max. His friends come from good families. He wanted to stay and it's not like Dad's a violent drunk. He loves us and tries in his way to show us. The house is a friggin' shrine to the two of us. He's really proud of us. He's just… got a disease."

"Oh, Chase, I had no idea it was that bad." Skye experienced a funny waver of something new inside her. A different kind of admiration that came from seeing beyond Chase Goodwin the super-hero to Chase Goodwin the boy with mettle. "I used to think you were gifted with natural ambition. You made it look like things came easy to you, but you've fought for everything you have, haven't you?"

"I have, Skye. I really have," he said with a resigned expression, hands going into his pockets. "And I feel like I should have been able to spare Flynn from going through any of the same things. I wish Cindy would have left him and taken Flynn a long time ago, but she stays, so I've done what I could. But you know what happened the other night? Flynn and I wound up in quite the man-to-man chat about his going off to college and what would happen after he left, what kind of arrangements I need to make for Dad and his mom and Flynn said, *He's my dad, too.* For the first time I felt like it wasn't all on me. Then I felt guilty as hell, but…"

"No, he's growing up and you have to let him have a say." She came forward a few steps. "He's right. You do. But I know what you mean. He's quite a bit younger than you are and these are big issues, but look at the decisions you were making at his age for the same reasons. He's a good kid, Chase. I know who the trouble-makers are, believe me. I chat with them weekly as they wait outside the principal's office. Flynn is the one who comes into the office because he found someone's keys in the parking lot."

His shoulders softened their tense line and he looked into her eyes in a way that seemed kind of bemused, kind of accepting, like he'd come up against something inevitable.

"Can I do something, Skye? It's not a come-on, I swear, but it's something I've wanted to do for a long time." He moved into her space.

She swallowed and held her ground, but had the feeling of a groundhog being cast in the shadow of a low-flying hawk. "What?" she prompted.

He set firm hands on her arms and slowly drew her against the heat of his big body.

Indecision had her hands rising nervously between them, but her arms folded as his wrapped around her and he molded her into his hard shape. He even set a wide hand on the back of her head to urge her into resting her cheek against the warm hollow below his shoulder. She was barefoot so the top of her head barely reached his collarbone and his jaw rubbed against her hair while he smoothed his hands reassuringly all over her back.

It wasn't an aggressive, sexual move. They'd shared some really personal things in the last few minutes and this was a sweet embrace to seal the connection.

It was something Terry would do.

That thought made her stiffen until she realize Chase was stiffening—

"Um—" she blurted, jerking away.

"Yeah, I really meant that to be just a hug." He eased his hold but left his hands loosely resting on her hips, allowing enough space for her to look up and see his rueful grin. "Let that be proof you're doing just fine at attracting a man."

It was the kind of boost her crushed womanhood really, really needed. They hadn't even kissed and he was hard? Her eyes began to sting and her heart rate skipped into an uncertain gallop.

"I desperately want to kiss you right now," he said gruffly, one hand rising into her periphery, hesitating, then resting on the side of her neck.

He was giving her time to decide and she'd already made this decision. As he set a possessive hand over her throat and tilted her chin with his thumb, she lifted on tiptoes, meeting the crush of his mouth.

And it was brilliant. No hesitation on his part. The opposite. Mastery. Hunger. He knew *exactly* what he was doing and it took her apart at the first indrawn hiss of her breath. In fact, she could hardly keep up under the onslaught of sensations. He kissed with firm, assertive masculine want, carefully grinding their mouths together, spreading dampness so their lips slid deliciously and a rush of excitement poured through her, culminating in a flood of wet heat between her legs.

Her arms curled around the back of his neck instinctively, mashing her tingling breasts into the hardness of his chest and even though he held her so close and tight it almost hurt, she loved it. His hands moved on her back, digging into her muscles and sliding low, encouraging her as she leaned her straining, reaching body into his. He caught her bottom lip in a gentle bite and lashed the plumped flesh with his tongue, then released it and swept to soothe the flesh before he delved into her mouth, flicking and coaxing her to play her tongue against his.

Oh God, she could barely breathe, but they only broke away to switch sides and threw themselves into another famished kiss, one she returned from a place of instinct and passion. She knew she ought to be having some kinds of thoughts, but her brain totally shorted out, leaving her flashfiring with bursts of excitement and contractions in delicious pleasure points. This was how it was supposed to be. She understood now.

Except, just as she was giving herself over to the mindless-ness of it, his hands tightened on her arms and he set her away, sucking a pained breath through his teeth as he said, "Dinner.

We have to leave now or we might not get out of here at all."

She looked at where her hands had trailed down to rest on his chest. Her trembling fingers rose and fell with his panting breaths. Her own lungs were gasping for oxygen while her head swam and giddy desire filled her.

Real desire. Crazy, *let's do it in the road* desire.

His hands moved restlessly up and down her arms. "Skye? I could really use your help here, 'cause much as we professional athletes have a reputation to uphold, I don't usually sleep with a woman this fast. Dinner first, for sure."

"You really want to, though, don't you?" she asked with wonder, needing to work up the courage to lift her lashes and read his face.

His expression flickered with bafflement, then slow understanding dawned and finally softened to tenderness. "No one since Terry? Really?"

"Not even a date. I'm using you. I'm sorry." She withdrew her touch, quirking a sheepish look up at him. "I need to get back in the game, Chase. Do you mind taking one for the team?"

His brows came together in pain at her metaphor, but an amused smirk danced around his mouth. "I don't know, Skye. Seems like a helluva favor to ask a guy when he's been wanting to make out with you for nearly a decade."

"You did not," she scoffed, backing up a step.

He sent her an impactful look that put a funny feeling low in her belly.

"I wanted to make out with you, too," she admitted nervously, stepping into a cavernous space, still not quite believing he could fully return what she had always felt around him, but wanting to.

He closed his eyes, hands fisting at his sides, reassuring her with the way he seemed to struggle for control. "That is not helping us get on the road, sweetheart. Now go fetch your purse so I can behave like a gentleman."

He kept his eyes closed and she knew she should do exactly what he said, but getting back here and continuing what they'd started is all she would be thinking about for the two-hour drive and two-hour dinner and...

Letting instinct and desire take over, she moved forward, slid her arms around his waist and lifted to press her lips near his Adam's apple.

His arms came around her, caging her in an embrace both possessive and protective, but stilling her from provoking him further. "You're sure?" he said.

"I even stole condoms from the health room. They're up-stairs. That sounds horribly premeditated, but I wouldn't have told you unless you seemed to want this, too and...you seem to. Which is really amazing to me when...." She licked her lips, encouraged by the way his gaze narrowed on her mouth. "Are you okay with, um—" She swallowed. "Kind of being my first?"

"Put me in, Coach."

Chapter Five

ဆာထ

SKYE WAS NERVOUS. It was dead obvious. What she didn't seem to realize was that he was equally nervous. *Talk about pressure.*

"They're, um, in here," she murmured, waving at the nightstand like he'd really come up here to see where she kept them.

"Skye, c'mere," he said, hearing a creak in his voice reminiscent of a far younger version of himself. Maybe that was a good thing. He didn't want her feeling threatened when he was so close to leaping on her.

She approached, all doe-eyed and tentative, her fine features accented with light powders of color, her hair sleek and shiny, but still innocent-looking with her feet bare and her bottom lip caught in her teeth.

He took her hands in as light a grip as he could manage when he wanted to be all over her. That kiss outside was still ringing his bell, but he had to scale back his hunger if he was going to make this as good for her as she seemed to need. Part of him stood back and shook his head at how wild this was, but mostly he felt privileged. He wanted her to know how it should be with a guy who was really into her.

His hands tightened involuntarily. He was *really* into her.

But it wouldn't work if she was scared.

Rubbing his thumbs over her knuckles, he said, "How long are your parents away?"

"What?" The question threw her expression into a confused frown, just as he'd hoped it would. "What do you mean—oh!" she broke into a grin of understanding, then played along. "Okay, um, they're gone all weekend. It's totally fine. They won't know you were here."

"Cool." He inched closer, sharing her conspirator's smile.

"I think the kids say 'sick' these days," she informed him.

"How about 'sweet'?" he asked, touching a kiss to the corner of her smile. "That seems about perfect for right now. You smell really good, by the way." He nosed into her hair, liking the way she shivered as he grazed her earlobe. "Like spring in Marietta."

"The jock is a poet?"

"I tell it like it is." His stomach muscles contracted under the exploring skim of her hand. He wanted to guide her touch, but letting her find her own way was nice, too. "Your skin is really soft." He smoothed his lips across her petal-smooth cheek. "Makes me want to kiss you everywhere."

In the back of her mind, a cynical part of Skye wondered if she was being seduced by a master, but even if she was, she didn't much care. He was really good at this, offering butterfly caresses down the side of her face with his lips, swirling exciting flutters through her with his suggestion.

Wriggling into the wall of his body, she found him hard again—still?—and the discovery made her instinctively hum a noise of approval and encouragement. Everything about him was so hard and sculpted to perfection. Stroking over his arms and shoulders and down to his waist, she kept pausing to dig fingers into his ungiving flesh, liking that honed, animal readiness in him. And he smelled good, too, like men's shampoo and clean laundry and something intrinsically Chase. He made her weak. All her bones softened as they stood there learning each other's shape and trading light kisses.

When she couldn't stand it any longer, she tilted her head back and fit her mouth to his. He released a groan of gratitude and relief and crushed her into him, just like outside. He'd been waiting for her to be ready, she realized, and suspected that was the last time she'd be given the lead.

Which suited her perfectly as he wiped her mind clean with a kiss that engulfed her. For long minutes, she could only cling to him while waves of desire intensified in her, each pushed by the way he rocked his mouth on hers, taking yet giving. She could feel his heart slamming behind her hand on his chest and trembled, shaken by the race of her own. The greatness of the feelings expanding in her frightened her a little, but his strength reassured her. His hunger, so undisguised yet controlled, was the real source of his seduction, wilting her into pure, feminine want that allowed him to guide her to the bed while they kissed and kissed and kissed.

The backs of her legs hit the mattress, but his arms hardened around her, keeping her on her feet. Lifting his head, he looked into her eyes as his hands began bunching her dress, climbing it up her thighs, higher. With the hem crumpled in his grip, he kept going, drawing it upward, revealing her panties and belly and bra.

She raised her arms, letting him lift it off completely, then braved his hot stare on her underwear, pretty things she'd put on in case this moment happened. His nostrils flared and he swallowed as he took his time memorizing the pale pink lace. One hand lifted and he traced the cup of her bra, fingertip tickling the plumped curve of her breast.

"I'm starting to worry I'm going to lose it before I get my clothes off. A man would *have* to be gay not to find you irresistible, Skye."

She smiled shakily and reached to undo his shirt buttons. He didn't help. Didn't even make it easy as he crowded her against the bed, but kept his hands firm on her skin, stroking lightly up her back as he dipped his head and kissed from her shoulder to her nape.

Tingles rushed down her chest to gather as sharp pinpoints at the tips of her breasts, sensitized buttons that he found with his thumbs after he loosened her bra and slid his hands around to her front under the cups.

"Oh my God," she murmured, stunned by how good it felt to be cradled in his sure hands, thumbs circling, sending rivulets of heat into her loins. His mouth nudged her bra strap down, then the other and she flicked it away herself, crying out a little when he dropped his head and kissed across the tops of her breasts and finally—"Oh my God!" she cried again, fisting a hand in his hair.

It was really good, really good. She couldn't think of anything else but the way tension seemed to gather and pull low in her belly as he sucked. When he shifted to the other one, her skin brushed his bare chest where she'd opened his shirt. His mouth was hot, wet, and he took his time as though he didn't want to stop licking and sucking at her.

Her toes curled and coils of tightness gathered in her center, making her whimper. When she thought she couldn't stand it any longer, he straightened, pulling her naked torso against his so he could kiss her again, hard. He caught a hand in her hair and tugged just a little, just enough for her to taste the primal energy of the action and react from a primitive place, communicating her excitement back to him in jagged noises and little scratches of pleasure and demand.

In a sudden move, he levered her onto the bed, making her gasp and cling, but he really was practiced at this because he was drawing away, skimming her panties to her knees, before she realized it was all part of his move. Before she could have a self-conscious moment, his hands went to his fly and without any hesitation, his own clothes were shed and cast away.

He was really, really hard. No performance issues there. Wow.

He took a condom from the drawer and set it on the pillow, then stretched out alongside her, holding himself on an elbow while his free hand went to her hip and snugged her into his heat, one raspy leg sliding over hers and trapping her half under him.

How did I get here, she wondered? But the thought flitted out of her consciousness just as quickly. He was stroking her from breast to hip, up and down again. Watching as he did, the expression on his face so intent she quivered. If she knew nothing else about him, she knew he had ferocious focus and sensed he was thinking of nothing else but her right now. This. Her heart nearly exploded with something that went beyond sexual excitement. It was something sharp and good and made her eyes sting.

He wanted her, really wanted her, and she wanted him right back.

The backs of his fingers petted softly across her mound, sending a jolt of sensitivity through her.

"Too soon?" he murmured, lifting his gaze to look into hers. "It's okay. I'm not trying to rush you, but I want to feel you against me. You're so soft, Skye." Leaning over her, he stroked her with his big body and kissed her again.

She splayed her hands over his naked back, moving under him to increase the delicious friction of skin against skin. Her center felt molten, so achy with arousal she had to catch back a sob. She licked into his mouth, trying to let him know how ready she was.

His hand returned to her thighs and his sharp knee pushed between hers. As heartening as it was to feel his erection against her hip, it took a lot of courage to let her legs fall open, but when she did. *Oh.*

He liked it, too. He groaned and pulled back enough to watch his hand shake as he caressed her, parting and soothing, delicate in the way he teased her, yet sure enough to convey he knew how to make this good. "You're so wet, Skye. You're killing me."

When he found her clit, she simultaneously wanted to arch into his touch and stop him from sending her over the edge. She settled on moaning, "Chase, I really want it to happen with you—"

"God, yes." He bit the condom packet open, rolled it on and covered her, hard thighs pushing hers firmly apart. It was a bold move, but the way he looked at her was incredibly tender. He kissed her as he entered her, both of them moaning at the exquisite, easy rightness of it.

The stretch and fit was—she almost cried it felt so good to have him deep inside her, so hard against flesh weeping with need for this. Him. She wrapped tight legs around him without thinking. It was a natural instinct, all of this feeling so perfect and right and no thoughts in her head except how good it was. So good.

He moved slowly at first, both of them drawing out the play, but it didn't last. She dug her heels into his buttocks, urging a stronger thrust and he responded like he knew what she needed. Like he needed this as badly as she did. She ached for him deeper and harder in places that had never been touched. Their pace grew animalistic and barely controlled and she loved it, drowning in sensation and passion and—

"Oh *God!*" she near screamed, ambushed by a climax that ran through her like a runaway train, sending her flying in all directions as release hit in a flash of blinding light and reverberations of pleasure so strong and sharp, they neared pain.

Hard hands bit into her shoulders and his powerful hips crushed into hers, tight, deep, his own release powerful enough she felt the pulses against her rippling walls, the oneness of it exquisite.

Oh God, she *loved* Chase Goodwin. She would love him forever for this.

Chapter Six

෨෨

THE BEST PART was the way he lingered and fondled as they came back to themselves, stroking and kissing and looking into her eyes. She ought to feel shy, she supposed, but she didn't. She was too grateful. Too enthralled by him.

"That was really amazing, Skye."

For her it definitely had been, but she took his words with a grain of salt, pleased by his compliment, but aware she could fall for him way too easily. This really was a do-over on losing her virginity and she would never, ever forget this. She was so glad it was him.

"I have to go," he murmured with what sounded like reluctance, but sent a shaft of chill into her heart. "I'll be right back. Don't go anywhere."

She realized he meant he had to pull away and go into the bathroom.

Should she get under the covers? Were they going to cuddle longer or, even better, do it again?

Her house alarm chimed, warning her that her front door was opening.

She sat up in panic, instantly remembering and silently cursing. No! Little feet scampered across her bottom floor and high-pitched voices called, "Auntie Skye, are you here?"

No, no, no.

Shooting to her feet, she hissed, "Stay here," to Chase and pulled the bathroom door shut on his startled expression in the mirror. Then she leapt into her walk-in closet to yank on sweats and a T-shirt, emerging as her five and six-year-old nieces trampled up the stairs and into her room.

"You *are* here. Mommy said you wouldn't be."

"I know, I told her I was going out." That's how they did things and it usually worked, but that darned Chase Goodwin with his distracting sexiness had sent her off playbook. "My plans changed and I forgot you guys were coming. Did she see Nana's canning jars? I left them on the counter. Let's go downstairs and get them." She herded the girls from the room, glancing at herself in the mirror on the way, expecting a disaster, but her makeup was only a little smudged. She snatched up a headband and smoothed her hair into place as they descended to her kitchen.

"Hi, Holly," she said, avoiding her sister-in-law's sharp gaze in favor of grinning at her youngest niece, two-year-old Chrissie. The toddler was obviously grouchy from being woken in the car. She didn't lift her head off her mother's shoulder or smile, but she held out a hand to Auntie. Skye kissed the tot's pudgy knuckles, not trying to take her, aware she would need time to wake up before she'd leave Mom.

"I totally forgot you were coming," Skye said, turning to the boxes she'd left stacked for pick up. "I'll carry these out for you."

"In a hurry for us to leave?" Holly asked with false brightness. "I brought the girls in because it looked like you had company." She made a point of scanning the empty deck through the windows. "Or does that truck outside belong to the pool boy?"

The weight of her middle niece came up against her thigh. "Is the pool ready, Auntie Skye? Can we go swimming?"

Skye gave Holly her best *die* look. "Not yet, sweetie," she said, stroking a hand over her niece's hair. "Next weekend, if the weather's good, you might be able to. If it's not, and your mom says it's okay, you guys could still come for a sleepover."

"Can we, Mom? Pleeeeze?"

Skye smiled inwardly. She loved her nieces to bits and didn't mean to use them in her chess match with Holly, but it was always satisfying to take the higher ground and do the woman a favor in retaliation for Holly's pillish behavior.

Holly's mouth tightened.

Skye picked up the boxes and turned toward the front room, but hadn't taken two steps before Chase trotted down the stairs, fully dressed and calm as you please.

"I'll take those for you, Skye. I couldn't see anything wrong with that modem, but if it's cutting out on you, I'd tell the cable guy to replace it and see if that helps. Hey." He greeted Holly with a chuck of his chin as he took the jars from Skye. "Chase Goodwin. Were you at Marietta?"

"No, Livingston. Holly Wolcott." Her eyes, bright with startled recognition, swung over to Skye's to grow narrow with a special kind of outrage. "I hear your little brother and his team are going to give our boys a run for their money this year."

"Be nice if we finally got a trophy with a date from this century," Chase drawled.

"Holly is married to Stan," Skye provided, not really appreciating Chase's attempt to cover things up. There was no winning with Holly. Not ever. Not for her.

"Nice to meet you," he said, then to Skye, "You should finish getting ready or we'll miss our reservation. Do I need keys to get these into the car, or…?" He hovered with enough male authority to propel Holly out the door before him, chin in the air.

"I can't wait to tell Stan I met you," Holly made a point of saying after she buckled all the girls into her hatchback.

"Say hello to him for me. I haven't seen him since graduation," Chase replied good-naturedly, coming back to the stoop, not touching Skye as they waved at the girls.

"She seems nice," he said with false sincerity when the car topped the driveway.

"Pah!" Skye choked. "She's going to break land speed records getting back to the ranch with this one. Smarmy cow! I mean, I don't care what she thinks of me, but to talk like that in front of the kids?" Furious, feeling the darkness of her messy life creeping back into her post-orgasmic buzz, she entered the house and headed for the stairs. "What time is our reservation?" she asked.

"I just said that to get rid of her. We don't have to go at all, if you don't want to."

Turning on the second stair, she impulsively held out her arms to him. "You are my hero."

He came forward and caught her with a little, "Oof." They shared a kiss and she felt him stir to life below his belt.

Wriggling her hips into that evidence of his desire for her, she said, "That is the nicest compliment any man has ever paid me."

He set a low hand on her butt and snugged her tight to the ridge of hardening flesh. "Allow me to compliment the hell out of you, then."

They went back to bed.

❧

"SKYE, THIS IS a really beautiful house," Chase said, stating the obvious, but he was mellowed out to the point of barely being able to talk at all. He was barefoot, wearing only his pants, and the floor had warmed with subfloor radiant heat as the sun set. He stood at the windows watching the sky purple and caught the reflection of his lover moving around her state-of-the-art kitchen with confidence.

"I know. I love it, I really do," she said, scraping a knife blade down a cutting board so the contents fell with a sizzle into a hot pan. The scent of frying garlic and onions and herbs burst into the air, making his stomach clench with appetite. "Sometimes it's a pain being so far out of town, but I was used to that at the ranch."

"Roads bad in winter?"

"Meh," she dismissed with a shrug. "It's Montana."

"Yeah." At first he'd liked being in the bustle of cities and having the convenience of just about anything within a few blocks of his apartment, but being back here for this long, he'd begun to appreciate the calm of rural living. You realized pretty quickly the difference between what you really needed and what you merely wanted. Getting a cheerful wave of *after-you* at a stop sign was a damned sight nicer than getting the finger in gridlocked traffic.

Spotting her tablet still on the table outside, he went to fetch it and brought her wine glass in as well. "You got a bug in this," he said, pouring it out and washing the glass. "You want a fresh one?" he asked as he dried it, eyeing up the delightful view of her bare shoulder blades in a white tank and the snug fit of yoga pants on her sweetly rounded butt.

"You don't mind?" she asked over her shoulder.

"You planning to get loaded?"

"No. Although I will admit to a certain amount of self-medicating while Terry and I were breaking up. I made myself go a month without drinking at one point, when I realized I was coming home to a glass every night. That didn't seem healthy so I quit and realized it was more of a habit I'd fallen into. I was just as happy if I made myself a tea."

"I know lots of people who drink within their limit," he said, pouring from the bottle in the fridge and setting it where she could reach it. "I'm not a crusader."

She lifted the glass, then paused. "Still going to kiss me if I taste like wine?"

"Hell, yeah, I am." He was going to kiss her whenever he wanted. They'd spent hours upstairs doing exactly that, among other things. Skye Wolcott was not only sweet and vulnerable, she was sensual and greedy and a bit of a screamer. He liked getting her off and he couldn't wait to do it again.

She blushed as if she could read his thoughts and took a quick sip before setting her wine aside. "You're going to make me burn your dinner."

He sidled up behind her as she turned to stir the boiling pasta, fitting her to his front as he explored the firmness of her waist and flat stomach. She smelled sweet and musky, a potent mix of both of them that went into his head like a drug. "If you hadn't kept me in bed instead of letting me drive to the falls, cooking wouldn't be an issue."

Sending a look up at him, she said, "You are so good for my ego."

A funny suspicion hit him. Did she think he was merely pandering to her? He let his hands fall away, disturbed.

"Thanks for bringing this in," she said, reaching out to her tablet and flicking the cover open. "I forgot I left it out there. Hmmph," she said as she touched the button to light the screen. "Terry, Terry and Stan. Look."

Terry: Call me.

Terry: I'm serious. I want to know who it is.

Stan: What?

"Holly is such a tattletale," she muttered.

"What's with you and her?" he asked. "It almost sounded like—" No, that couldn't be right.

"What?" she prompted.

"Like a competitive rivalry," he admitted with a shrug. He breathed that dynamic and was sure he'd heard the shove in her voice and the line drawn in the sand. "You said you were close to your brother. Does that bother her?"

"That's part of it, but we both used to barrel race," Skye surprised him by saying.

He shouldn't be surprised, of course. She had the body of an athlete. Her movements were economical and sure as she moved to drain the pasta and stir vegetables into the onion and garlic sauce. Of course she would have been a helluva horsewoman, growing up on a ranch.

"I didn't know that about you. I never went out to the rodeo or watched any of the competitions. Too many other things going on and..." He shrugged. "Horses aren't my thing. Closest I got was loading alfalfa pellets onto a truck."

"Blasphemy!" she declared.

"Should I show myself to the door right now?"

"I'll let it go for the moment, but only because you show so much potential as a mount."

He chuckled, liking the way she could be naughty and funny at the same time. "Why thank you. I look forward to further opportunities to be jumped."

They shared a laughing, sexy look. Then something popped in the pan and she shook herself back to reality and said, "I really am going to burn dinner."

A few minutes later, she dished up a simple but delicious plateful of carbs that made him nod with approval. They sat at the island, his leg crooked open so he could graze the side of her hip with his knee. He hadn't felt this magnetized to a female since… Hell, he honestly didn't know if he'd ever felt it this strong.

"So you used to win at the barrel races?" he asked, still curious about her rivalry with her sister-in-law.

"I did, which was especially hard on Holly because she really needed the prize money. Her father's place has never done anything like ours, and we've had our struggles. It was actually a big deal for her to marry Stan and be a rancher's wife after she went through all those years of scraping by. I get that and I've always tried to be understanding and not take her jealousy to heart, but I had a horse to feed, too. I wasn't cheating. The fact is, I was better than she was."

A woman after his own heart. No false modesty or overconfidence. She worked hard, recognized what she deserved and made it happen.

"She still hates you for it," he guessed, more than aware how awkward it was to be the object of envy and animosity for honest accomplishments.

"Terry calls her my nemesis. Oh my *gawd* did she love it when he came out. The baby thing, I swear she had Chrissy to spite me, knowing how bad I wanted kids. Which I shouldn't say because that sounds like she doesn't love her kids and she does. She and Stan are actually a really good match and she and Mom get on well. They're very similar, both super practical and have their own territory staked out at the house so they don't step on each other. Me, I'm an interloper if I'm there. I load the dishwasher wrong and spend too much time in the barn or with the kids when I could be helping out in the house. And then I have this." She waved to the exposed beams of her ceiling.

"How dare you marry into a family of building professionals," he said.

"Exactly. And Terry loved to spoil the girls rotten with gadgets and swing sets and whatever else they wanted. That's why he put in the pool. She blames me, of course. He was too generous and made Stan look bad, but if we brought out modest birthday or Christmas gifts, well, we could afford better so…" Skye sent a frustrated growl to the ceiling. "She's such a piece of work."

"Screw her," he dismissed.

"I wish, but she's family. And this?" She motioned between the two of them. "I couldn't have an affair with just anybody. It had to be with someone famous. That's how she'll see it. Like I somehow did this to *show* her."

"Is she going to have it all over town?" he asked. More importantly, "Do you care?"

She paused in twirling noodles onto her fork. "I'm getting tired of having my laundry aired. After the other day—" She flashed him a look. "I'm not ashamed, Chase. I have no regrets, I swear, but I can see how this is going to be the juiciest steak for people to chew on, how that lonely Mrs. Baynard fell for the smooth-talking playa. That part bugs me."

The damp of suspicion frosted into certainty inside him. "Is that what you think I did, Skye?"

"No." Her brow crinkled into a small scowl, but she kept her gaze lowered.

"'Cause I don't do pity fucks."

She lifted her face and dropped her jaw. "That's a yucky thing to say."

"It's a lousy thing to accuse me of."

"I didn't!" she said, but her scowl stayed in place and her gaze dropped again.

"Not out loud," he groused, biting across his fork. "But you're thinking it."

"I'm not." Her breath went in and out on a huff. "But I do know how to use the internet, you know. I've seen the women you're usually with. They're not pathetic school secretaries from small town Montana."

"Oh, snap out of it," he growled. "We knocked each other's socks off and it had nothing to do with who we are outside the bedroom. If you want to hang onto feeling like a victim, that's your business, but I went upstairs with you because I like you, not because I couldn't leave town without getting laid."

"You don't have to be like that about it," she said hotly, cutting him a dismayed look. "I know I've been staging the longest running pity-party in history. I just find it hard to believe that someone like you, who seems to have so much of the world in the palm of his hand, could want me. I'm nothing special."

"And that's exactly what makes you special," he said with his palm up to indicate her amazingness. "Who I am gets in the way of my relationships all the time. People want to be with the guy who's famous and has money and gets them in front of a camera. You don't want anything to do with that idiot. You're willing to have a conversation with the real me and listen to me bitch about my problems. Am I excited by the idea of someone catching us holding hands and posting it so we can go through another round of public scrutiny? Hell no. But do I want to walk down Main Street holding your hand because I like touching you? You bet I do."

"Really?" She gave him her high school look. "You want to keep seeing each other? I mean, after tonight? Like, while you're here?"

Longer, maybe, he thought and a strange unsteadiness rippled inside his chest. All those old warnings flashed about not getting hooked into staying in this town.

Nevertheless, he heard himself say, "Yeah." And he felt himself regressing to about thirteen years old, asking his first girl to go steady. "Do you?"

She smiled, tucking her chin to hide it, but her cheeks colored up with a pink so warm he felt it trickle heat through him.

"Okay." She wrinkled her nose, glancing back up at him. "But, like, publicly?"

"You lead on that one," he said, giving in to temptation and reaching up to skim her headband off her hair so the tresses fell forward in a swing of shiny dark brown.

"Why'd you do that?" She tried to catch his hand before he spun the headband like a Frisbee toward the sofa.

"Because." He cupped the back of her head, drawing her into a buttery kiss. "I've kept my hands off you about as long as I can manage."

Bracing a hand on his thigh, she smiled a womanly smile. "I like your hands on me, you know. A lot. What time did you say you have to be home?"

"We've got hours."

"Suh-weet," she teased against his growing smile.

Chapter Seven

ഔരു

SITTING ON THE edge of her bed at one thirty, he insisted she not get up to see him to the door, but he wanted her number. "I'm texting you now so you have mine. Let me know when you're awake. I have to take Flynn to practice, but maybe I really can buy you dinner tomorrow?"

"I usually go out to the ranch on Sundays. Wanna come?"

"What time? I'll have to see what Flynn's doing—"

"I was being facetious. It'll be awful."

"Really?"

She liked that protective edge in his tone, like he was drawing a sword.

"Just big brother acting like a dad. I can handle him." She set her head on his thigh and lightly bit one of his fingers.

He evaded her and sifted his fingers through her hair, something he'd done a million times tonight. Oh, she was hopelessly infatuated with him and his sexy, tender, proprietary nature.

"I'll figure something out and come if you want me to. I don't like leaving you without knowing when I'll see you again, Skye." The room was dark, but she felt the pierce of his glittering gaze.

"I'll be at work Monday," she reminded. "You have practice in the afternoon on the field."

"That's too far away," he grumbled.

She grinned. "Sneak out of the house tomorrow night."

"A fine example to set," he said, a smirk in his voice. "But I'm tempted."

"On a school night, no less," she scolded.

"See? It's a good thing I didn't make a play for you back in high school. I never would have had the strength to leave town."

She suspected that was supposed to be a compliment, but it was a chilling reminder that he had a career to get back to and she a life here she loved. They were both still and silent a moment, as if he was thinking the same thing.

"Find out when Flynn works next," she suggested, sitting up next to him. "Bring some steaks over and you can barbeque. It'll be like buying me dinner only better."

"Tuesday, I think," he said, leaning to give her a lingering kiss, one still tainted with that moment they'd recognized how impermanent this was.

She refused to dwell on it. For this moment, they were perfect. "Thank you for tonight, Chase."

"It'll be more than tonight," he growled against her lips.

৪৩

SUNDAY TURNED INTO a bit of a wash. They texted flirty banter until she had to run out to the ranch and knew she'd lose service. He wasn't happy about that, but the football team was having a meeting about an upcoming game and Chase had to attend so his phone would be off too.

The team was on such a winning streak at the moment, talk of their chances this year had actually wound up being the salvation for an otherwise uncomfortable family dinner. Even her mother, who wasn't a particularly fervent sports fan, was keeping tabs on the team via the local paper. For some reason she seemed to think Skye had insider knowledge because she worked at the school, but Skye gave all the credit to Mitch Holden.

And clenched her teeth over Holly's blithe, "I hear that new coach is a hunk. Doesn't he also teach computers or something?"

"Government," Skye provided. "Livingston wanted him, but we got him." *Winning.* Then she again raised the topic of having the girls for the weekend.

Tell me what he said, was the message from Chase that greeted her when she came back into service at seven o'clock that night.

I'll be home in twenty. Will call you. Can you talk? she replied, then pulled back onto the road.

He was waiting in her driveway when she came down it.

"How did this happen?" she asked, heart taking flight as he lifted her off her feet in a bear hug.

"Flynn's at the movies. I only have an hour."

They didn't even close the garage door in their hurry to her bedroom, but afterward, as they lay curled in a tangle of limbs, he asked, "Well? Was Stan a jerk about it?"

"I said you bought me dinner and that Holly misunderstood."

He lifted his head to angle a dismayed look at her.

"I'm sorry I lied, but I don't know how to explain this. I don't even know how it happened."

"Yeah," he groaned in bewilderment, dropping his head back onto the pillow. "Flynn was all, *Wanna tell me where you went tonight?* when I picked him up last night."

At the mention of the boy's name, Skye lifted her head off his shoulder and glanced at the clock. Chase looked too and sighed, pulling away with reluctance. As he dressed, he gave her a disgruntled look.

"And still no dinner," she teased.

"That's your fault. You jumped me in the garage."

"You're a pushover, Chase Goodwin. Learn to put up a fight." She rose to dress, kissing him at the door a few minutes later.

"This is already old," he said, looking at the keys in his hand. "We have to figure out something better."

She didn't know what that would be without tipping off the whole town they were sleeping together. Well, sharing a bed. Not sleeping, which seemed to be what Chase was taking issue with.

Skye had to wonder if it was worth the effort to hide their affair when something in her demeanour the next day seemed to radiate signals that she'd had a man in her bed on the weekend. More than one person commented, "You're in a really good mood," and "You look really nice today." Two teachers even went so far as to ask in an undertone, "Are you seeing some-one?"

"It's a nice day," she prevaricated. "Everyone's whistling."

True, but no one else had dressed with Chase Goodwin in mind, anticipating that he'd be here sometime around three. Wearing a floral-print dress with a fluttery skirt, she kept her eye out for his arrival. When the team started practice, she picked up the envelope she'd set aside this morning, shrugged on her light sweater and set off through the gymnasium to the back field.

SO CR

CHASE WAS ON the surly side today, having received a call this morning that complicated what was already a balancing act here in Marietta. Getting back to his team and playing ball was his goal, for sure, and they only wanted him to come out for an assessment and a check up next week, but the season was over for them and he'd barely settled in here.

Since when did he want to, he wondered?

Right. There was the answer to that one. Brunette hair and a green and yellow dress fluttered in the breeze. Jagged mountains and blue sky and puffy white clouds provided a stunning backdrop as the fabric of her dress pressed to her knock-out shape.

Skye was turning into his own personal bottle and he didn't know how he was going to give her up.

It took her a while to reach him, circling the field on tip-toed heels to where he was working with the team's quarterback, showing him how to work his shoulder to keep it supple, but build power for chucking.

He lost the plot, barely able to take his eyes off her, liking everything about the way she moved.

"Go run a few laps," he told the kid as she arrived, then greeted her when the boy was out of earshot. "Ms. Wolcott. This is a nice surprise. Did you come all the way out here to see me?"

"I did. And I brought the flimsiest of excuses I could find." She handed him the envelope addressed to the Parent Or Guardian Of Flynn Goodwin. "No use wasting a stamp when you're right here. It's the finalized game schedule."

"Aren't you conscientious of taxpayer money." Through her bra and the light weight of her dress, he could just make out the way the breeze had hardened her nipples. Or maybe she was reacting to him. That was a heady thought.

"Not really, or I would have brought everyone's. Now quit looking at me like that because Tommy Reid has his camera on us."

He turned his head and saw the boy aiming his mobile phone at them. "Hey! Knucklehead! What did coach say about phones on the field? Bring it," he ordered, waving the kid in.

Tom's shoulders sagged as he ran the phone to Chase.

"Now apologize to Ms. Wolcott. I'm not going to say what kind of move that was, but you and I both know. That was rude, dude."

Tom looked between them, confused. "You mean Mrs. Baynard?"

Chase sent her a faintly exasperated look.

She shrugged. "I married out of high school. It's the name everyone knows. I didn't see the point in changing it."

"Just apologize and get back out there," Chase grumbled, pocketing the phone. When the kid was gone, he said to Skye, "Listen, I got a call this morning. I have to fly to L.A. next week, see the team doctor and have a few tests."

"Oh." Her cheerful expression faded to somber. "Are you coming back?"

"Yeah. I think so." Pretty sure. He tucked his hands in his back pockets, watching the boys and listening to the calls from the quarterback, brooding. He glanced back to try to interpret her frown.

"But you're not leaving until next week," she said with an attempt at optimism.

"Yeah, but we have that game in Bozeman this weekend," he reminded. Whose dumb idea had it been to sign on as assistant coach slash chaperone and tie up all his time?

"I've got the girls this weekend anyway," she murmured, gaze clouded and focusing on the middle distance.

"You want to come?" he asked, aware it had been in the back of his mind since he'd finished his call.

"To Bozeman?" she asked, startled and dubious.

"L.A."

"Oh." If anything, she looked even more askance.

That annoyed him. It couldn't be that big a stretch for her to imagine he'd want her to come with him, could it?

Mitch's piercing whistle made them both look. Max called for the boys to break for water and Skye took a shaky breath. "I'll, um, think about it," she said, brow still gathered as she waved at the coaches and headed back into the school.

Ten minutes later, the boys were running suicides. Mitch was on one side of him, Max on the other, arms folded, drill sergeant expression firmly in place.

"So you two kissed and made up?" Mitch said.

"Beg your pardon?" Chase returned, hearing the flick of danger in his tone. Damn. That was probably more revealing than he'd needed it to be, especially with Mitch standing right there, but seriously.

Max's brows shot up. He eyed Chase like he read a lot more in his expression than Chase's frozen features meant to convey.

They all looked straight ahead again, but Chase could sense Mitch's interest. The guy was new to Marietta, young but confident enough to earn the boys' respect. Keen. In good shape. It was pretty easy to imagine he'd make a play for Skye if she showed an inkling of interest. That made Chase hate the guy a little bit, for moving to Marietta with what looked like a desire to stay.

He sent a disgruntled glare in Mitch's direction.

Mitch lifted his hands in a *not gonna touch it* gesture and took a few steps up the field, clapping his palms and shouting encouragement as the boys started to flag.

"Hmph," Max snorted, then he offered a muted, "Uh-huh," under his breath.

Chase said nothing, but every hair on his body was primed for a wrong signal from Max, fairly daring him to make something of it. Women could say men were lousy communicators, but they got messages across just fine with grunts and sneers.

"And then what happens?" Max asked after the boys had

trampled the grass in front of them again and Mitch was out of earshot. "When you leave?"

"I'm working on it," Chase snarled. You didn't throw away a career like his, but you didn't throw away a woman like Skye without giving things an honest shot either. What if they really had something?

And yet, it was so new, what did he know? Maybe her dismayed reaction had been a signal that things were dying out on her side.

They didn't have a chance to talk it out properly until he was turning steaks on her grill on Tuesday. The weather had turn gray and drizzly so she was inside baking the potatoes in the oven and tossing a salad while he tried not to demand answers when she seemed to have retreated to a remote headspace.

He made himself wait until they sat down at her dining room table, a candle lending warmth to the atmosphere when rain was gusting against the windows and the air felt heavy and damp.

"I guess it's short notice to put in for time off," he said as an opener.

"I have some time I could use," she murmured, pushing green flecks of onion deeper into the melted butter pooling in her baked potato.

"But you don't want to," he surmised.

"That's not it. It's just… Chase, I don't do that sort of thing. Run to L.A. mid-week for a couple of days. I'm not saying I don't travel. We honeymooned in Mexico and did the Keys one year because it was on our bucket list. And Vegas, of course, which was a four-day weekend, but…" She shrugged.

"Is it the cost? I intend to buy your ticket. You're my guest."

"I can afford my own ticket," she rushed to assure. "No, I'm talking about what kind of person I am. It's the trunk of the elephant we're not acknowledging. You don't live here and I do.

I can go to L.A. with you, but in a couple of weeks you'll be gone for good. I'm not saying I want more. I realize this is just this." She drew a circle over the space between their plates. "I'm not trying to pressure you. It's the opposite. I don't want to get too serious when…" She shrugged. "I already know it's going to hurt when you leave."

"And you won't even consider coming with me when I do."

He wasn't entirely comfortable saying that and the way she paled told him how surprised she was that he had.

He sat back and rubbed his hands on his thighs. "I realize that's fast. And I'm not saying it would turn into something permanent, but right now I can't see walking away in a few days and writing this off as a nice little holiday romance. I see potential, Skye. Don't you?"

Her heart was hammering her throat, making breathing nearly impossible. She took a sip of wine, but her head was already swimming. In some ways, everything he was saying was a dream come true, but she knew who she was and he apparently didn't realize who he was.

"Chase, I don't have grand goals like you. I had one dream growing up: to marry a nice man who wanted kids and raise them here in Marietta. I love it. It's why I sank my claws into the school secretary job and refuse to let it go. I know I could have gone to college and become an accountant or something, but when I finally do have a family, I want summers and Christmas break off with my kids. I have really great friends here who stuck by me through a really crummy break up. I want to be here for them if and when they need me. My family is here. This is my home." She waved, indicating the house. "I'm not made to live large and back up someone of your caliber."

"Okay, stop. If you think you'd be homesick, fine. I'll accept that, but do you hear how you're limiting yourself? If I had told myself all those years that I wasn't the right stuff to be a professional athlete because of where and how I grew up, I would have proved myself right and I'd still be at the feed store. I'm not going to sit here and listen to you tell me you can't date a professional athlete because you're only a school secretary. First of all, school secretaries are pretty freaking exciting. I can speak from experience on that one. And you *are* dating a professional athlete. It's your jam. Pretending it's not is like living Terry's kind of lie."

She sat taller. "It's my *jam*?"

He groaned. "It just came out. You hang around all day with those kids and their lingo rubs off. You know what I mean." His pained frown grew serious, impatient even. "But come on, Skye. We have time to work out the long term stuff if you'll at least try a road trip before you write us off."

"It just seems like a really big step when…" She eyed him, working up her nerve. "Would you ever consider making Marietta your home again?" she asked in a small voice, quickly stuffing a bite into her mouth, sure she knew the answer and it wouldn't be good.

He sighed and looked out at the blustery day, not one of the nicest here by far. His lowered brows weren't encouraging. "I don't usually come back for more than a day or two and it was usually for Flynn, but Dad will always be here—which is not why I'm talking about us getting more serious," he said firmly, cutting off any suspicions she might have before they grew. "I'm not looking for a babysitter for him or anything. Cindy seems to want that job and she can keep it."

She watched him comb his fingers through his hair.

"But most of the guys keep their wives in a major center, so the travel isn't too bad. It wouldn't be very practical to live here, but I won't say no outright." He gave her another impactful look, this one letting her know he viewed himself as considerably more open-minded than she was.

She set her chin, still stinging from his calling her a closet self-limiter.

"If all goes well with my shoulder and nothing else happens, I could be playing another ten years at least. After I retire, I was aiming to go into coaching."

"Which would be more of the same travel and everything."

"That isn't written in stone, but yeah, it could be."

"You don't want to go back to school?"

"For interior design?"

She slitted her eyes, telling him he wasn't funny.

His mouth quirked briefly, then he said, "I've thought about it a lot, but I've never been sure what to take. I like sciences. Maybe I could get my teaching diploma. Work at the high school with you. Summers and Christmas off."

Feeling mocked for her low aspirations, she asked the deal breaker. "Do you want kids?" She could barely get the words out. Her chest felt too tight.

"Honestly?" His tone said she didn't really want his answer. "Given my childhood, kids were not something I pictured for myself. But I could see it now." The timbre of his voice went through her to her bones, lifting her hot eyes. She found him waiting for her, his expression incredibly tender. Everything in her stopped, then started up at double speed.

"I'd be waiting again," she blurted. "Waiting for you to finish playing, waiting for us to move back here, waiting…"

He reached across and gently crushed her hand. "Would you open your pretty eyes and look at us? I don't see either of us dragging our feet very long with anything."

She smiled through lips she was clamping so they wouldn't tremble. Maybe he wasn't declaring love, but it was quite the declaration of honorable intention.

Yes, he looked very intent. All that wonderful focus she used to admire in him was narrowed onto her right now and it was terrifying yet exhilarating.

"Is this really how your mind works? Even when you were hitting a tee-ball in little league, you were already convinced you'd win the World Series one day?"

"You can't find a place that isn't on your map. Did you go into a barrel race planning to lose?"

"No."

"Don't go into your next relationship planning to fail, either," he said, releasing her to pick up his steak knife. "Play to win."

Chapter Eight

80C3

M AYBE THE REAL difference between her and Chase, Skye thought as she wheeled her horse after a calf, was that she rarely tried anything she didn't know she had a good chance of winning. Barrel-racing had been a strong event for her, but she could have competed in calf-roping. She knew how to do it. Others had been better though, so she'd stood back from those contests.

Dropping to the mucky ground, she heeled the calf and used her knee on his neck to hold him long enough to get the syringe from her vest and jab it into his unhappy hide. Stan wasn't a fan of giving shots without cause, but this critter had an infection that was being stubborn. Stan had told her to keep an eye out for him while she was on her Sunday ride and now she'd got him. Job done.

Satisfied, she released the calf and started trotting back to the house, whimsically thinking that the black SUV picking its way down the potholed drive looked like Chase's, but he was in Boze—

The truck stopped, the door opened, and his tall frame stood on the running board. He waved at her.

She gave an excited kick and Pancake broke into a gallop. She crouched low over his neck as he ate up the quarter mile.

Slowing him as they neared the fence and floating on his cantering gait, she saw Chase grinning at her. "Damn, woman. I thought you were going to jump right over us."

"Might have if we were just starting out, but we've been riding for hours. We're both done in." She patted the horse's neck, breathless as she asked, "What are you doing here?"

"Flynn and I drove the Patterson twins home. Their mom said yours had called over looking for some attachment for her sewing machine. She asked if I'd mind dropping it on my way back to town."

"She's got the girls making spirit flags in the team colors for the pep rally. It's what they did back in the day, when Mom was in Home Ec." She let him see her bemusement over that one. Not the support part, but Home *Economics*? Good Lord, women had come a long way. "You're a good sport to play courier," she added, well aware that to ranching folk this distance off the main road wasn't out of the way, but it could sound like a funny request to townies. Ducking to catch Flynn's eye inside the SUV, she greeted him. "You're back early from the game. Don't tell me you lost. I'll have to tell Mom to make black arm bands instead."

"Other team couldn't field enough players, had to forfeit," he said, looking at her curiously.

"Easy win, but we'll take it, right? Listen, I'll meet you guys at the house, otherwise I really will have to jump the fence." She nodded at the fence line to the barn.

Chase followed her look. "I'll walk with you. Flynn can drive up to the house. Mind Flynn?"

"What? But—" As Chase left the keys on the seat and stepped away from the SUV, Flynn grumbled a dubious, "I...guess." He slid out of the passenger side and came around the back of the vehicle to cast a confused glance between Skye as she dismounted and Chase as he stood from climbing through the fence. "Do I, like, give the thing to Mrs. Wolcott or…?"

"Just knock on the screen at the back. She'll be in the kitchen. Might even be in the garden," Skye assured him.

"Drive slow," Chase reminded. "Watch for the kids."

"Oh, and would you please tell Coralee, she's the older one, that I'm in the barn? She wanted to help me brush down Pancake. Thanks, Flynn."

With a confused shake of his head, Flynn climbed into the driver's seat and crawled down the rest of the winding drive.

"I thought you might be here. That's why I didn't mind coming by. Do *you* mind?" Chase asked, pacing on her left while she held Pancake's reins in her right hand.

"No." She couldn't help her smile, even though she felt oddly shy. They might have made love on Tuesday, and flirted at the gym on Wednesday, and taken their time together on Thursday while Flynn did a four-hour shift at the restaurant, but they'd both been tied up all weekend, barely able to text. She had messaged him Friday afternoon when her time off had been approved and he'd sent her a smiley face and a heart in return, but this was their first face to face since then.

Galloping hoofbeats thundered from a distance, growing louder. Stan and Holly crested the south hillock, returning from their own Sunday ride, not that Skye had ever had the lack of class to speculate on what kind of 'ride' it was.

They all met at the barn, Coralee leading a lost-looking Flynn into their midst.

"Here," Flynn said to Chase, handing over the keys with a significant jangle. "I parked right out there." *We can go now*, his tone said.

"I want to say hello to Stan. It's been a while," Chase said, stepping forward as Stan dismounted and held out his hand to shake. Chase didn't flinch from Stan's dirty palm or the smell of the barn or the sweat on humans and horses.

"Indeed it has," Stan agreed, as welcoming as any Wolcott to a guest on the ranch, but there was a hint of reserve. "No need to ask what you've been up to since graduation," he added, but his tone held an inquisitive, *But what are you doing* here?

"Or you," Chase said with an indulgent nod at Coralee where she carefully set out grooming tools on the bench beside Pancake's stall. "You know my brother, Flynn?" Chase introduced.

"Seen him around." The men shook hands and Stan introduced Holly, then Coralee.

"We saw you at Auntie Skye's when we came to get the canning jars," Coralee said to Chase.

"You did," Chase agreed smoothly.

"Fixing her modem, I believe," Holly said with her most sickeningly sweet smile. "I guess that's what we're calling it these days?"

The silence was awful, but Skye suspected the reaction between the speechless adults would have been hysterical to someone watching them. Holly pinned a triumphant look on Skye, one that made Skye's face sting with a flush of mortification, but then Holly caught her husband's eye and her gaze widened with shame. Stan shot a look of deep regret at Flynn, but Flynn was staring at Chase, dumbfounded.

Chase, meanwhile, gave Holly a hard stare that said, *Do you know how hard I throw? I can aim wherever I want.*

She paled and had to slink around behind her horse to hide from him.

Poor batters, Skye thought as she handed off Pancake's bridle to Coralee.

"I'll put the horses away, Holl. Go tell Mom we have two more for dinner," Stan said with a hard note in his voice.

It was a mind-your-manners set down, one Skye appreciated, but Chase didn't have to stick around for a dinner full of awkwardness. Flynn looked like he wanted to step into a sci-fi machine and transport to another planet.

Chase just said an affable, "Thanks. They're not expecting us at home until late anyway," and she tripped a little more in love with him for being so easy-going.

The conversation shifted to horse talk. Coralee couldn't believe neither of their guests had been on a horse, ever. When Chase asked what they could do to help, Stan and Skye said in unison, "Stay out of the way."

"Besides," Skye added. "You might hurt your shoulder."

That prompted Stan to ask after the injury.

Chase explained it wasn't his throwing arm. He had fallen on it after diving to catch a line drive. "The worst of the pain's gone, but it's getting that hand over my head," Chase explained, demonstrating his pitch in slow motion. "I can do it, but it acts up when I push it. Things go wild."

"He almost broke the neighbor's window the other day," Flynn supplied. "So embarrassing."

"Only if you keep telling people," Chase shot back, both of them wearing the Goodwin grin that made Skye's heart swoop and soar.

"You're in town until you're fully healed?" Stan asked.

Skye heard the underlying query. *How long are you planning to fool around with my sister?*

Skye caught Chase's gaze as he replied, "My plan was to stay through Homecoming, but things are in the air. I have to fly out for an assessment this week."

"In L.A.," Skye said, taking refuge in watching Coralee where the girl brushed Pancake's drying side. "I'm going with him."

Boom. News detonated. No more hiding in the closet.

Except she kind of stayed behind Pancake in the stall, not quite slinking, but little better than Holly at that moment.

"What's El-aye?" Coralee asked, bless her.

"Los Angeles. It's in California," Skye explained.

"Where Uncle Terry moved to?"

"He's in San Francisco. That's a different city so I won't see him, but yes, they're both in California."

They finished up with the horses and headed into the house, Stan quizzing Flynn on his post-secondary aspirations and the football team's prospects while Coralee skipped ahead and Chase lagged behind with Skye.

"Thanks," he said ruefully.

"Sorry." She eyed him sheepishly. "Did he look like he wanted his shotgun?"

"Little bit. So did Flynn."

"Really? He doesn't approve of me?"

"The opposite, actually." His face lifted, taking on a kind of rueful pride. "You know the other day when that kid tried to get another clip of us on his phone? The rest of the team got all over him for it after you left. 'Mrs. Baynard's nice,' they said. Which is very true," he confirmed, tilting a possessive look at her. "But I was still impressed by how many came to your defense."

"Peer pressure, when it's directed well, can be a good thing I guess," she said, blushing a little.

"It's not just that. I know that's why you love this place so much, Skye. To be honest, this visit has been great for me, too. Yeah, there was a bit of autographing at first, but people don't care about that so much as what my brother is planning and how my father is doing. Real stuff. If I hadn't grown up here, I'd think they were being nosy, wanting to sell it to a magazine or something, but they feel like it's their business to know because this community is like a family. It's nice."

"It is," she agreed, nodding, heartened that he understood, but as they paused on the stoop, she realized that didn't make their decisions easier. Just because he appreciated why she loved Marietta didn't mean his career could be put on hold so he could settle in with her and start the family she'd wanted years ago.

"Skye?" Her mother leaned into the open back door. "What's this I hear about you going to L.A.?"

Chapter Nine

❧❧

HOLDING SKYE'S HAND through the airport, Chase had one thought: he wanted to put a ring on it. He reminded himself they were still trying things out, that being on the road lost its glamor pretty fast and Skye was a homebody at heart, but he was so damned proud to have her at his side it was button-busting.

She had her Alice In Wonderland look firmly in place as she followed where he led, tugging her away from the autograph seekers as quickly as he could, into a limo and across the insanity that was midday traffic in L.A. In the elevator to his apartment, she goggled at the view through the glass wall. When they entered his condo, which was not the penthouse but a damned nice piece of real estate all the same, she walked without a word from the spacious living, dining, kitchen area out the glass doors to the pool and patio, gazed at the ocean, then went into the master bedroom and came back past the two guest rooms, one for Flynn, one for weights.

"This is incredible," she finally said, sounding intimidated despite the fact she lived in a very nice place herself. "How does it feel to be so rich and famous?"

"I don't feel rich or famous," he dismissed, hooking an arm around her waist to pull her nervously twitching body close. He was too practical to think about his bank balance or popularity in those terms. It was always about security for himself and his family, setting a good example for Flynn and boys like him, keeping the team's morale where it needed to be. Not doing anything stupid and blowing his chances.

"Don't be modest along with everything else, Chase Goodwin. It makes you too much the perfect package."

"Are you calling me irresistible? I'll take it." He loved the way her lashes fluttered with shy confusion as her body softened with acceptance of his. Sexual heat was charging in him, fueled by the possessive excitement of having her in his home. He didn't want to think about what he'd do if she hated being here. Everything in him wanted to cement her presence here for all time.

Some of his aggressive need might have flavored his first kiss. She drew back briefly, a question in her eyes. Then she lifted her mouth to his, letting him crush her lips, offering herself up for what he needed. *That* was why he really needed her in his life, no matter which kind of world they occupied. She met him halfway and it was more than erotic. It was heart-moving.

Which helped him remember to be gentle with her, despite the pulse of ravenous need that burst in him. She was strong and sexual, but slender and feminine. Easily bruised. He stopped just short of leaving a love-bite on her neck, palms so enamored with the firm curve of her ass, he couldn't find the will to pull away and undress her.

She rubbed herself against his erection, inciting him, a little sob telling him she was growing as anxious as him and just as fast. Dear Lord, they were right for each other, breaths humid and hot, bodies trying to occupy each other's space.

He was stronger, of course, and backed her into the sofa, nudging her to balance against its back. He allowed enough space between them to do what he'd been wanting to all day and opened her wrap dress, then pushed between her legs, almost busting his fly when he saw the damp of her ivory panties.

He'd licked her out the other day and she'd loved it. He wanted to do it again, but he wanted inside her at the same time. He jerked his pants open, wanting the heat, wanting to fill her and lose it.

A distant voice said, *Condom*, but he shook it off, baring himself so he could rub against satin and softness. She tongued into his mouth and he scooped a breast out of her bra cup, loving the feel of her hard nipple scraping his palm. His scalp tightened as they rubbed and fondled, her heels behind his thighs, urging him on.

Get the condom, fool. But it was miles away, in his bag by the door. He didn't want to leave her for a heartbeat. Rather, with this lack of firm commitment between them, the opposite imperative was riding him. Put a baby in her. Tie her to him in a way that couldn't be broken. She had so much love to give. It would strengthen their foundation and they'd last forever.

And it would be cheating to do that to her.

With a curse, he locked his arms firmly around her, holding her tight to the place where his heart slammed with primitive determination.

"Like a pair of damned teenagers," he said, hearing the growl of maturity and male demand in his voice. "Your brother really will have to get the shotgun if I don't start showing some control." He nuzzled his lips against her hair, fairly quivering with the effort to restrain himself from biting and devouring.

When she lifted her head, there wasn't a shred of concern in her expression. More like, *Okay*. Her lashes were heavy, her skin flushed with arousal. She licked her lips and stared at his mouth as if it was her salvation.

He groaned and kissed her hard, punishing her a little for putting it all on him, but she gave back as good as she got, nearly upending all his good intentions.

"You know what you are, Skye Wolcott?" he accused when they came up for air and he pulled her to her feet. "Dangerous."

She gave a throaty laugh. "Really?" Throwing off her dress, she walked toward the bedroom with hips swinging, wearing only her bra, panties, and high-heeled sandals. The way she pulled off her headband and threw it down was both invitation and dare. Shooting him a look over her shoulder, she said, "You jocks are adrenaline junkies, aren't you? What are you complaining about?"

He wasn't. He really wasn't. In fact, right this second, he was excited to take a risk. Wanted to throw away consequence and take a fast, reckless joy ride.

He managed to snag the handle of his bag before he followed her, though, and fumbled protection onto himself before he joined her on the bed.

ɛɔɞ

SITTING BY THE pool late the next morning, Skye fairly purred. After all the attention Chase had shown her since they'd begun sleeping together, her confidence as a woman was pretty high, but she had still appreciated his insatiable appetite last night. She'd loved how close he'd come to losing control, more than once, but she was aware of a wistful yearning today. A light wish that he had lost control completely and started a baby in her.

She wasn't that girl, though. Locking a man into marriage with a pregnancy was the last thing she'd ever plot to do, but she'd seen him with the teenagers and watched him with her nieces the other day. He was awesome with kids. They'd all gone outside after dinner to play baseball with the girls' plastic bat and ball. The bases had been the raspberry patch, the apple tree and the corner of the garden. The dog dish had been home plate. The picture of him picking up her baby niece and carrying her in a race after Stan, so she could tag him, had been priceless.

The way they'd made love last night, so utterly wrapped up and devoted to each other, would have been the perfect time to conceive a baby.

But perhaps not the best time in their lives or their relationship.

Still. She sighed, aware they had more to think about and talk about before big decisions like that were made.

He had left while she slept, leaving a text promising to meet her after lunch. She'd had a light brunch of scrambled eggs and toast, brewed some coffee, and now she was sipping it, romance novel cued on her tablet, coconut-scented sunscreen tingling on her skin. If this was the way an athlete's wife spent her time, she could get used to it.

Her phone released the crack of a bat and a roar of applause—the ringtone she'd downloaded for his texts and calls. Picking it up, she glanced at the screen.

They want to trade me. Will be tied up for the afternoon.

Her heart stopped. She didn't know what that meant. Was it good news? Bad? How was he feeling? How should she? Was it because of his injury?

Was it because of *her?*

That was her first question when the alarm system buzzed with his entry. By then she'd watched the desk jockeys on the sports channel discuss what the two teams would gain and lose if the trade went through.

She stood from the sofa and tried to decipher his stiff expression. "It wasn't because of that stupid explosion of mine, was it?"

Surprise flickered across his face. "No." He frowned a small scold. "Of course not. That's old news. No, this was about me being out and my team not making the playoffs. They want to make some serious changes for next year. I was called in for assessment so the new team knows I'll be solid by spring training. They were looking like a shoo-in to the series at the beginning of this one, but only wound up playing post-season because the rest of the field was compensating for their pitcher. He's hit a bad streak." He shrugged. "It happens, but they want options next year."

"How did the assessment go?"

"Good. I actually chucked a few good ones. Not as fast as we'd all like, but close enough."

She linked her hands before her, made uncertain by the remoteness in his demeanor.

"You must have been shocked," she hazarded, trying to draw him out.

"I was. Am." He ran a hand down his face. "All I could think was, Wrong side of the country. I have veto rights, Skye."

It took a moment for the realization to sink in that he was asking her to weigh in. He was worried about what this meant for her. Them.

"But you're saying you have a chance to play with a team that has a really good chance in the playoffs. That's like... You could go to the World Series, Chase."

He nod-shrugged.

Her stomach bottomed out. She swallowed, then acted on instinct and went across to him, pleased when his arms came around her as she crashed herself into him.

"We'll figure it out," she promised. They had to. *She* had to, if she meant that much to him. "I can't hold you back from that."

He hugged her tight. Some of the tension left his hard back.

The light stubble coming in on his chin caught her hair as he rubbed his jaw against her temple. "Sure? 'Cause it means a red-eye tonight. They want me out there tomorrow."

"You want me to come with you?"

"Of course. Will you?"

She had the rest of the week off, but... "I only packed for two nights."

They both chuckled at the absurdity of her argument.

"I don't know how to be a jet-setter!" she argued.

She learned pretty quickly though, landing bleary eyed the next morning, too early to get into the hotel and finish sleeping.

"They want me at batting practice, meet the guys, all that. Will you do me a favor?" Chase asked her in the limo. "They hooked me up with a property agent." He waggled his phone. "Will you look at whatever she shows you? See what you think?"

Half-convinced she was dreaming and would wake in her bed on Copper Mountain any minute, she agreed.

And even though it killed a few hours while she waited to check in, she found it overwhelming. The woman's questions drove home for her that she didn't know all that much about what Chase liked or disliked. The heavy traffic and skyscrapers were pure culture shock and she grew more and more turned around and confused as the day wore on. She earmarked one as promising for its media room and proximity to the ball field, just so the woman would take her back to the hotel for a nap.

Chase woke her, spooning in behind her.

"Hi," she said sleepily. "How'd it go?"

"Good. I set the alarm on my phone. We have to go out later. One of the guys is having everyone over. Meet and greet." The last was said on a yawn. His arm settled heavily across her waist as he drifted into sleep.

She came awake just as quickly, injected with nerves and questions. Which guys? What kind of everyone? Another big reservation loomed. He had his own community and she didn't know if she would fit into it any better than she knew what he looked for in a living space.

By the time she'd showered and dried her hair, he was sitting on the side of the bed, looking groggy.

"What do I wear?" she asked anxiously. Her wrap dress seemed too casual. "Should I go down to the lobby? See what the shops have?"

"He said barbeque and bring a bathing suit if we want to swim. Jeans should be fine."

She wore heels with hers and put on her big hoop earrings, leaving her hair loose. "Okay?" she asked when she was ready.

He wore a blue button shirt over blue jeans and sneakers and nodded approval at her sheer yellow peasant top over a white cami. "You look nice."

"I'm nervous," she admitted in the car. "Are you?"

"I was this morning," he said, playing with her fingers where he'd drawn her hand to rest on his thigh. "First day at a new job is always the worst, right? But you shouldn't be."

"I've only had one job," she confessed, but didn't mention that she felt like this casual dinner was a kind of interview. Would she be accepted for even an entry level position as Chase Goodwin's spouse?

They arrived to a sea of high-end vehicles, boisterous conversation and children running to and fro. The men were big and muscled and oozed so much confidence it was an assault to the senses. The women wore real diamonds, designer jeans, and airs of superiority.

Their host and his wife, Don and Riki, welcomed them and Riki began introducing her around. It wasn't horrible, but it wasn't easy. Skye faced a cross-section of society every day at the high school. She recognized the female cliques immediately: the cheerleaders, the fashionistas, the stay-at-home moms and the career women with their own brand of intimidating confidence.

And she knew she was summed up dispassionately as The New Guy's Date. Not a wife, possibly not here for the season, so no use investing more than a few polite smiles.

She'd never been one to try penetrating these tight circles when it had been a means of teenaged survival. It was one of the reasons she and Terry had got together, she supposed. He'd felt like an awkward outcast and so had she. They'd gravitated to each other at the fringes, discovering similar tastes in movies, books, and music. It had been easy and had saved her from risking herself in this sort of environment.

Standing on the sideline of a group of women whose crossed legs and body language closed her out, she reminded herself that she hadn't come here to lose. This wasn't just about her comfort zone, but what Chase expected of her. She had to at least try and if they cut her down, well, Holly was good for one thing, at least. She'd learned to be philosophical about that sort of thing.

Picking up a thread of the conversation about trying to match tiles and drapes, she waited for a break and asked, "Which part of the city are you in? I was trying to get my bearings today when I was with the agent. Chase and I could use an insider's opinion."

There. She knew exactly what she was doing, putting them in the lofty position of advising her, but she had managed to sneak in that nice tidbit about the depth of her relationship with Chase. It pushed them all into sitting back, opening the circle to view her with new eyes.

Two ladies warmed right up to her, one saying, "Come over tomorrow and look at what we have. It's an area still in the middle of redeveloping, so parts of it are shady, but it's on the uptick and an easy drive to the stadium."

One gal, however, the Queen Bee type, turned her attention

to Skye.

Here it comes, Skye thought, and dug in her heels.

⁊⁋

CHASE DIDN'T LIKE that Skye had been lured away from him, but it was the sort of thing that happened at any party. Men talked sports and power tools, women talked babies and home décor. He spotted her outside, something in her profile reminding him of her interactions with Holly, and extricated himself from the conversation he was in.

This was it. Some trophy wife with an inferiority complex was going to scare her all the way back to her safe life in Montana.

"…high school?" he heard as he approached. "How lucky for you to get a second crack at such a good catch."

"Very," Skye said in the tone he'd learned meant she was stuffing her feelings into the bottom of her sensitive heart.

She startled when he set his hands on her waist from behind.

"Hey," he said, smoothing hands on her to try easing her tension. "Ladies." He eyed the troublemaker.

"Skye was just telling us how you met in high school, but didn't date."

"True. I wasn't smart enough to make a play." He looked at Skye. "Probably because you were all the way out at the ranch and I was stuck in town without a car."

"Oh, you grew up on a *farm*," the woman said with false delight.

They're not all like this, he wanted to say to Skye. Two of the other wives exchanged looks that told him they expected nothing less from this blond with the bitchy smile.

"Mom keeps a garden and a few chickens, but we don't really grow anything but cattle," Skye corrected politely. "And it's twelve hundred acres, so we call it a ranch."

"Twelve hundred," blondy repeated in a tone that said, *I see what you did there.* "Land in Montana must be pretty cheap."

"It was a few years ago, when the economy was so bad. We had the place appraised when Dad died and it barely topped twenty million. We were disgusted, not that we want to sell. Wolcotts have been on it since pioneer days, but I talked to Terry's mom not too long ago." She glanced at Chase as she mentioned her former mother-in-law. "She said she'd price it closer to thirty if we were testing to see who would bite, and still up around twenty-eight if we were serious. Million," she clarified to blondy. In case she wasn't getting the message.

Chase could hear the hiss on the bottle stopper, protesting the pressure. He made an excuse and steered her into the kitchen where their hostess was eager to pick Skye's brain about how to handle a disagreement with her son's teacher.

ॐ

SKYE WAS COMPLETELY drained by the time they returned to Marietta and the scrutiny wasn't over by any means. Chase hooking his arm around her after practice and kissing her openly was duly noted.

"Um…?" Chelsea questioned with a perplexed look on her face when she saw Skye Monday. "Did you have anything you wanted to share?"

"No," she said, both sheepish and defensive.

Somehow she'd imagined going away with Chase would fill her with confidence that they were right for one another. Instead she was less secure, wishing they hadn't gone public because if they didn't work out, she'd be the talk of the coffee shops again and really couldn't face it.

At the same time, she loved being with him, walking down

Main Street exactly as he'd said he wanted to, holding her hand, stopping to chat with locals, waving at the Homecoming parade floats, feeling part of the very fabric of this community she loved so much. She saw people she hadn't seen in ages. Joelle was back in town, she noticed with a wave, thinking she'd have to make a point of having coffee with her and catching up properly.

Evenings like this were like a family reunion. She couldn't imagine ever feeling as comfortable and happy in the fast-paced, rotating door of Chase's world.

The switch had flipped to Fall while they'd been away and the air was crisp in the morning and their breath visible when they arrived to watch the Homecoming game Friday night. Her nieces were doing a brisk business with their spirit towels, but took a break to greet Auntie Skye and ask after Chase and Flynn.

"They're inside, getting ready for the game," Skye answered Coralee, then saw Logan, friends with Stan since grade school and a teacher over at Livingston now. She often caught up with him at different regional or faculty events. He carried a little girl of about four and was talking with a woman Skye wasn't sure she recognized.

They stopped to look at the flags and Skye said, "Hey, Logan. Who have you got there?"

"You can't see her. She's invisible."

His flirty wink took Skye by surprise until she read the girl's body language. She looked like a small animal fearing she'd be stepped on in the bustle of the crowd streaming around them.

Not unlike how Skye had felt when Chase had been mobbed by autograph seekers at the airport. Invisible would be awesome, she thought with private commiseration.

"Do you remember Samara? She was only here for senior year," Logan said, drawing forward the woman beside him. She was around Skye's age, fair with dark hair.

"You were a year ahead of me, I think," Skye said. "Are you

back for good?"

Samara explained she was freshly moved into a recently renovated heritage house that Skye had heard Terry's mother covet more than once. Her daughter kept herself tucked anxiously into Logan's protective grasp, but watched as the girls offered Samara a flag.

"I don't know how long we'll stay tonight," Samara said with a glance at her daughter. "But thank you. This will be fun to wave as we cheer," she assured the girls.

"Who will you be cheering for, Logan?" Skye challenged lightly.

"The home team, of course," he said, acting indignant, like there was no doubt, even though he was notorious for shifting sides when he was at work. To prove it, he added a dry, "This time," as he walked away, leaving them all laughing.

"Big news about the trade," Holly said. "What does it mean?"

Skye looked up from admiring her nieces' work. "It means Chase has a good chance at playing in the Series next year," she responded mildly.

"That's not what I meant."

"I know what you meant," Skye said, feeling her mouth go tight as frustration took over. Why hadn't she and Logan ever clicked as more than friends? *He* was sticking around, looking like a family man. And there was Holly, staring at her like Skye had chosen to fall for Chase deliberately to spite her when he was the last sort of man she'd been looking for. "Did it ever occur to you that you got exactly what I always wanted, Holly? The right guy who wanted to stay here and make a life? You think I'm living the dream, but it's not what I wanted."

She turned to walk away and barreled right into Chase's chest.

He caught her by the arms. His face was like a vengeful

god's carved into obsidian. "I was coming to find you. To ask you to sit on the field with us." He released her like she was covered in barbs.

Oh hell.

"Of course," she said, and tried to find a smile, but it was impossible.

℮℥

THE LAST THING, the very last thing Chase wanted tonight was to stand on a podium and have the entire town applaud and cheer him for something he was proud of, but that was costing him the first and only woman he'd ever been serious about.

He couldn't give her what she had here. He'd tried to help her navigate the week with *his* community, but the wives didn't have the all day contact or the unified goal that a team did. Making new friends and feeling accepted was easy when you came into a new group loving the sport and wanting to win as much as everyone else did.

Skye was bright and funny and warm, but she didn't flourish among strangers the way she did in her element. *Here* was her team, where the students rushed up with a last-minute question about decorations for the dance, and parents greeted her by name and she kept the entire program on schedule, including ensuring the previous Homecoming court was here to crown this year's batch.

He'd been the King his last year. What's her name, that cheerleader he'd been dating, had been the Queen. He'd give anything to go back in time and be standing here now with Skye by his side, keeping her from marrying the wrong guy and—

Hell. No, he wouldn't give away all that he'd struggled to achieve. His father was here tonight, watching Flynn play and slapping Chase's back after he accepted his award, breathing stale beer breath into his face.

Staying hadn't been an option. Where would Flynn be if he had?

Flynn had worked himself back onto the team and scored the winning touchdown. The fans went wild, the place was in a roaring great humor as the stadium emptied, and he and Skye were ominously quiet as he drove her home.

His things were there now, not in his old bedroom in the house he'd bought for his father, but taking up space in hers. He liked the way she had made him feel at home there with a section of the closet and a drawer in the bathroom.

He wished he'd been able to give her the same sense of welcome.

But he hadn't. He feared very much that he couldn't.

They went to bed ignoring the tension and made love. It was good, really really good, but bittersweet. Afterward, holding each other in the dark, he said through a throat that felt like it was coated in sandpaper, "You won't come with me when I leave, will you?"

෧෮෪

SKYE CLOSED HER eyes, even though it was dark, trying to catch back a sudden well of tears.

"I don't know," she admitted agonizingly.

Chase cursed and released her, turning to sit on the edge of the bed. For a long minute he just sat there, the stretch of his tanned back bowed. Then he stood and went into the closet. She heard the zip of his duffel and thought he was packing to leave.

Her heart leapt after him and she sat up, trying to catch up to it, ready to stop him, but he reappeared. Still naked, he came back to sit on the edge of the bed. Leaning out one long arm, he clicked on the lamp and showed her a wedding ring.

Oh my God. Her heart rolled like a tumbleweed, fast and uncontrolled down the valley opening in her chest.

"This isn't what you think. Not quite," he said. "I always carry it. It's a bit of a charm for games. It was my mother's. There were so many games when I didn't have anyone in the stands, I got in the habit of carrying it as a placeholder, but it's also a symbol of a broken marriage so it would be bad mojo for me to propose to you with it."

Her equilibrium took a dip and a turn. She shifted, settling the blankets across her waist as she watched his thumb and finger work the plain band of gold.

"Then why…?" she prompted, voice so thin it almost wasn't there.

A flinch of painful memories tore at his expression. "She left it on her note for Dad that said she was leaving. She and Cindy were friends and Cindy had moved in because she'd walked out on her own husband. Her and Dad started fooling around and she was five months pregnant when Mom realized what was going on. I know Mom had to leave. Sometimes I even think we all enable Dad where Mom was strong enough to draw the line, but I'm still kind of mad at her."

"How old were you? Did she ask you to go with her?" Her inner being ached for the boy he'd been. It must have been so hurtful and awful.

"Nine. She lived above the dollar store for a few years. I went back and forth until she remarried and moved to Florida. By then Flynn was four. I couldn't leave him. Cindy was barely scraping by. I was already watching Flynn so she could work and I got my own job as soon as I could to help her out."

"You shouldn't have had so much responsibility pushed on you that young," she murmured, unable to help herself.

"It's not that. And I don't have mommy issues or an abandonment complex. I just remember keeping this in my room in those early days, thinking Mom would come back for it. I used to think, if *I* had a wife and she left her ring and told me she was leaving, I'd go to her and give it back to her and tell her I wanted her to keep wearing it. I'd do whatever I had to so she would come back. It was a kid's view of the situation. Obviously it wasn't that simple." His mouth twisted with frustration.

"But you still wanted your father to fight for her. To win her back and put your world into order again," she guessed.

"That, but it also molded my feelings on marriage. I promised myself that if I married, it'd be for life. No fooling around with another woman and messing up my kids with drinking and divorce."

Her breath bottomed out. Was he telling her that if she couldn't match that commitment, they weren't meant to be? She searched his expression, but it remained somber and inscrutable. He pressed the ring into her palm.

"That's a promise to you, Skye. Stay here in Marietta if you have to, but I'll come back for both of you."

"But—" If she took this ring, he'd have no one in the stands again. "Chase," she said helplessly, not wanting to protest when this was such a huge thing to offer her, but she couldn't do that to him.

"I realize we live a lot faster outside of Marietta. I've been rushing you, I know that. I do want to lock you in, Skye. I know, in here," he tapped his chest, "that we're meant for each other. But take some time if you need it. I'll keep coming back to you, trying to talk you into coming with me."

"Oh, Chase." She squeezed the ring so hard it hurt her palm. "You make me feel like such a coward!"

"I'm not trying to—"

"No, listen." She dipped her head against his chest, lips grazing the smooth skin near his shoulder. He smelled good and felt even better. Manly and smooth and firm. If she'd only shown an ounce of courage and foresight back in high school, a willingness to compromise and *move*, she might have been with him all this time. They might have had half-grown kids by now and so many good memories she'd be delirious. "I've always had such a terrible crush on you and I was convinced you were out of my league. I still can't believe you want me."

"I do, Skye. I don't know how to convince you—"

"Shhh. It's my turn." She tilted back her head and let him see all the frightened bunnies cavorting through her mind, but she tried to let the other stuff shine through too. The part where she admired him with every blood cell in her. Her pulse was racing and just being close to him made her feel more alive than she'd ever felt. "It's not easy being in love with the most amazing man ever."

"Yeah? You love me?" His features softened with deeply touched emotion. "Sweetheart," he choked and crushed her into his arms, hot lips pressing a hard kiss to her temple. "I love you, too."

They had to kiss then and it was loving and sweet and tasted just enough with hesitation on her part for him to life his head and prompt, "But?"

"Don't laugh at me, okay? I have to explain how small my aspirations are for you to fully understand why this is so big and scary for me." She drew back a little, pulling in a cleansing breath. "Mom is a homebody. It's the only thing that she and Dad ever fought about on a regular basis. She wouldn't ride out with him, preferring to stay in the house or the garden, maybe visit the neighbor at Christmas and only go into town for the doctor or the fair. I'm honestly not much better, but at least I live in town. You're starting to laugh."

His big body was shaking.

"I'm sorry, I don't mean to, but you really are living large by comparison, aren't you?" he said with a chuckle. "Look at you, going to the gym."

"Sometimes I drive into Bozeman just for the day, to shop," she stated loftily, making him laugh even more. "It's not an actual diagnosed phobia," she defended, able to mock herself, but aware she would always be the nesting sort. "It's just that I prefer to be in my own place and do things at my own pace, whereas the way you live is really, really big. And fast. It's hard to get used to."

"I understand, I do," he insisted, hugging her. "I will give you time, Skye."

"But I used to think, *Mom, just go for a ride with Dad. It would make him so happy.*" She pulled back and smoothed a hand along Chase's square jaw and lightly kissed his gorgeous lips. "I want to make you happy, Chase. So much. I want to keep trying if you do."

His hand came behind her head and he pressed his lips to her forehead, throat working a hard swallow before her eyes as he said, "You'll come with me when I go? Help me find a place to live and make it a home. That's what you're saying?"

"I will."

He whooped and tackled her onto the mattress.

Chapter Ten

ഇൗൠ

Thirteen months later

SKYE WAS ALMOST dancing out of her skin, she was so excited when she let Terry and his partner, Abe, into their apartment. Chase weighed her down with his arm across her shoulders, a little reminder to stick to plan that she appreciated, but she was *bursting*.

Terry kissed her and immediately started investigating the floor plan of the penthouse while Abe shook hands with Chase.

"Congratulations. I hate you for winning. I was betting on the other guys, but that last game! Dear God, man, I thought it was going to be a shutout," Abe said.

"I gave it my best shot," Chase drawled, rolling his pitching shoulder, ever modest.

"I like what you've done here," Terry remarked, sending a nod at the oversized photo above the fireplace. He always maintained that photos of couples should never be more than five by seven and never, ever displayed so prominently.

This one was mounted in an exceptionally tacky border as a bit of a joke, blurry because it was blown up from a screen cap of a video, but the shocked excitement on both their faces made up for it. The final game of the World Series had just finished and a sportscaster had asked Chase the famous question, "What are you going to do now?"

As Skye had run into his arms, he'd shouted, "I'm getting married!"

Iced champagne had been poured all over their kiss and the entire thing had made the rounds on the internet for days.

"That was a wedding gift from Shazandra, one of the other wives." Shazandra had become one of Skye's closest friends and Skye sometimes thought that if she hadn't risked everything to stick it out with Chase, she would have lost out on more than just his love. She wouldn't have the sisterly relationships with women she hadn't expected to appreciate so much or the cool new career she'd started for herself as a virtual assistant. It allowed her to make her own hours so she had vacation time pretty much whenever she wanted it, well beyond just summer and Christmas.

"Might look better in the den," Terry mused.

Which is where she'd had it until she'd heard he was going to be in town. Oh, she was giddy with how amazing her life was these days.

Terry picked up Chase's winning ball, signed by the entire team, encased in its plexiglass box. "This, too," he decided.

"I invited you to dinner, not to redecorate," she protested, beginning to quiver with excitement, exchanging looks with Chase who was laughing at her as much as with her. "But speaking of dens and redecorating, you had a question for Terry, didn't you?" she prompted Chase, so obvious it was pathetic.

"Right." He played along because he was an exceptionally good sport. "We're headed back to Marietta next week and I'm going to need to repaint the den at the house. What did you have on there? Oil or latex?"

Terry gave Skye his weariest look. "You think you're funny,

but you're not."

"What?" she insisted, barely holding onto a straight face as she delivered her oh-so-carefully plotted line. "You always agreed that when it was time, we'd turn the den into a nursery. If you really want to repaint it for us—"

Terry dropped the ball so it thumped onto the carpet by his feet. His eyes grew misty and he opened his arms to her.

She ran into them and hugged him tight, waiting for the lift and spin.

"I thought you'd pick me up and twirl me around," she complained when he only hugged her with aching gentleness.

"I don't want to break you," he said, voice moved. He kissed her cheek. "I'm so happy for you, Skye. So happy." His grin was as wide as hers.

"I knew you would be. And I am super happy, Ter. Thanks for divorcing me."

"Anytime, kid," he joked, both of them working to hold back tears as they laughed.

Later, snuggled in bed with her husband, she sighed blissfully and said, "I feel like *I* won the World Series."

"This is better, trust me," Chase said, molding her breasts and flat belly, all still tingling with orgasm, to his relaxing body. "And winning the World Series is pretty freaking great, so that tells you how incredible this is."

She reached to pull his mother's wedding ring to the front of its chain around her neck so it was more comfortable, then checked with her thumb that her own rings were straight. A hum of contentment escaped her and she cuddled closer to Chase's heat, nuzzling her lips into the crisp hair on his chest.

"Chase?"

"Mmm?" He was half-asleep.

"I'm glad we're going back to Marietta, but I like being here, too. I don't care where we live, so long as I'm with you."

"That's good, 'cause I'm probably gonna be traded to Florida next month."

"Serious—Oh, you!"

"I'm kidding, I'm kidding," he insisted, laughing and trying to stop her from pinching his stomach.

It was two months and it was Washington, but she didn't mind. Marietta was their real home and it was always there, waiting for them.

The End

Sing Me Back Home

A Montana Homecoming Story

Eve Gaddy

Dedication

For Maverick. I hope you're having fun swimming every day,
chewing on sticks, eating all the treats you want, running the
opposite direction when someone calls you, and eating dinner at
least four times a day. I miss you, sweet puppy.

Acknowledgements

Many thanks to Jane Porter for allowing me to be a part of the Tule team. You all rock! Everyone involved is so supportive and so fun to work with. I'm having a blast. I also want to thank Katherine Garbera for recommending me to Jane. Thanks, Kathy!

Chapter One

&)(&

H E HEARD IT through the grapevine.

In Marietta, Montana, the grapevine was Sally Driscoll, the barista at the Java Cafe. Along with Carol Bingley, manager of the pharmacy, she knew everything there was to know about the town and its citizens. Or thought she did, anyway.

Most mornings, Jack Gallagher stopped at the Java Cafe on the way to work. Ordinarily, he didn't pay much attention to Sally. But today the gossip hit him in the chest like a kick from a horse.

"Dr. Gallagher, have you heard the news?"

"What news?" he asked, resigned, knowing Sally would hold his coffee hostage until he answered.

"Maya Parrish is in town. You know, the famous model."

As always, her name gave him a jolt. Pleasure. And pain. "Her sister lives here. I imagine she's in town to visit her." He'd seen Maya a few times over the years, but only from a distance. They had managed to successfully avoid any closer interaction.

"No, not for a visit. Maya and her daughter are here to stay," Sally said with relish. "They've moved into her great-great-great grandmother's house on Bramble Lane. The one old Dina Parrish lived in until she died a few months ago."

Maya's ancient aunt had left her the house on Bramble Lane? Maya and her daughter had moved into a house the street over from his and he hadn't even known it?

Speechless, Jack stared at the barista. Maya, his high school love, the woman who'd broken his heart all those years ago, was home to stay.

Well, shit.

"Isn't that cool? Who would've thought Maya Parrish would move back to Marietta?"

Not him, that was for sure. Sally probably didn't know of his and Maya's history. Probably. It wasn't a secret, though, so she might. Since she was waiting expectantly for a response, he said, "No, I hadn't heard that. I'm running late, Sally. I've got to get to the hospital. Could I have my coffee now?"

Jack tried his best to put Maya out of his mind after that, but that proved impossible. After he rounded on his hospital patients, he went to his office. Many of the town's doctors had offices in the medical building across from the hospital, since it was so conveniently located. Jack had moved his own office into it shortly after the building was completed. He'd been back in Marietta since he finished his Family Practice residency and had never regretted coming home.

He was beginning to regret it today, however. His first patient, Eileen Delaney, should have clued him in.

He walked into the exam room and spoke as he washed his hands at the sink. "Hi, Mrs. Delaney. How have you been?"

"Not good, Doctor." She patted her heart as she often did, though as far as Jack knew, she'd never had any evidence of coronary artery disease. "I'm not feeling at all well. I don't think these allergy shots are working. What's the point of getting jabbed all the time if it doesn't do any good?"

Jack sighed inwardly. They went through the same exact conversation whenever Mrs. Delaney came in for her weekly allergy shot. The shot she insisted only Jack could give her. She didn't *trust* Jack's nurse, Vera Lancaster.

The problem wasn't one of trust, he knew. The two women had been at odds ever since Mrs. Delaney accused Vera of fixing the results of the bake-off at the Marietta Fair, causing Mrs. Delaney to lose to her archrival. Vera denied doing any such thing and maintained that Mrs. Delaney's cooking was not as good as she thought it was. The feud had been ongoing for several years now. Naturally, Vera couldn't stand Mrs. Delaney either.

"I can stop giving the shots to you any time," Jack said, knowing what her answer would be. "Just say the word."

"No, no. I'm here. Might as well take it." She chattered on, talking about Marietta High School Homecoming, coming up in a few weeks. "Who do you think will be elected to the Homecoming court?"

"I have no idea. Gina hasn't mentioned the Homecoming court," Jack said, referring to his daughter. And as far as he knew, she didn't care. Now, the football team and players were another matter altogether. Though school had only started a couple of days previously, Gina had a crush on one of the football players. She didn't realize her old man knew about it. He'd have to be an idiot not to, since Gina was constantly on the phone or texting to Mattie Guthrie or one of her other friends, and Kevin Taylor was one of their main topics.

He was still dwelling on his baby girl being old enough to be interested in boys when Mrs. Delaney brought up another subject.

"Have you heard about Maya Parrish?"

"Yes," he said, hoping to head her off. "I understand she's moved back to town."

"That's right." Nodding decisively, she added, "I hear she's divorced."

Jack made a noncommittal sound though he was well aware of Maya's marital status.

Mrs. Delaney leaned forward and said knowingly, "Maya never took his name, you know. There's something odd about that."

Not really, he thought. "A lot of professional women keep their maiden name."

Mrs. Delaney sniffed. "I don't hold with that foolishness."

Jack squelched the urge to defend Maya. What did it matter what Mrs. Delaney thought?

"Didn't you and Maya date in high school?" She raised an eyebrow and damn near winked at him.

"Yes," he said in his most imposing, abrupt voice. It had no effect on Mrs. Delaney. That was the problem with someone who'd known you all your life.

"Maya's little girl is the same age as Gina," she went on. "The girl's name is Carmen. Carmen Collins." She sniffed again.

He'd known Maya had a daughter, but had forgotten she was around Gina's age. Great. Daughters the same age meant they'd see each other at school functions. Maybe Carmen wouldn't have the same interests as Gina. His and Maya's paths didn't necessarily have to cross.

Oh, get over it, he told himself. *All that was years ago and you've both been married since.* Running into Maya again shouldn't be a big deal. He'd probably find out he wasn't even attracted to her anymore.

Still, by the end of the day, Jack had developed a nervous tic every time someone brought up Maya. Which was every single patient. He wished he had "Yes, I know Maya Parrish is home to stay" tattooed on his forehead. Even that wouldn't stop the talk, though.

He had a feeling nothing would.

₧₨

RETURNING TO MARIETTA had been the right thing to do, Maya thought as she shopped in the local grocery store for a few things she needed to make her famous variation of the dessert, Death by Chocolate. Moving had been the right thing for Carmen as well as herself. Months ago, when Carmen's father, Graham Collins, had told them he was getting remarried and moving to Europe, Carmen had been terribly upset. While she liked her father's new wife, she wasn't ready for him to move so far away. The promise of trips to Europe to stay with Graham and Adele didn't seem to help much, either.

But for Maya it was a sign. There was nothing keeping her in Texas now. Her company, Maya's Models, was slowly becoming Internet only, so she could base herself anywhere. Over the early summer, Carmen had been on the verge of getting in with the wrong crowd at her school, which gave Maya that much more reason to move.

As for Maya herself, she'd never thought she'd be back to stay. But over the years she'd found that she missed Montana and the mountains. And oddly enough, she missed small town life. Her sister Amy lived in Marietta now too. Another person who'd lived elsewhere and returned.

Maya had especially missed Montana during the Texas summers. The coolness of Montana summer mornings beat the hell out of Dallas traffic jams in the sweltering heat of the summer all to hell and back.

Marietta had grown, of course, but it was still a small town, with that lovely small town flavor. Of course, there was also the "everyone knows everything about you and your business" angle of living in a small town, but that seemed a small price to pay for such a great place to raise her child. Marietta was a beautiful place, situated to the north of Paradise Valley, in between the Absaroka Mountains and the Gallatin Range. Copper Mountain rose to the west of town, lending dignity and majesty to the view with its purple and white peaks, and the green of the Evergreens and spots of yellow where the Aspens had only just started to turn.

There was only one possible fly in the ointment. One tiny little thing she was worried about. Living in the same town as Jack Gallagher again. Dr. Jack Gallagher now. Along with the mountains and her family, she'd left Jack behind when she left Marietta to pursue her modeling career, in Dallas, Texas.

Jack Gallagher. Her *almost* fiancé, whom she'd *almost* jilted at the altar, the night of their high school graduation.

සටෙ

MAYA HAD PLENTY of time before she needed to worry about seeing Jack again. Right now, she was driving to the high school with her daughter in tow. Some bright soul had decided the Spirit Club should have a party shortly after school started, so that all the students and parents could get to know each other. The same bright soul had also decided to make it a potluck supper. Maya had volunteered to make her famous Death by Chocolate dessert. It was always a crowd pleaser. Not to mention, it was one of few desserts Maya knew how to make.

She asked Carmen to help her carry everything in, since she not only had the glass compote full of the dessert, but also various bags of paper plates, napkins, and plastic cutlery. So much for that promise. Maya hadn't even turned off the car before Carmen dashed off to see some friends. "Carmen, wait," Maya called, watching her daughter's retreating back. *Typical,* she thought. Determined to make only one trip, Maya balanced the heavy dish in one hand and the bags in the other and headed for the gym doors.

Holding the compote carefully, she reached with her other hand for the double wide doors just as they swung open. She jumped back to avoid being smacked by them, losing her precarious grip on everything, including the dessert.

"Da—darn it!" she yelled, just in time to see her beautiful masterpiece slide right out of her hands and land upside down on the door mat in front of the entryway. She stared at it with her mouth open, then looked up, prepared to rip someone's head off.

"Don't you look where you're go—" Maya broke off staring into those gorgeous green eyes she'd never forgotten. "Jack?"

"Maya," he said, looking as taken aback as she was. "I'm sorry. I should have been more careful."

She bit back the obvious response, wondering why in the world the glass serving dish hadn't broken, and why she'd thought it a good idea to bring anything glass to a high school party. The dish looked intact, though, but the dessert's lovely layers were a thing of the past. The stupid thing had taken all afternoon to make, an afternoon she'd spent cooking when she should have been working.

Jack and she knelt down at the same time, bumping foreheads. They both drew back as if burned. "Let me help," he said. "Maybe we can salvage it."

"Oh, sure," she said, dripping sarcasm. "We'll just turn it over and hope no one notices the nasty dirty crap from the floor on the top." Why did it have to be Jack? And why now? She'd known she'd run into him after moving back to Marietta, but she'd hoped to have more time before seeing the man whose heart she'd broken all those years ago.

He didn't look heartbroken now. Sexy, good-looking, smoking hot, maybe, but sure as hell not heartbroken.

He flashed her his trademark smile, another thing she'd never forgotten. "Do you have a piece of cardboard? That will make it easier to turn over without losing all of it."

Maya fished around in her bags and came up with a large paper plate. Jack took it, deftly sliding it beneath the dish and flipping the whole thing upright. "Here you go. We can scrape the top layer off and it will be good as new."

Death by Chocolate looked more like death warmed over. What had started as layers were now a jumbled mess, the remaining whipped topping sprinkled with little bits of dirt and debris.

"Just leave it alone," she snapped, trying to wrestle the dish back from him. "You've done enough."

He had the nerve to grin at her. "It's a dessert, Maya. Not a priceless work of art. Besides, there's plenty of food. Here, let me." Rather than continuing to struggle, she let go of the dish. Taking the serving spoon from her unresisting hand, he carried the dessert over to the trashcan and scraped off the top layer. "There. It's fine." He handed it to her.

"That depends on your definition of fine." She inspected her once beautiful dessert and sighed. "At least the serving dish isn't broken." She should have known better than to use a glass compote, but that's what she always used to serve this dish.

Jack picked up her bags from the floor and opened the gym doors. Resigned, Maya accepted his help and walked through.

"It's good to see you again, Maya. I'd heard you moved back to Marietta recently," Jack said walking beside her towards the food tables. "How are you liking it?"

Heartbroken, hah! she thought. He was all grown up and smoothly sure of himself. "It's not as if I've never been back," she reminded him.

"Living here is different from visiting."

"True. A lot has changed, especially here at the high school.

The old gym was nothing like this one." Maya looked around, taking in the polished basketball court, the retractable bleachers, the giant scoreboard hanging above it all. "How did they pay for it?"

"Fundraisers and generous donors," Jack said. "Same goes for the new football stadium. Have you seen it yet?"

"Yes, I went to the first game with my sister Amy. Go Grizzlies," she added, smiling.

"Everyone is excited about this year's team. We have high hopes for them."

"I take it Marietta is still football crazy."

He laughed. "Did you ever doubt it? Marietta hasn't changed that much."

Apparently not. "There are some tables set up against the far wall," she said, gesturing towards the long tables, decorated in red and white, the school colors. "We can take all this stuff over there."

"You never said whether or not you liked being back," Jack prompted.

Maya set down the compote, wincing again at the looks of it. "I like it. It's Carmen I'm not so sure about."

"Your daughter?" he asked, as he set out the paper and plastic goods Maya had brought.

Maya nodded. "She's fifteen. Not a good age to uproot her and move across the country, but when I inherited the house on Bramble Lane from my great-great-aunt, I decided it was a sign." Especially since it had coincided with her ex marrying and moving to Europe, and no longer having alternate weekends with their daughter. "I wanted a fresh start for both Carmen and me." Maya glanced around, looking for Carmen without success.

"A fresh start?" he asked.

"It's a long story. But both Carmen and I needed a change."

"You must have liked Texas, since you've been living there

ever since you left Marietta."

He'd kept up with her. The knowledge perked her up. She didn't want to analyze why. "I did. I still do. But Carmen started to get involved with the wrong crowd and I wanted her out of there before she got in any deeper."

"Marietta High is a good choice, then. My daughter Gina is Carmen's age. She's in Spirit Club, too, obviously. I'll ask Gina to be sure and introduce Carmen to some of her friends."

"That's very nice, but maybe we should just see how it plays out without our help. They're pretty contrary at this age. At least, Carmen is. The last thing we want is for them to think we're pushing them to be friends."

He laughed. "You're right about that. Okay, we'll leave them on their own."

He seemed about to say something, but a woman Maya didn't know came up and took over the conversation. Jack introduced the two of them, but the other woman clearly had no interest in Maya, choosing instead to hang on Jack's every word.

As Maya started to wander away she heard the woman, whose name she'd already forgotten, say, "Can you believe someone brought *that*?" pointing at Maya's dessert. "I'd be afraid to eat it."

Jack's eyes met hers and she could tell he was struggling not to laugh. "I think it looks delicious," he said firmly, scooping a large portion onto a paper plate.

"Oh, Jack, you should have a piece of my chocolate meringue pie. Now *this* is delicious." She pointed to the paragon of pies, as yet uncut, its fluffy, whipped topping perfectly browned and just begging to be eaten.

At that exact moment, a foam football came sailing over Jack's head to land on top of the pie, splattering chocolate filling and meringue all over Ms. Perfect Pie's white blouse.

Chapter Two

&)(&

To Maya's surprise, her dessert's appearance didn't seem to bother anyone, except, of course, Ms. Perfect Pie. It certainly didn't faze the boys, who dug into everything on the tables with abandon. The girls were more discerning in what they ate, but she noticed a number of them, not including Carmen, had gone for her Death by Chocolate. Of course, they ate the chocolate pie that had been flattened by the football as well, so that didn't say much beyond teenagers would eat anything.

"So, you and the doc, huh?" said a voice at her elbow.

Maya turned to find one of her old friends, Tamara Casey, standing beside her with a knowing smile on her face. The two of them had kept up with each other sporadically through the years and Maya had made a point of seeing her whenever she returned to Marietta for a visit. Tamara was heading the "pick up" committee of one of the Spirit Club's fundraisers.

"Ha-ha. There is no 'me and the doc.'"

"Oh, really? You two looked pretty cozy when you came in the gym. Heating up that old flame again?" Tamara waggled her eyebrows.

Maya couldn't help laughing. "All that happened a long time ago. So, no, there's no firing up the flame." Which was, on her part at least, a big fat lie. She glanced over at Jack, who was surrounded by women. "Besides, Jack appears to be on everyone's 'most eligible bachelor' list. Especially that one," Maya added, nodding at Ms. Perfect Pie.

Tamara pursed her lips. "Too true. Velma is newly divorced. She's like that with all the single men. As for Jack, though," she leaned in to whisper, "he never dates anyone more than a few times. And if he's slept with anyone from Marietta since his wife died, she's not talking."

Interesting. And a little surprising. After all, he'd been a widower for a long time now. "I remember Amy mentioning Jack's wife died suddenly. Some kind of accident, I remember. It's been several years now, hasn't it?"

"Yes, it has. I'm not saying he hasn't had sex since then, but he's been awfully discreet if he has."

"He hasn't dated anyone seriously since she died?"

"Not that I know of," Tamara said. "And I would have known. Nothing stays secret long in Marietta."

"That's the truth." Maya glanced over at Jack, still surrounded by women. "Do you know what happened? Amy didn't know much."

Tamara nodded. "It was horrible. Brianna was crossing the street and a car ran a stop sign. She lived for a few hours, long enough to say goodbye. Gina was only ten when her mother passed. Jack doesn't talk about it, and no one brings it up."

"No, I don't imagine they do."

"You'd have liked Brianna," Tamara said. "Everyone did."

They went on to talk of other things, but Maya couldn't help wondering what Brianna Gallagher had been like. Having seen her picture in the local paper a number of years ago, she knew the woman had been beautiful. Jack had met and married her when he was out of state, during medical school. That, and what Tamara had just told her, was the extent of Maya's knowledge about Jack's late wife.

A short while later, Maya heard a commotion over by the food tables. Expecting another football mishap, she glanced over and saw her daughter, clearly distressed, her face turning red and blotchy, visible even from a distance.

As Maya rushed over, Carmen puffed up before her eyes. The boy she'd been talking to scrambled out of the way as quickly as he could, leaving Carmen to turn redder and more swollen by the second. As Maya reached her, Carmen clutched at her throat. "Can't ... breathe ..." She turned wild, beseeching eyes to her mother.

Maya's world stood still and her mind blanked for a moment. She realized Carmen must be having an allergic reaction to something. Before she could speak, Jack was at her side. "Does she have an epinephrine auto injector?" he asked her.

Adrenaline for allergic reactions? "No. She's never ... No, we don't."

"I need adrenaline right now," he said in a voice she'd never heard. He didn't shout, but he said the words clearly and forcefully. They'd drawn a crowd and Jack, busy with calming down Carmen, snapped again, "I need an auto injector of epinephrine. The nurse's office will have one if no one else does."

Maya started to go, but a woman handed Jack something. "Here, Dr. Gallagher. I have another one too, if you need it."

"Thanks." He took it and immediately shot the medicine into Carmen's thigh. "This will help," he told her frightened little girl. "You should be able to breathe easier very shortly."

"What if she can't?" Maya asked. She thought she sounded oddly calm, but her mind had been shrieking since she first saw Carmen puff up.

"We give her another shot. But she's already breathing easier, so it's helping. Come on, let's get her to the Emergency Room."

"We called 911," another woman told him. "But they didn't know how long it would take."

"I'll drive. That will be quicker." He picked her up and started toward the door, taking Maya's agreement for granted.

Heart pounding, Maya followed.

ဆၣ

SOME TIME LATER, Maya followed Jack out of Carmen's 'room' at the hospital—one of several curtained off cubicles in the Emergency Room of the Marietta hospital. "Are you sure she's all right?"

He answered patiently, though she'd asked him the same question several times. "Carmen responded well to the treatment. To be safe, we'll keep her here a few hours, but I don't expect her to have any further problems."

"But she might," Maya said anxiously. "You said it was a possibility."

"A remote possibility," he said, and patted her shoulder. "At this point it's very unlikely. She's in the hospital, Maya. We'll take care of her, I promise."

"I know. I can't help but worry."

"Entirely natural. She's your daughter. Of course you're worried."

"Carmen has never had an allergic reaction before. Nothing this severe, anyway. It scared the hell out of me. How do I make sure this doesn't happen again?" Now that the immediate danger was past, the stress settled in to wreak havoc on Maya's nerves. She'd done all right during the crisis. Afterward was a whole different story.

Jack spoke soothingly. "You can't. The best she can do is try to avoid the allergen and keep an injection pen with her at all times."

"You really think she's allergic to grapes? She's eaten them before with no problem." The epinephrine injection had made the swelling in Carmen's throat subside so that she could breath. Once at the hospital and after further treatment, she had improved even more rapidly. Jack and Carmen had then discussed in detail what she'd eaten. Apparently, she was in the process of eating grapes when she started to feel 'funny.'

He nodded. "Yes, I do. She said she felt fine until after she had eaten several grapes. Her throat began to close up immediately. She swears she didn't eat anything else. Even so, she could have drank something without thinking about it. I drew some blood and sent it to the lab to be certain. We should have the results soon. However, the fact that she was actually eating the grapes when she went into anaphylactic shock is a strong indication that they're the culprit."

Anaphylactic shock. Just the words were enough to scare her to death. "I'm really glad you were there. I don't know what would have happened if you hadn't been."

"I've seen a number of these reactions before. It wouldn't have taken you long to recognize what the problem was, too. I just happened to be quicker."

While she had known Carmen was in distress, Maya wasn't sure she'd have known that Carmen needed epinephrine. But thank God Jack had. Several important things had resulted from the experience. First and foremost, Carmen was going to be all right. Secondly, she and Carmen were now aware of her allergy and what to do if it happened again. "Thank you," she said.

Jack smiled and patted her on the shoulder again. "Carmen's going to be fine. Be sure and fill the prescriptions I gave you."

"Don't worry, I will." Carmen would have an auto-injector

of medicine to keep with her at all times, and Maya intended to see that every place her daughter frequented would have one too.

Plus, she'd make sure Carmen knew that she needed to carry her injector with her everywhere. No exceptions.

Maya watched Jack walk down the hall. Who would have thought all those years ago that Jack would become the doctor who saved her little girl's life?

∞⃝

INDECISIVENESS WAS NOT in Jack's makeup. So, the fact that the following day found him staring at his cell phone screen between every patient irritated the crap out of him. Why was he debating asking Maya out? *Do it or not*, he thought, *but make up your damn mind.*

He'd dated since Brianna died. In fact, he'd been out with half the single women in town. Once, at any rate. One date didn't mean anything. Except this was one date with Maya Parrish. Who, if anything, had only grown more beautiful over the years. More beautiful, more fascinating, sexier . . .

The sizzle was still there. For him, he thought, remembering his reaction to Maya prior to Carmen's crisis. Maya felt something too, he was sure of it. She had looked as shocked as he was when they touched. When their hands met his had tingled. How crazy was that?

Not one of the women he'd dated since Brianna died had sparked more than a mild interest. He'd liked them all, but he'd rarely been tempted to have more than two dates with the same woman. He'd loved his wife very much, and he knew he always would. But Brianna had been gone for a long time now. Jack had thought his sex drive had died with her, but it came back with a vengeance the moment he saw Maya again, up close and personal.

One part of him said, "Oh, hell, yeah. Go for it." The cautious part yelled, "Are you nuts? Remember what happened last time you got involved with Maya."

He went with "hell, yeah" and punched in the cell phone number she'd given him. "Hi, Maya. It's Jack," he said when she answered.

"Hi." She sounded surprised. "Are you calling about Carmen? She's fine. She went to school this morning."

"That's great. Glad to hear there were no permanent ill effects."

"I can't thank you enough. I was scared out of my wits."

"An allergic reaction like Carmen had is frightening, especially if it's the first one you've seen. And even more so, when it's your daughter."

"That's the truth."

"Checking on Carmen wasn't the only reason I called. I know it's last minute, but do you want to go to dinner tonight?"

Silence. "Um . . . You're asking me on a date?"

"Yes."

More silence. "Do you think that's wise?" she finally said.

He laughed. "Obviously, or I wouldn't have asked you." When she hesitated again he added, "It's just dinner, Maya." But was it?

"All right. Thanks. Casual or dressy?"

"Casual. I'll pick you up at seven."

After hanging up, he realized he was grinning like a fool. Wise? Probably not. But irresistible? Oh, yeah.

Chapter Three

৪৩

"WHY ARE YOU getting dressed up?" Carmen asked Maya later that afternoon. She came in and threw herself on Maya's bed, flat on her back and spread-eagled. "Aren't you going to the movie with Aunt Amy and me?"

"No, I'm going to dinner." Having changed three times, Maya contemplated a fourth. "Do you like this one, or this one?" she asked her daughter, holding up two different outfits.

Carmen ignored the question. "Dinner? With who?" she asked suspiciously.

"Dr. Gallagher."

"You have a *date*?"

Maya turned around and looked at her daughter, who was now sitting up on the bed. Only a teenager could look so incredulous at the thought of her mother dating. "Yes. I've had them before, you know," she added dryly. Not to mention, Carmen's father had remarried. What was so shocking about Maya having a date?

"But . . . but you just met him."

"Actually, I went to high school with him." And almost married him, Maya thought. "Why are you frowning?" After placing both outfits on the bed, she rifled through her closet and pulled out another sweater. She held it under her chin and looked in the mirror. *You look like a corpse in that color*, she thought, sticking it back in the closet quickly.

"He's my *doctor*. Isn't it like, illegal for you to date him?"

Maya laughed. "He's not *my* doctor. And even if he were, it wouldn't be illegal for me to date him."

"Whatever," Carmen said with a shrug. "His daughter's a snot."

Maya stifled the urge to tell her to get over it. "Why do you think that? You've only just met her."

"She thinks she's hot sh—snot," she amended hastily when Maya gave her the evil eye.

"Well, I'm not going out with her. I'm going out with her father." She held up an outfit in either hand. "Now, which one of these outfits should I wear?"

"The black one," Carmen said, and left.

Which, since that described both of them, was no help at all.

ಸಾಂ

"YOU LOOK AMAZING," Jack told Maya when he picked her up that evening.

"Thanks." She had finally decided to wear dark skinny jeans, ass kickin', black, Louboutin boots, and a double-breasted black knit jacket, loosely buttoned over a lacy black camisole. Did it say something that she was wearing all black? No, she decided. Unless, it meant she wanted to look her best.

Jack didn't look so bad himself. He wore jeans and a black leather jacket over a cream colored button down shirt. His eyes were the same gorgeous green she remembered gazing into as a teenager. She noticed again that he'd filled out and put on some muscle in the intervening years. He must have caught her staring at him, because he gave her that slow, sexy smile she'd always loved.

Damn it.

After they got in his black SUV and buckled in, he said, "I thought we'd go to the Long River Cookhouse. The rainbow trout is fantastic." He glanced at her. "Unless you've become a vegan or something."

She smiled. "No, and not vegetarian either. I eat fish, fowl and beef." She thought about that for a minute. "And chocolate, of course."

"Still think chocolate should be its own necessary food group?"

"I can't believe you remember that," she said, laughing.

"I bought you a lot of chocolate. It's hard to forget that." He glanced at her. "*You're* hard to forget," he added.

He probably says that to all the women, she thought, pleased by the comment anyway. "You managed to forget me, though."

"Forget? No." He shook his head. "I moved on. Eventually." He paused and added, "And so did you."

"True enough."

Maya didn't ask Jack about his wife. If he wanted to bring her up, he would. But she couldn't help wondering about his wife and his marriage. Like her, she knew Jack had married fairly young. During medical school from what she'd heard. Unlike hers, his marriage had lasted. Maya didn't regret her marriage since it had given her Carmen, but if she were honest, she knew she and Graham should never have married in the first place. They were much better suited as friends. She shook off that thought. Her ex was the last person she wanted to think about tonight.

"I've been to the Cookhouse once or twice with Amy when I came back to visit. Who's that guy who plays the piano there? Is he still there? He's got a funny name. Older guy with a white beard and bushy eyebrows."

"You must mean Fly."

"That's it. Is he still there?"

"Sure is. Fly is pretty much a fixture now."

Silence fell. Surprisingly, it wasn't terribly awkward. As they drove to the restaurant Maya looked at the countryside, enjoying being driven for a change. The Long River Cookhouse was built beside the Yellowstone River, almost at the V where the Yellowstone and Marietta rivers met. Marietta itself lay at the northern end of Paradise Valley. Several mountain ranges surrounded it, but the two visible as they drove south were the Absaroka Mountains to the east, and the Gallatins to the west. Both ranges rose high and magnificent above the valley, their peaks already snow covered though it was only early September. Winter came early in the mountains.

The wheat fields danced golden in the wind, waiting for harvest. Cattle grazed in other fields, dotting the landscape everywhere. This part of Montana was mainly cattle country. Although Maya knew there were horse ranches in the area, horses were not as prevalent. Some horse ranches had been there for years, but a number of them were newer.

"I didn't realize until the Spirit Club get together that our daughters are the same age," she said.

He smiled. "I didn't know either until one—several, actually—of my patients told me this morning."

"Several?"

He shot her an amused glance. "Maya Parrish is big news in this town. Not to mention, a fair number of my patients are old enough to remember the two of us were together in high school and they wanted to make sure I knew you had moved back."

"I'd almost forgotten how small towns work," she murmured. "Lord, that was years ago. Don't tell me they're matchmaking already."

"Okay, I won't tell you."

Maya laughed and changed the subject. "Does Gina ride?"

"Yes, she rides at my brothers' place, but I don't make it out there very often."

"That's too bad. You used to love to ride."

"Between my practice and being a single parent, I can't seem to find the time." He glanced at her. "I'm sure you understand that, since you're a single parent yourself."

Maya nodded. "It's tough sometimes, that's for sure. But getting back to riding, Carmen has already asked me if she could learn to ride. Is there any place you'd suggest for lessons?"

"Olivia Canaday teaches riding out at Lane's End. Western and English. She's great with kids. Give her a call."

"Thanks. I'll do that. How are Wyatt and Dylan?" She remembered the younger Gallagher brothers as being as wild as they were good-looking. "Are either of them married?" She couldn't imagine it, but she still remembered them as Jack's pain in the ass little brothers and not the grown men they were now.

"No. Dylan came really close, but they broke up a week before the wedding. No one knows why. Wyatt says he's too busy with the ranch to worry about women."

"Do you believe him?"

"Of course not," Jack said, and they both laughed. A few minutes later, they arrived at the restaurant, a charming wood and stone building with a wide wooden porch that started on the side of the building and wrapped around to the back.

The hostess knew Jack and she knew who Maya was too, welcoming her back to Marietta. She chatted briefly as she led them to a quiet table in a corner, next to the bank of plate glass windows that overlooked the Yellowstone River. She left leather covered menus with them and told them someone would be with them shortly.

The Cookhouse wasn't a fancy place, but it was a pleasant,

cheerful place with a fun, family atmosphere. Tonight it looked a bit fancier than usual, with white tablecloths, upholstered chairs, candles flickering and a vase of white roses and bluish-purple delphiniums at each table.

"Did you ask for this table?" Maya said after they'd given the waitress their drink orders.

"Because it's romantic?" He smiled and shook his head. "Every time I come in with a single woman I'm not related to they seat me here."

"I'm crushed," she said. "And here I thought I was special."

"You are."

Surprised, she looked up at him. There had been a note of sincerity in his voice that sent a tingle up her spine. She tingled when he touched her, tingled when he spoke. His voice had deepened with the years and was now a beautiful bass and . . . sexy, damn it.

"Now that we're here, we should take advantage of the seating," he continued. "We wouldn't want all that romance to go to waste."

"How do you propose we do that?" She'd heard of a silver-tongued devil. Jack Gallagher was a golden-tongued one.

He didn't say anything, just smiled into her eyes and took her hand. His thumb stroked her palm gently. Maya sucked in a breath. He was holding her hand for crying out loud. That shouldn't make her feel . . . dizzy. Dizzy, tingling. Good Lord, you'd think she'd never been on a date.

When the waitress arrived with their drinks, he let go of her hand. Red wine for Jack, white for her. It occurred to her that while she knew almost nothing of Jack as an adult, he still reminded her vividly of the boy she'd loved. Except he was older, more sophisticated, and even hotter than he'd been before.

They studied the menu, both of them deciding on the trout,

one of the Cookhouse's specialties, and giving the waitress their orders.

"I thought it would be more awkward when we saw each other again." Maya sipped her wine and added, "We didn't exactly part friends." Might as well get it out in the open. If they were going to see each other regularly, either at school functions or in a more personal way, they had to talk about the elephant in the room sometime.

"No, we didn't," he said with a wry smile. "You've changed since you left Marietta."

"I would hope so. I'm a good bit older."

"No, it's not that. We're both older. A lot older."

She laughed. "Gee, thanks. Nothing a woman likes better than to be reminded of her age."

"You don't need to worry. You don't look a day over thirty."

"Flatterer."

"Truth."

She felt absurdly pleased.

He took a sip of wine and went on. "The younger Maya would have avoided the issue of our mutual past as long as possible. That girl avoided possible controversy rather than meeting it head on."

"Like I did when I didn't tell you about my job offer in Texas until the night of graduation?"

He smiled, a little ruefully. "Yeah, like that."

Remembering, she sighed. "At the time it seemed like the only way to break the news. I'd been trying to tell you for weeks, and I just couldn't do it until I no longer had a choice. I can look back on it now and know that was the wrong choice. I wish I'd gone about things differently."

"I'm not sure how you broke the news would have made a difference. I didn't respond well either. All I heard was that you were leaving. I could have listened to you, instead of giving you an ultimatum."

"True. But I can't blame you. Well, much," she added. "After all, we were almost engaged."

"Almost. But I think it was more in my head than yours. You wouldn't commit to a real engagement. You said your parents thought you were too young."

"They did. And obviously, I was too young."

"Still, I could have been a little more understanding rather than telling you to choose me or the job." He shook his head with a chuckle. "You told me you chose the job and I could shove it."

"I don't remember saying that." She remembered crying into her pillow, though.

"I do. It was the first time a woman told me to take a leap. Unfortunately, it wasn't the last. I'm a slow learner."

Maya laughed. "Oh, I doubt that."

Different courses came and went. They talked sporadically until they both had their entrees in front of them.

Maya almost moaned when she took her first bite of fish. "This trout is delicious."

Jack agreed and changed the subject. "We saw you in the magazines, you know. The town is very proud of you."

"Too bad my seven-year-old sister was the only one who believed in me." Amy had been almost as starry-eyed about Maya's career as Maya was herself.

"I believed in you, Maya."

She stopped with her fork halfway to her mouth and stared at him. "It sure didn't seem like it at the time," she blurted out.

"I'm sure it didn't. In my defense, I was young and oblivious. Totally focused on college and medical school. Totally concerned with myself and my career. I knew you would succeed in modeling or whatever you chose. In my mind, though, your career was more flexible. So when you told me you'd accepted the job in Texas—" he shrugged. "I was too busy feeling hurt and angry to really consider your feelings."

"You've changed too," Maya told him. "The younger Jack would never have admitted that."

"As you so aptly pointed out, I'm older now." He laid his hand over hers on the table. After a moment of hesitation, she turned her hand over, so that they were palm to palm.

Oh, God, Maya thought, gazing into his eyes. Not only dizzy, but tingling. *My arm is tingling. Actually tingling.* Chemistry. Instant chemistry, just like there had been all those years before. Did he feel it too? From the look in his eyes, she thought he did.

"Why don't we table this discussion?" he said. "We've talked enough about the past. Let's talk about here and now."

"What about it?" she asked warily.

He released her hand to take a sip of water and lean back. "Tell me about your business. I know it's called Maya's Models, but I haven't heard anything else about it. Believe it or not, the busybodies don't seem to know much about your work."

She hadn't imagined that gleam in his eye. Maybe he didn't want to come on too strong when they'd only just reconnected. Which was a good thing. Wasn't it?

"Maya?"

Aware she'd been thinking about other things than business, she answered. "I haven't been back in town long. I guess that's why more people don't know about it. My company is a headhunting firm for models. I have a lot of contacts from my modeling days and afterward, when I went into the management side of the agency."

"When did you go into management?"

"Shortly after I found out I was pregnant with Carmen. I modeled maternity clothes until I had her and then switched over." She laughed ruefully. "I discovered I liked eating and had no desire to starve myself back into my pre-pregnancy weight."

"A wise decision," he said, looking her over appreciatively.

"I thought so," she agreed. "Anyway, after several years working in downtown Dallas, I was tired of the commute and tired of missing so much with Carmen. So a few years ago, I started an online agency that brings together models, photographers, modeling studios, and basically anything else to do with modeling."

"Is it Internet only?"

"No, but it's getting there. I haven't quite managed it yet. With video chats of all kinds to not only talk to people but see them as well, it can almost feel like being there." Once she had her assistant completely trained, she could let her do the necessary traveling, or at least most of it, especially the international traveling.

"How much do you travel?"

"Not often. I traveled a lot when I first started the company, but her father and I shared custody, so I was able to plan my trips during his time with her. He recently remarried and moved to Europe so Carmen and I came here."

"I'm glad you did."

"So am I," she said slowly. But that didn't mean she was ready to immediately jump into a relationship the moment she returned to Marietta. Not with Jack, not with anyone.

But Jack was sure tempting her.

Chapter Four

∞CR

"**D**O YOU WANT to come in?" Maya asked Jack when he walked her to the door.

He glanced at his watch. "Sure, but I can't stay long. I told Gina I wouldn't be late."

"Carmen is staying with my sister tonight."

Idle conversation, he wondered, shooting her a speculative glance. Or something else?

"I didn't mean that the way it sounded," she said, flustered.

He couldn't resist teasing her. "How did it sound?"

Now she looked annoyed. "You know very well what it sounded like. Like I was dropping the biggest, most obvious hint possible. I said the first thing that came into my head. I wasn't inviting you to jump into bed with me."

Jack laughed. "I didn't think you were. Which is too bad." Really too bad, he thought. Maya was without doubt one of the most beautiful women he'd ever known. Long, dark hair, classic features, a perfect complexion. Gray eyes, rimmed with a darker gray, unusual and compelling. An angel she wasn't, though. More like a siren. "You blew me away when I first saw you tonight."

Her lips curved. "Good. I meant to."

"You always did have a wicked streak." As a teenager, Maya had been pretty, but now she was downright dangerous.

"What would you have done if I had been dropping a hint? If I invited you to stay?"

He didn't have to think about that. "I'd have taken your hand and walked with you to your bedroom and—" he put his hands on her waist and gently pulled her closer—"I'd have done this." He kissed her. Slowly. Reacquainted himself with that luscious mouth. Her beautiful mouth he'd been thinking about since he saw her up close for the first time in years.

Maya moved closer. Instant heat flared between them. He took the kiss deeper, until he drowned in her taste, her scent, the feel of her arms around his neck and her soft curves pressing against his chest.

Jack broke the kiss, but he couldn't make himself move away. Maya wasn't unaffected either. Her breathing was fast and her lips were parted, wet from his kiss. As he stared at her, she ran her tongue delicately around her lips, making them, if possible, even more inviting.

"Damn." He kissed her again, harder, more briefly, and resolutely set her away from him. "I have to go home."

"Yes. You do."

"I want to kiss you again."

"I know. I want to kiss you again too."

He was tempted. Oh, man, was he tempted. Instead, he turned around and walked to her door. Once there, he turned back and looked at Maya, standing where he'd left her. "I'll call you. Soon."

"Good." Her smile could have seduced a dead man, and Jack was far from dead.

He left before he said to hell with it and devoured her.

☙❧

THOUGH MAYA TRIED not to work on the weekends, she couldn't always swing it. Saturday morning found her tying up loose ends. She had just finished a video chat with a client when Amy brought Carmen back from her house. Carmen ran off immediately.

"Hi to you too," Maya muttered, watching her daughter go. "What's up with that?" she asked, turning to her sister.

Amy and Maya looked nothing alike. Whereas Maya was tall and nicely curved, with long dark brown hair, gray eyes and a creamy complexion, Amy was short and voluptuous with short, light brown hair, blue eyes, and to her disgust, freckles. She always complained that she shouldn't be saddled with lack of height, overly generous curves and freckles to boot, especially since freckles were out of place with her body.

Amy had been a concert pianist with the Philadelphia Philharmonic Orchestra for several years shortly after graduating college. Everyone, including Maya, was surprised when Amy abruptly left the orchestra, returned to Marietta and began teaching piano lessons out of her home. Amy rarely spoke of her time with the orchestra, although once after several margaritas she'd admitted to Maya that she'd left because of a failed love affair. But that was all Maya had gotten out of her.

Amy snorted. "Men. Or, in this case, boys. We saw Carmen's heartthrob at the movies. He pretended he didn't know her. Needless to say, she's heartbroken and furious and the hours she spent talking to me and on the phone and texting last night to her friends were not nearly enough to thoroughly dissect the issue. I imagine she's going to call one of her friends. Again."

"Poor baby." Nothing was worse than being humiliated by a boy you liked. "He's the one she was talking to when she went into anaphylactic shock at the potluck. He used some pretty fancy moves to get away as fast as he could. Turkey," she added.

"I heard that." Amy smiled ruefully. "About forty-seven times. I wouldn't be a teenager again for anything."

"Me neither," Maya said. "Want some coffee? I just made a fresh pot."

"Sure." Amy followed her into the kitchen, accepted a cup of coffee, added milk and a couple of packets of artificial sweetener, and sat at the table. "So, Maya, spill. Inquiring minds want to know."

"You mean about my date?"

"No, about the dry cleaners. Yes, the date. What else?"

"There's nothing to spill. I had a date with Jack last night. We had a nice time. No big deal."

"Your nose is growing," Amy observed dryly. "Come on, Maya. Out with it. Was the old zing still there?"

Maya laughed. She had never been able to hide anything from her sister, even though they were ten years apart in age. "Yes." She patted her heart. "And then some."

"I knew it! Did you sleep with him?"

"Amy!"

"What? Carmen isn't anywhere near. It's a reasonable question. Did you?"

"No." Remembering the kiss, she flushed. "We hadn't seen each other in twenty years. At least, we haven't been close enough to speak before the potluck and then later at the hospital."

"If nothing happened, then why are you blushing?"

Maya eyed her sister, then sighed. "I didn't say nothing happened. I said I didn't sleep with him." But she'd sure been tempted. "We kissed," she added.

"All that blushing for a kiss?"

"It was a hell of a kiss." Before Amy could probe further, Maya's cell rang. She had a feeling it was Jack, even though his name didn't come up on the screen. "Hello."

"Maya, it's Jack."

"Hi," she said, aware her voice sounded as goofily happy as she felt.

"Do you have plans tonight?" he asked.

"Other than taking Carmen to a party, no."

"Gina's going to a party too. I imagine it's the same one. Do you want to have some dinner?"

"I'd love to. I'm taking Carmen and her friend Mattie to the party, so it will have to be after that."

"Sounds good. I'll pick you up around eight."

Maya put her phone in her pocket and found Amy staring at her. "Oh, sister, you've got it bad."

"Don't be ridiculous. It's just a date."

"The second one in as many nights."

Maya felt almost giddy. Maybe she and Jack were both reliving their teenage years. Except, she didn't feel anything at all like she had as a teenager. No, they were all grown up now. "Why don't you do something useful and help me find something to wear?"

"If you insist. Dressy? Casual?"

"He didn't say."

"So, something to make his eyes fall out of his head?" Amy asked, eyes twinkling.

"Absolutely," she said, and led the way to her bedroom.

ഏറജ

JACK DROVE TO his office Saturday afternoon wondering what his brother Dylan's latest injury was. He didn't ordinarily work on weekends other than making rounds. But he was always willing to open when family or close friends called. Since Dylan wouldn't have called him for something minor, he hoped it wasn't too bad.

"Thanks for meeting me," Dylan said when he arrived a few minutes after Jack. "It's just a scratch, but that damn Wyatt's as bad as a woman." Still griping, he sat on the exam table. "Wouldn't shut his mouth until I called you."

Scratch my ass, Jack thought, glancing at the torn bloody white undershirt covering the wound. "Good for Wyatt. I'm glad at least one of my brothers has some sense. How did you do it?" he asked, unwrapping the shirt from around Dylan's arm.

"Fixing the fence. Damned barb wire."

Just as he'd thought, Dylan's idea of a scratch wasn't the same as Jack's. "Hate to tell you, but Wyatt was right. You need stitches. And a tetanus booster."

"Oh, man," Dylan complained. "You know I don't like needles."

"It won't heal well, and knowing you, will undoubtedly get infected, especially if I don't stitch you up. Buck up, cowboy."

They talked while Jack set up the instruments and injected the wound area with a local anesthetic before beginning to stitch him up.

"Hear you're going out with the Heartbreaker again," Dylan said, as he started stitching. "She's a looker, I'll give you that."

The Heartbreaker was the name his brothers had given Maya when she left Marietta—and Jack—behind. They'd been young, but old enough to give Maya a name that had stuck, at least within the family and he suspected elsewhere too. "You're not going around town calling her that, are you?" That would be great for Maya to hear.

"Would I do that?" Dylan asked, sounding hurt.

"Yes, but you'd better not."

"Relax. She won't hear it from me." He raised an eyebrow. "At least three different sources in Marietta told me you two were an item again. You work fast." Dylan winced as Jack continued stitching, pulling each thread carefully through the skin. "Damn, that hurts."

"Thought you were a tough guy?"

"Tougher than you, Whipper," Dylan retorted with his favorite nickname for Jack. Wyatt, a little older than Dylan, had nicknamed Jack 'Ripper' for Jack the Ripper. At the time, Dylan couldn't pronounce his R's, so Ripper became Whipper.

"In your dreams," Jack told him. "Maya and I aren't an item." Yet. He could hope, though, couldn't he? "We've only had one date."

"Yeah? You gonna leave it at that?"

Thinking about being with Maya again, Jack smiled and shook his head. "Hell, no. We're going out again tonight."

"You dog," Dylan said. "Watch out you don't get burned again."

Good advice. But it was already far too late to be careful.

80CB

"NO, THAT'S NOT it," Amy said, lounging on Maya's bed. "It's cute, but not sexy."

"Who says it has to be sexy?"

"You did when you said you wanted to make his eyes fall out of his head."

Okay, she had a point. "What about these boots? They're new." She held up a pair of black suede ankle boots with a low, stacked heel.

"I don't think I've ever seen so many boots. How can you wear them all?"

"I work in fashion," Maya defended herself. "I have to dress the part."

"Maya, you work from home most of the time now."

"I didn't always. Besides, I video chat. I'm not a model any longer, but I still have to look good." Sighing, she rubbed her hand over the suede. "Besides, I love shoes. Especially boots."

"For real? I hadn't noticed," Amy said dryly, waving a hand at the closet. "But I guess the fact that you have a separate closet for shoes should have clued me in."

Maya ignored her sister, concentrating instead on the clothes in her other bedroom closet. Most of her dressier clothes were in closet in the spare bedroom, but the master closet held a mix. She was considering adding a large, walk-in closet to the master bedroom, but she knew it would cost more than she could afford right now. Moving had taken a big chunk of her disposable income.

"How about this?" She pulled out a baggy mid-thigh length sweater and a pair of black leggings.

"You know the drill. Try it on," Amy insisted. As Maya pulled the sweater over her head, her sister added, "You're lucky I love you. Otherwise I'd hate you for what you look like in clothes."

"You could look just as good if you'd buy some new clothes once in a while."

"Yes, because I'm so tall and slim, I'd look great in something like that." She flicked a hand at the outfit Maya had just taken off.

"I'm not slim."

"Of course you are. I suppose you don't think you're tall, either."

Amy's height, or lack of it, had always been an issue for her. "You're petite. There's nothing wrong with that."

"There's nothing right with it, either," Amy grumbled.

"What do you think?" Maya asked after putting on the leggings and boots as well.

Amy looked her over critically. "If you want him to think you're a bag lady, sure. Didn't you try that sweater on? Whatever possessed you to buy that? Even you can't make that thing look good."

Looking at the oversized, muddy brown sweater in the mirror, Maya couldn't argue. "It was on sale. At the time, I thought it was cute. It went with some boots l like."

"Well, it's hideous," Amy said.

"Don't hold back, Amy. Tell me what you really think."

Unabashed, Amy laughed and went to the closet. "Here. Try this." She handed Maya a cowl necked, silvery gray sweater dress, belted at the waist and hitting mid-thigh. Then she disappeared into the shoe closet, emerging with faux lace-up black boots that stopped just above the knees.

Maya didn't argue. She put everything on and waited for her sister's response.

"That's it," Amy said, grabbing up her purse. "My job is done," she declared. "Now I have to go. I have a piano lesson in half an hour." She shook her head. "Unfortunately, with a child who has neither aptitude nor desire. His mother is convinced he has talent, but then, his mother is totally tone deaf, so that's not surprising. Call me after. I want details."

"Maybe there won't be anything to tell."

"With you wearing that outfit? Not likely." Amy gave her a "get real" look and left.

Chapter Five

ഉ൭

C ARMEN WALKED INTO Maya's room a short time after Amy left. "Mom, can I spend the night with Mattie tonight? She's having a sleepover after the party. Charlie's going to pick us up."

Mattie lived with her brother Jesse Guthrie and his new wife, Charlie. Maya had carpooled with them before, besides knowing Jesse's family from way back.

Although Carmen and Mattie Guthrie had bonded immediately upon meeting each other, unfortunately, the same couldn't be said of Carmen and Mattie's best friend, Gina Gallagher. Maya wasn't certain what that was about, but she suspected it had something to do with a boy.

"Sure, that sounds fun. Who else is going to the sleepover?" Maya asked.

Apparently just now noticing the clothes and boot bomb that had exploded over Maya's bed, Carmen asked, "What's going on? Why are all your clothes everywhere?"

"Amy was helping me find something to wear tonight."

"You're going out *again*? With who?"

"Dr. Gallagher."

"You went out with him last night," she said accusingly.

"And I'm going out with him again. Why, does it bother you?"

Carmen shrugged. "I don't know. I guess not. It just seems kinda weird."

Weird that she was dating period, or weird that she was dating Jack? Maya didn't ask. "I wish you and his daughter could be friends." Probably a mistake to say so, but she felt like she should make the push. No matter what happened between Jack and her, she didn't want their daughters to hate each other.

Carmen looked surprised. "We are friends. I thought you knew?"

"That's news to me. Last I heard you two couldn't stand each other."

Carmen put her hands on her hips and gave Maya the look that every mother of a teenage girl was familiar with. The one that said, 'Mothers are so clueless.' "Mom, that was so last week. Gina's really sweet."

"Really? Well the other day you said she was a snot. What changed?"

"Some of the other girls were giving me a hard time about, um, well, you know. The potluck? When I swelled up? In front of Kevin?"

"I'm sorry you had to go through that, honey. But I'm sure Kevin didn't think a thing about it." Except Maya knew that wasn't true. She'd seen the boy take off like he was running from the Zombie Apocalypse.

"Yes, he did. He ran away. And then, at school he made fun of me too. I wanted to *die*, right there," she said dramatically. "But Gina had come over and heard them and she told them to get a life and she hoped they had an allergic reaction one day, and then they'd know what it was like."

"That's nice that she stuck up for you."

Carmen nodded. "And she told Kevin he was a lame ass—I mean, butt—and told me I shouldn't pay attention to him. I thought she liked him, but she said not anymore."

"She sounds like a smart girl."

"Yeah. And I told her what Kevin did to me at the movie and she thinks he's a big fat jerk. Which he is." Carmen went off to call Mattie.

Teenagers, Maya thought. They changed not only by the day, but sometimes by the hour.

She started to hang up the clothes strewn over the bed when it hit her. Carmen and Gina were both going to the slumber party. They'd be gone all night. And she had a date with Jack.

Maya pressed her hand to her stomach. *Butterflies? Really? How old are you?*

❧❧

"I THOUGHT WE'D go to Rocco's," Jack said when he picked up Maya later that evening. "You like Italian, don't you?"

"Love it," Maya said. "But are you sure we can get in? It's Saturday night, after all."

"I made a reservation." Which hadn't been easy. He'd bribed the hostess with the promise of a date with his brother Wyatt. Luckily, she hadn't wanted a date with Dylan, because no amount of threats or coercion could make Dylan go on a date arranged by someone else. Wyatt was more easy-going. Not to mention, Jack hadn't yet collected his winnings from Wyatt for the last poker game they'd played with the guys, so he could hold that debt over his brother's head if he gave him any grief.

When they arrived at the restaurant, he helped Maya out of her jacket and had to remind himself to breathe. She wore a belted grayish-silver sweater dress that hit her mid-thigh and another pair of those sexy high-heeled boots she favored. The dress hugged her curves, with a wide neckline that dipped just low enough to show tantalizing glimpses of creamy skin. With the boots and the short dress, her legs looked a million mouth-watering miles long.

She was trying to kill him. And she was succeeding.

"Is the hostess another person who always seats you and your dates in a romantic, out-of-the-way corner?" Maya asked after she slid into the dark red leather booth. Red candles flickered and dripped in the straw bottomed wine bottles. The high backs of the booth shut out the other diners and muted much of the ambient noise, leaving them in a cozy, intimate setting. The beautiful mural of Tuscany with its pastel golds, greens and blues on the wall beside them added to the romance of it all. A waterfall was nearby, the faint sounds of trickling water adding gentle notes to the instrumental music playing softly in the background.

"No. I asked for it."

Their eyes met and they both smiled. "We're moving awfully fast, aren't we?" she asked after a moment.

"Not yet." He reached for her hand over the red and white checked tablecloth. Maya turned hers over, so that they were palm to palm. "But I'd like to."

Before Maya could speak, the waitress came to take their order. "They have a Chianti here that I really like." Jack told Maya releasing her hand. "Would you like a glass?"

"Yes, that sounds good. I haven't looked at the menu yet," she told the waitress apologetically.

Jack ordered their wine and the waitress went off to get it.

Maya studied the menu. "I'm going to have the Portobello ravioli. Have you had it?"

"No, but I've heard that it's good. I usually get Lasagna. I always think I'll order something else, but the Lasagna is so good I end up getting it nearly every time."

They ordered dinner and sipped their wine, sharing an appe-
tizer of crab cakes.

"What happened to the adventurous boy I knew?" Maya
asked. "You ordered Lasagna. Everyone orders Lasagna at an
Italian restaurant."

"I save my adventurous nature for *other things*," he said,
lifting an eyebrow and giving her a suggestive smile.

Maya laughed. "Oh, please, tell me you didn't say that."

He lifted a shoulder. "I'm out of practice."

"Apparently so," she said, obviously teasing.

If you only knew how true that statement really is, Jack thought.

Later, during dinner, Maya asked him, "Do you still play the
guitar?"

"Sometimes." Not very often since Brianna had died. It
wasn't until the last year or so that he'd begun to play again. He
even sang a little occasionally, though his voice was even rustier
than his guitar playing skills. "What brought that up?"

"The music." She smiled. "Do you recognize the song playing?"

"Of course. An instrumental version of Clint Black's 'State
of Mind.'"

"It's a pretty song." Eyes dreamy, she sighed. "Songs really
do bring back memories. You used to sing that when we were in
high school, remember? I always wanted you to sing it to me,
but you never did."

"As I recall, you liked Clint better. He was the one you really
wanted to sing to you."

"I never said that," she said indignantly. "I always thought
you were great."

He held up a hand. "Please. You plugged in that cassette
every time you got in my car."

"I did have a thing for Clint Black," she admitted. "But so
did all my friends. After the fiftieth time or so, you refused to let

me play that tape in your car." She laughed. "But at least you gave it to me, instead of pitching it out the car window like you threatened at first."

"I knew better. I just liked to tease you."

"We had fun, didn't we?"

"We did." He held her hand and wished she was closer. "But now we have the best of both worlds. Past and present."

"With a long gap in between," she added. They were quiet a moment, listening to the fading notes of the song. "Jack?"

"Hmm." He carried her hand to his mouth and kissed the pulse beating at her wrist.

"I'm really liking the now."

Her skin was soft, like running his hands over silk. Jack imagined that all of her skin felt that way. "I am too." He kissed his way up her arm, smiling when he heard her draw in a sharp breath.

"What are you doing?" she asked.

"I thought that was obvious," he said, amused.

"You're kissing my arm."

"Yes. If we weren't in a restaurant I'd be kissing other parts of you." He raised his head and smiled at her.

Her lips curved into a smile. "Then what are we waiting for?" she asked.

&c&

JACK TOOK HER to his house. It was closer by a couple of minutes. At the moment, that seemed like too much longer to wait. He kissed her in his SUV. They made it into the house before they started ripping off each other's clothes. At the door, he kissed her again. Once inside, he backed her up against the wall and kissed her like he'd wanted to since the night before. Only this time was better, because he knew they weren't going to stop.

He slid his tongue in her mouth, explored it, tangled tongues with her. With their mouths still fused together, he cupped her breasts in his hands, sighed, breathed in her scent. Light. A little spicy. A lot sexy. Her breasts were lushly perfect and he wanted her naked, now.

Maya put her arms around his neck and pressed up against him. He put his arms around her and cupped her rear, slowly raising the dress. Maya raised her leg, wrapping it around his hips to pull him closer. Hands under her dress, he slid one hand up her leg and over her bare skin. He kept going until he reached the smooth skin of her butt, caressing it with both hands. Bare skin. Oh, God, she was wearing a thong.

Maya untied the belt at her waist, letting it fall to the ground. "Take off your shirt," she said huskily, attacking the buttons. When she finished, he slipped it off his shoulders and let it drop to the floor. He wanted to take her up against the wall, on the table, on the floor. But even more, he wanted her in his bed.

"You can't carry me," she said when he scooped her up in his arms. "I'm too heavy."

Jack laughed. "Not in this lifetime, honey."

In his bedroom, he set her down and pulled her dress up over her head and off. Jack gazed at her and nearly swallowed his tongue. She wore a low-cut peach bra, peach thong panties, and high heeled black boots that came up just over her knees. He felt his brain short circuit, barely aware of her soft laugh.

Maya put a foot on his bed and began to unzip the boot. "Oh, no you don't," he said. "That's my job." Slowly, carefully, he drew the zipper down, kissing the skin as it was revealed, drawing the boot off and tossing it aside. He repeated the process with the other boot.

She helped him unzip his pants, push them down and off, his boxers following. He helped her take off her bra and panties and then they were on his bed and he was holding her in his arms, skin to skin, mouth to mouth, sex to sex. He kissed her mouth, her neck, her breasts, her belly. Kissed those long gorgeous legs he'd dreamed of wrapped around him. He pulled a condom out of his bedside table drawer, one of the boxes his brother Dylan had given him months ago, telling him to go get laid again before he drove everyone crazy.

Maya took it from him, opened it and rolled it down, her hands making him crazy as she did it. Jack knew he should take his time. Should seduce her slowly. But it had been far too long for him to slow down.

But Maya didn't want slow either. She urged him on, with her hands, her lips, her tongue tasting his skin and her heart beating as fast as his. She opened her legs, and he drove inside her, seating himself deep. He pulled out, thrust in again, and again. She cried out, her body clamping down on his, and he exploded inside her.

Jack rolled off her, not wanting to smother her, but he wasn't ready to let her go, either. He put his arm around her and snuggled her up against him, angled her head upward and leaned down to kiss her mouth.

"Hmm," Maya sighed deeply.

"Hmm," he echoed. That was about all he could manage too.

Chapter Six

ഇരു

MAYA LAY WITH her head against Jack's chest, listening to the steady beat of his heart. They hadn't spoken for some time beyond a word or two here and there.

"Are you okay?" he asked. "You've been awfully quiet."

"I'm better than okay." She rose on her elbow to look down at him. His dark hair fell over his forehead. Those gorgeous green eyes were at half-mast, his mouth was curved in a sexy smile. She wanted to eat him up. "I'm wonderful," she said.

"Yeah, you are." He pulled her head down and kissed her lips. "Wonderful is a good word."

Maya laughed. "Flatterer."

"Hey, you said it first."

"I meant I *feel* wonderful." Wonderful, marvelous, contented, happy. Pick any one of them, she thought.

He smoothed his hand over the bare skin of her butt. "Yes, you do feel wonderful."

She laughed again. He kissed her again. They dozed. They woke and made love, more slowly this time and every bit as deliciously good as the first time. If she'd known it would be like this between them in high school, she wouldn't have been a virgin when she left Marietta. In fact, she might not have left town at all.

⁸ºСᴚ

"I DON'T WANT you to go," Jack said very early Sunday morning. Making love to Maya again was probably a physical impossibility, but he was willing to give it a try. He had a lot of libido stored up.

She sat on the edge of the bed with her back to him, still naked. "I know. I don't want to go either. But I have to get home to shower and change before I pick up Carmen. And you need to pick up Gina. Plus, you have to drive me home."

Jack sat up and moved her hair aside to kiss the nape of her neck. "I have a better idea." He slid his hands around to cup her breasts and play with her nipples.

She relaxed against him, sighing as he caressed her. "I'm sure you do." She turned her head and kissed him. "But we don't have time."

He slipped his hand down to the juncture of her thighs. "We could shower together. Here. We can be quick," he said, his fingers exploring her wet heat.

"You are a wicked, wicked man," she murmured.

He rummaged in the bedside drawer for a condom, then got out of bed and picked her up. She wrapped her legs around him and kissed him as he walked toward the bathroom with her. He reached into the shower and turned the water on, kissing her with his hands beneath her butt, supporting her against the cool shower door while the water heated, steaming up the room as his own blood heated to a boil.

He wanted to explore her slowly, to take his time and kiss and caress every womanly curve and every secret place. Wanted to learn her, steep himself in her. *Next time*, he thought, stepping beneath the warm spray, lifting her up and plunging inside her warmth, her wetness, as hard as he'd ever been. Maya kissed his neck, scraping her nails against his skin, as she held on tight and rocked with him on a wild ride. Once, twice, he thrust inside of her and came, as she shattered around him and called his name.

He let her down slowly, spread shower gel on his hands and started to soap her. She took the gel from him and massaged it over his chest, and lower. He felt a little dazed, a lot consumed. He'd never spent a night like the one before, not even, he was guiltily aware, with Brianna.

It's just sex, he thought. Great sex, but still, it couldn't be anything more. Regardless of their past, they were almost strangers. Two people who hadn't spoken in twenty years. Two people who, once they reconnected, couldn't keep their hands off each other. Which wasn't a surprise. Not really.

It's just sex, he told himself again. *Amazing sex. Mind blowing sex. But sex. You know, sex that you've only had twice in the five years since Brianna died.* The sex that in no way came close to what he'd just experienced with Maya.

It wasn't as if he'd fallen in love with Maya again.

Was it?

⚭

MAYA ENDED HER video chat with her assistant, uneasily aware she hadn't been giving Cindy her full attention. *This is ridiculous*, she thought. *Three days later and you're still all gooey inside. You've had sex before. It was good, sure. Great even. But there's no need to be all starry-eyed over the experience.*

Except that she was. Not only starry-eyed but gobsmacked. But damn, surely she was allowed to be a little stunned after a night like that one. Who wouldn't be after sex that had completely blown her mind?

You can't possibly have fallen for him so fast. You don't even know him, not really.

Her cell rang and she answered, her heart beating a little faster when she saw Jack's name on the readout. "Hi."

"Hi. I don't have long, but I wanted to ask you and Carmen over for dinner tomorrow night. I have the afternoon off and I thought I could grill some steaks."

Talk about gooey. Her heart melted like chocolate in the sun. It pitter-pattered for all it was worth. Jack was asking her and her daughter over for dinner. That meant something. It meant acknowledging they were a couple to the two most important people in their lives, their daughters. She should think about it before plunging in.

"Maya?"

Oh, hell, it wasn't as if he was asking her to marry him. Thinking was overrated. "Yes, we'd love to. What can I bring and what time do you want us?"

"Around six, since it's a school night, we'll want to finish early. And if you don't mind, bring a salad. I like to eat them, but hate to make them."

Maya laughed. "I can do that. See you then."

ఴoca

NATURALLY, MAYA COULDN'T decide what to wear to Jack's house. Something casual. Not too sexy. The girls would be there, after all. But then, she didn't want to look like a bag lady either, as her sister had accused her of the other night. Finally, she settled on tight black leggings and black suede spike-heeled ankle boots. A deceptively simple white long sleeve, fitted scoop neck T-shirt came next, to which she added a slim black leather waist length jacket with faux quilting on the shoulders and arms and left it unzipped.

Carmen came in as she was finishing up. Looking over her mother critically she said, "You sure are taking a lot of trouble over what to wear to a backyard cookout."

"No, I'm not," Maya said automatically.

Carmen sniffed the air. "You're wearing that super expensive perfume, aren't you? The one you bought in Paris and save for special occasions."

Good Lord, the child had a nose like a bloodhound. "It happened to be the first one I picked up," Maya said blandly, knowing that Carmen didn't for a moment believe her.

"This is like your third date with Dr. Gallagher," she persisted. "If you don't count Sunday night when he came by, or Tuesday when you met him at the diner."

"Nobody likes a cookie counter." Maya held a chunky gold necklace around her neck. Wrinkling her nose, she selected a slim silver and turquoise one.

"I'm not counting cookies. I'm counting dates."

"Nobody likes a date counter, either."

Carmen sat cross-legged on Maya's bed and watched her while she searched for matching earrings. A few seconds later she pulled out big silver hoops. Perfect.

"You two are like, dating. *Dating* dating," Carmen added, emphasizing the word.

"Yes. I suppose we are," Maya agreed cautiously.

"Like, exclusively?"

Maya turned around to look at her daughter, who seemed uncharacteristically solemn. She and Jack hadn't talked about exclusivity. Maya hadn't thought they needed to, she'd just assumed they were exclusive. But Carmen didn't need to know all that.

"Yes. Does it bother you?"

Carmen shrugged. "Daddy got married again. And then he moved to Germany."

Bless her heart. Her daughter was stressed about being uprooted again. Or she was worried about a stepfather to deal with. Or both. "Don't worry, we won't be moving again."

"But you could get married again." She picked at imaginary lint on the bedspread. "Daddy did."

Married? Sure she could. Someday. "Dr. Gallagher and I are just dating, honey. We enjoy each other's company. There's nothing serious going on." *Yet,* came the unspoken rider. Could this . . . affair be serious? Did she want it to be serious?

She didn't know. She liked being around him. Enjoyed talking to him. She loved the sex. But serious? No, no, no. Not yet.

Maya walked over to Carmen and ruffled her hair, then sat beside her. "I know it's been hard on you having your father move so far away. But you're going to see him at Thanksgiving. And you still video chat with him at least once a week."

"It's not the same."

Maya put her arms around her and hugged her. "I know." After a moment she said, "Is something else bothering you? About your dad? Or me?"

Carmen's voice was muffled when she spoke, since she still had her face buried against Maya's chest. "Daddy and Adele are having a baby."

Typical Graham, she thought angrily. He told Carmen before he told Maya, never considering that Maya could have smoothed the way and perhaps made Carmen feel better. As for herself, she couldn't have cared less if her ex and his new wife had one new child or ten. But Carmen did.

"Your father loves you, Carmen. He loves you a lot."

"I know. But he's going to have a new baby now. He might just . . . " her voice trailed off, then she said, "He might forget me."

Graham was clueless and annoying, but he loved Carmen.

"No he won't. You're his first born and he loves you very much. Besides, you're impossible to forget," Maya said, trying for a lighter note. "Do you want me to find a weekend soon so you can go see him? Maybe take off a Monday or a Friday?" With all of her business traveling, Maya had points enough to fly both of them whenever and wherever she wanted.

"I don't know. Maybe."

"Think about it and check your school schedule. I'll check into flights." Maya glanced at the clock. "Are you ready to go? It's time."

"Okay." At the door, she stopped and said, "There's a new app for the tablet that Gina and I could play. It's not expensive. Can I get it?"

"What kind of app? It's not one of those blow-'em-up ones, is it?"

"Of course not. We don't even like those. It's a fashion app. You can dress the models and everything. You get to design outfits and then see what they look like on a model. It's cool."

Fashion was better than death and mayhem. "All right, but I want to see it. And don't think I didn't notice how you slipped that in there."

Carmen laughed and left the room.

Fashion. Fortunately, Carmen was interested in designing clothes, not modeling them. While Maya had enjoyed modeling, it wasn't a career she necessarily wanted her daughter to embrace.

Chapter Seven

ഔ൫

LATE WEDNESDAY AFTERNOON Gina answered the door to Maya and Carmen. The girls immediately took off to test out Carmen's new app for her tablet. Jack was nowhere to be found, and apparently, Gina hadn't felt the need to point her in his direction. Carrying the bowl of salad, Maya walked through the living room and headed for a swinging door, which she assumed led to the kitchen.

She pushed it open and stopped. She saw his legs first. And then his rear, which looked particularly fine in an old, faded pair of blue jeans. With the oven door open, he was bending down over it, cursing softly and reaching one hand inside. Just what he was doing she couldn't figure out.

"Hi. I come bearing salad."

"Hey." Jack emerged from the oven holding a large spatula. "Did Gina let you in? I didn't hear the doorbell."

"That would be hard to do with your head stuck inside the oven," she agreed. "What are you doing in there?"

After closing the oven and setting down the spatula, he took the salad from her and set it on the counter. "Salvaging potatoes. Two of the damn things exploded. The remains are not pretty."

He looked her over with an appreciative gleam in his eyes. "You, on the other hand, look good enough to eat."

She smiled. "Cute. Weak, but cute."

Putting his hands on her waist, he pulled her to him. "Wow, you smell as good as you look."

"You smell a little like burned potatoes."

"Can't win 'em all," he said and kissed her.

She returned the kiss, wrapping her arms around his neck and meeting his tongue with hers. Her brain shut down and she could only feel. His hand beneath her jacket at the small of her back. His other hand sliding over her rear to bring her closer. His lips locked to hers, his tongue doing a tango with hers as heat swamped her. He backed her up against the swinging door and took her deeper.

"Better watch out," she murmured between kisses. "This door isn't stationary."

"I know. It's my door," he said, kissing the pulse racing at the base of her throat.

Her head fell back and she sucked in a breath, trying to think, but it was no use. Her brain was addled.

The swinging wood door bonked her in the head. Maya yelped, coming down to earth with a bang.

"Dad, what's going on? We're hungry," Gina said, pushing the door open as Jack dropped his hands and smothered a laugh. Following right behind her, Carmen came in too.

"You hit Ms. Parrish in the head with the door, Gina."

"Oh, sorry Ms. Parrish."

"Don't worry about it. I shouldn't have been standing in front of the door."

Gina turned to her father, while Maya rubbed her head. "We're *starving*."

"Why were you standing there?" Carmen asked her.

When she wanted, Carmen's eyes were extraordinarily sharp.

Maya suspected she looked more mussed than she had when she came in, but she hadn't had a chance to even smooth her hair. Luckily, Jack distracted Carmen before Maya could come up with an answer. He picked up two apples from the fruit bowl and tossed one to Gina and the other to Carmen. "Scram. That should hold you until I get dinner ready."

"You exploded the potatoes again, didn't you?" Gina looked at the bowl sitting on the floor by the oven, containing burnt bits of potato. She heaved an exasperated sigh. "Didn't you poke holes in them?"

"Yes, Ms. Smarty, I did. They still exploded." He glared at the remains of the offending potatoes. "They hate me."

Gina gave him a superior look. "Dad, potatoes aren't alive. They can't hate you." With that, the girls walked out.

Maya couldn't hold back her laughter any longer. "'Dad, potatoes aren't alive,'" she repeated in Gina's exact tone. "I love it."

"I raised a smart ass," he muttered. "I must have poked forty holes in the stupid things."

"There, there," she said, still laughing. "Let Maya fix it."

"How do you salvage exploded potatoes?"

"Mash them."

"I never thought of that," he said, seeming struck by the idea.

"Do you cook a lot?" she asked while he found what she needed to mash the potatoes.

"Some. I can grill. I'm good with breakfast, even though I don't often have time to cook it. I can make sandwiches. But pizza is my specialty," he added modestly.

"Really? You make homemade pizza?"

"Who said anything about homemade? I know where to pick up the best pizza in town."

"Oh, good. Tell me where, because the last one I bought

was terrible."

"I'm a man of many talents," he said. He caught her hand and pulled her close to him. "For instance—" He cupped her face in his hands and kissed her. Deliciously, slowly.

Maya's eyes fluttered closed and she sighed. "Yes, you are."

It was a wonderful evening. Maya hadn't had as much fun in a long, long time. Good food, good company, and the two girls were funny and entertaining, only rolling their eyes a couple of times when they caught Maya and Jack gazing foolishly at each other. After dinner, the four of them played a game, a variation of dominoes called Chicken Foot that had them all laughing. Even though she'd never played before, Carmen cleaned up at the game, beating them all soundly.

The girls went off to Gina's room. "We can't stay long," Maya called after them. "Tomorrow's a school day."

She and Jack sat on his couch and talked for a little while longer. "Carmen and I should be going," Maya said, reluctantly.

"Okay." He kissed her.

"Soon," Maya murmured and kissed him.

"Okay," he repeated, and kissed her again.

"I really, really have to go," she said against his lips.

"Mom," Carmen said in disapproving tones, "you said we had to go soon."

"Busted," Jack murmured, lifting his head and smiled at Maya.

"By both of them," she said, looking over at the two girls, who exhibited identical censorious expressions.

∾℀

THE FOLLOWING EVENING, Jack was reading a medical journal when Gina came into his study. He smiled at his daughter and asked, "Are you going to bed already?"

She rolled her eyes. "Dad, it's only nine o'clock. I'm not a baby."

He hid another smile. "You're right about that. I didn't realize what time it was." He'd been having a hard time concentrating, mainly because he couldn't stop thinking about Maya. She and Carmen had plans with Maya's parents, who were in town for the night, so Jack knew he wouldn't see her until the weekend.

Gina wandered around the study restlessly, looking at the bookshelves, picking out books and putting them back, and sighing a lot.

A sure-fire sign that she had something on her mind. He knew a cowardly urge to hope the problem wasn't about boys. He sucked at that sort of thing. Gina didn't want to hear that Jack didn't trust one single teenage boy with his little girl. She'd say he was being overprotective, and he was. But Jack had been a teenage boy, and he knew how their minds worked.

"Did you want to talk about something, honey?" he asked her.

She shot him a glance and shrugged. "You won't want to talk about it. You never do."

Boys, damn it. "Gina, you know you can talk about anything with me. Out with it. What's wrong?"

"It's about Mom. You don't like to talk about her."

Jack felt a pang of guilt. Gina was exaggerating, but she did have a point. He didn't avoid conversations about Brianna, at least not with Gina, but he rarely initiated them. It always saddened him to think that Brianna was missing so much with their daughter and with him. "What about your mother?"

Gina sat in the comfortably shabby overstuffed chair where Jack often sat to read—anything except medical journals. He read those at his desk. Curling her legs up under her, Gina began plucking at the fabric of the chair. Another sign of troubled thoughts.

"I miss her," she said, her tone so sad it broke his heart.

"I know you do. I miss her too."

"Do you . . . do you still love Mom?"

Now he knew what was going on. He should have realized from the first. "I'll always love your mother. You know that."

Gina still looked troubled. She looked up and met his eyes. "You kissed Ms. Parrish."

"Yes," he agreed cautiously. "I like her."

"You're dating her."

"Yes," he said again. And he meant to continue. Where it was going, he didn't know but in the meantime he wanted to be with Maya.

"You really like her, I can tell."

Was it that obvious? Even to his daughter, who, like a typical teenager, didn't usually notice much beyond her circle of friends? Or was it just the kiss she witnessed that gave him away? Gina had seen him kiss women before. Hadn't she? He thought about that. Maybe she hadn't. "Does it bother you that I'm dating someone?"

"I don't know. I like Ms. Parrish. Carmen and I are friends and her mom is cool. But—" she hesitated, then said, "I feel like we're just forgetting Mom."

Tears welled in her eyes. The eyes that looked so much like her mother's. Jack's heart turned over. "Come here," he said huskily.

Gina got up and crawled into Jack's lap, as she had as a little girl. She didn't fit quite as well, with her long legs, but she was still his baby. He put his arms around her and kissed the top of her head. "We won't ever forget your mother, Gina. She'll be with us, in our hearts, for as long as we live. No matter what happens in the future, we'll have our memories of your mom and know how much she loved us."

"Promise?"

"Cross my heart," he answered. "She'd want us to be happy, Gina. Your mother wouldn't want us to grieve forever."

"Does Ms. Parrish make you happy?"

Thinking about Maya, he smiled. "Yes, she does. Very happy."

"Okay." Gina got up and walked to the door. "Dad?" He looked at her, thinking how grown up she was getting. "I hope you're being *responsible*. That's important, you know." She left before he could answer. Which was a damn good thing, because he hadn't a clue what to say.

Oh, my God. He'd just been lectured about safe sex by his fifteen-year-old daughter.

❧

MUSIC. MAYA HEARD music. And not soothing music, either. Had she set her alarm? She cracked open an eye and looked at the clock. Five a.m. The music came from her phone. She grabbed at it, trying to make the obnoxious noise cease. Who the hell was calling her at five a.m.? "Hello." She held the phone away from her ear. The readout said it was her assistant. "Cindy? What's wrong?"

"Maya, thank God you answered," Cindy said. "I thought you might have turned off your ringer."

Maya sat up, swung her feet to the floor and rubbed her eyes. "What happened? Are you all right? Did we lose a big client?" Cindy wouldn't have called this early unless it was something serious.

"No, everything's fine. Well, not exactly fi—" Her voice cut off and Maya heard muffled sounds. What in the hell was going on?

Cindy came back on the line. "Sorry, I had to—"

She must have dropped the phone again, but this time Maya heard the unmistakable sound of someone throwing up. Sincerely glad she had a cast iron stomach, Maya waited.

A short time later, Cindy spoke again. "I hate to do this, but can you go to Los Angeles?"

"Los Angeles? Today?" Oh, damn. She remembered now. Cindy had a meeting with one of their biggest clients, a photography studio in LA that supplied Maya's Models with a number of the photographers they used for freelance projects.

"I've been sick all night," Cindy moaned. "I kept hoping I'd get better but—" she gulped—"I haven't."

"No, that's obvious. Shoot me the details and I'll catch the first flight out. Please tell me it's this afternoon and not this morning."

Cindy assured her the appointment wasn't until late that afternoon, which meant if she was lucky she could make it to LA in time. Minutes later, they hung up and Maya received a text with the details of the meeting on it.

By the time she'd called Amy to ask her to take care of Carmen, booked a flight out of Bozeman, woken Carmen and told her what was going on, choked down some coffee, showered, dressed and packed a carry on, it was late enough to call Jack. Amy was taking Carmen to school and would pick her up as well. If Maya drove like a crazy woman, she'd make it to the Bozeman airport in time to catch her flight.

Naturally, Jack didn't answer. She remembered he'd said he had early rounds, so she left a message and told him she'd call him later with details. That is, she *tried* to leave a message, but since cell phone reception was spotty on the way to the airport, she wasn't sure he'd get it.

Great start to the day.

Chapter Eight

∞ℭ℞

"WHAT HAPPENED TO Dylan?" Jack asked his brother Wyatt. He and Wyatt had met at Grey's after work to have a beer and play some pool. Gina had stayed home to "do her homework," which he knew meant anything but. She'd probably gotten on the phone the minute he walked out the door.

"Dylan stayed home with Lulabelle," his brother said, referring to one of their mares. "She's ready to foal any day now." Wyatt checked his cell phone. "He'll call me if she does. 'Course I can't hear it over the noise in this place. I put it on vibrate."

"I hate cell phones," Jack said.

"Since when?"

"Since this morning. I've been playing phone tag with Maya all day. Either the reception is bad, the messages she's left me are garbled, or she doesn't answer and it goes straight to voicemail."

"Trouble with the Heartbreaker, bro?"

"No, smart ass." At least, he didn't think so, but since he couldn't talk to her he didn't know. "Stop calling her the Heartbreaker, or I'll break your face."

Wyatt laughed. "You and what army?"

Jack considered it briefly, but even though punching Wyatt would be satisfying, he couldn't do it. His patients would hear about it without fail, and every single one of them would disapprove of Jack punching one of his brothers, no matter how much said brother deserved it. "Ha. You've forgotten what happened last time."

"Probably, since I haven't been in a fist fight with you since you went to medical school."

"Some of us are responsible professionals."

"Yeah. Must be a drag sometimes," Wyatt said. "Now me, I don't have to worry about my image. Or women either."

He had a point. "I'm not worried about women," he said, focusing on Wyatt's last comment.

"Obviously, or you wouldn't be dating the—"

Jack glared at him, daring him to complete the sentence.

"Maya," he said with a grin, as Jack sank the eight ball.

"Add it to your tab?" Jack asked, racking the balls to start a new game.

Wyatt shrugged. "When's the wedding?"

Caught in the act of breaking, Jack's shot went squirrely. "Damn it, you did that on purpose."

"It's a logical question. You sure as shit haven't been sleeping with any other women since Brianna died. Figure that means you're serious."

Jack felt a pang of guilt at the mention of Brianna, but brushed it aside. He opened his mouth to explain that his sex life hadn't been quite that dismal, but thought better of it. His sex life, or lack thereof, was his own business. "Who said anything about marriage? We're just getting to know each other again."

Wyatt smirked at him. "Whatever you say, bro."

After that, Jack's game went to hell. He couldn't stop thinking about Maya. Maya and the M-word. Marriage.

IF JACK HADN'T been so preoccupied, he'd have cared more that Wyatt was cleaning up at the pool table. Where the hell was Maya? he wondered for the hundredth time. If just one of those calls had been more clear, he would know. As it was, he missed being with her. One night and he already missed her. And he didn't like it.

Since Maya had returned to Marietta and she and Jack had gotten together, everything had been going great. Blue skies all the way, baby. Jack knew what could happen when everything seemed too good to be true. Great times, right up until everything went to shit.

Brianna's death had taught him that. They hadn't had the perfect marriage, but they'd had a damn good one. They'd loved each other, loved their child, they'd believed in their marriage and that they'd grow old together. Instead, Brianna had been hit by a car, while crossing the street. Sudden, shocking, devastating death. She'd lived long enough to say goodbye to Jack and Gina. And then she was simply . . . gone.

God, he didn't want to dredge up those feelings again. He'd pulled himself together and soldiered on. He couldn't fall apart. He had his daughter to think of. He had to be strong. He had to deal. Over time the pain had lessened, fading from razor sharp to a dull ache. But he'd never forgotten it. Never forgotten that first surge of grief, the feeling of the bottom dropping out of his world, when the woman he loved had left him.

"Your shot," Wyatt said. He took a swallow of his beer, then set it down again. "Jack? Are you okay?"

"Fine." He sank two more balls, then missed an easy one, because he couldn't get Maya off his mind.

Jack hadn't thought about another woman for longer than a day or two until Maya came back into his life. The sex was fantastic. Strangely enough, that was part of the problem. He and Brianna had loved each other, enjoyed each other, been comfortable with each other. But if he were honest, he had to admit he'd never experienced anything like the white-hot fire that exploded between him and Maya when they came together. That couldn't last, could it?

Maybe he was overthinking the situation. He did that sometimes. He should just enjoy what was going on now and not worry about the future.

"Are you gonna play or what?" Wyatt asked.

Damn Wyatt for making him think too much. He and Maya were having fun. They enjoyed each other. They enjoyed the sex—who wouldn't? They cared about each other, sure. That didn't mean either one of them was ready to commit to anything serious. There was no need to get his shorts in a twist. Especially not over anything his brother said. He took his next shot and missed.

"Eight ball in the corner pocket," Wyatt said, and sank it. "Game over, bro."

Yeah, he was doing great if Wyatt could beat him at pool. "You're a sneaky bastard, aren't you?"

Wyatt grinned. "Double or nothing?"

"You're on," Jack said, determined to wipe that smart-ass grin off his brother's face.

෨෬

MAYA FINALLY REACHED Jack late that night. At first, she got his voicemail, but before she could hang up in frustration, he came on the line.

"Maya?"

"I'm sorry. Did I wake you? I know it's late, but I haven't been able to reach you all day."

"No, that's okay. Where are you?"

"Los Angeles."

She heard rustling. "Sorry, dropped the phone. Los Angeles as in California?"

"Yes, I had an emergency business trip. My assistant was ill and I had to take over for her."

"Do you have to do this often?"

"Not often, but occasionally. Anyway, I'm sorry it took so long to get in touch. I'll be home late tomorrow afternoon." She could imagine him right now, lying in bed shirtless, the stubble on his jaw making him look a little bit scruffy and a lot wicked. She wanted to be there with him. Badly.

In fact, she'd missed him far more in the hours since she'd left Marietta than she would have believed only a few weeks ago. You'd think she was madly in love.

Oh, crap. She *was* madly in love. With Jack Gallagher. Again.

"Maya? Did you hear what I said?"

"Sorry. Something about the football game tomorrow night?"

"Gina is going with Mattie and a group of girls that Gina says includes Carmen. Charlie Guthrie's taking them and then they're spending the night at Mattie's."

"I remember now. But Charlie just had them spend the night. Is she sure she wants them all again?"

"She said since it's an away game they'd be back late, so they might as well all sleep over."

A big smile spread over her face. "I don't suppose you want to come over tomorrow after I get home?"

"I don't suppose I would. I know I would," he said.

They talked for a while longer and then hung up. Maya felt giddy. Ridiculous at her age, but that's how she felt. She hugged her pillow and shivered, thinking about making love with Jack again. And when she fell asleep, she dreamed of him.

ॐ

MAYA HAD CALLED Jack from the airport and he was waiting for her at her house when she drove up. Minutes later, he had her backed up against the wall, his hands sliding beneath her dress and hers already wrestling with his shirt buttons.

Her lips clung to his. His hands were busy unzipping her dress, then pulling it down. He unhooked her bra, pushed her panties down her legs and suddenly she was standing there wearing only her suede platform sandals. His mouth left hers to cruise along her jaw, her neck, heated kisses pressed against her pulse, then dropping lower to her breasts. Maya wrapped her legs around him and he strode to the couch. He let go of her and dazed, she watched him unbutton and unzip his khakis, slide them off along with boxers in one smooth motion.

She pulled him down beside her, barely gave him time to roll on the condom before she straddled him and lowered herself onto him. He was hard and hot and felt so good she wanted to scream, and when his hand slipped between them to caress her, she did scream. He kissed her, put his hands on her hips and helped her rock until she was flying again, higher and higher. Jack groaned. She moaned. She squeezed tight, feeling him shudder, as he said her name and pumped inside her one last time before he came.

They didn't speak for a long time. Eventually, she bit his shoulder gently and sighed. "That was some welcome home."

"I don't think I can move."

"Me either. Why do we have to?"

"Food," Jack said. "I need food."

"I have frozen pizza."

"Yeah? What kind?" She told him. "Diet pizza? Really?"

"Of course. What did you expect? I may not be at my model weight, but I still have to work at it to be able to get in my clothes. Did you think I was just magically slim?"

"Yes."

Maya laughed. "I eat what I want when I go out, but at home I'm usually very careful."

"Don't you have anything else?" he asked plaintively. "I could call for a pizza delivery, but we'll have to get dressed. Or one of us will."

"I'll get dressed. You can order. I like vegetables," she added as she picked up her scattered clothing and went to her bedroom to find something comfortable to wear.

They ate pizza and watched a movie, part of one, anyway. They talked about Maya's business trip and whether she needed to hire another assistant, and about Jack's nurse's running feud with one of his patients. He wouldn't tell her who his patient was but she knew anyway, since Vera's and Mrs. Delaney's feud over the bake-off was common knowledge.

They made love and talked and made love again. Maya hadn't been this happy in a long, long time. The night was magical. Marvelous. Perfect.

Until she told him she loved him.

Chapter Nine

ഇരുതു

MONDAY AFTERNOON MAYA met Amy at the Java Cafe. "Let's sit outside," Maya said after they picked up their lattes.

Amy looked at her curiously. "Okay, but it's a little chilly."

Maya didn't care about that. She needed to talk and she wasn't anxious to broadcast what she had to say to every person in the cafe.

"What's wrong?" Amy asked when they sat down.

Maya sipped her latte, burned her tongue and frowned. "I did something stupid. I knew it was a mistake the moment I said it, but by then it was too late. I'd already opened my big mouth."

"Just guessing, but does this stupid thing you did have something to do with Jack?"

"Who else?" she asked glumly.

"Is it really that bad?"

Was it? "I think so."

"What did you do? Why do you think you screwed up? Last I heard, you two were well on the way to being madly in love."

She snorted. "Yes, that would be the problem. *One* of us was. I told him I loved him."

"Oh." Amy looked at her for a moment. "Not a good idea, I take it."

Maya drummed her fingers on the table. "I told him I loved him and he said . . . nothing."

"Nothing?" Amy repeated.

"Absolutely nothing."

"Awk-ward," Amy said, emphasizing the first syllable.

"Tell me about it," Maya said. Thinking about that moment still made her want to cringe. "Then he kissed me. Every time I started to open my mouth, he kissed me."

Amy laughed. "And that's a problem?"

"You're damn right it's a problem. It's called avoidance." She fell silent, thinking about it.

"So what happened after you told him?" Amy prompted.

"Obviously, he didn't want to talk about it. So, we didn't. We both spent the rest of the night pretending I hadn't said the 'L' word."

"I'm impressed that you managed not to say anything else. I'm sure I would've had to say something."

"I started to ask him if it was too soon, but I didn't want a repeat of him staring at me with nothing to say." She smiled briefly. "I seduced him instead."

"That sounds like a good plan," Amy said, laughing.

"The rest of the night was okay. In fact, it was good. But ever since he left the next morning, things have been weird."

"Define weird."

"It's more of a feeling I get than anything he's actually done. He hasn't broken things off or anything like that. He hasn't been mean or combative. He's been a little distant. Stand-offish. Then last night I asked him and Gina to come over for dinner and he said no. He said he had to make early rounds today."

"Maybe he did," Amy said reasonably.

"Ha! He makes early rounds all the time. This is the first

time he used it as an excuse not to see me."

Amy frowned. "When did this happen?"

Wrapping her hands around her cup, she said, "I told him late Saturday night. Early Sunday morning technically." She drank some more coffee, stewing over Jack's reaction to her confession. She shouldn't have told him. Clearly, he didn't feel the same. Or, at the least, he wasn't ready to hear it. Maya didn't know what had possessed her to blurt out her feelings. She used to have more sense. Of course, she hadn't ever been so madly crazy about a man either. For sure not her ex-husband. Not that she remembered, anyway.

At first, she'd shrugged off Jack's reaction, or done her best to. He'd seemed fine later that night. Better than fine. They spent the remainder of the night, or most of it, having fantastic sex. And if Jack wasn't on the same page about the great sex, then he was the best faker she'd ever known.

Amy laughed. "Oh, Maya. You're overreacting. It hasn't even been two days."

"Trust me, I'm not overreacting. You didn't see his face." Nothing had been the same since. "I thought our relationship was going somewhere. Maybe I was wrong. Maybe he just wants to have fun."

Amy patted her hand. "Why don't you just ask him? Talk to him, instead of jumping to conclusions."

Was she jumping to conclusions? There was one way to find out. "You're right. I'll go see him tonight."

ॐ

"HEY, MS. PARRISH," Gina said, answering the front door. "Come on in. Is Carmen with you?"

Oh, man. Maya's here, Jack thought, looking up from the toaster he was trying to fix. Maya. In the flesh. In the very beautiful flesh, wearing tight black leggings, man-killer black boots and a cream-colored sweater that kept slipping off her shoulder. *I am so screwed.*

"Not this time," Maya told Gina pleasantly. "Why don't you go call her?"

Gina took off for her room. Leaving Jack, and the toaster, alone with Maya. She walked over and stood beside the couch, looking at the toaster parts spread all over the coffee table.

"What in the world are you doing to that toaster?"

"Trying to fix it." And doing a mighty crappy job of it.

"I think it's dead. Why don't you just throw it out and get a new one?"

"It was a wedding present," he said, immediately wishing he'd kept his mouth shut. For reasons he didn't understand, Brianna had loved the stupid toaster.

"I see." She said nothing else, but sat beside him and crossed one long, gorgeous leg over the other. The sweater slipped again and he saw smooth, creamy flesh. Why had he wanted to avoid her? Oh, yeah.

Maya had told him she loved him.

"We need to talk," she said.

Talk. Exactly what he'd been trying to dodge. He continued fooling around with the toaster, which really was hopeless at this point. Maya was right. He should throw it out, but he knew he wouldn't. "What do you want to talk about?"

"I'm fairly sure you know." Maya tilted her head, considering him. "I've never seen you so uneasy."

Jack started to deny it, but couldn't.

"I'm sorry I made you uncomfortable," she continued. "I didn't mean to."

"You didn't make me uncomfortable." Which was as big a lie as had ever come out of his mouth.

Maya hitched up her sweater. He couldn't figure out why.

She'd simply switched shoulders, exposing the skin of the other one.

"Call it what you want, but ever since I told you I loved you, nothing has been the same between us."

Jack looked into her eyes. He did not want to talk, and he sure as hell didn't want to talk about love. Why did Maya have to complicate matters? Why did she want to label what was between them? Why couldn't they just continue on, enjoying each other, having fantastic sex, and not have to *talk* about it, for God's sake?

"I don't know what you're talking about," he said. "Everything's fine." *Liar, liar.*

Her eyes flashed. "Everything is a long way from *fine*. I told you my feelings. That doesn't mean you have to reciprocate. But you don't need to freak out, either. It doesn't have to mean anything beyond those are my feelings and I wanted you to know."

Part of him admired her for putting herself out there as she had. The other part didn't like it at all. What did she expect him to say? Did she really think he believed she wasn't upset by his response, or lack of it?

"I'm fine," he repeated. "You're the one who's decided we need to analyze every damn thing."

Her eyes flashed again and narrowed. "Pardon me. How stupid of me to suggest we have an honest discussion about our relationship."

"I didn't say you were stupid. But I don't see why we need to talk. There's nothing wrong with us. Why can't we just go along the way we were? Why do we have to *discuss* anything, for God's sake?"

Now, she was really pissed. Fine. He wasn't too happy himself.

She stood. "We don't. We don't need to talk about one

damn thing. Ever."

She started toward the door. He got up as well. "You're overreacting, Maya."

Maya turned around and looked at him incredulously. "I'm overreacting? Did you really just say that to me?"

He shrugged. "That's the way I see it."

"Really. That's the way you see it." She opened the door and sent him a scathing look. "The way I see it is you can stick it where the sun don't shine." The door slammed behind her.

"Wow, she's really mad. What did you do, Dad?" Gina said.

"Nothing." He ran a hand through his hair and scowled at the door. "Why do you think I did something? Maya's the one being completely unreasonable."

Gina looked a little skeptical. "Did you two break up?"

Well, shit. Is that what had happened? "I don't think so," he told Gina. "She's just upset. She'll get over it."

"Dad?"

He looked at his daughter.

"I don't think you get girls at all." She didn't wait for his response, but went off to her room, shaking her head.

He couldn't argue that. *Women*, he thought in disgust. *Who could understand them?*

Chapter Ten

M AYA DROVE STRAIGHT to Amy's house. On the way, she
called her daughter to check on her. Fortunately, Carmen
was on the other line and didn't want to talk long, which was
fine with Maya. She wasn't sure how much longer she could
bottle up her anger.

"Are you alone?" she asked Amy when she answered the
door. "Are you expecting anyone?"

"Yes, I'm alone and no, I'm not expecting anyone." She
opened the door and stepped aside. "What's got you so worked
up?"

Maya brushed past her and paced the room, her stride
lengthening as she did. She could never sit still when she was
angry, so she paced. "I went to see Jack. To talk to him,
honestly. I wanted to reassure him that I hadn't meant to freak
him out." She snorted in disgust. "That was the dumbest idea I
ever had. Do you know what he did?"

"Just a guess, but made you mad as hell?" Amy sat on the
couch, then added, "I wish you'd sit down. You make me tired
just watching you."

Maya ignored her comment and continued to stride around

the room. "He sat there and said everything was fine. Fine!" She kicked the couch in frustration, then grabbed her foot, hopping on the other. "Damn it!"

"It doesn't pay to hit or kick inanimate objects. Back up," Amy said. "I need more details. Take it from the top."

"Gina let me in. He was sitting on the couch fixing a toaster—a toaster for God's sake—and I said he should just throw it out. It was in a thousand pieces." Amy looked perplexed. "He said it was a wedding present," Maya continued. "Which, of course, made me feel like slime for suggesting he throw it out."

"How were you to know that?"

"I couldn't, of course. Especially since he's never once spoken of his wife to me." Maya shrugged. "It doesn't matter. I tried to talk to him, but he wasn't interested. He said we didn't need to discuss anything. According to Jack, everything is just fine. I'm overreacting." She paused and added the clincher. "And then, he said I was stupid."

"What?" Amy sat up straight and goggled at her. "He actually called you stupid?"

Maybe he hadn't. Even so, that's what she had taken from the conversation. "No, but he implied it."

"Somehow I can't imagine this scene."

"I don't have to imagine it. I was there. After he implied I was stupid, he asked why we had to 'analyze every damn thing,'" she said making air quotes around the phrase. "I wanted to kick him."

"Did you?"

"No, but he would have deserved it if I had. I told him we didn't have to discuss anything, ever, and then I said he should stick it where the sun don't shine."

"Gee, Maya, you could have been more forceful about it. Why'd you let him off so easy?"

"Are you laughing? You are! Don't you dare laugh. This isn't funny."

Amy gained control of herself. Maya decided to ignore the tremor in her voice when she spoke. "Maya, you had an argument. At the risk of you biting my head off, don't you think you are overreacting just a teensy bit?"

"No," she muttered. "Maybe."

"The two of you need to cool off. It sounds like he was being almost as unreasonable as you were."

"Almost my foot. He's the one being completely unreasonable, not me."

"Give it some time," Amy advised. "And after you've both had a chance to cool down, try to talk to him again."

"Because it worked out so well last time, you mean? No, thanks. If Jack wants to talk he can come to me."

ఆలన

NOW YOU'VE STEPPED in it, Jack thought. The week from hell had just gotten worse. He looked from his nurse Vera's angry face to Mrs. Delaney's even angrier one. But really, they were grown women. Why couldn't they act like it?

"I beg your pardon," Mrs. Delaney said in arctic tones. "You want me to—to—"

Jack interrupted. "I suggested that you and Vera make up and you allow her to give you your weekly shot. She's more than capable of doing it."

Mrs. Delaney stared at him as if he'd lost his mind.

Vera's bosom heaved and she glared at him for all she was worth. But she kept her mouth closed. She wouldn't say anything in front of a patient, no matter how angry she was.

"And if I refuse? I don't want that woman touching me."

He could all but see the icicles hanging from her words. He slipped into a pleasant fantasy.

"I'm sorry to lose you, but that's your decision, Mrs. Delaney." To Vera he added, "Fax her records to Mrs. Delaney's new doctor. Have you chosen one or would you like me to recommend someone?"

It would almost be worthwhile to say those words aloud simply to see the reactions of the two women.

He sighed. "If you refuse, of course I'll continue to give you your shot. But I urge you both to consider burying the hatchet." He walked to the door and said, "I'll leave you to talk about it. I'll be in my office if you need me, Vera."

છેલ્લ

HE WAS GOING to pay for this. Vera wouldn't appreciate his comments any more than Mrs. Delaney had. His nurse could make his life miserable if she wanted. But what difference did it make if the last week was any indication of how things were going?

He hadn't talked to Maya for more than a few minutes since Monday evening. Today was Friday. The end of a very long week. Take Tuesday, for example. He and Maya had run into each other at the Java Cafe that morning. He'd assumed she'd gotten over her snit.

"Do you want to grab some dinner tonight?" he'd asked.

She looked him up and down, as if he were gum on the bottom of one of her fancy-ass boots. "Sorry. I have to wash my hair."

"Still pissed at me?"

"No, not at all," she said, dripping sarcasm.

If her goggling eyes were any sign, Sally, the barista, had heard every word. Great. The news that he and Maya were on the outs would be all over Marietta by nightfall. Or more likely, lunchtime.

It annoyed the hell out of him that just because he didn't

want to talk everything to death, Maya was pissed off at him. He hadn't seen Maya since, or talked to her either. He'd decided she could come to him once she got over herself. He had a feeling he might be waiting until Hell froze over.

Someone knocked on the door. Vera probably. "Come in."

Vera stepped inside his office. Miracle of miracles, she didn't look angry.

"Did you two call a truce?" he asked without much hope.

She nodded. "We did."

That shocked the hell out of him. "You're kidding. How did that happen?"

"Well, we talked to each other. She told me her side and I told her mine, and we actually listened to each other this time."

Stunned, he asked, "That's all it took? You two have hated each other for years. A simple conversation and suddenly you're friends?"

Vera laughed. "I wouldn't call us friends. But we're not enemies anymore. We decided life was too short."

Life's too short. Brianna's life had been. His thoughts must have shown on his face.

"Oh, Doctor, I'm sorry. I wasn't thinking."

"Don't worry about it. I'm just glad you two aren't at each other's throats anymore."

"I suppose." She looked at him closely. "Are you all right, Dr. Gallagher?"

"I'm fine." Yeah, he was great. Maya was giving him the frozen shoulder and showed no signs of thawing, all because he didn't want to talk. And why didn't he want to talk? Because he didn't know what to say.

He wanted Maya. He wanted to be with her, make love to her. But love? He wasn't ready for that. He wanted things to go back to the way they were. Fun and easy. Love complicated everything. It didn't last either. You never knew when it would be snatched right out of your hands.

"You don't look fine," Vera said bluntly. "If you don't mind my saying, you look like something my cat dropped on the doorstep." Thank God, she took herself off after that observation.

The day didn't get any better. He dragged himself home and looked in the refrigerator to get a beer, but of course, he didn't have any. Instead, he picked up a soft drink and took it to the couch, determined to do nothing. Relax. That was the ticket.

"Dad, have you seen my red sweater?" Gina rushed into the living room and began pulling up cushions, checking behind chairs, and shoving magazines off the tables. Her magazines that were supposed to be kept in her room, but never were. She insisted she keep every stinking one "in case she might need them." For what, he didn't have a clue.

"No. Why do you need it?"

She shot him an exasperated glance. "For the game, of course. We have to leave in half an hour. I need to get there early because the Spirit Club is going to sit together." She took another look at him. "Is that what you're wearing?"

Crap. He still wore his work clothes, khakis and a button down shirt. He'd totally forgotten he'd promised not only to take Gina to the game, but to stay and watch it himself. He didn't know why it mattered to her, since she'd vanish with her friends the minute they got there. Not to mention, she was sitting with the Spirit Club, so she wouldn't even know he was there. But a promise was a promise, so he went to his room and changed into his jeans and a lightweight sweater.

Jack only waited on Gina ten minutes. Almost a record. "I see you found your sweater." He started the car and backed up. "Where was it?"

"Um, in my room."

Buried under God knew how many dirty clothes, he bet. He

was too tired to say anything, so he let it pass.

It was a good game. Close, and their team, the Grizzlies, were ahead at halftime and they looked like they might hang on to win. He'd discovered he was hungry after all, so he went to the concession stand at halftime, like everyone else in the stadium.

Everyone, including Maya.

Chapter Eleven

ജ‍ൽ

MAYA HAD GONE to buy candy during halftime. Candy was a crutch, she admitted, but she only allowed herself to have it for certain very good reasons. Heartache made the top five. Maybe it was because she was thinking about him, wondering if he was at the game that she knew who had walked up behind her, before she turned around. Of course, it was Jack. Who else would it be among the hundreds of people attending the game? She turned around, smiled at him and said, "Hi."

He looked surprised, then relieved. "Hi." He hesitated then added, "How are you?"

"Good." *I've been a lot better*, she thought. "How about you?" How about *that* for inane conversation?

"Good." He cleared his throat and repeated, "Good."

It was small of her, but it made her happy to see him so uncomfortable. She launched into her plan. Clearly, waiting for Jack to make a move wasn't working, so she'd decided to prod him a little. "I wanted to tell you, I'm not angry anymore."

"You're not?" He didn't look as if he believed her. "So . . . we're okay?"

No, you idiot, we're not okay. Fortunately, she had to tell the person behind the counter of the concession stand what she wanted. It gave her time to remember her plan. Kicking him wasn't included in it. Darn it. Maya took her drink and M&Ms— she deserved chocolate, lots of chocolate, after this encounter— and waited for him to place his order and receive it. They walked away together and when she judged there wasn't anyone too close by, she said, "Of course we're okay."

In the process of opening his candy bar, he shot her a sharp glance. "You still want to talk, don't you?" He took a big bite of his candy, irritation written all over his annoyingly handsome face.

"No. I changed my mind."

His hand stopped halfway to his mouth and he stared at her for a moment. "You changed your mind." It wasn't a question. "I thought you were pissed because we weren't talking and now you're saying you're fine with that. Why don't I believe you?"

Maya shrugged. "I have no idea. Obviously, I misread the situation." Jack was looking at her as if she had two heads. She began to cheer up.

"What does that mean?"

She hadn't opened her M&Ms yet, so she transferred the bag to the same hand holding her drink. Patting his arm, she said, "We had a fling. It was fun and now it's over. No biggie. It's time to move on."

"But you said—"

She interrupted him, managing to give an amused chuckle. "Oh, Jack." She shook her head in a pitying manner. "Haven't you ever heard of heat of the moment? I got caught up in the"— she gave him a limpid look and finished—"passion. I didn't *mean* it. It's just something people say." She lifted a shoulder and gave a tinkle of laughter. "I'm sure you know how it is."

His eyes had narrowed and his jawline hardened. "No, I can't say that I do. And I didn't think you did either."

"Come on, Jack. We're both adults here." Though she hadn't relied on that person in years, she summoned up the woman, who could work underneath high power lights all day, change enough outfits to go through an entire wardrobe, and live through the chaos of fashion week, all without breaking a sweat. The woman who could smile through hunger, through her feet killing her, through aches and pains that wouldn't quit, through heat, cold, illness and exhaustion. The woman who, whatever happened, smiled for the camera.

She regarded him with her most indulgent glance and laughed. A laugh that said, "You poor, deluded thing," and she could tell he knew it. "I suppose I should tell you, I've been dating someone else."

His eyebrows shot up. "You're dating? We haven't even broken up and you're seeing someone else?"

"Did I misunderstand again?" she asked innocently. "I know we didn't come right out and say it, but I thought after Monday night we were both on the same page. But then, I'm known to be stupid at times."

"I didn't call you stupid," he ground out.

"Again, my mistake. But yes, I've been dating someone. I met him when I was in Los Angeles, but since you and I were still . . . involved I only talked to him briefly. He gave me his number and said to call him if anything changed. So that's what I did. After you and I had our little spat and decided to call it quits, I called him and let him know I was free." She stressed the word free, loving the incredulous expression on his face.

"*We* never decided to call it quits," he said grimly.

"Of course we did. You made it clear you weren't looking for anything complicated, or God forbid, permanent. Obviously, we broke up Monday night." She could tell he was getting madder by the minute, but she was careful to keep her expression mild and clueless.

"And in the what, three days since, you've started dating another man."

Maya looked at him blankly. "Yes. Why not?"

"Who is he? What's his name?" he asked suspiciously.

She gave an airy wave of her hand—the one holding the M&Ms. "Rolf. Rolf Siegrist." A name she'd conjured out of thin air. She uttered a happy sigh. "He flew out to see me that very day."

"Do tell," Jack said.

"Isn't it funny how everything happens for a reason?" she asked him.

"Hilarious."

∞∞

BROKEN UP MY *ass*, Jack thought, watching Maya walk away. That was so not what he'd intended and Maya damn well knew it. Maybe she was right, though. Even though he didn't believe for a minute she'd begun dating already, she seemed serious about the fact they'd broken up. If they had, Jack didn't have to worry about dealing with messy emotions, conflicted feelings, guilt, or anything else. No, he could be alone the rest of his life, wondering why the hell he'd let Maya walk out of it.

She'd told him she loved him. And she'd meant it. He didn't believe one word of what she had said just now. She wanted to stick it to him, and she'd figured out a great way to do it.

Face it, he told himself. Maya might not be dating anyone right now, but she wouldn't be alone for long.

His head hurt. It hurt because he couldn't sleep, and he couldn't sleep because he missed Maya, and he missed her like crazy, even though they'd only been together a couple of weeks, and every time he shut his eyes he realized what a fool he'd been, and if he could have reached it, he would have kicked himself in the ass.

And yet, something still held him back. Something stopped him from going to her, from groveling, from admitting he'd made a terrible mistake and he didn't want to let her go. Was it pride? Maybe, but if so, that wasn't the only reason.

Was he in love with Maya? Could he really have fallen in love with her—again—so quickly? Is that why he'd panicked when she said she loved him? He remembered how she'd looked. Naked. Beautiful. All that smooth, creamy, silky skin. Gray eyes, dark and slumberous. Her lips swollen from his kisses, her hair tousled from his hands. Her heart in those dark, passionate eyes.

Like hell it was heat of the moment.

ഔരു

SATURDAY MORNING STARTED off badly and it only got worse. Maya had thought she would be able to sleep in that morning. Since she was short on sleep from her Jack Gallagher induced insomnia, she'd hoped to make up some of it by sleeping late. Instead Carmen—Carmen, the girl who never voluntarily woke before noon—woke her up at the crack of dawn, or what seemed like it anyway.

"Mom, why aren't you awake? We need to leave in twenty minutes and I need you to help me. I can't find my new jeans."

Maya buried her head in her pillow. "Go 'way."

Carmen plopped down beside her, making the mattress bounce with her enthusiasm. "C'mom, Mom. You've only got twenty minutes to get ready and it takes you that long to drink your coffee. We're supposed to be at the gym at nine."

Maya groaned, rolled over and cracked open her eyes. There sat her daughter all bright-eyed and annoyingly chipper. "Coffee," she croaked. "I need coffee."

Carmen ignored her desperate plea. "You didn't forget did you? It's the White Elephant drive."

White Elephant? What in the world was Carmen talking about?

"You did forget," she accused. "The Spirit Club, well, mostly their parents, are starting pick up this morning. You said you'd go with one of the drivers to pick up stuff and help sort it for us to sell or take to charity."

Maya sat up and rubbed her eyes. "I did no such thing."

"Sure you did. They asked for volunteers, and I said you would. We had the meeting the night you went out of town." Carmen frowned. "I know I told you about it."

"No," she said grimly. "You did not."

"Oh. Maybe I didn't. But you have to go, Mom!"

Of course, I do, she thought darkly. "Fine." Maya threw back the covers and got out of bed. Fixing Carmen with the evil eye, she pointed her index finger at her and said, "Go make my coffee."

"But—"

"Don't tell me you don't know how. It's time you learned. Six cups of water, five scoops of coffee. And find a to-go mug and pour some in there when it's ready."

She stumbled into the bathroom, knowing she barely had time to shower, much less wash her hair. In record time she'd showered and dressed, pulling on her oldest, most comfortable pair of jeans, running shoes, a white T-shirt, and a cream-colored loose knit cable sweater she loved, though she didn't wear it often anymore, because it was almost as old as her jeans. She ran a brush through her hair and decided in favor of coffee over makeup. Driving around picking up other people's junk did not, in her opinion, require makeup. The driver would have to take her as she was. They could call it a White Elephant sale all they wanted, but those ominous words "or give it to charity" sent a chill through her bones. She knew what they'd get. Anything and everything people wanted to get rid of. In other words, junk.

Minutes later, they were out the door, with Carmen still whining over her lost pair of jeans.

"If you'd clean up your room once in a while, you might be able to find things," Maya snapped, her head aching from lack of caffeine.

"I *did* clean it up! I cleaned it up, like Monday."

"Guess again."

"Well, it was sometime not too long ago." Carmen relapsed into injured silence, which was just fine with Maya.

She grabbed for the to-go mug and swore when the top came off. Carmen giggled, since she'd said a word she tried not to use around her daughter. Maya glared at her, daring her to say anything. After putting the top on firmly, she backed up and into the street. Sighing with relief, she downed a big gulp of coffee. And nearly gagged trying to swallow it.

"What in the h—world did you do to this coffee?"

"Nothing. I did just like you told me."

Cautiously she tried another sip. *Oh, good Lord.* "Did you use a filter?"

"You didn't tell me to. I did just like you said," Carmen repeated smugly. "You never said anything about a filter."

Technically, she hadn't. She still wanted to bang her head against the steering wheel, but since her head already ached, she refrained.

"What are you doing?" Carmen asked a couple of minutes later. "This isn't the way to school."

"It is if you go to the Java Cafe first."

"But Mom—"

"Don't even. I. Am. Getting. Coffee. Period."

"You don't have to be mean," Carmen said, and her voice wavered.

Maya felt like a worm. As she should. She reached over and patted her daughter's knee. "You're right. I'm sorry. I'm tired and I really do need coffee, but I shouldn't have been short with you."

Carmen shrugged. "That's okay. I guess it's kinda sorta my fault, since you said I forgot to tell you." She shot Maya a mischievous glance. "Except, I did tell you," she added, sotto voce.

Maya laughed. "Whatever you say, honey."

The day could only get better, right?

Chapter Twelve

෨෪

"ALL RIGHT, EVERYBODY. Listen up," Tamara Casey said.

They had gathered in the gym, but the custodian had forgotten, or never known, to pull out any stands to sit on, so everyone at the meeting was standing around. By the time it occurred to anyone that they could pull out the bleachers themselves, the meeting was halfway over.

At least, Maya hoped it was.

"There are still donuts and coffee," Tamara continued, waving a hand at a table set up along the wall. "Be sure to get all you want before you leave. We still don't have a firm date for the sale, since we want to collect as much inventory as possible to make as much money as possible. As you know, this money will have a dual purpose. It's earmarked in part for sports uniforms. Not football uniforms, but uniforms for some of the other sports." She smiled. "Yes, we do play other sports at Marietta High." Everyone laughed and she went on. "The other part of the money will be used to start a fund to help critically ill Marietta High School students and their families. It will be an emergency fund to be accessed according to need and how much we have in it, of course. It's going to take several weekends to organize it for maximum benefit."

A woman raised her hand. "Where are we keeping all this stuff?"

"The sale will be in the gym and the high school has given us a couple of empty rooms to utilize."

Tamara was good at this sort of thing, Maya thought. Now she was glad Carmen had volunteered her services, since it was for such a good cause. Someone else asked another question and Maya allowed her mind to wander.

Not for long, though. Her gaze settled on Jack, who she thought looked ridiculously good for this early on a Saturday morning. But he was used to early rising. When he had patients in the hospital, he made rounds daily and from what she gathered, they were often early. He wore a dark tan and brown plaid shirt, along with jeans and running shoes. He *should have* just looked like a normal guy. Unfortunately, he looked good enough to eat.

But that was sure as shooting not in her plans.

Thinking about those plans, Maya only half heard the rest of Tamara's spiel about how to categorize the donations. She started paying attention again just in time to hear hers and Jack's names read off, as one of the pairs picking up items. Anxious to see how he was taking it, she glanced at him to see him giving her that damn sexy smile she kept dreaming about.

Remember the plan, she told herself. *Throwing yourself at him is not part of it.*

ഇൽ

JACK GLANCED AT Maya, sitting beside him on the passenger side of his SUV. While she wasn't hugging the window, neither was she leaning toward him. She looked different from her usual persona. Whether it was her hair hanging straight down her back, her obvious lack of make up, or her clothes, he wasn't sure. She often wore jeans but these jeans had seen better days, and he didn't think the holes in them were a fashion statement. Ditto her sweater, which while it was pretty, was not exactly new. But the kicker was that instead of a pair of those man killer boots she liked to wear, or even a good pair of cowboy boots, she wore running shoes. Running shoes with a hole in one toe.

Today, Maya looked nothing like a model. Not that she looked bad. Being Maya, she couldn't look bad if she tried, but she wasn't the usual put-together professional he was accustomed to seeing.

He liked her this way. She was a woman of many moods, and recently, she'd ranged from mad as hell, to totally indifferent, to maddeningly offhand. He had discovered that her moods fascinated him. With the exception of the 'mad at him and wanted to kick his ass' one, that is. As far as he could tell, her current mood was a cross between grumpy and grumpier.

He made a couple of comments to make sure he was gauging her mood correctly. Judging by her responses—a grunt, nothing, and another grunt—grumpy was spot on.

He gave her space and tried to decide what his next move should be.

After a mostly sleepless night, he'd known that he had to do something to put things right with Maya. His feelings for her weren't a fluke, and the way he felt wasn't because of her undeniable beauty, or even the great sex. In the pre-dawn hours of the morning, he had finally admitted he loved her. He still felt uneasy about the two of them. But not uneasy enough to "talk" about it.

Unfortunately, she wouldn't go for anything less.

"What a coincidence, huh?" he said, breaking the long silence.

She gave him a look that would have withered a lesser man. "I'm tired, I've had too much coffee and I don't want to be here. Must you talk?"

"How about that Tamara putting the two of us together?" he continued, ignoring her complaints. The two of them being together was in no way a coincidence. Early that morning, long before the meeting started, Jack had called Tamara and asked her to make sure he and Maya worked together for the pick up detail. After worming part of the story of their break up out of him, she'd agreed. Needless to say, he hadn't told her much, but he'd thrown himself on her mercy, and softhearted Tamara had quickly approved.

When Maya didn't respond he said, "I was surprised when she called our names. I guess Tamara hasn't heard about your new man."

"What new"—Maya broke off, catching herself, though not in time.

Jack smiled. *Too late, sweetheart,* he thought. *You gave yourself away with that one.* "Ralph, wasn't it?"

"No, it was Rolf."

"Ah, yes. Rolf. How are things going with him?"

"Not too well. I'm not sure we're going to work out," she said airily.

"That makes sense. With him being imaginary and all."

"He's not imaginary," she said indignantly. "Whatever gave you that idea? He's quite real."

"Oh? My mistake."

He said no more until after they'd finished at the next house. "Isn't it funny how things happen for a reason?" he said, chuckling. "You and I breaking things off, you and Rolf getting together, and now you and I working together."

"I'd hardly call it working together," she said to the window. "We're driving around picking up other people's junk."

"One man's junk is another man's treasure," he said, as if he'd thought up the saying himself.

"That's what I like about you, Jack. You have such a fascinating way of repeating platitudes."

He grinned and pulled up to the first house on the list. They loaded up a cane-bottomed chair badly in need of re-caning and refinishing, assorted clothes, and a plastic box full of what appeared to be McDonald's Happy Meal toys. The next house was only a few minutes away from the first. There, they picked up more clothes, more broken down furniture, and a dorm-room sized refrigerator. As they loaded it into the back of his SUV the door fell open, and Maya turned away hastily, coughing and choking. He couldn't blame her. The smell was overwhelmingly noxious. The people had simply left everything on the curb for them to pick up at their convenience, so he didn't have to worry about offending them. "Charity or the dump?" he asked Maya.

"For the refrigerator? The dump. No one could get that dead animal smell out of it."

"No argument here." He drove to the dump before their next pick up, since he really didn't want his vehicle to take on such a disgusting smell. He couldn't guarantee the refrigerator door would stay shut, and besides, he imagined the smell would continue to seep out even if it did.

"Where to next?" he asked Maya, who was looking over the list.

"Since we're out here at the dump, we might as well continue on out of town and pick up from that direction, working our way back toward town." She read off an address and he headed that way.

In the fall, the countryside around Marietta was just turning from hues of green to hues of gold and golden brown. Harvest was nearing and the fields were thick with the season's yield.

This time of year, Jack often thought he'd like ranching as well as his brothers did. But then winter would hit and he'd be very grateful he didn't have to be up before dawn breaking the ice on the frozen water troughs, forking out hay to feed the cattle, taking care of the horses, and everything else running a successful ranching or horse breeding operation required. At those times, he was really glad he worked in town at the hospital or his office. He still had to get up at the crack of dawn sometimes, but there was a lot to be said for a warmer environment.

At the next house, an ancient farmhouse far out in the country, the old rancher and his wife had totally forgotten about promising items for the sale. They wouldn't hear of them leaving without anything, so Jack and Maya not only had to wait on them to scramble around gathering up what could only be called junk, they also had to listen to the garrulous old rancher's monologue on what was wrong with the current generation's morals, manners and addiction to electronics.

The minute they got back in the SUV and Jack had driven part way down the dirt drive, Maya succumbed to the giggles she'd been trying to hold back during the old man's tirade. Jack grinned and kept driving. "Do you get the feeling he's mad at their kids?"

"Ya think?" She wiped her eyes. "The best part was when he kept talking about 'my damn kids and their damn electronics.'"

Jack laughed too. "Yeah, did you notice the satellite dish on his roof? Do you suppose he doesn't consider that electronics?"

"I doubt it. Anything to do with the TV is different, I'm sure." A few minutes later, she said, "You're going the wrong way."

"No, I'm not."

"The next house is south of here. You're heading west."

"I know. I intended to."

"Why?"

He turned off the dirt road and drove around a fallow field, until he reached a big oak tree in another field, this one planted with winter grass. He parked, rolled down the windows, got out and reached in the back to pick up an old blanket before going around to open Maya's door. She didn't move but stared at him perplexed, until he reached in and unbuckled her seatbelt.

"What are you doing?" He stood at the open door waiting for her to get out.

"It's time we talked," Jack said. "I'm not fighting *eau de* stinky dead animal, while we do."

Chapter Thirteen

ಐ೧ಜಿ

MAYA CLIMBED OUT of the truck and stood for a moment, watching Jack. He didn't go to the big tree as she'd expected, but started walking in the green field. He strode along, never looking behind him until he reached a small clearing.

Curious to see what he had to say, she followed.

Jack spread out the blanket and waved a hand. "Let's sit down."

They both did so. "What's that smell?" Maya asked. "It smells like"—she sniffed the air—"it smells like mint."

"It is. Or it was. We're next to a mint field that was harvested last week."

"I'd forgotten they grow mint around here. I bet it's beautiful when the fields are green."

Jack didn't say anything, but seemed fine with allowing her to ramble. After talking for several more minutes, she ran out of mundane conversation. She wasn't sure why she was delaying any kind of real discussion. Wasn't this what she had wanted? "What do we need to talk about?"

"You and me."

Maya raised an eyebrow. "I thought there wasn't a you and

me. Besides, I'm dating someone, remember?"

"I remember." He smiled. "Rolf. Your imaginary new boyfriend."

"What makes you so sure he's imaginary? Don't you think another man could be interested in me?" *No, not when you look like you do today*, she thought.

Jack stretched out on the blanket, propped up on one arm. "Maya, I think any single, uninvolved man who isn't interested in you is either dead or gay. But that isn't the point."

"You're wrong. Rolf is very real." At first, she thought she'd made him up, but then she remembered why his name had come to her so easily. She'd met the wizened little man at dinner in Los Angeles, the week before her fall-in-the-floor fight with Jack. Rolf had been extremely charming, married, and almost twice her age.

"What's the problem, then?"

Sitting cross-legged, she shifted to a more comfortable position. "He's a bit older than me. More than a bit, honestly."

"How much older?"

"Forty-six years. Or maybe forty-seven."

Jack started smiling. "Besides a little difference in age, what's the problem?"

"He's married, and he loves his wife."

"I can see how that would be a problem." He turned over to lie on his back. Deciding what the hell, Maya followed suit. For a few moments, they lay comfortably side by side, watching the clouds, feeling the occasional sharp, cool breeze slide over them.

"Brianna and I used to take a blanket outside and lie on our backs and watch the clouds. It was one of her favorite things to do. She saw so many different things in their shapes. To me they were just clouds. Pretty clouds, but nothing more. Even when she pointed out what the shapes were, I couldn't see them. Usually, anyway."

"Jack?" He turned his head to look at her. "That's the first time you've said Brianna's name to me. In fact, I think it's the first time you've mentioned her period."

He frowned. "No it's not."

She let her silence speak for her.

He put his arm across his forehead. "Maybe you're right," he muttered.

She knew she was, but he had to admit it to himself.

A few moments later, he continued. "After the barbecue Gina said she wanted to talk. I thought it would be about boys. But no, she wanted to talk about Brianna, but she was afraid I'd get mad or upset with her. She said I never talk about her mother."

"Is she right?"

"Sort of. I wouldn't say I never talk about Brianna with Gina, but I don't very often. I don't unless someone else brings her up."

"Why?"

He was quiet for so long she didn't think he would answer. "It makes me sad," he said simply. "I think of everything she's missing, especially with Gina, and I get sad and then I feel like shit, so I try not to talk about her. Sometimes I try not to even think about her. Which also makes me feel like shit."

Maya raised up on her arm and looked at him. He still lay on his back with his eyes covered by his arm. Her heart went out to him. "You miss her. There's nothing wrong with that."

"I know. But since you moved back and we got involved . . . " he hesitated, then added, "I don't think about her as much." He sat up and she sat up too. Taking her hand, he rubbed his thumb over her palm and went on. "All I can think about is you. The way you look, the way you smell, the sound of your voice. I think about being with you, or I wish I were with you, talking to you"—he looked straight into her eyes—"making love to you. Damn, Maya, I can't stop thinking about you."

Her heart beat faster. "And that's a problem because . . . "

He didn't answer directly. "I don't know. I know she's gone. She's been gone for five years, but I've never felt like"—He stopped.

She wondered if he'd ever talked to anyone about his wife's death. Had he shared his grief with anyone? "Never felt like what, Jack?"

"I never wanted to move on until you came back. Hell, I've barely had sex since Brianna died. Until you."

His admission didn't surprise her. It touched her heart. She squeezed his hand. "It's okay to love Brianna. It's okay to miss her. No one is trying to take that from you, Jack. I'm *glad* you loved Brianna so much. That's part of what makes you who you are. You're loyal and loving and that's a good thing." She asked him a question, though she already knew his answer. "After Brianna died, did you go to grief counseling?"

His laugh held no humor. "Are you kidding? I'm a doctor. I know how to deal with death, Maya."

"I'm sure you do. But it's different when someone you love dies."

He let go of her hand and shrugged. "Grief counseling is a good thing, for some people. But I didn't see the point for me. I'm not comfortable laying my feelings out for everyone to see. It's my grief, my business. I handled it."

Maya didn't point out that obviously his handling of the matter left something to be desired. "Do you feel as if you're being disloyal to your wife, because you're enjoying being with me?"

"That would be stupid, wouldn't it? Brianna's dead. It's not as if I had an affair when she was alive."

"No, but maybe that's the problem. Your head knows Brianna is gone, but your heart hasn't quite accepted it."

೭೦೧೪

YOUR HEART HASN'T quite accepted it. Was that the problem? Could it really be that simple? Jack wondered.

"You should talk about her with someone, Jack. A counselor, your brothers, me. But you need to talk to someone about Brianna."

"Oh, that sounds reasonable," he said sarcastically. "I should talk about my dead wife to the woman I've fallen in love with. Yeah, that would be smart." Why the hell was she smiling at him?

"That's the first time you've admitted you're in love with me."

Damn. "That isn't how I wanted to tell you."

Her lips curved upward. "I don't think you wanted to tell me at all. Which is why you panicked when I told you how I felt."

"I didn't panic. Exactly."

Maya laughed. "What would you call it? You became distant. You made excuses not to see me. You absolutely refused to talk when I came over Monday night. You acted as if it would be the worst thing in the world to discuss anything important."

"I still think talking is overrated." He got up to walk around. He didn't feel like stretching out and his legs could only stay so long in the uncomfortable position he'd been sitting in.

Jack felt Maya's hand on his arm and saw she'd gotten up too.

"I'm a good listener." Her eyes were dark gray and filled with compassion.

"You're not going to let this go, are you?"

"What do you think?"

He sighed and picked up the blanket, folding it over his arm. "I think you're a very stubborn woman."

"Right the first time," she said.

They walked back to his SUV. He tossed the blanket in the back seat, but didn't get in. Instead, he opened the tailgate so they could sit on the back end.

"I thought you said the truck was too stinky?"

"It's been aired out long enough." He hoped. They both sat and silence fell. Maya was waiting for him to say something and he didn't have a clue how to start. How did he talk to the woman he was in love with about the woman he had married, lost, and still loved?

"Brianna was crossing the street. Minding her own business, obeying traffic laws—the woman wouldn't have jaywalked on a bet—and the son of a bitch ran the stop sign and hit her. He didn't stop. Hit and run. Some bystanders got the license."

"Did they catch him?"

"Yes. He got the maximum sentence, ten years. Unless he gets early parole, he'll be in for five more years." Jack was glad the man couldn't hurt anyone else, at least until he got out of prison, but it didn't bring Brianna back. Nothing would.

"The doctors operated on her, they did their best to save her, but her injuries were too extensive. She died a few hours later."

"Were you able to talk to her before she died?"

He nodded. "She knew she was dying. Gina and I were both with her when she passed. She talked to us, kissed us both goodbye, and then she was gone."

"I'm glad you two were able to be with her. I'm sure it comforted her to have her family with her. It must have been a comfort to you and Gina as well."

"A comfort?" He shook his head. "No. Nothing about her death was a comfort to me." Once started he couldn't stop. "One moment Brianna was alive and the next she was dead. I couldn't do a damn thing to save her. It wasn't a disease we could fight. I couldn't fix her injuries. My medical training made no difference. I was helpless. I couldn't stop *my wife* from dying."

Maya didn't speak. She held his hand in both of hers and looked at him with such understanding, such compassion, such *love* that his heart turned over. He didn't think he would be so understanding or so compassionate in the same situation.

Talking to Maya hadn't magically made him feel better. But—and he didn't know why—it had helped. He remembered what Brianna had said to him shortly before she died. She'd rested her hand on Gina's head and looked at Jack with all her love in her eyes. "Be happy, Jack. Promise me you'll be happy," she said fiercely. "Don't mourn me forever. It isn't fair to you or to Gina."

He'd soothed her, tried to pretend there was no need for deathbed promises. They'd both known she was dying, but he couldn't say it. As if not speaking of it, would stop it from being true.

"Promise," she'd whispered.

And he had.

Chapter Fourteen

෨ඏ

MAYA DIDN'T KNOW how long they sat on the tailgate of his SUV. Had she been wrong to convince him to talk to her? She didn't think so. From what she'd gathered, most people tiptoed around the subject of his late wife. She wouldn't do that. Brianna was a part of his life and his daughter's life, and she always would be. Maya understood that. Now, Jack had to understand that he could move on with his life without being disloyal. That loving a woman, a living woman, didn't mean he'd forget Brianna and all that had made her special.

She had talked enough. This was something Jack needed to figure out for himself. He knew how she felt. And, she knew that he loved her. So, she would wait.

"Whose field is this?" she asked, an unwelcome thought suddenly occurring to her.

"My brothers'. Why?"

"They might not appreciate us driving into the smack dab middle of their field."

"First off, it's the edge of the field. Second off," he added and smiled, "I'm not going to tell them. Are you?"

"I wouldn't dare. They already don't like me."

"Sure they do. What makes you think they don't like you?"

Maya started singing the song *Heartbreaker*. Jack laughed until he was holding his sides. "You knew what they called you?"

She gave him a pitying look. "I'd have to be pretty stupid not to. Everyone in town knew it, and they all had to tell me. I left two days after graduation and during that time, twenty-five people must have told me what your brothers thought. And said."

"Sorry."

"Why? They were just looking out for you. Wyatt and Dylan, I mean. Most of the others didn't have such a good motive."

"That was then. Wyatt and Dylan don't hate you now."

Maya wasn't sure about that but she didn't argue. Jack looked at his watch. "We'd better get going. We still have several stops to make." He put his hands on her waist to help her out, but instead of putting her down, he boosted her up, wrapped his arms around her and kissed her.

She kissed him back, then pulled back to look down at him. Taking his face in her hands, she smiled at him. "Does this mean we've made up?"

"What do you think?" he asked.

"I think yes," she said, and kissed him.

✂〇✃

"WHAT ARE YOU doing, Dad?" Gina asked him when she came in his study Sunday afternoon. She plopped down in the other easy chair and watched him quizzically.

"Playing the guitar." *And doing a mighty crappy job of it*, Jack thought irritably. Who knew the song would be so hard to play? It hadn't seemed so hard years ago when he first played it.

"You've been playing the guitar a lot lately. What's up with that?"

He struck a sour note and winced. How was he supposed to sing if he couldn't play the melody worth a shit? "Nothing's up. I'm playing the guitar. That's nothing new."

Gina looked at him skeptically. "You haven't played this much, not in a long time. And you haven't sung in like, forever."

She was probably right. It had taken him years after Brianna died to even pick up the guitar, much less play it. But he'd started playing again about a year ago. Recently, he'd started singing a little along with it. Man, was he rusty.

"What's that song? It's pretty. I've never heard it, have I?"

"I don't know." He told her the title. "It's an old one. By Rod Stewart."

She gazed at him blankly. "Who's Rod Steward?"

God, I'm old, he thought. "Never mind."

"It's pretty," she repeated. "But you sound like you're practicing. Why are you practicing?"

"I'm not practicing. I'm just messing around." She didn't say anything, but the look she gave him said loud and clear that she didn't believe him. Her next question made him sure of it.

"Didn't you say you and Ms. Parrish were going out tonight?"

He went back to playing the chords and struck another off-key note. Great, he was getting worse, not better. "Yes."

Gina gave a peal of laughter and clapped her hands together. "You're practicing for Ms. Parrish, aren't you? You're going to sing to her! Woo-hoo, go Dad!"

Damn it, he could feel his face heating. "Are you finished?" he growled.

"Do you want me to help? I can tell you if it sucks or not. You know, like a music critic."

As if he weren't already nervous enough. "Thanks," he said dryly. "I'll take my chances."

"You look nervous. Why are you nervous?"

Jack sighed and put aside the guitar. "Come here," he said, and patted his knee.

Gina sat on it, looped her arms around his neck and said, "Okay, Dad, spill."

"Once upon a time—"

"Dad! What's going on?"

He laughed and told her.

⁊

"I HOPE YOU don't mind going to the Cookhouse again," Jack said after he picked up Maya that evening.

"Why would I mind? The food is great and I love the atmosphere."

"Good. I want to take you to Beck's Place sometime, too. It's more upscale and dressier, and they've got a chef who's great. But I've always had a soft spot for the Cookhouse. And I wanted to bring you here tonight."

When they walked in, they were told there would be a short wait on the table. Jack said they'd wait outside and led her through the doors near the plate glass windows to the porch overlooking the Yellowstone River. Small outdoor lights illuminated the porch, and as the night wasn't totally dark, the river was barely visible. The sound of water flowing shut out other background noise. Rushing water and vegetation mingled in a sharp, crisp smell. There was no one else on the porch. They both stood looking out at the river. Jack put his arm around her and she leaned against him, happy to be with him again.

"I'm glad we're not mad at each other anymore," Maya said.

"I was never mad at you," Jack said.

"That's all right." She looked up at him with a smile. "I was mad enough at you for both of us."

He laughed and kissed her.

The hostess came out and told them their table was ready. To Maya's surprise, she led them to a table toward the middle of the room, closer to the piano, and nowhere near the cozy, romantic one they'd shared the first time they ate at the Cookhouse. "I thought they always seated you at the other table?"

"I asked to sit at a different table tonight. Fly is playing. We can see better from here."

Yes, they could see better, but it was also much more difficult to talk, since the only time they could hear each other well was when Fly took a break. They ordered their drinks and dinner. When their wine arrived, they toasted each other and from then on talking and hearing anything over the piano grew progressively more difficult.

Jack didn't seem to mind that every time either of them raised their voice to be heard, there was a lull in the music. Maya felt as if people were staring, and sneaking a peek around them, she discovered this was true. She began to wonder why in the world anyone would ask to be seated at this table. In fact, she realized as she looked around, their table seemed to be in a special place, particularly close to the piano. After a while, Maya gave up trying to communicate, sat back and ate her food, drank her wine and listened to the music. Jack continued to try to make conversation, not very successfully.

Fly had a large and varied repertoire. He played everything from songs that had been popular in her grandparents' day to current hits. The only genre he didn't play, she noted, was Rap. Probably not Hip Hop either, she suspected.

She couldn't imagine why, but Jack seemed nervous. He wore a baby blue button down dress shirt, jeans and boots. Typical attire for many of the men around Marietta. Though his shirt was open at the neck, she noticed him tugging at it and running a finger underneath the collar, as if it were choking him.

When the waitress asked if they wanted dessert, Maya declined. At this point, all she wanted was to get away from the noise and pray that her headache would subside when she did.

Jack patted her hand and squeezed it. "This is nice, huh?"

Yes, nice and loud, she thought, but she smiled and nodded.

"Are you sure you don't want dessert?" he said loudly.

Maya shook her head, marveling that he could be so clueless. She excused herself to go to the restroom, thinking that surely by the time she returned, he would have paid the check and they could leave.

No such luck. Jack wasn't at the table when she got back.

Chapter Fifteen

ಬಿಂಬ

MAYA SAT DOWN and began searching in her purse for some aspirin. She had just pulled out her emergency supply, gotten out a couple of pills and swallowed them when she heard Fly say, "My friend Jack here has a special request for his lady."

She jerked up her head and stared at the older man. Beside the piano, Jack sat in a chair, holding a guitar and looking extremely uncomfortable.

"Take it away, Jack," Fly said with a grin and a flourish.

Jack said something to Fly and then adjusted the microphone on the stand in front of him. "This"—he started to say, wincing when feedback reverberated throughout the room. A number of the other diners laughed. Jack laughed too, adjusted the mic, blew into it, tested it, and said, "Take two." He looked more relaxed, but Maya's heart had started to pound the moment she heard Fly's first words.

"This is for Maya," Jack said. "It's a song I hope she remembers."

Fly started on the piano, Jack joined in with the guitar, strumming a few recognizable chords before he began to sing

Rod Stewart's version of *Have I Told You Lately That I Love You*.

"*Our*" *song*, Maya thought with her heart melting. *We danced to that song at our high school prom*. Maya blinked back tears and put a hand over her heart, which beat faster by the minute. Never in her life had a man sung a song directly to her. Jack sang and played the guitar in high school, but he'd never done what he was doing tonight. A song. Just for her.

She couldn't have said what the music sounded like to others, but to her the song was perfect. Jack looked at her and sang to her as if she were the only person in the room, the only woman in the world. Her heart turned to total mush.

When the final notes died away, he set the guitar aside and walked directly to her. Her heart slammed against her ribs. She had to remind herself to breathe. He took her hand and pulled her up, then knelt down on one knee in front of her, still holding her hand. She choked up and couldn't have spoken if she tried.

"Maya," he said. A look of consternation came over his face. "Wait a minute." He patted his pockets, pulling something out of his front jeans pocket.

"Oh, you're not—you can't be—are you—" she started to say.

"I hope I am, because if I'm not, I'm making a total fool out of myself," he told her. He cleared his throat and started over, holding a beautiful diamond ring in his hand and looking at her with love. "Maya, have I told you lately that I love you?" he asked.

"Oh, Jack, only you." She laughed and said, "Why yes, you have."

"Maya, will you marry me?"

She nodded, unable to speak for a moment. "Yes," she whispered, then said it again, louder. "Yes, I'll marry you."

Jack slid the ring on her finger, then stood and took her in his arms. "No doubts?" he asked.

"Not a one," she said, and threw her arms around his neck. "Now, kiss me."

He grinned and kissed her, a sweet kiss, full of love and promise.

The restaurant erupted into laughter and applause. The noise faded away as they stared into each other's eyes, and it was only the two of them standing together.

"I love you," she said.

"I love you, too," he told her, and kissed her again.

ᔕᔐ

MAYA AND JACK told both the girls that same evening. Gina had already known of her father's plans to ask Maya to marry him, but Carmen hadn't. However, Gina was over at Carmen's when they came home and when they broke the news, neither of them was surprised. Gina had texted the news to Carmen before she even came over.

"Gina, you should have let Carmen's mother tell her," Jack said.

"Why? We're going to be sisters. I'm not keeping a secret like that from my sister."

"What if she'd said no?" Jack asked her.

Carmen laughed. "No way. Mom must've tried on a gazillion outfits before she decided on which one to wear."

The girls went off and Maya and Jack relaxed on her couch. Maya leaned her head against Jack's shoulder and held out her hand, admiring her engagement ring. It was a gorgeous ring, she thought, simple and elegant. A single round diamond with smaller diamonds encircling it and set in a platinum band, it was exactly what Maya would have chosen.

"How did you manage to get a ring so quickly? We didn't even make up until yesterday."

"I have my ways," he said, raising his eyebrows.

She laughed. "Seriously, Jack. How did you do it?"

"I'm friends with a jeweler over in Bozeman and he had several. I thought I might give you a placeholder until I saw this one. It looked like you to me."

"It's perfect." A tiny bit loose, but she'd wrapped tape around the bottom of the band and would get it sized tomorrow. "When do you want to get married? Christmas?"

"Christmas? Are you kidding? Too far away."

"It can't be Thanksgiving. Carmen's going to Germany to see her father."

"Too far away, anyway. How about next weekend?"

She laughed until she saw he was serious. "Next weekend is Homecoming. Our own daughters wouldn't come if we had it then."

"Oh, I forgot about that."

"I don't know how. Everybody in town's been talking about Homecoming for weeks."

"I had other things on my mind." He swung her legs up over his lap and laid her back on the couch before kissing her soundly. "Such as convincing a beautiful woman named Maya to marry me."

After more discussion and a lot more kissing, they agreed on a date two weeks after Homecoming. Maya and Jack were kissing when Carmen and Gina came in just then. "Gross," they said in unison.

Maya started giggling.

"Get used to it," Jack said, "and go away."

Which of course, they didn't. "Mr.—um—Dr. Gal"— Carmen started to say.

"Hold it right there," Jack said. "We are now Jack and Maya to you two."

"You want me to call you Jack?" Gina asked.

"Very funny. Carmen, I want you to call me Jack."

"And I want you to call me Maya," Maya told Gina.

"We just wanted to know if Dr—I mean, Jack, would play the song for us that he played for my Mom tonight."

Jack groaned. "No. That would be a big fat no."

"Dad, come on. We won't laugh, we promise."

"No. Once is enough."

"Never mind, girls," Maya said with a gurgle of laughter. "I happen to know someone, who caught it on her phone. She just emailed it to me."

Jack turned pale. "Somebody *videoed* it? And is texting it around? You're kidding, right?"

"Afraid not. Technically, she's sending it by email. It's too long for a text message." She picked up her cell phone, pulled up the email, punched a few other buttons and handed the phone to the girls. They immediately started giggling and took it with them into the other room.

"You're a cruel woman, Maya."

She patted his cheek. "Have I told you lately that I love you?"

The End

Home For Good

A Montana Homecoming Story

Terri Reed

Dedication

Writing is never done in a vacuum. Thank you to Jane Porter for asking me to write a story for Montana Born Books. I enjoyed stepping into your world. Thank you to Leah Vale for all your input and advice. And a big thank you to the whole Tule Team for your hard work and support.

Dear Reader,

When I was asked if I wanted to write a story set in the fictional town of Marietta Montana I couldn't resist. I fell in love with the town and the community, both real and fictional.

I hope you enjoyed Joelle and Matt's journey as they realized that what they were longing for was right in front of them.

You can learn more about me and my books at www.terrireed.com.

All my best,
Terri Reed

Prologue

ଘଡ଼

THE DOORS TO Marietta Hospital swooshed open, the sound mimicking Joelle Winslow's panicked exhale. She hesitated on the threshold, the warm sun of a Montana spring at her back. She was too scared to walk forward and too afraid not to. Somewhere inside the walls of this large brick and mortar building lay her father.

A heart attack, she'd been told. One he'd ignored until he'd collapsed. So like him to not seek help.

From the moment she'd received the call, an invisible hand had clamped around her throat. The choking sensation worsened with each mile that brought her closer to home.

She prayed for strength and stepped inside the hospital. Chilled, air-conditioned air prickled her skin. The sedate, hushed voices of those moving through the lobby created an eerie, almost surreal atmosphere. After the harried pace of New York City, her home for the past seven years, the foreign peacefulness made her feel out of place.

But then again, she'd always felt out of place in Montana. At least the second time she came to live in the state.

At the nurses station, she asked for her father's room and

was given directions to the cardiac care unit. Not a fan of enclosed spaces, she bypassed the elevator and took the stairs. She easily found her father's room. For a long second she stared at the white, unremarkable door, bracing herself for what waited on the other side. Would he live? Would he be happy to see her?

She hoped and prayed so.

She knocked lightly before turning the knob and stepping into the room. The beeping of monitors hooked to her father echoed in her head. Her heart constricted, setting off a throbbing pain that radiated outward, making her shake. He lay propped on the bed, his handsome face gaunt. His eyes were closed and she was grateful to have a moment to collect herself as the reality of his condition stole her breath and tears burned her eyes.

She would not cry. He would not like that. Crying was a sign of weakness. She would not be weak. Not in front of him. She pressed the heels of her hands against her eyes, forcing back the tears.

Once she had herself under control, she took a shuddering breath and moved to the side of the bed where a chair had been pulled up, most likely so that Ava, Dad's housekeeper, or Matt could sit with him. She was grateful neither was here now. She wanted this time alone with her dad.

She sat and gathered her father's hand in hers, careful of the IV protruding from the blue vein on the backside of his rough and weathered hand.

Not sure whether he could hear her, she spoke softly, "Please, don't die. I love you, Dad. I wish you knew that." Why was it so easy to say those words with him unconscious?

There was no response, just the beeping of the monitors gauging his heart rate and his breathing. She watched the little squiggly lines of the monitor, mesmerized by the pattern as it began to change, the rhythm increasing along with the beeping of the monitor. Concern flooded her. What was happening?

"Joe?"

Startled, she nearly jumped out of her skin. Her gaze yanked from the monitor to her father to find his gray, unfocused gaze on her.

"I'm here, Dad." She gave him her bravest smile.

"You came."

She hated the stunned note in his tone. Did he really think so little of her? "Yes. As soon as I heard. I'm going to stay until you're better. You are going to get better." He had to get better.

"Follow your dream," his voice came out hoarse and weak, nothing like the strong, bold and larger-than-life man she knew.

"What?" She leaned closer unsure she heard him correctly. He'd never said anything like that to her before.

"Promise me." His fingers curled over hers, his grip surprisingly strong. A good sign, she hoped. "Promise me, you'll follow your dream."

"Of course, Dad. I am." Emotion clogged her throat, increasing the choking sensation. She sucked in a breath, fighting for oxygen. She wanted to tell him about her life, her work. About the things she'd accomplished. There was so much she wanted to say yet the words were held captive inside, as they always were when it came to him.

He licked his lips. "Water." She spied a pitcher on the counter. She moved to pour him a glass and held it to his lips. He drank then turned his head away from her. "Where's Matt?"

She stiffened. "I don't know."

"Go find him." His eyes closed. "I need him."

A fist of pain slammed into her chest. Of course he did. It was always Matt he needed. Never her, his own flesh and blood.

And once again she was being sent away. Why did that hurt so deeply? She should be used to it by now.

On wooden legs, she left the room to do his bidding and

headed to the nurses station at the end of the hall, confident they would know how to reach Matt.

Before she reached her destination, the elevator doors opened and a tall, dark-haired man stepped out.

She froze, struck by the sheer beauty of the man Matt Locke had become. Dressed in jeans and a plaid work shirt, he exuded a rough and tough masculinity that had her female senses jumping to alert mode. She stepped back as if putting more distance between them would temper her involuntary reaction.

His dark eyes widened a fraction before his features settled into wary welcome.

The sudden, loud shrill of an alarm coming from her father's room pulsed through her in shocking waves. Doctors and nurses rushed into the room.

Matt barely spared her a glance as he brushed past her and followed the doctors. She hurried after him, stopping in the doorway. A crushing weight settled on her chest as she watched the doctors work to save her father from crashing.

Were heart attacks contagious? She put a hand over her aching heart.

The heart monitor attached to her father's chest screamed with one long static beep until someone flipped off the switch. The silence descended, deafening in its completeness.

The doctor called her father's time of death.

An all-consuming, soul-deep sorrow gripped Joelle.

She sank to her knees and cried.

Chapter One

❧

Six Months Later

*C*OMING HOME TO *say goodbye.*

Joelle Winslow halted inside the big red barn that housed her late father's prized thoroughbred horses and let her eyes adjust to the dim interior. High wood beams stretched the length of a football field. Bridles hung from hooks at each metal stall door where thousands of dollars of horseflesh munched away oblivious to the turmoil about to be thrust into their lives. Her life.

A frosty breeze coming in from the pasture brought the hint of winter. In a few short weeks, the crisp, dry fall Montana air would give way to piles of snow and drive the inhabitants of Marietta inside. But not today.

On this late September morning, Joelle intended to spend a few moments alone with her horse and her memories one last time before returning to the life she'd made for herself in New York City. If the day went as she planned, she'd be heading back to her apartment on the Upper Westside by nightfall.

Awareness shimmied up her spine. She wasn't alone. She spun around, her gaze landing on the man emerging from the shadows. Matthew Locke.

Her heart hiccupped. She hadn't seen him since the funeral last spring. Even through her fog of grief, she'd noticed how handsome he'd become over the years, from cute teenager to grown man. That day he'd worn a tailored navy suit that had emphasized the width of his shoulders. She'd been surprised by his attire since she'd never seen him wear anything but ranch clothes, like he had on today.

His jeans fit snuggly on his long, lean legs and his wide shoulders filled out the navy flannel shirt with the sleeves rolled up to reveal muscled forearms, liberally covered with dark hair. Her gaze lifted, bypassing his eyes, not ready to see his disapproval, to the well-worn cowboy hat on his head and the tuffs of dark hair peeking out from beneath. She'd always thought he had great hair.

The corner of his mouth twitched, drawing her attention to the hard set of his jaw, emphasizing the unyielding angles and planes of his face. Her heart thumped in her chest, but she ignored the jolt of attraction. This was not the time or the place. Never would be. Not with him.

Her father's pet project.

Her childhood nemesis.

Okay, that probably wasn't a fair moniker. Matt had never done anything overtly mean to her.

Only crushed her tender heart with what he'd said in confidence to his friend, RJ, that summer day long ago. Matt hadn't known she was hiding in the hayloft.

His words had cut her deeply, to the marrow of her being. Even now, in the very place where her world had shifted, the echo of his words rubbed at the raw wound, threatening to reduce her to a quivering mass of hurt.

But none of that mattered now. Or wouldn't soon.

Once she accomplished the task that had brought her back

to Montana, she'd be done with the past. She had a promise to fulfill. A nervous flutter hit her tummy. Matt would not like what she'd come here to do, but she couldn't let him derail her plans. Her father had rarely asked anything of her. He hadn't needed to. He'd had Matt.

But she'd given her father her word, made him a promise and to honor her father's last request hinged on accomplishing today's goal, despite the turmoil she knew it would cause.

Self-consciously, she dragged a stray lock of hair behind her ear. She hadn't taken the time this morning to do more than dress in jeans, a long sleeve t-shirt, her old barn coat and worn boots. She'd barely brushed her hair before throwing the tangled mass into a rubber band at her nape after brushing her teeth. At least her breath would smell minty.

She smiled. "Hello, Matt."

"We weren't expecting you." Matt's smooth voice rubbed at the edges of her frayed nerves.

And just like that the old hurt surfaced, making her back teeth grind together with irritation. "What? I'm not welcome? I do own half the estate."

Her father, bless his soul, left equal shares of the ranch to his only child—Joelle, and to Matt. Even in death her father had made it clear he thought of Matt as the son he had always wanted. Her father hadn't known what to do with a girl.

She scuffed the toe of her riding boot into the dirt, wishing she could scrape away the hurt flooding through her as easily.

"Of course you're welcome here. This is your home." Matt's placating tone inched her annoyance up a notch. "I only meant that I would have driven to Bozeman and picked you up at the airport."

She bit the inside of her lip. When would she learn to control her response, not to mention her tongue? Matt always brought out her claws. Contrite at her jab, she softened her voice. "It was late. I didn't want to bother anyone. I rented a car."

She'd also wanted a way to quickly and easily escape back to New York without having to rely on anyone else. Once she told Matt why she'd returned and what she wanted, he'd probably chase her off the ranch with a pitchfork.

"Ava will be happy to see you."

Affection for her father's housekeeper and cook filled Joelle. Ava had stepped in to be a surrogate grandmother to both Joelle and Matt. She'd been devastated when daddy passed. They all had been. "She stayed on after Daddy's death?"

"Of course she stayed on. As well as Chuck, Randy and Mick."

The hands who had been with the Winslow Estate before she was born.

Guilt for not keeping in contact with those at the ranch pricked her. Her gaze slid away from Matt to stare out the weathered barn doors. The grassy meadow layered in shades of gold glistened with dew in the morning sun. Her decision would affect not only her and Matt, but also everyone who worked on the ranch.

But what choice did she have? She had a promise to keep.

In the horizon, Copper Mountain stood sentinel in all its majestic glory over Paradise Valley.

From the stall to her right Star snickered. The pungent odor of hay crunching beneath his impatient hooves assaulted her senses. The horse could sense her mood. They'd always been in tune to each other. She missed him so much. She wished she could take him with her but the city was no place for a horse. Besides, Star was one of the ranch's best studs. He'd fathered numerous prizewinners. No, Star was an asset of the ranch and needed to remain here. But he was hers for now.

She pulled his tack off the hook next to his stall. Matt

reached to help her. She leveled him with a quick look. "I remember how."

"Just trying to help." He stepped back with his palms up and heaved a sigh.

A familiar sound. One that grated on her like sandpaper.

When she was six her mother had divorced her father and taken her away. For two long years, she begged and pleaded to return home to the Montana ranch. Finally her wish was granted. She'd been ecstatic until she'd come home to find her father had taken in an orphaned boy, four years older than her. She'd been resentful and yet fascinated by the silent kid. He'd had her father's attention so of course she followed him around, hoping and needing to be included. But Matt had been unwilling to let her into his world. He'd tolerated her but kept her at arm's length. Just like her father. Neither man had had much use for her. At least in the end, her father had expressed an interest in her happiness.

After saddling Star, she led him out of the barn with Matt following close behind. She hitched her foot into the stirrup and lifted herself onto Star's strong back.

Matt stroked Star's neck and gazed up at her from beneath the brim of his hat, his expression hid in the shadows. "Be careful. Don't stray beyond the river. There's a cougar roaming the area."

"We'll be fine." It wasn't like she didn't know the lay of the land. The ranch had been her playground as a child. The meadows, the pastures, the river and the mountains beyond. While her dad had been grooming Matt to take over, she'd been allowed to roam unfettered.

She spurred Star into a lope leaving Matt behind. The cool mountain air touched Joelle's face like a caress. Her dark hair escaped from the band holding the strands back. The exhilarating feel of the wind blowing through her hair made her smile.

An unexpected sense of nostalgia hit her, twisting her insides up.

The memory of the first time she'd ever sat a horse and rode by herself begged for her attention. She'd been four and Dad had sat her on a big mare named Kitty. The feeling of power, of pride that her daddy was teaching her how to be like him had expanded within her little girl's chest; she'd thought she might burst.

From that moment on, she'd loved riding. It was the one thing she and her dad had in common. A bittersweet melancholy washed over her. She wished her dad were here now. She wished he could see how successful she was and that she was doing as he'd asked and following her dream.

She spurred Star on. There was a sense of freedom on the back of a horse, feeling the beast's powerful body beneath her, knowing she controlled the animal, yet the unpredictability of the horse sent excitement revving through her veins. She left the main part of the ranch for the north pasture. She stopped to open the gate and heard the thunder of hooves on the ground. Shielding her eyes against the sun, she watched Matt approach on an unfamiliar, beautiful quarter horse with a red coat and white socks.

He pulled up on the reins and slowly walked his horse through the gate. Star blew out a loud huffy sounding noise much like the one Joelle stifled as she re-latched the gate.

She swung back into the saddle. "What are you doing?"

"What I do every morning," he replied. "This is Amber. She's rehabilitating from an injury and needs to be exercised."

So he decides to follow her? "Isn't that why Daddy built the arena?" She nudged Star with her knees to get her walking again.

Matt and Amber fell into step on the left. "We use the arena during the winter months."

Of course she knew that but having him tag along on her ride galled her. She'd wanted to enjoy the peace and quiet of big sky country before heading back to the tall, concrete jungle of skyscrapers that made up New York City.

They rode in companionable, if not comfortable, silence through tall grass damp with the night's dewy kiss. The river running through the valley glistened in the autumn sun, the water glinting like specks of glass floated on the surface. Overhead a hawk circled, the bird's massive wingspan dark against the cloudless baby blue sky.

She leaned back, turning her face upward, watching the bird for a moment before closing her eyes and absorbing the feel, the taste of being in Montana. She breathed in deep the scents of pine and fir trees, enjoying the fresh, crisp air filling her lungs. Imprinting the sensory impressions on her heart. An ache formed in her chest. She'd missed this. And would miss it once she returned to the life she had built in the city.

"Beats the smells of subways in New York, huh?" Matt asked, amusement dancing in his tone.

Her eyes snapped open and her cheeks heated. Sitting upright in the saddle, she slanted him a glance. As far as she knew he'd never left the state of Montana. "What would you know of New York subways?"

"I've been there a time or two. Good way to get around town but I'd take a horse over a subway train any day of the week."

The air left her lungs in a rush. "Recently?"

"I go east at least once a year on ranch business. I take in a Broadway play or a Yankee's game."

She twisted in her seat so she could fully see him. "You've come to the city and not visited me?" Why did that sting? It shouldn't bother her. They weren't family. They weren't even friends. They were…she didn't know what to call them. Him.

He shrugged. "I've thought about it. But I figured you wouldn't welcome the intrusion."

A protest formed but the truth of his words hit her in the middle like a fist, making her swallow her denial. If he'd shown up on her doorstep, she'd have thought he were there to check up on her like she was an errant kid. Daddy hadn't been happy when she'd gone away to school in the Big Apple. And even less happy when she didn't return home after graduation. Though she didn't understand why he was upset, it wasn't like he wanted her underfoot either.

A sneaking suspicion flared deep inside. "What kind of ranch business?"

He looked away but not before she caught the flash of panic in his eyes. He never was a good liar. "You were checking up on me, weren't you?"

"Clark was worried. He wanted to make sure you had everything you needed and lived in a safe place."

She rolled the admission around her mind. Matt had spied on her at her dad's request. She should be angry, yet she couldn't work up any steam. She felt strangely cared for.

At least Dad had died knowing she had a good job.

And now she had a chance to be a partner in a business. If things went according to her plans, that was. So much hung in the balance and she had very little time to make her move. A move that would fulfill her promise to her dad. But she would need Matt's cooperation.

She licked her lips. The bite of guilt made her overly warm in the thick wool jacket. She owed him an apology. For so many things. The frog in his bed the second night after she'd returned home. The orange juice in his cereal—that one never got old. Telling one of the Wright sisters—for the life of her she couldn't remember which sister—he had a fungus right before he asked her to prom.

Joelle wasn't sure if Matt ever knew why the girl had turned him down. Not one of Joelle's finer moments. At the time she'd been so mad at Daddy for giving Matt a new saddle and telling her she hadn't earned one. Her fourteen-year-old self hadn't understood why he'd received a gift and she hadn't. But the saddle hadn't been a gift but recompense for taking on so much of the everyday labor of the ranch.

While she'd been a pampered child with no work ethic. A sad fact of reality that had been a hard lesson to learn those first few months out of college. Not that Daddy had given her a chance to develop a work ethic. Around the ranch, her job was to stay out of the way.

Go do your homework had been Daddy's mantra.

And she had, earning herself a 4.0 and a wallop of a scholarship to one of the best art schools in the country. Even that hadn't impressed her father.

But pride kept the words of apology from spilling out. Instead, she settled for a mediocre olive branch. "Next time you come to New York, please stop by. I'll take you to one of the best Italian restaurants this side of the Atlantic."

He tilted his Stetson back. "Do they have Carbonara?"

She laughed. "Yes, they do. Though that seems a little fancy for you. I remember when I made Zuccati for you and Dad. It didn't go over well." Few of her attempts to cook and impress had gone over well.

He wrinkled his nose. "Squash isn't a favorite, but who can resist anything with bacon in it?"

The gesture took her back to their childhood. She could always tell when he didn't like something. But he was always too polite to come out and say so. Unfamiliar affection spread through her chest. "True that."

His answering grin nearly knocked her out of her saddle. She liked the way his eyes crinkled at the corners. He had really nice eyes when he wasn't mad at her. Dark and mysterious, yet open and inviting. Why hadn't she ever noticed that before? Probably because she usually only brought out his anger. And he hers.

This moment of camaraderie was strange and comfortable all at the same time.

"Joe? Why did you come home unannounced? That's not like you."

Her heart squeezed tight at the nickname. Her dad was the only one she ever let get away with shortening her name. A reminder of his unrequited desire for a son.

Not ready to answer his question, she tugged the rein to the right, turning Star back toward the ranch. Matt followed suit. "I'll race you back."

"No." Matt's stern tone brought her up short.

She halted Star but kept her gaze on the sprawling estate in the distance. The world-class horse barn and indoor arena stood off to the left of the main house and to the right a bunkhouse for the year-round hands and an old pole barn, now used for storage.

The two-story farmhouse, built circa 1906, evoked memories. Some good. Some not-so-good.

After Mom had left, ripping Joelle away from her dad and settling them in California, Dad had remodeled the farmhouse. He'd gotten rid of the white siding and had the outside redone in tones of brown to blend in with the sweeping landscape. Inside was up to date and modern. Ironically, Dad had put in all the things Mom had wanted to do—state-of-the-art kitchen, a peek-a-boo fireplace in the master, all new bathroom fixtures.

To this day Mom complained, even though she'd started a new life in San Francisco and didn't regret leaving Montana. But Joelle hadn't like the city and had made Mom's life miserable until she finally relented two years later and allowed Joelle to return to the ranch. To find her dad had found himself a son. And then to realize a few years later how her being there hadn't been wanted by anyone.

"Hey, talk to me," Matt said, concern lacing his tone.

A flicker of surprise prompted her to look his way.

"Are you okay?" His brows pulled together. "You're not sick or something, are you?"

Empathy formed a lump in her throat. He'd lost so many people in his life. She hadn't meant to make him worry. Hadn't even realized he would worry over her. She swallowed hard. "No. Nothing like that."

She needed to tell him now. *Stop hesitating.* Get it over with like ripping a bandage off. "I came home because—" *Spit it out already.* "I have this wonderful, once-in-a-lifetime opportunity to buy into a jewelry design company."

His face cleared. He stared at her with no visible emotion. "How nice for you."

"It will be." She wanted to make him understand how much this meant to her. Make him understand that she would be fulfilling the promise she made to her dad. "We have a space in SoHo, which is a part of the city south of Houston Street. It's very trendy, but one of my partners had a connection through a friend, and we can have the place for a steal. Then there's the equipment we'll need and the supplies and such." She was rambling but couldn't seem to stop herself. And the more she talked the more distant his expression became. "So there's some risk involved, but I firmly believe our business will do well. We have a business plan and vendors as well as wholesalers lined up and orders already coming in for some of our test designs."

"I see." He took off his hat and swiped a hand through his thick, dark hair. Her gaze followed the tracks left by his fingers. "What does this have to do with you coming home?"

She met his gaze. The wariness there made her tongue stick to the roof of her mouth. She forced out the words that she knew would change things forever. "I want to sell the ranch."

Chapter Two

ഇ൚

M ATT'S CHEST CONSTRICTED so tight, he thought he might suffer a heart attack. The horse beneath him shifted as if sensing his upset.

Sell? Joelle wanted to sell the ranch? What would he have if they sold? Nothing. And he'd have no one. Pain knifed through him. Pain mixed with anger. His fist tightened on the smooth-edged pummel of his saddle.

Now her impromptu visit made sense. She had an agenda. One that would rip the rug out from under him and everyone else on the ranch.

He clamped his teeth together to keep from saying something he might regret. He needed a moment to gather his thoughts as Clark had taught him.

Never react until you take a moment to think, he'd say.

Taking a deep breath, Matt surveyed the home he'd come to love since arriving seventeen years ago. The land of rolling hills, wide-open spaces, and the buildings that held treasured memories. The only place he'd felt like he belonged since a drunk driver killed his parents'.

Three months after that fateful, tragic night, Clark Winslow showed up at the fourth foster care home and whisked twelve-year-old Matt away to live with him on his ranch. Clark and Matt's dad had been best pals as kids and Clark had fought the courts to gain custody of his best friend's orphaned son.

To Matt, who'd spent the first twelve years of his life in Montana's largest city of Billings, the ranch was an adventure. And a healing place for a traumatized kid whose whole world had been turned upside down in the blink of an eye.

Clark had taken Matt under his wing, helped him to process his parents death, to come to terms with the anger and unfairness of life. Learning from Clark all there was to know about breeding and rehabilitating horses had given Matt purpose, focus. He'd devoted every moment to the ranch since the day he'd stepped on to the property. He had grown to love Clark like a second father. And had mourned Clark's death six months ago.

For the second time in his life, Matt had buried a parent.

And now Clark's only daughter wanted to destroy his legacy.

One last slap in the face for the man who'd provided for her, loved her and cherished her, despite her wild and unruly ways. As her father's right-hand man, Matt knew the relationship between father and daughter had been a difficult one. Sometimes down-right testy. He wouldn't let her sell the ranch. He couldn't.

Matt slid his gaze to the beautiful woman sitting on the back of the big roan, a horse nearly as unruly and wild as the rider. He didn't want to, but he couldn't ignore the fact she'd grown into a beauty that had only been hinted at during her gangly teen years. She'd filled out in all the right places and her face was fuller, softer. Dark lashes trimmed her pretty blue eyes and a rosy hue from the cool air brightened her cheeks. Her thick dark hair now hung loose down her back and shone in the bright morning sun.

She watched him with a wary and expectant look, which made his stomach burn.

Joelle had been a burr under Matt's saddle since the moment

they'd met.

Four months after Matt came to live on the ranch, this little girl with long dark pigtails, arrived in a blur of pink bows and ribbons.

Clark's ex-wife had sent Joelle back to live with him. For good.

And Joelle had not taken kindly to finding an intruder in her home. Matt didn't need a degree in psychology to know she viewed him as competition for her father's affection. At first, she'd followed Matt around like a lost puppy. He couldn't go anywhere or do anything without her tagging along, getting in the way. His shadow, he'd call her. She'd done everything she could to make Matt's life miserable. No doubt in the hope he'd go away.

He'd learned quickly to stay out of her way. To engage as little as possible and to turn the other cheek as the Good Book advised. Which, on occasion, had been difficult. Especially when she messed with his things or told potential dates he had a disease.

He couldn't say he'd been sorry to see her go off to college. Life on the ranch had settled into a calm and peaceful place. Her infrequent visits, though welcome by everyone on the ranch, caused a whirlwind of chaos.

"I'm sorry to spring this on you so suddenly, but this oppor-tunity came up so quickly and I need to move on it," she said.

"This is a big decision, Joelle," he managed to reply in a relatively civil tone. "One that can't be made lightly."

"I know that."

Her tight tone was tinged with something else. Desperation? What did she have to feel desperate about? Joelle always succeeded at everything she attempted. She was smart and talented.

"It is a big decision," she went on. "My decision. I'm doing what I promised Dad I would."

No way would Clark have told her to sell. "And what exactly is that?"

"Follow my dream. He made me promise before…" She looked away, blinking rapidly.

A piercing ache throbbed in Matt's chest. He rubbed a hand over his jaw. Joelle had been the last one to talk to Clark before his heart gave out. In some ways, Matt suspected Clark had hung on to life long enough to see her before passing on. Matt had a hard time believing Clark had meant for her to sell her half of the ranch to fulfill her dreams.

"I'm only telling you first as a courtesy," Joelle pressed, having regained her composure. "I could have gone straight to Dad's lawyer."

He arched a brow and held onto his temper with both reins. "We'll need to talk to Ren Fletcher. Find out the exact terms of your father's will."

Matt had been honored and humbled to find out he'd been gifted with half of the estate. Never in his imagining had he considered Joelle wouldn't want the ranch. Or rather that she would want to take her half of their inheritance out in cash.

"You could buy me out," she said. "Then nothing changes."

Like he had that kind of money on hand. Not.

"You'll own everything and I can buy into my new business. My new life. Please, don't fight me on this. Promise, you won't fight me."

Her words hurt like the sharp tips of a dart. He didn't understand her. Why would anyone want to live anywhere else except here if they could? This was their home. One day she might want to come back. He had to preserve Clark's legacy. He'd also promised Clark he'd watch out for Joelle. Make sure she never wanted for anything. Clark had loved his daughter, he just hadn't known how to relate to her.

"I can't make you that promise." He nudged Amber and started her walking back to the stables. Behind him he knew Joelle and Star followed.

After settling Amber back in her paddock, Matt stalked to the house, stripped off his boots and went to Clark's office, now Matt's domain. He sat in the large captain's chair behind the mahogany desk and grabbed the landline phone to dial Clark's lawyer, Ren Fletcher.

Fifteen minutes later, Matt hung up. With a heavy heart, he ran his fingers through his hair. According to Ren the law would stand behind Joelle if she insisted on selling. She'd need to file a property partition with the courts and the court would then require the estate to be sold and the proceeds divided. Unless Matt could buy out her interest or talk her out of selling. The latter wouldn't be easy, but he didn't have the kind of money necessary to buy her share and wasn't sure he'd qualify for a loan.

"Was that Ren?"

Matt jerked his gaze to where Joelle hovered inside the office door. She'd shed her barn coat and boots. She'd plaited her hair into two braids. For a moment he was transported back to their youth. Sadness whispered through him.

How many times had she entered the office while Matt and Clark sat at the desk, Clark teaching Matt the ins and outs of running the ranch's books? Matt would look up to see Joelle hovering, witness the wistful look on her face until she realized he was watching her. Then her eyes would darken and her chin would jut out. She would stomp in demanding something or other. A new doll, a new dress and new car. Anything to make Clark take notice of her.

But Clark was gone now. And Joelle was ready to leave the ranch behind for good. Matt couldn't let that happen. For better or worse, this was her home. His home. He nodded.

"What did he say?" she asked.

"We have a meeting with him in two hours."

Her eyebrows twitched. "Okay. I need to shower and change. I'll meet you there."

"We can ride together."

"I'll be leaving straight from there for Bozeman. My flight leaves at six p.m."

So typical of Joelle. Drop a bomb then flee. "This isn't going to be resolved in one afternoon. Ren said the first step is to have the property appraised."

"How long will that take?"

"Days, weeks." He shrugged. "I don't know. Then you'll have to file something called a partition lawsuit."

Her eyes widened. "A lawsuit? Come on, can't we handle this between the two of us like rational adults."

He pressed his lips together to keep from smiling. Rational and adult were two words he wouldn't normally use when describing her. Some part of him knew that wasn't fair. She'd grown up. She was a college graduate with a degree and a career. "How much money do you need to invest into this business and by when?"

"Five hundred thousand up front by next Tuesday or they'll look for another investor." Her blue eyes bore into him. "I want this, Matt. You of all people should understand the importance of honoring the promise I made to my dad."

"I do understand." Clark had been the kind of man that inspired loyalty. Matt was glad to know Joelle felt some sense of allegiance to her father. But was selling the ranch the only way? "We could pull that much out of the equity."

Her unwavering stare sent unease creeping down his spine. He had a feeling that wasn't a solution she agreed with.

"I want to sell my half interest."

His throat closed. The knife in his chest twisted. He swallowed several times before he managed to speak. "Why? This is your home. One day you may want to return for good."

She shook her head, her chin jutting up in that stubborn way he remembered all too well.

Irritation itched through him like a burlap sack sliding across his skin. "You're not thinking clearly. Obviously, you're still grieving. You need more time."

"Don't patronize me." Her gaze narrowed. "I don't need more time. I'll contact a real estate agent and see about an appraisal. In the meantime, I'll take the money from the equity. I'm sure Ren can make that happen."

He scrambled for a reason to keep her here so he'd have time to convince her not to sell. "It's Homecoming week. The Marietta Grizzlies have been on a winning streak. We have a really good chance of winning the big game against Livingston on Friday. This would be a good opportunity for you to see your friends in person. I know Andie McGregor was sad you didn't make it home for her wedding in August."

Indecision warred in her eyes. Her bottom teeth tugged on her lip. The zing of desire rippled through his system, catching him off-guard. His pulse skittered. His mouth went dry.

Whoa! No. So inappropriate. This was Joelle. Clark's daughter. No way would Matt disrespect Clark's memory by being attracted to Joelle. He wasn't even sure he liked her.

His gaze lifted to meet her eyes. The arrested, questioning look on her face sent heat climbing up his neck. No way could she tell what he'd been thinking. Could she? "The alumni dinner is on Saturday."

She blew out a breath. "I'll give you until Monday to come up with an alternate plan. Otherwise, I'm filing the lawsuit."

"Does that mean you'll stick around?"

After a hair's breadth of hesitation, she nodded and then fled.

Matt dropped back into the chair. Great. Unless a miracle happened and he came into a windfall, he had five days to convince Joelle she was making a mistake by selling.

☙☙☙

STUPID, STUPID. WHY had she agreed to stay?

Because for a moment she'd found herself rendered mindless by the attraction crackling between them like a live electric current.

Unsettled and overwhelmed, she flung herself face down on her bed. The frilly pink ruffles tinkled her nose.

She didn't want to stay. Every second in this house sent slivers of pain sliding deep into her heart. Everywhere she looked were memories waiting to assault her.

And she certainly didn't want to be attracted to Matt. He was a constant reminder that she was a disappointment to her father. She resented Matt and wasn't even sure she liked him. Honestly, she hardly knew him. And didn't want to. She'd made her choice one summer day. No longer would she trail behind him like a puppy, no longer would she yearn for his acceptance. Not when she knew he wished she hadn't come home. That her father hadn't wanted to take her back when her mother had insisted.

Poor little unwanted Joelle, a mocking voice inside her head taunted.

Bile rose to make her gag.

Flipping over, she stared at the ceiling. Unicorns danced from a mobile hanging overhead. A keepsake from one of the numerous camps her father had shipped her off to during the summers.

A knock sounded at the door.

She popped up to sit on the edge of the full-sized bed.

"Yes?"

The door opened and Ava stepped inside, her face beaming. Her graying hair was trimmed short in a boyish style that made the diminutive woman appear like a pixie. She wore an apron over a plaid flannel shirt and dark denim jeans. Small horseshoe-shaped earrings swung from her lobes. The Christmas gift Joelle had sent last year. "It's true, you're home."

A rush of love flooded Joelle. With a small cry of joy, she went into the older woman's arms. The hug was warm and comforting. Joelle inhaled the scent of vanilla clinging to her. "You're making French toast."

Ava laughed and pulled back to look at Joelle. "I am. Hungry?"

"Starved."

"Get cleaned up and come on down," Ava said. "I can't wait to hear what you've been up to."

Her words pierced holes in Joelle's momentary happiness. Knowing she needed to tell Ava before she heard the news from Matt, Joelle took Ava's hands in hers and led her to the bed where they both sat. Shoring up her courage, Joelle told Ava why she'd returned. "I made Dad a promise. I know this is a risk, but I have to take the chance. I might not get another one like this."

Ava listened quietly until Joelle was done. "You're taking a chance with all of our lives."

Scored to the quick by guilt, Joelle countered, "Not if Matt buys my interest, then things will stay the same."

Ava touched Joelle's cheek. "Change is a natural part of life, dear."

Agitated butterflies danced in Joelle's tummy. "You don't think I should do this?"

She was quiet for a moment. "I want you to be happy. That's all anyone of us have ever wanted."

Frowning, Joelle realized the full extent of what giving up

her half of the inheritance would mean. "If Matt can't buy me out, you could come to New York with me."

"We'll see." Ava stood. "I know you'll make the right decision. And we'll honor whatever that decision is. Who knows, maybe the new owners will want to keep everyone on. Either way, we'll be okay. You do what you need to do." She kissed Joelle's check then headed for the door. "Come down when you're ready to eat."

A dull ache took up residence in the middle of Joelle's chest. She rubbed at the spot. Ava had always been so kind and supportive. Joelle thought it might be easier to deal with anger than acceptance. She wouldn't feel as guilty if she had to fight for her dream.

This was turning out to be harder than Joelle had imagined. But she had to go through with her plan to buy into this business. She wanted to be a success. She wanted to finally make her father proud of her.

ജാരു

THREE HOURS AND forty minutes later, Matt and Joelle left Ren Fletcher's law office on the corner of Third and Main Streets in downtown Marietta. The crisp fall air did little to alleviate the sick feeling settling in the pit of Matt's gut. Though Ren had prepared him during their phone call, knowing that he had little to no say in what happened to the estate left him queasy.

The lawyer had laid out their options—Joelle could file a property partition lawsuit in which case the courts would require all assets of the estate to be sold and divided. Or they could form an LLC partnership, at which point, Matt or another party could buy out Joelle's interest in the ranch.

He didn't like either option. He wanted things to remain as they were. But that wasn't realistic. And he was nothing, if not realistic.

"If we hurry we can make it to the bank before lunchtime." Ren had agreed that taking the money Joelle needed now from the equity was feasible and would be factored in when the time came to sell. In any case, it would take a few days for all the paperwork to be processed.

"Great." Joelle stopped to zip up her red leather jacket. She'd changed after their ride into black pants tucked into knee high black boots and a starched white blouse. The red leather belt at her waist matched her jacket. The ornate silver buckle matched the silver necklace peeking through the open V of her top. Her dark hair had been caught at her nape with a silver barrette that also matched the buckle and necklace. Even her earrings coordinated.

His gaze went back to the pendant nestled against her creamy skin. "Are those your designs?"

She touched the necklace. "Yes."

Impressive. "I like them."

Her cheeks pinkened. "Thanks."

She acted as if a compliment from him shocked her. Surely, he'd paid her compliments before. Hadn't he? Matt adjusted his hat and walked down Main Street toward the brick building of the First Bank of Marietta where Clark had done all his banking.

"Oh, look." Joelle stopped in front of the Copper Mountain Chocolate store. "Is this Sage's place? Callan told me her sister had hung up her spurs to become a chocolatier."

Sage Carrigan had been a barrel racer until she'd decided to turn her passion for chocolate into a business. "You keep in touch with Callan?"

Joelle pressed her nose against the glass to peer inside. "Yep. We Facebook. Wow, look at those truffles."

"Sage's business is booming. People come from all over for her chocolates. In fact, Marietta is becoming more and more a tourist destination for people passing through to Yellowstone. There are several local artisans taking up shop." His gaze snagged on her necklace again, giving him an idea. "Let's cross the street."

"But the bank's on this side."

"True, but there's someone I want you to meet." He took her elbow and propelled her across Main to the gift store run by Sabrina Kelly.

"Cute name," Joelle commented as they entered the shop called When I Was In Paradise…

Matt spied Sabrina at the back of the store stocking a shelf with packaged handmade gingerbread pumpkins from the Copper Mountain Gingerbread and Dessert Factory. "Hey, Sabrina."

The thirty-something glanced up with a smile. "Hi, Matt." Her gaze darted to Joelle and back. "What can I do for you?"

"I wanted to introduce you to Joelle Winslow."

Sabrina's gaze widened. "Oh. Hello." The two women shook hands. "My mom talked highly of your father. I was sorry to hear of his passing."

"Thank you," Joelle said. "Who's your mom?"

"Was Esther Kelly. Mom passed a few years ago." Sabrina gestured to the shop. "I inherited this from her."

"Ah. I'm sorry for your loss. It's a nice store." Joelle turned curious eyes to Matt.

"Joelle makes jewelry," Matt stated. He turned his attention to Sabrina "She's talented. I was thinking that you might be interested in selling some of her work here." He pointed to Joelle's neck. "These are her designs."

Joelle stared at Matt like he'd grown a third head. He gave her an encouraging nod.

Sabrina stepped closer to inspect Joelle's accessories. "You made the whole set?"

Joelle's smile was tight but Matt saw the pride in her gaze. "Yes, I did."

"They are lovely," Sabrina stated with warm sincerity. "I would definitely like to see more. Do you have a catalogue?"

The flare of surprise lit up Joelle's eyes before she tucked her arm through Matt's. "Not yet. But I will. We really must be going. It was nice meeting you, Sabrina."

Matt had no choice but to follow Joelle as she practically dragged him from the gift shop. Once they were outside she let go.

Planting her hands on her hips, she said, "What was that about?"

"Your jewelry screams Montana," he replied. "Seems like Marietta would be the best place to be selling your pieces."

She touched the silver pendant at her neck. "This isn't remotely western. This is Celtic."

"It would sell well here just the same," he insisted. "Sabrina had been impressed. I'm sure the other shops in town would, as well."

She frowned. "Selling in boutiques isn't in our business plan. We hope to be in major retailers across the country."

"Assembly style? Do you really want everyone wearing the same design?" That didn't sound at all like Joelle. "Where's the uniqueness? The specialness of your work?"

Her blue eyes darkened. "You don't know what you're talking about," she huffed and strode away.

Maybe not, but he'd seen the spark of interest.

And noted her defensiveness.

Hope bloomed within his chest. Maybe she wasn't as set on her path as she wanted him to believe. Could he set her on a new path? One that included keeping the ranch? If memories and her father's legacy wouldn't do it, maybe her passion for jewelry could.

Chapter Three

ଚ୦ଓ

T HE TRIP TO the bank was both a success and a failure for Joelle. Yes, she could take out a line of credit against the equity on the ranch, however doing so would put the estate in a precarious position and the paperwork wouldn't be completed until next week. It seemed her dad had already taken out a line of credit to build the new arena and to put her through college. Another reason for her to feel guilty. Great.

And she wasn't sure how she felt about being dragged into the gift shop, presented to the owner and then put on the spot to promote her jewelry designs. Though Sabrina Kelly had liked the silver set Joelle had on, Joelle wasn't convinced her pieces would sell well in Marietta. To her they were more urban and too fashionable for the sleepy valley town.

However, she could hear her college mentor Jason Dixon's voice in her head saying, "Never overlook an opportunity."

Maybe there was a market for her pieces here in Marietta. Hmmm. She'd have to run that by her partners.

But what stunned her the most was Matt's encouragement. That he'd even noticed what she had on had been a surprise. She hadn't taken him as a man who paid attention to women's fashion accessories. During their youth, he hadn't taken an interest in anything she had done. Why was he doing so now?

Was this some ploy to change her mind about selling her share of the ranch?

Their next stop after the bank was Styles Realty Company. Elinor Styles, the owner, greeted them with a smile that grew wider upon learning they might be selling.

"We can do an appraisal for you early next week." She waved over a well-dressed man in his early thirties. "This is Tod, he'll be handling your account." She quickly explained the situation to him.

Tod's gaze traveled up and down Joelle, lingering at her chest before moving to her face. "Hello, it will be my pleasure to help you."

Joelle nearly laughed at the sleazy attempt at flirting with her. She'd had her fair share of comeons over the years. A single woman in New York City learned quickly how to shoot down unwanted, would-be suitors.

"You'll be dealing with me," Matt cut in, his voice sharp. He stepped closer to Joelle.

Interesting. Matt wasn't normally so protective of her.

There was no mistaking the irritation flashing in Tod's eyes before a professional smile slipped into place. "Of course, Mr. Locke. I'll check my schedule for next week and call you with a time."

"That's fine," Matt said as he slipped a hand to the low of Joelle's back, clearly staking a claim. "I'll expect your call. Good day." With that Matt propelled Joelle out the front door and down the sidewalk.

Curious, she said, "You don't like Tod Styles much, do you?"

"No, not at all. He cheated on Chelsea Collier back when they were engaged."

"Ah. I see." And she did. Matt was an honorable man who kept his word. Just like her dad. To both men, a man who would cheat on his woman was a man who wouldn't think twice about cheating in other areas of his life. A man not to be trusted. "Is there another real estate agent in town we could use?"

"It will be fine. I trust Elinor. Just not her son." He stopped in front of the Main Street Diner. "Are you hungry?"

"No." She patted her tummy. "I ate more than my fair share of French toast this morning."

He glanced inside. Joelle followed his gaze to the red-haired woman working behind the counter. She was very pretty. She'd heard he had a thing going on with some woman named Rose Hart, a waitress at the diner in town. In a community as small as Marietta, everyone knew everyone else's business and Joelle's high school friends kept her informed of the local gossip through Facebook.

If all went as Joelle planned then Matt could build a new family with Rose.

A perplexing knot formed in her gut. Why on earth would the thought of Matt starting a family bother her?

Joelle swallowed down the unpleasant taste of confusion, which suddenly appeared in her mouth. "You go ahead. I'll just wander a bit."

He gave her a quick smile. With his hand on the diner's door, he paused to say, "Eve Oliver works at the Jave Café."

Joelle perked up. She hadn't seen Eve since graduation. "Thanks. I'll head that way."

They parted. Matt ducked into the diner. Joelle watched him sit at the counter. The pretty woman said something to him and he laughed.

A tightness banded across Joelle's chest. She forced herself to turn away and make her feet move. She didn't care whom Matt saw or what he did. She would be leaving in a few days. She was so ready to start her new life. Ready to follow her dream. Without ties to the ranch, or Matt.

⁊❦

"SOUNDS LIKE YOU'VE had a stressful day," Rose commented, her amber-colored eyes regarding Matt with a mix of concern and compassion.

He ran a hand through his hair. He'd removed his hat while eating as he'd been taught by Clark, and the hat occupied the seat next to him. "I can't lose the ranch, Rose. It's all that's left of Clark."

"Not to mention your home," she said quietly.

"Right." He wrapped his hand around the mug of coffee she'd set in front of him while ignoring the BLT he'd ordered. He couldn't bring himself to eat. His stomach was tied up in knots.

The whole morning, from the moment he'd realized why Joelle was home had stretched his nerves taut like fence wire. The pressure was making his head pound.

"If you had the money to buy her out, would you?"

"Yeah, sure. But I don't."

"You could take out a loan against your half," she suggested.

"That's true," he said. "But then I'd owe the bank. I don't take much of an income from the estate. I never saw the need before. Maybe if I had, I'd have a nest egg with which to buy out Joelle."

"You should tell her how you feel. Tell her how much the ranch means to you and what selling will do to you."

"I'm sure she knows."

"Probably. But you aren't exactly a master at communication." She softened the criticism with a smile.

He grunted in acknowledgement and grinned.

Rose rolled her eyes and said, "Maybe she needs to hear it from your lips rather than infer the importance of the ranch."

"Yeah, you could be right."

She gestured to his untouched plate. "You want me to wrap that up for you?"

"Please."

Rose took his plate and disappeared in back. She was such a sweet woman. Thoughtful, kind. Even-keeled. Nothing like Joelle.

With Rose, Matt felt calm. She was easy to be around. No drama, no hysterics. They had a great deal in common. Granted they'd only been dating for three months and were still in the beginning phase of a new relationship, but he had a good feeling about where things were headed.

Behind him, the ding of the bell over the front door signaled a new customer. From a booth to his left he heard a female gasp. Then a squeal of delight. He turned to see Callan Carrigan slide out from the booth and pounce on Joelle, who'd entered the diner.

The two women hugged. Joelle's happy smile made Matt's breath catch the way it did when he witnessed the morning sun exploding over the eastern horizon.

"I take it those two are friends?" Rose said, drawing Matt's attention.

"Yes. Kind of odd, considering they are as opposite as could be." Callan, a petite brunette, was as tough as they came. A tomboy to Joelle's girly-girl ways.

"Opposites attract. Even in friendships."

"I guess." His gaze strayed back to Joelle. Her blue eyes sparkled. She glanced his way and winked, catching him off-guard. What was that about?

He swiveled back to face Rose and found her watching him. He self-conscientiously changed the subject. "So, are you planning on going to the Homecoming game Friday night?"

She hesitated. "Maybe. We'll see."

"Order up," the cook called out.

"Excuse me." Rose walked away to pick up several plates and deliver them across the room.

Joelle slid onto the empty seat beside him. "That was fun."

"Seeing Callan?"

"Yes, especially after seeing Eve, too. Callan had to get back to the Circle C. But we're going to get together while I'm home."

"That's good to hear. Just so you know, she likes to hang out at Grey's Saloon. She's become a pool shark." Maybe he could enlist Callan's help in convincing Joelle not to sell.

A gleam entered her blue eyes. "Ohhh. I've never been in there. Or the Wolf's Den, for that matter."

Of course not, she'd been only eighteen when she left Marietta. And when she came home while Clark was alive she'd stayed on the ranch, not in town. "The Wolf's Den is not a place for you."

Her eyes narrowed. "Says who? You're not the boss of me."

His mouth twitched. "I'm not trying to boss you. Just giving you some friendly advice. The place can be rough."

Joelle sniffed. "We'll see."

Rose stopped in front of them. "Hey, Matty, did you want some pie?"

He inwardly cringed at the nickname. He hadn't had the heart to ask Rose not to use the moniker. Joelle's chuckle chafed.

"Yeah, Matty, pie?" Joelle mocked. Slanting her an irritated glance, he said, "Stop." Her eyebrows inched upward. "What?"

Shifting his attention to Rose, he said, "Rose, this is Joelle. Joelle, Rose."

"Nice to meet you," Rose said, with utmost politeness.

"Likewise," Joelle said, her voice devoid of any inflection.

Matt squirmed in his seat, inexplicably uncomfortable with

these two women meeting. "I'll take a piece."

"Me, too," Joelle piped up.

With a nod, Rose dished out two slices and set them on the counter in front of Matt and Joelle. "I made the pie this morning."

Matt stared at the red goo oozing from the sides of a flakey crust. Cherries. Not his favorite. Not even on his list of doable fruit. Not after the summer he'd gorged himself on the tart, round orbs and got so sick he thought he'd die.

He picked up his fork. For Rose...

"Uh-oh, "Joelle said. "Matty doesn't like cherries."

Her singsongy voice ratcheted his annoyance. He nudged her with his elbow. "It's fine."

She gave him a dubious look. "Since when?"

"I didn't know," Rose said and reached for his plate.

He held on to the side of the plate, hating to see the shuttered look in Rose's eyes. "It's okay. I'll eat the pie. You made it, so it has to be good."

She tugged. "You don't have to."

"But I want to," he insisted and gave the plate a pull. Too hard.

The slice of pie slipped off the plate and landed in a heap on his lap.

"Ooops," Joelle said. "But that was very entertaining." She took a forkful of pie off her plate and made a big show of eating the gooey mess.

Compelled by some unseen force that wanted to show up Joelle, he stabbed his fork in the glob of pie soaking his lap and took a mouthful. As soon as the sweet and biting confection hit his taste buds, his gag reflex kicked in. He sealed his lips to keep from spitting out the goop. He forced himself to swallow. The cherries went down but hit his stomach with a bounce. Clenching his jaw tight, he glared at Joelle.

She smiled. "This is really good." Joelle pointed her fork at Rose. "So you're a baker and a waitress. But your accent isn't from here. You sound like a Texan."

Rose merely smiled and quickly came around the counter with a rag in hand. "Is there anything else you two would like?"

Joelle slipped off the stool. "Nope. I'll wait for you outside."

Shaking his head at Joelle's abrupt departure, he waved off Rose's attempt to clean the spilt pie. He took the rag and wiped off as much as he could before taking out his wallet to lay down enough money to cover the bill and give Rose a generous tip. "Sorry about the pie."

She scooped up his cash. "No worries. You have a lot to contend with right now."

"Can I see you later?"

A strange, almost sad, expression crossed her face. "Not tonight. Excuse me." With that she was off waiting on other customers.

He'd upset Rose. Frustrated with the situation, he grabbed his hat and left the diner. He found Joelle on the sidewalk talking to an older woman. Carol Bingley. The town gossip.

As he joined the ladies, he noticed Joelle's face had lost some of its color. Concern arched through him. He moved to stand beside her.

Mrs. Bingley's gaze swept over Matt. She raised a black drawn-in eyebrow. "My, did you have an accident?"

"Ms. Bingley," he said tipping his hat and ignoring her question. "How are you today?"

"I'm doing well, Matthew." She patted Joelle's arm. "I was telling Joelle, here, how proud Clark was of her."

"Yes, he was," Matt agreed.

"I understand you two were at the bank today," Carol said, her eyes glinting with interest. "And the real estate office. Is everything all right at the ranch?"

"Everything is good," Matt assured the woman. "If you'll excuse us, I'd like to get on the road before the sun sets."

"Oh, of course. It was nice to see you both."

Placing a hand at the small of Joelle's back, he guided her down the street to where he'd left the pickup parked in front of Fletcher's law firm.

Once they were on their way back to the ranch, Matt said, "Thank you for not saying anything about wanting to sell to Ms. Bingley."

"She'd be the last person I'd confide in," Joelle replied. "Dad used to say if you wanted everyone to know anything, just tell Carol Bingley."

Matt laughed. "Yeah, Clark and Carol weren't exactly on good terms most of the time."

"Especially after my mom left him. The town gossips were convinced Dad had driven Mom away. It wasn't true." Joelle shrugged. "Mom just wasn't cut out for ranch life."

He sent her a curious glance. She'd never talked about her mom to him. He'd only seen Gloria twice—at Joelle's high school and college graduations. He remembered Gloria as elegant and reserved. "Makes me wonder why they married."

"I know, right?" Joelle leaned back. "It wasn't like Dad hid the ranch from her." She sighed. "I think Mom liked the idea of living in the Wild West but she was a city girl from Philadelphia."

"How did your parents meet?" Matt had never felt comfortable asking Clark questions about his failed marriage.

"Funny story. The summer after Mom graduated from college, she headed west on a road trip that was supposed to last a week before she returned and started a job teaching at an elementary school. But instead, she stopped in Marietta and never left." Joelle snorted. "Well, until I was six and she decided she'd had enough."

"But she didn't head back to Philadelphia?"

"Nope. She hadn't made it to California so that's where she took me. Then she met Bob, remarried, sent me back to Dad and the rest, as they say, is history."

His fingers flexed around the steering wheel. He hadn't realized the timing. Joelle must have felt unwanted by her mother, and then to arrive home at her dad's only to find Matt there. So much of her behavior made sense now. His heart twisted. "I thought you wanted to return to the ranch?"

Her gaze met his briefly then bounced away. "I did."

But now she wanted to leave. Just like her mother. However unlike Gloria, Joelle had lived in the city for nearly seven years. He just needed Joelle to want to come home. To find her dream here in Marietta. To realize how much she belonged here. He turned down Railroad Avenue.

"Where are we going now?" she asked as they cruised down the once residential part of town. But like a lot small towns that had out grown the main thoroughfares, a few of the houses had been converted to places of business.

He brought the truck to a halt in front of a clapboard house with a wide porch. The sign hanging below the eaves read Jenkins' Fish and Game. And then another sign had been attached to dangle below the original sign. In sparkly letters B. Dazzled Western Bling glittered in the waning afternoon sunlight.

"Oh, no," Joelle said, her gaze going from the sign to him and back. "Let me guess. Another person you want me to meet?"

He laughed. "Yes. I want you to meet Bailey Jenkins. She opened her shop up this summer. She's also a jewelry maker."

The look on Joelle's face let him know she was humoring him as she climbed out of the truck and headed up the stairs.

Inside, the store gleamed and glistened. All sorts of feminine things blinged and twinkled, causing Matt to tug at the collar of his shirt. He spotted Bailey behind the register.

She smiled as they approached. "Hey, Matt. How are you?"

"I'm good, Bailey." He tipped his hat. "You?"

She stepped back and put a hand on her very round belly. "As you can see I'm expecting. And engaged to Paul Zabrinski."

"That's fantastic." Matt would have to remember to congratulate Paul.

"Congratulations," Joelle said. "Do you know what you're having?"

Bailey shook her head. "We're going to wait and be surprised."

"That's what I would do, too," Joelle shared.

Matt's gaze shot to her. She'd considered having kids?

An unexpected image of her holding a baby in her arms grabbed him by the throat and wouldn't let go.

"You okay?" Joelle's concerned touch jolted through him, kick-starting his stalled breath.

"Maybe you should sit down," Bailey offered. "You look like you're about to pass out."

He waved off both women. "I'm fine. A bit too much girly stuff in here."

"Yeah, right." Joelle eyed him for a moment before turning to Bailey. "I hear you're a jeweler."

"I am." Bailey gestured to the many ready-to-wear shirts, coats and pants with glittering studs in fanciful patterns. "I mostly B-Dazzle, as you can see."

"Joelle is a silversmith," Matt said. "She's wearing a set she recently made. Don't you think your customers would be interested in her work?"

Bailey admired the pieces on Joelle with oooh's and aahhh's. "I would love to feature your work. In fact, if you'd be interested I could use some help here. We could display and sell your art.

In exchange you could help me out while I'm on maternity leave."

Joelle's smile was full of good-natured affection. "That's such a tempting offer but I couldn't. I'm only here through the weekend. Then I have to return to Manhattan. But we could talk about ordering some pieces." She sent Matt a grateful glance. "Matt has convinced me that Marietta might be an untapped market."

A small victory. Now if he could only convince her to stay. But what would it cost him?

Chapter Four

❦

THE NEXT DAY, Joelle awoke early and took Star for a ride. Matt didn't join her this time, which was oddly disappointing. Strange considering she'd spent most of her youth resenting his presence. Now she was missing him? What was wrong with her?

Apparently he'd been busy caring for one of the pregnant mares. According to Matt, the mare, Daisy, would foal sometime in the next few days. Joelle hoped she was still here for the birth. She'd forgotten how much work and excitement went in to the birthing of a new foal.

Not that she'd been allowed to participate. Dad hadn't wanted her anywhere near the gritty aspects of the breeding process, including birthing.

Her pragmatic side saw the birth as another asset of the estate. Matt had said the new foal was already spoken for by an Oklahoma rancher. Though the foal would stay on the Winslow Estate until weaned. But her romantic, wistful side loved babies of any sort.

She found herself envying Bailey Jenkins, soon to be Mrs. Zabrinski. Bailey had glowed as she'd talked of her unborn child and her fiancé. Joelle had liked the woman and was excited at the prospect of placing some of her pieces in B. Dazzled. That made two stores in town that were interested in her designs.

Of course, she would work up a variety of pieces so the stores didn't have the same styles. She hated to admit it, but when Matt had asked about her designs being unique, he'd hit a nerve.

She wanted to make distinctive and one-of-a-kind pieces. And she could do that down the road. After making this new company a success. She needed to make this company a success to honor her father's last request.

Pushing away the niggling doubts that success wouldn't come to pass, she enjoyed her solitude. Other than in her apartment, in New York there was no such thing as aloneness. There were people everywhere at all times of the day and night.

This peacefulness was a rare treat. One she hadn't realized she missed.

She breathed deep, letting the refreshing fall air fill her lungs, chasing away the cobwebs of a restless night's sleep.

She wasn't sure what had kept her from slumber. Anxiety and guilt over selling her part of the ranch? Seeing Matt with the red-headed waitress at the diner?

Or spending the evening with him eating popcorn and watching an action flick? One of the few things—popcorn and action movies—they'd ever found in common growing up.

Joelle hadn't expected to feel the spurt of possessive jealousy that had gripped her when she'd walked into the diner and seen Matt and Rose, both of them leaning toward each other as they conversed. They were only talking, separated by a counter and a plate of food, but there'd been an intimacy to their conversation that had clawed through Joelle, making her feel like an outsider.

The way she'd always felt when she'd found her dad and Matt holed up in Dad's office or in the barn or seen them riding away from the stables, leaving her alone.

But there was a hollow feeling lingering in the pit of her stomach now. She chalked it up to grief over Dad and/or her dismal personal life. The last guy she'd dated had been more interested in his guitar than her.

However, seeing Callan had been an unexpected treat. Callan had always pushed Joelle to step out of her comfort zone when they were kids. Callan was fearless, willing to try anything and always went after what she wanted. Joelle had always admired that about her. She couldn't wait to catch up some more with her. And the idea of dancing or shooting pool at Grey's appealed to her. Matt's reaction when she'd mentioned the Wolf Den had been priceless. She smiled with a spurt of amusement and turned Star homeward. She may just have to check out the Den and see what all the fuss was about.

Joelle returned to the barn, groomed Star and then put him out in the pasture to graze. When she entered the house, Ava had breakfast waiting. Blueberry pancakes, hashbrowns and bacon.

"I'm going to get fat if I eat like this every morning," Joelle teased. Though she ate every last scrap on her plate.

Ava laughed. "I'm sure the guys would give you some chores to work off the food."

"Actually I was thinking of packing up my room." Time to put away the little girl world of pink frilly pillows and unicorns.

Sadness crossed over Ava's face like a shadow. Joelle's heart squeezed tight. It wouldn't be just her own past she was packing but Ava's as well. Ava had been a huge influence on so much of Joelle's girlhood.

Ava took off her apron. "There are some empty boxes in the old barn. I'll show you." She led the way out of the house.

The old barn had been built around the same time as the original farmhouse. Painted a traditional red, the structure was weathered and in need of some love. Inside had become a storage shed of sorts. Old machinery, discarded tack and a variety of miscellaneous stuff her dad had never gotten around to getting rid of.

"I never realized how much of a pack rat Dad was," Joelle said, fingering the broken and cracked leather of an old saddle.

Ava moved to a corner where empty boxes had been stacked. "He had a hard time letting go of anything he deemed valuable."

Joelle spied a beat-up steamer trunk. "What's in that?"

"Don't know," Ava said.

The lock was busted on the trunk. Joelle opened the lid. Inside lay a treasure trove of memorabilia of her father's life. A stack of letters tied with string. From the return address she guessed they were his letters home from Vietnam. He'd been wounded during his first tour and sent home. He'd limped from shrapnel in his heel but it hadn't stopped him from making a success of his life. Joelle hadn't known about his time in the war until she was a teen when he finally shared his injuries history with her.

She shifted the contents and found several old yearbooks. And photos. Lots and lots of photos, some black and white and ancient-looking. She picked up one picture and studied the image. Her dad as a teen with a stern-looking man and a smiling, dark-haired woman. They stood in front of the farmhouse, before it was remodeled. Her throat closed with grief and melancholy. She'd never met her grandmother or grandfather. They had passed on before she was born.

Dad had told her once that Grandfather Winslow had been an accountant for the copper mines and had bought the ranch as an investment, but had fallen in love with the land. He'd dubbed the place Winslow Estate. Joelle always thought that a funny moniker because the title conjured up images of a mansion and groomed lawns like the ones in upstate New York. A farmhouse, barns and bunkhouses didn't exactly equate to estate.

"You look like your grandmother," Ava commented from over Joelle's shoulder.

"Thank you." Finding this piece of her family history created a strange burning in her chest. She tucked the photo into the waistband of her jeans to free her hands to carry usable boxes back to the house.

For the next several hours, she sorted through her dresser drawers, her closet and the vanity/desk in her room. She made piles to be taken to Goodwill, piles for the dump and piles to keep. She'd put the photo of her dad and grandparents in her suitcase so she wouldn't forget to take it with her when she returned to New York.

She had just stepped onto the bed and reached for the unicorn mobile when a knock sounded at the door. "Come in."

The door opened but she was concentrating on the mobile. She couldn't quite get the ring off the hook in the ceiling. She wasn't tall enough. With her arms stretched overhead, she jumped up, hoping if she could provide some slack the ring would slip off the hook. She came down on the soft bed and lost her footing. With a yelp, she wind-milled her arms, fully expecting to fall off the edge of the bed, but two strong hands gripped her by the waist.

"Whoa, there."

Startled by Matt's voice, she twisted to see him.

Bad move.

Her body tilted, completely throwing her off balance. His arms slid around her, warming and bracing. She found herself clenched against his hard, muscled chest. Her heart hammered against her ribs. She put her hands on his shoulders to steady herself and stared into his handsome face. His eyes danced and a smile played at the corners of his mouth.

For a moment the insane thought of kissing him marched through her mind like a band in a parade. She forced the unruly idea down. But she couldn't dismiss the heat in her cheeks as easily.

"Sorry, you startled me," she said, liking the feel of his shoulders.

Big, hard and muscled. Heat radiated from him in waves. The scent of hay and horse and man clung to him and teased her senses. She breathed in deep, filling her lungs.

A bolt of desire struck her, lighting a path of fire straight to her center. A panicked flutter hit her tummy.

Before she could process all the implications and ramifications of the moment, he easily lifted her off the bed and set her on the floor. His hands slid to grip her hips. His fingers hot against her skin where her shirt had ridden up.

She felt branded. Claimed.

Which was ridiculous.

He'd stopped her from falling. And she was overreacting to his nearness. But for some reason she couldn't bring herself to step back. And he didn't let go.

"What were you trying to do?" His smooth voice washed over her, creating little shivers over her flesh.

Her hands remained on his shoulders, the soft feel of his shirt belying the strength of his muscles beneath. "Trying to take down the mobile."

He glanced up at the unicorns swinging over the bed then his gaze dropped back to meet hers. "I'll take care of it."

She nodded. His grip loosened.

Slowly, she let her hands slide down his arms, over defined biceps to strong forearms exposed by the rolled-up sleeves of his work shirt. The rough tickle of his arm hairs rasped against her palms. Reluctantly, she stepped back and let her hands fall to her side.

Thankfully, he'd removed his boots before coming inside. He stepped onto the bed, his white socks bright against the pink lace coverlet. With efficient movements, he detached the mobile's ring from the hook and then stepped down. "Here you go."

She took the mobile and carefully laid it in a box to keep, aware her hands shook. Her reaction to him was so out of the normal, she didn't know what to think.

"You've been busy," he stated, his voice devoid of inflection.

"I'm almost done." With one room. The thought of packing up the rest of the house was daunting. She hoped it wouldn't come to that. Matt had to find a way to keep his share of the ranch and hopefully hers. "How's Daisy?"

"Good. The foal is in position and should come before the weekend's out."

She rubbed her hands together. "That's so exciting."

He gestured with his chin toward the boxes. "Care to take a break and head into town with me? I've volunteered to help the high school football team with a car wash fundraiser this afternoon."

She remembered the fundraisers from her own high school days. "That sounds fun."

"Bring a change of clothes," he advised. "You know how these things go."

"Yes, I remember." They'd be sopping wet from head to toe by the time they were finished. "I wonder if the Daltons will set up an apple cider stand. Their apples are the best I've ever eaten."

His eyes twinkled. "They usually do."

ഊരു

MATT COULDN'T TAKE his eyes off Joelle. Her smile took his breath away. Every time she laughed, his gut tightened. She had a bucket of water in one hand and a big sponge in the other, but she had so many admirers helping her and clamoring for her attention, she wasn't getting much work done.

Water clung to her jeans, making the fabric mold to her skin and emphasizing her curves. She'd worn a waterproof shell over her shirt and had the hood over her hair and tied beneath her chin.

He shouldn't find her so appealing. But he did.

Earlier in her room, he'd had to use every ounce of self-control he possessed not to kiss her. To not slide his hands beneath her shirt and feel more of her silky skin. She'd been so cute standing on the bed wrestling with the mobile. And when she'd lost her balance, he'd reacted, not realizing that touching her, holding her, would wreak such havoc with his senses. With his mind.

But any man with a pulse would find Joelle attractive. As evidenced by the circle of available, young bucks who'd stopped in to help shortly after Matt and Joelle showed up. Men who weren't on the list of volunteers.

Matt yanked his gaze away and grabbed a sponge out of a bucket. With both hands, he wrung the water out with a vengeance.

He had no business finding Joelle desirable. Guilt crimped his heart. He shouldn't be interested in another woman while dating Rose. It wasn't right, wasn't honorable.

Thinking of Rose made him frown. She hadn't answered the phone last night when he'd called. They'd developed a habit of talking at nine in the evening on the nights they didn't get together. Of course, he'd been almost an hour late in calling. After dinner, he and Joelle had watched a movie that ended close to ten p.m. Maybe Rose was mad at him? But she hadn't struck him as the passive aggressive type. Maybe she'd been out? He didn't think she was seeing anyone else but they'd never talked exclusive. He mentally shrugged. Tonight he'd drive in to see her.

With that firmly decided, he soaped up the mayor's sedan with vigor, resolutely keeping his eyes on the car.

"Dude, ease up." RJ McCreadie stood close by with his thumbs hooked in to his belt loops. He was a tall, lean, slow-walking, slow-talking guy who'd taken newcomer Matt under his wing in junior high. "Did the car do something to offend you? Or was it the mayor?"

The community of Marietta included the rural ranches in a wide berth from the Gallatin Mountain range, through Paradise Valley and to the Absaroka Range. So even though the Winslow Estate and McCreadie were a good fifty miles apart, they were still considered neighbors. And good friends.

Dropping the sponge back in the bucket, Matt said, "No, neither one. Just feeling edgy."

RJ let out a low chuckle. "Yeah, I don't blame you."

"What's that supposed to mean?"

RJ nodded toward the passel of guys surrounding Joelle. Matt's blood pressure shot up.

"Man, she may have been a pain in the backside as a kid, but wow." RJ whistled through his teeth. "She's grown up and then some."

Matt grunted since he really didn't want to verbally admit the truth in his friend's words.

"Hard to think the pigtailed brat that used to torment you is now a beautiful, funny and smart lady," RJ said.

"When did you talk to her?" Matt practically growled.

"While you were getting the supplies ready," RJ replied, his gaze trained on Joelle. "I remember one summer at the fair—I think we were fourteen—and she followed you around like a puppy dog."

He remembered that summer. She'd tagged along with him and his buddies; wanting to ride every ride they did, even though she was too small. She'd made his life miserable. But he'd ditched her in the fun house. He'd felt bad until he saw her later with her friends. "More like a poodle with sharp teeth."

RJ grinned at him. "Does she still bite?"

Running a hand through his hair, Matt lowered his voice to confide in his friend. "She wants to sell the ranch. Or at least her share."

"Oh, man. No way!" RJ shook his head. "You can't let her."

"I don't have much say in the matter. It's her inheritance." He picked up the hose and rinsed soap off the car. "Unfortunately, I don't have the funds to buy her out."

"Then marry her."

"What?" Matt swung around to face RJ, his hand still pressing the nozzle lever. Water spray hit RJ in the face.

"Hey!" Rj stumbled back. "I don't need a shower!"

Releasing the lever, Matt grumbled, "Sorry. I can't believe you just suggested I marry Joelle."

Wiping off his face, RJ shrugged. "Why not? It would solve your problem."

"First off, I'm dating Rose. Second, Clark would not have approved and third, we don't get along. We could never be a couple. Besides, she's determined to buy into a startup company in New York City. She doesn't want to live on the ranch." RJ's lips twisted in a dubious grin. "Right. So this thing between you and Rose is serious?"

He shrugged. "I—don't know. We've only been dating a few months. These things take time."

RJ snorted. "Dude. Either you know or you don't."

Matt's gut churned. He really liked Rose. She was sweet, kind, generous…he could go on and on with all her positive traits and fill a book. He'd yet to see her angry or grumpy even.

But it was early in the relationship. They were both putting their best foot forward. He enjoyed her company. Found her attractive, but…he couldn't say he was in love with her. Not yet, anyway. He hoped those feelings would develop.

"As for Clark," RJ continued. "The old man would tell you to do whatever was necessary."

Tucking in his chin at the absurdity of RJ's words, Matt said, "Not going to happen. It wouldn't be right toying with Joelle's affections just to gain the ranch." He lifted one shoulder in an agitated shrug. "Besides it's Clark's words to Joelle that has her set on this path. Before he died he told her to follow her dream."

"Then change her dream," RJ said his tone implying that would be an easy feat.

"I won't manipulate her."

RJ shrugged then ambled away. "Suit yourself."

"I will, thank you." Matt went back to spraying down the sedan.

Marry Joelle! Ha! There was no way he would ever consider something as preposterous as that. They barely tolerated each other.

Okay, that wasn't true exactly. There had been enjoyable moments together since she'd returned. After the initial shock of her plans wore off, that is. The first part of their ride yesterday morning had been very pleasant, peaceful. Something he'd like to do again with her. She sat a horse well. But she always had.

The drive to and from town had been nice, too. They'd talked. Actually had conversations about life and the past and he'd enjoyed it.

Showing off her designs had been fun. Seeing her blush at his praise of her work had been pleasing. Last night, she'd been companionable. He hadn't felt the need to fill the empty spaces.

He'd been content, relaxed.

And there was that moment of insanity when he'd held her in his arms earlier today. The effects of which lingered in his veins, making his pulse beat a little too erratically for his peace of mind.

But a few instants and some flickers of attraction didn't make for a lifetime commitment.

No, his best course of action was to convince her to stay in Marietta and sell her designs in town.

A thought flittered through his mind. His breath stalled. She could have her own design company at the ranch. The old barn could be converted into a workshop. Or they could build a new one. The possibilities exploded in his brain, solidifying the idea. He could move to the bunkhouse if she wanted the house to herself.

"Hey, need some help?" Joelle stopped beside him.

Matt stilled and glanced over his shoulder to see several disappointed males watching them. For some reason his ego puffed up. She'd left the others to wash the black SUV and had come over to be with him.

To help him, he amended. She was being kind and thoughtful. And he shouldn't read any more into her presence than that.

He turned off the hose. "The only thing left is to dry this baby." He picked up two shammies and tossed one to her. "Here."

She caught the rag with a grin and moved to the other side of the car. They both started at the front and quickly, efficiently worked their way to the trunk.

"There." Joelle tossed her wet rag onto a growing pile.

"Yep, all done." He jammed his hands into his front pockets to keep from reaching over to push a lock of stray hair from her cheek.

"Good." She tucked her arm through his. "Now can we

please get some Dalton Cider? Judy Dalton baked Apple Cake. I've missed Apple Cake."

Heat spread through him and his chest expanded. They weren't a couple but he sure liked having her on his arm, pressed to his side. More than he should. He'd better be careful or he'd find himself in serious trouble. "Then let's feed you some Apple Cake."

Chapter Five

ഇൻ

JOELLE SLIPPED HER feet in a pair of two-toned, brown and turquoise cowboy boots that she'd found in the back of her closet. She'd forgotten about them. They'd been a gift from her dad on her sixteenth birthday. Amazed they still fit, she twirled in front of the full-length mirror hanging over her bedroom door. The bling on the back pockets of her jeans sparkled in the overhead light. Her ruffled, pale blue, sheer top billowed. She was meeting Callan and Andie at Grey's Saloon and she was ready to shoot some pool.

When she and Matt had returned to the ranch after the car wash, there'd been a message from Callan that she would be shooting pool at the popular bar and restaurant and hoped Joelle would show up. Joelle had then called her friend Andie and asked if she'd go, too. Andie had been over the top enthusiastic about joining them. Joelle couldn't wait to see her friends. And that fact really surprised her.

Yes, she'd kept in touch with both women through Facebook, but she hadn't realized how lonely she was for friends who really knew her.

Applying a touch of lip gloss, she was ready to go. Grabbing her purse and the keys to the rental car, she headed outside. The cool evening breeze swept through her loose hair.

"Hey, wait up!" Matt strode toward her from the barn.

She stopped next to the red sedan she'd rented. Her heart did a little jig in her chest at the sight of him. Tall and lanky yet muscled in all the right places. No extra pounds on the guy. He'd changed into dry denim that showed off his long, lean legs. A gray thermal t-shirt molded to his well-defined chest. He pushed back his black Stetson as he halted in front of her.

"Nice boots," he said.

She pointed her toe. "My sixteenth birthday present."

"I know. I picked them out."

A stunned warmth filled her chest. "No way! Really?"

He grinned. "Yep. Clark didn't know what to get you. We'd seen those in the window of a Western wear store on a trip into Bozeman. I told him you'd like them."

"That's—sweet." And touching. He'd have been twenty at the time. To think he'd known she'd appreciate the boots filled her with affection. "I do like them. I was always afraid to wear them because I didn't want to get them dirty. I should have packed them when I went to college."

But she hadn't wanted any reminders of home. In retrospect that was just plain silly. The Western look was so hip in the city. Always had been, probably always would be. But fashion hadn't been driving her.

"You going out?"

"I'm meeting Callan and Andie at Grey's."

"Could you spare a moment before you go?"

"Sure." Wariness spread through her chest.

"I want to talk about the ranch."

A rush of guilt made her cringe. "Can we do this tomorrow?"

"No. I need to say what I need to say."

"Fine." She braced herself. "Hit me with it."

He took off his hat. "When your dad took me in, he didn't just give me a home, he gave me a place to belong. After my parents died I was so alone, so adrift. I had no future that I could see."

In the waning light, the vulnerable expression on his handsome face broke her heart.

"I know it was hard for you having me here," he said.

Her chest tightened. He had no idea. "It was. And I didn't make it easy for you either. I was a brat. I'm sorry."

He flashed a quick smile. "You were." He sobered. "But I can only imagine how difficult it was for you to return and find me here. I never meant to cause you pain. I never meant for you to feel like I was taking your father away from you."

Old hurts sliced through her but she refused to give them any space. He'd lost his parents and her dad had opened his heart and his home to Matt. Joelle ached for Matt's losses, for his pain. Though she'd lost her dad six months ago, there were times she felt like she'd lost him the day her mother ripped her away from Montana and took her to California.

And again the day she overheard Matt in the barn telling RJ he wished she'd never come back to the ranch. That Clark hadn't wanted her to return.

"It's not your fault," she assured him. "You were a kid, too. Right? I know life was better for you and Dad when I wasn't here."

Matt shook his head. "That's not true. Clark loved you."

She swallowed back the denial. "I'm sure he did in some ways. But you said it yourself, he didn't want me to come back."

He frowned and confusion crossed his face. "I never said that."

"I heard you tell RJ that."

Matt stared at her, then dawning lit his eyes. "You were in

the barn?" He shook his head. "I was fourteen. I didn't mean it."

"But it was true. There were times when it felt like Dad preferred you to me. He liked you better. He'd wanted a son. He didn't have much use for a daughter."

"Hey, now that's not true. He loved you and was so proud of you. He would brag all the time about your good grades and later about your accomplishments in college. I'll admit he didn't know how to raise a girl. What man does? At least not without some guidance. Which Ava tried to provide. But your dad was too stubborn to ask anyone for help on anything." He shook head. "He never preferred me."

Though she agreed her dad had been one stubborn man, she didn't buy that Clark hadn't preferred to spend time with Matt over her. "Well, in any case, he's gone now and I have to let go."

"I agree."

Surprised, she raised an eyebrow at his understanding.

"You do have to let go of your anger," Matt said.

Offended by his words, she straightened. "I'm not angry anymore."

The dubious expression on his face said he didn't believe her. "You haven't made peace with Clark's memory. I can't speak about your relationship with your mother."

The relationship with her mother was complicated. She and Mom were working on forming a new, adult connection. Mom had even agreed to counseling. "I'm trying to make peace with Dad's memory by fulfilling my promise to him."

"No way would Clark have meant for you to give up the ranch."

A protest rose within her, but he held up a staying hand before she could speak.

"Look, this ranch is my home," he said. "I can't lose it. If I had the money to buy you out, I would. But I don't."

She sucked in a breath. "Matt—"

"Hear me out," he said. "I've been thinking. Why don't you start your own company and run it here on the ranch? You could sell your designs in town, in Bozeman, Livingston and online. You could even sell them to shops in New York and other places. But make the ranch your base of operation."

Every word stabbed into her, making her hurt. She understood how he felt. She hated that she was putting him in this position. But she had her own needs to think of, her own plans to implement, and her own path to follow. Didn't she? Was it selfish to want a life away from Marietta, away from the ranch? To want a life that was her own, on her terms?

"Matt, I think the best solution is to form a partnership and then sell my portion. It would be a win, win solution."

The dejected set to his shoulders called to her. She clenched her fist around her keys to keep from reaching for him while her other hand tightened on the car door handle. She yearned to comfort him, to put her arms around him and tell him it would all work out. But they didn't have that kind of relationship. And she honestly didn't know how life would turn out for any of them.

She opened the door and slid into the driver's seat. "I'm sorry, Matt."

"Me, too." He stepped back as she closed the door.

As she drove away, she glanced in the rear view mirror. He slowly made his way back to the barn. Back to the life he wanted. The life her father had provided for him. And her.

Tears burned the back of her eyes. She blinked to keep them at bay.

The life she didn't want. Right?

જ્જ

AFTER CHECKING ON Daisy and ensuring all was progressing as

expected, Matt drove his pickup truck to town and straight to Rose's bungalow at the end of Collier Ave. across from the town recreation center. He parked behind her little two-seater sports car. He wasn't sure how she afforded the roadster on a waitress' salary but then again he didn't know that much about her. She was always very vague and cryptic about her past. He mentally shrugged. Her past didn't matter a lick to him. He figured she'd get around to filling him in when the time was right.

For now, he needed her to lend an ear. He vaulted up the front porch stairs. From inside the house he could hear the television.

He felt so foolish for practically begging Joelle not to sell. And telling her his idea of running her own company out of the ranch had fallen flat. She hadn't been the least interested.

At Rose's front door, he tried the screen door but it was locked. He rang the bell. The house went silent. A moment later, she opened the wooden door and appeared on the other side of the screen door in a belted deep purple robe. Her red hair spilled over her shoulders in a massive mess. She was so pretty.

He should have felt more of a jolt of something seeing her like this but—he shook off the thought.

He was too upset to feel much of anything, he rationalized.

"Hey, Matt." Her soft voice came to him on the evening breeze.

"Hi. Did I catch you at a bad time?" He should have called first. But it wasn't that late, but maybe she had an early shift and was retiring for the night.

"No, I was just reading." She leaned against the doorframe and crossed her arms over her chest. "What can I do for you?"

Taken aback by her reticent reception, he plucked his hat off his head. "Can I come in?"

She shook her head. "No."

The rejection confused him more than stung. "Okay. Is

something wrong?"

"I don't know, you tell me. Is something wrong, Matt?"

His fingers rolled the edges of his hat. "Yeah. I did like you suggested and talked to Joelle. Told her how much the ranch means to me. But she won't change her mind."

"I wouldn't give up on trying," Rose said. "She might surprise you and come around."

"I doubt it." He peered at Rose. Why was she staying on the other side of the door and not letting him in? "Have I done something to offend you?"

She smiled, a sad sort of smile that confused him. "No. You've been the perfect gentleman. It's just—" She stopped as if she were searching for the right words. "You and I aren't right for each other."

Whoa. Where'd that come from? "Why not? I thought we were getting along just fine."

"Oh, we get along just fine. I like hanging out with you. But we don't have sparks the way you and Joelle do."

Her words knocked him back a step. "Excuse me? Whatever sparks you think you saw between us the one time you saw us together, were sparks of anger."

"Not from where I'm standing," she countered. "I saw the two of you at the car wash today. You two couldn't keep your eyes off each other."

Rose had been there and hadn't come and talked to him? He felt offended more than hurt.

He shook his head to deny her words, but he'd only be lying to himself. Yeah, okay, sure. He was fighting an unexpected and unwanted attraction to his childhood competitor, but that didn't mean his feelings for Joelle went any deeper. He wouldn't let them go any deeper. Especially, not now that she'd made it clear she was leaving no matter what he said or did. "Rose, there's nothing between Joelle and me. Never will be."

"Too bad because all that passion and affection could ignite into something wonderful if you'd let it." She straightened. "And that's what I want. You and I are comfortable together. It's nice. Easy. We're like a favorite pair of slippers." She sighed. "I want what I see between you and Joelle. I want sparks." Her index finger wagged between her and him. "You and I? No real sparks. Friendship, yes. But no passion."

He opened his mouth to protest her declaration but then clamped his lips together. He searched his heart and found nothing there beyond friendship. His shoulders sagged. "I'm sorry."

She waved away his apology. "Don't be sorry. We're friends. Right?"

"Right." He put his hat on. "You're one special lady and someday you'll find a man who gives you sparks."

"Goodnight, Matt," she said and closed the door.

The click of the lock sliding home echoed in his head as he drove through town. Was he destined to be alone? And homeless?

He turned down First Street and for some masochistic reason, cruised past Grey's Saloon. Joelle's rental car was parked halfway down the block. He pulled into the next available spot and shut off the engine. He sat there for a long moment wrestling with himself.

Why had he stopped?

He wasn't going inside.

Why would he go inside?

He should check on her, make sure she can drive herself home.

She was a big girl. She'd know not to drink and drive. She'd call him if she needed him. *She's fine. She's with Callan and Andie.*

Hmmm. Maybe he could catch a moment alone with Callan and ask her to talk to Joelle, convince Joelle to stay in Marietta.

That sounded like a good plan. He just hoped it didn't backfire and push Joelle further toward selling.

Grey's was hopping for a Wednesday night. The booths along the wall facing the bar were full. Wooden tables were scattered throughout the place. Most were occupied. Matt saw several people he recognized as he searched for Joelle. She wasn't sitting at a booth or table. He turned his attention to the scarred wooden bar.

Jason Grey and another bartender Matt didn't know were tending to the line of customers. Matt stepped up to ask Jason if he'd seen Joelle when his gaze hit the large mirror on the wall behind the two men. In the reflection, he saw Joelle. She was at the back pool table, a cue stick in her hand. She was smiling at Dillon Sheenan, who flanked her on one side while Lane Scott took a position on her other side.

A burning knot cramped Matt's chest. His gaze narrowed and his hand clenched the edge of the bar. Joelle flipped her hair back and laughed at something Lane said.

Matt's jaw clenched tight. Those two were too old for her.

A mocking voice inside his head reminded him both men were his age.

Dillon was a player who liked to keep things light. Matt couldn't have him adding Joelle to his list of conquests.

And Lane...empathy stirred in Matt. The former marine had served his country and returned home a double amputee. Though looking at him, one couldn't tell with the jeans covering his prosthetic legs. Matt liked Lane but he wasn't the right man for Joelle.

Was there a right man?

"What can I do you for?" Jason Grey's gruff tone silenced the mocking voice inside Matt's head.

"Nothing, thanks. I found what I was looking for." Matt pushed away from the bar and headed toward the back.

He stopped next to Andie and Heath McGregor.

"Hey, nice to see you." The six-foot-tall, curly-haired construction worker stuck out his hand.

"You, too." Matt shook Heath's hand and smiled at Andie, a willowy blonde with bright blue eyes. Hard to imagine she was an electrician. She was pretty enough to grace the cover of a magazine. "How's married life treating you?"

Andie's smile lit up the room. She snuggled closer to Heath. "Wonderful. And it's so wonderful having Joelle home."

"Yes, yes it is." Matt was surprised that he meant the words.

His gaze slid to Joelle. She leaned over the table, the cue set up for a shot. Her face was a study in concentration. Her blouse dipped, revealing an edge of lace. Heat shot through Matt. Joelle's gaze lifted from the white ball and met his. For a second her eyes widened, then the blue in her eyes darkened and a small, sexy smile lifted the corners of her lush lips.

Matt's mouth went dry.

She took the shot while holding his gaze.

A cheer went up as the yellow-striped ball rolled into the pocket.

Joelle straightened and high fived Callan. Dillon handed her a martini glass filled with a frothy pink concoction. Matt's fingers curled as she clinked her glass to Dillon's beer bottle and then took a ladylike sip.

"How many of those has she had?" Matt asked Andie through clenched teeth.

"Just the one." Andie's voice held amusement. "She's schooling them royally at billiards."

Who knew she played pool? He hadn't. He didn't know that much about the adult she'd become. And strangely he wanted to know her. Not because she held his future in his hands but because he cared for her in ways he'd never expected or wanted.

And that scared him more than losing the ranch.

Chapter Six

ಬಂದ

POINTING THE CUE stick to the far corner of the green pool table in the back of Grey's Saloon, Joelle called the shot, "Eight ball, corner pocket."

On the juke box a country rock song played, the tempo matching the beating of her heart.

"Yeah, right." Lane Scott smiled, leaning against the side of the table. He was tall, handsome and athletic-looking. His marine tattoo peeked out from beneath his black t-shirt. "There's no way you can pocket the ball clean."

She slanted him a grin. "Watch me."

The shot would be easy if she weren't so aware of Matt's brooding gaze tracking her every move. She'd been surprised to see him standing across the table with Andie and Heath, her new husband. And more surprised by the thunderclouds on his face. What had him all twisted up?

As she pretended to study the table and the angle of her move, she surreptitiously glanced at Matt. His Stetson was pushed forward making shadows on his face from the low lighting. He'd changed into clean jeans and a blue chambray shirt that he filled out well. Had he come here to check up on her?

The thought should irritate her. Especially in light of his confession that he'd being doing so since she left home. But for some strange reason a warm and fuzzy haze filled her. Must be the Red Appletini she was drinking.

She straightened, picked up the martini glass and downed the last few sips.

"Another?" Dillon asked, his smooth-as-whiskey voice caressing her ear.

"I'm good." She set the glass aside and smiled at him.

The guy was eye candy, all lean muscle and dark Irish looks, and charming to boot. If she were any other woman, she'd be falling at his feet, but he just didn't do it for her. Nor did Lane. Oh, there was nothing wrong with either man, they were good-looking, charismatic and knew all the right words to make a girl feel pretty. But her type was more the dark and brooding, hard-to-get-type guy.

But then again, her track record with guys wasn't that good, so maybe she needed to reassess her type. In New York City they came a dime a dozen. Musicians, actors, Wall Street types. All the guys she'd dated were of a similar build and disposition.

Sort of like another certain someone she knew.

Matt.

The thought rocked her back a step. To cover, she grabbed the chalk cube and rubbed the tip of her stick against it, liberally applying a coat of blue dust.

She forced back thoughts of Matt. He had no place in her life.

Concentrate!

The last thing she wanted to do was scratch in front of Matt.

Lining up the shot, she pulled the stick back three times to get her rhythm, then sent the stick forward. The tip kissed the white ball perfectly, leaving a blue mark and sending the small orb shooting forward while spinning counterclockwise as she'd intended. The white ball banked off the cushioned side of the table, changing direction enough to by-pass the solid blue ball blocking the black eight ball. The white and black balls kissed then each ball shot away. The white ball veered horizontally across the table, while the black ball dropped neatly into the far corner pocket.

"Whoo, whoo!" Callan pumped a fist in the air. "That's the way to do it."

Joelle blew out a relieved breath. She looked for Matt, wanting to see his reaction, but he wasn't standing across the table anymore. She frowned; disappointed he hadn't seen her make the shot.

"Well done," Dillon said, tipping his beer bottle at her.

"Where'd you learn to play like that?" Lane asked.

"That's what I'd liked to know, too." Matt's voice sent a shiver down her back. He was close. She could feel waves of energy cascading over her.

She whirled around to find herself trapped with the pool table at her back and Matt standing arms length away, feet apart, gaze burning.

Annoyed by the way her heart bumped, she let loose the first words that came to mind. "Hi, Matty." She put her free hand over her mouth. "Oops, only Rose is allowed to call you that."

His brows dipped together. But he didn't say anything.

She could feel everyone watching them. Growing uncomfortable under Matt's unrelenting stare and regretting her catty remark, she directed her attention to Lane. "I learned from some of the best players in Brooklyn. My college friends and I would take the train out to play most weekends. It was cheaper than the clubs in the city and more fun."

"It's getting late," Matt said, his voice low. "And you've had enough to drink tonight. I'll drive you home and tomorrow we can return for your car."

She tucked in her chin. She didn't like his highhanded tone or the fact that he felt it necessary to drive her home. One drink was all she'd had.

Before she could respond, Dillon spoke.

"I'll see she makes it home safely."

Callan wedged herself between Dillon and Joelle. "Nope, that's my job."

"You shouldn't drive either," she said to Callan. "You've been drinking, too."

She grinned. "One beer. Only half empty."

Tenderness filled Joelle, tamping down her irritation. Matt and Callan both were protecting her. They were her friends. That's what friends did. Not that she needed protection from Dillon or Lane. Despite their flirtiness, she had nothing to fear from them. And she wasn't falling down drunk, though she was a lightweight when it came to the hard stuff so driving would be irresponsible.

Or maybe she just wanted to ride home with Matt.

That was a thought she didn't want to examine too closely. Or at all.

Joelle pushed out her bottom lip in a pseudo pout. "Fine. I won't drive. But I'll go with Matt. We are going to the same place after all."

After hugging Callan and Andie with promises to see them at the Homecoming football game on Friday, and saying goodbye to the others, Joelle allowed Matt to lead her outside to his pickup truck. The hand he held to the small of her back was warm and sent little flashes shooting through her. She was surprised she wasn't lighting up the whole street like a firecracker on the fourth of July.

She slid onto the passenger's seat and waited for him to climb in and start the engine. Once again she owed him an apology. "I'm sorry for that crack about Rose. I shouldn't tease you. I'm happy for you. You must care for her a lot to let her call you Matty."

He remained silent as he drove through the quiet town and headed down the rural road that would take them to the ranch. Outside the cab of the truck was dark. The moonless night didn't offer any relief. Inside, the tension bumped up against the windows. Joelle's mood plummeted. Matt must be really mad at her to not even banter back. The silence stretched. She sank lower in her seat and tipped her head back.

"I don't like having Rose call me Matty, either," he finally said. "But I couldn't bring myself to stop her because then I'd have to explain."

Joelle sat straighter. "Okay."

She could barely make out his features from the lights on the dashboard. His jaw was tight. His gaze trained ahead on the road. She wasn't sure what to do with that information. Ask him to explain? She bit her lip. Debating questioning him or letting him have his privacy.

"My mom called me Matty."

His softly spoken words hit her like a sucker punch to the gut. Tears pricked her eyes. Of course. That made total sense. Remorse for all the times she'd badgered him with the nickname choked her. His angry reaction had covered his pain and grief and sorrow. She blinked to clear the blur of tears. "I'm sorry. I never knew."

"I never told you." He let out a heavy sounding breath. "I should have. It might have made things easier between us."

She laid a hand on his arm. "What were your parents like?"

She'd never dared ask that question. He'd made it clear from the get-go the topic of his family was off-limits. The little she knew of Mr. and Mrs. Locke came from her father and snatches of overheard conversations.

The muscles of his forearm beneath her hand bunched as he flexed his fingers on the steering wheel. "They were great parents. Dad managed a sales and marketing team for a Fortune 500 company. Mom stayed home. They'd tried to have more children but God only blessed them with me."

Joelle's heart clutched. She squeezed his arm. He took his hand off the steering wheel. When she removed her hand, he grabbed it and laced his fingers through hers. His roughened, work-worn palm fit snuggly against her own palm. He had big hands. Strong hands. Hands made to work. But hands that could be tender, too. She'd seen the way he was with the horses, the gentle manner he used to bring an injured animal comfort.

"They had a car accident, right?"

"A drunk driver swerved into their lane and hit them head on." His voice cracked.

This was hard for him to talk about. She didn't want to push, but she wanted to know, to understand, him better. Her throat ached with sympathy. She squeezed his hand. "I'm so sorry."

He blew out a noisy breath, clearly struggling to talk. "The guy died, too." Matt let out a sharp scoff. "He'd had four times the legal limit in his system. The police suspect he was suicidal. He'd lost his job a few weeks before and was deep in debt. But the authorities couldn't prove it." Matt shook his head. "Not that it mattered whether he wanted to die or the crash was an accident, the man had driven while intoxicated. And took my parents from me."

"That's awful." Tears burned her eyes again. She wished there was a way to heal his wound.

"You weren't with them when the crash happened, right?" She prayed he wasn't. She could only imagine the survivor's guilt he'd shoulder if he had been.

"No, they'd gone out for a date. I was off with some buddies. Bowling." He let out a mirthless laugh. "I hate bowling."

That was a small comfort to know he hadn't witnessed the accident. "I'll never ask you to bowl."

That earned her a small smile. "Clark and my dad were friends growing up."

"I know. Dad explained that part to me. After I calmed down enough to listen." She'd been so shocked and enraged to find a boy in the house. It had taken so much energy and effort to talk her mom into letting her return to Montana and then to find her dad had brought in a replacement child. She'd been so hurt. Lashing out had been her way of dealing with her pain. Childish? Yes. "Dad did a good thing by taking you in."

Matt squeezed her hand. "Thanks for that."

He slipped his hand from hers as he brought the truck to a halt at the front porch of the farmhouse. They climbed out and walked to the front door. Matt pushed the solid piece of wood open. She stepped through. When he didn't follow, she asked, "You're not coming in?"

"I need to check on Daisy." He tipped his hat and sauntered toward the barn.

Part of her wanted to go with him but her head was spinning, not only with the effects of the alcohol but also with the knowledge he'd shared a part of himself with her. A part he hadn't shared with the woman he was dating. What did that mean?

As she made her way to her bedroom, she decided it meant nothing more than their friendship was deepening. They'd known each other more than half her life. He'd always have a special place in her heart. That of a long time friend.

But she couldn't help the tiny part of her that wished it could be so much more.

☙❧

AFTER SAYING GOODNIGHT to Joelle, Matt headed inside the barn, when what he really wanted to do was follow her inside and up the stairs to her room. But that wasn't going to happen.

He had no business letting his attraction to Joelle cloud his mind. She was already worming her way under his skin as it was, something he'd never imagined happening.

Nor had he expected the possessiveness that had gripped him at Grey's tonight. He hadn't liked seeing Joelle with Dillon and Lane, who were practically salivating over her. A primal urge to lay claim to Joelle had driven him to intercede.

That she'd come almost willingly had only ratcheted his fascination.

Though it had been her apology that had busted a crack in the shell around his heart. Opening up about his parents had been hard. Clark had been the only person he ever talked to about his mom and dad. And now Joelle.

He reached Daisy's foaling stall, a small enclosed shed-like structure away from the other horses. Straw covered the floor. She paced, her tail swishing wildly. She nosed at her flank as her muscles contracted, preparing for the birth. He quickly cleaned the stall then bandaged the mare's tail to prevent the foal from picking up any dirt on its way into the world. He retreated to a position where Daisy couldn't see or hear him but he could see into the stall. It could be minutes, or hours, now.

Joelle would want to be here.

He hurried to the house. Joelle had left the hall light on. Her thoughtfulness expanded the warmth in his chest. He quickly vaulted up the stairs and knocked at her door. A few seconds later she answered. Her sleep-mussed dark hair cascaded over her shoulders. She wore a long, black t-shirt that fell to her knees. She was so painfully beautiful. His chest ached. For a moment he forget why he was there. The yearning to pull her into his arms pulsed through him. Grabbing a hold of his self-control, he stepped back when everything inside of him wanted to step forward. He broke out in a cold sweat.

She blinked sleepily at him. "Matt? Is everything okay?"

"The foal's coming," he managed to say in a somewhat normal tone.

Her eyes widened. Excitement spread across her face. "Cool. Let me throw something on and I'll be right there." She shut the door.

Needing a moment to reclaim his sanity, he went back downstairs and into the kitchen for a drink of water.

When Joelle joined him in the kitchen she had on one of his old flannel shirts, sweatpants and her old worn boots. She carried her barn coat in one hand. She'd gathered her hair up in a messy bun held with a claw-like clip. Her face was clean of makeup and so pretty in the soft glow of the overhead light.

"Hope you don't mind I borrowed your shirt," she said. "It was in the laundry room."

He liked the idea of her wearing his shirt. "You're welcome to whatever you'd like."

They left the house and went back to the barn. He set up a hay bale against the wall far enough away for Daisy not to be bothered by their presence but where they could observe her. They sat in companionable silence to wait for the foal.

Joelle shifted, clearly uncomfortable.

Matt moved so that he had his back propped against the wall. He positioned her in front of him so that she could lean her back on his chest. Her bun hit his chin. She reached up and removed the clip, letting her hair fall. He breathed in her scent, a heady mix of flowers and vanilla. It felt so good, so natural to wrap his arms around her. The hours ticked by. Joelle dozed off in Matt's arms. Tenderness filled his heart.

Daisy grew more restless, going from standing to lying down and back again. Somewhere around five in the morning, her water broke. But something was wrong. Daisy grew agitated. Pawing and pounding at the ground with her hooves.

Worried, Matt woke Joelle and instructed her to call the veterinarian, Noah Sullivan. While she hurried to the house to use the phone, Matt did what he could to help Daisy foal. But nothing seemed to be working.

The vet arrived as the first rays of morning peeked over the mountain range.

With Joelle at his side, Matt greeted Noah with a handshake. "It's been nearly a half hour since her water broke." He ran a hand through his hair and anxiety churned in his gut.

Noah, a soft-spoken man in his early thirties, put a calming hand on Matt's shoulder. "Take a deep breath. It will be all right."

Matt hoped so. He hated to think of anything happening to the foal or Daisy.

The vet worked quickly and efficiently, repositioning the foal so that its feet, head then body slipped out. Matt and Noah worked to clean the foal and attend to Daisy.

When both mother and son were bonding, Noah said goodbye with the promise of returning to check up on the pair.

Joelle clapped her hands. "Ahhh, he's sooo cute." She leaned against the stall door.

Matt joined her, slipping an arm around her waist. "He's a beauty. He already has strong lines."

Joelle yawned and leaned into him with a sigh. Affection flooded his veins. He liked having her so soft and pliant within his embrace.

"Come on, we should get some rest." Matt kissed the top of her head and steered her back to the house.

They met Ava in the kitchen. She had a breakfast casserole baking in the oven. "You two look beat."

Slipping onto the stool at the counter, Joelle told her about the foal. "It's a shame he's already spoken for. I'd love to have him."

Matt glanced at her, hope spurting to life. Did that mean she was changing her mind about the ranch?

"But I couldn't exactly keep a foal in my apartment in New York, so that wouldn't work," she continued. "Plus, if I were to take a horse it would have to be Star. Hmmm, I wonder if I could find a place to rent a stable outside of the city."

And just like that, Matt's hope withered. Along with a part of his heart.

Chapter Seven

80CR

FOUR HOURS LATER, Joelle awoke from a nap. She lay on her bed reliving the foaling. It had been messy and wonderful. She'd never witnessed a birth before. Her dad had forbidden her from the barn when any of the mares were foaling. In fact, Dad had pretty much kept her out of the day-to-day operation of running the ranch. Oh, she could groom and ride Star and occasionally he'd have her ride a horse he was rehabilitating because she was lighter than him or one of the hands.

She sighed, wishing he'd have let her into his and Matt's world. Maybe then she'd have more of an affinity for keeping her inheritance.

Eyeing the boxes stacked against the wall, she decided to take the ones marked for donation into town. After dressing in a pair of tan corduroy pants, and a light-weight red sweater, she brushed her hair and tied it back in a low ponytail with a colorful ribbon she'd found in the drawer of her vanity set. She slipped on a twisted silver and multi-colored glass-beaded necklace and matching earrings. She left the house and went in search of Matt.

She found him in the arena with a pale palomino. She

climbed on the rungs of the fencing to watch. The horse stood with its back leg drawn up. Matt talked gently to the animal, coaxing her to drop her leg. The palomino was having none of it.

"She's a stubborn cuss." Chuck, one of the old time ranch hands came to a stop next to Joelle.

"Like someone else I know," Joelle said at his teasing. Chuck had hired on the ranch under her grandfather and stayed on when Dad took over. Nearing seventy, he had gray hair, a weathered faced and a kind smile. "What's wrong with her leg?"

Leaning on the fence, he said, "Endocrine-related laminitis, a disease that inflames the laminae, the connective tissue between the pedal bone and the hoof."

"What stage of recovery is she?" Joelle asked.

"Day twenty. She had a new shoe glued in. The bone is healing but she's still unwilling to put weight on the leg. The vet will be out again later today to see if there's more going on." Chuck pushed away from the railing. "I figure you're waiting to talk to Matt. I'll go relieve him."

Chuck walked into the ring and took the reins of the bridal. He and Matt conversed for a moment, and then Chuck led the limping horse away while Matt headed in her direction. He wore a green Henley shirt with the sleeves pushed up. His long legs were encased in a pair of worn work jeans. She liked to watch him walk, liked the way his body rolled with each step. As he stopped in front of her, he pushed back his hat and wiped a hand over his stubbled jaw. Apparently, he hadn't shaved this morning. She liked the scruffy look almost as much as she did when he was clean-shaven and dressed for a night out. Last night, he'd been so handsome when he'd shown up at Grey's. Today was no exception, just different.

"Did you get some rest?" he asked.

"I did, but I take it you didn't?"

He shook his head. "Nope. There's work to be done."

Asking him to show her the work balanced on the tip of her tongue, but she swallowed the words back. She was leaving, selling her portion of the ranch, learning the ins and outs of the business now would be a waste of both their time. "Hey, so I need to go get my rental and I want to take some stuff I boxed up to the charity drop-off."

"Sounds good."

An hour later, she was sitting behind the wheel of her rental, the boxes loaded in the backseat.

Matt held on to the driver's side door to ask, "You positive you don't want me to come with you?"

"No, I'm good. I want to stop in at the dress shop. I didn't bring anything dressy enough for the alumni dinner," she replied. Having him tag along on a shopping trip probably wouldn't settle well with his girlfriend.

"All right then. Be careful." He shut the door, patted the top of the car and then sauntered back to his truck.

He was even good-looking from the backside. All lean, long and well muscled. Tearing her gaze away, she tuned in a pop station on the radio before pulling away from the curb. She stopped by St. James Church's donation center and unloaded the boxes. She'd always loved the old world feel of the church that took up a good portion of the block. The early settlers of Marietta had built the structure with money made from the copper mines. The Winslows had attended here since arriving in Paradise Valley.

Joelle's heart squeezed tight with a wave of nostalgia. Her father had helped fund the refurbishing of the pews inside. She remembered every Sunday sitting in the third row with her dad, Ava and Matt listening to the pastor and staring at the beautiful stained glass windows. Maybe she'd attend this Sunday. She wondered if Matt still went to church.

Her next stop was the dress boutique. The lovely shop, scented with a subtle jasmine fragrance, had a wide variety of clothing from fancy undergarments to pretty special occasion wear. Soft music played from overhead speakers and the low lighting helped to create a soothing ambiance.

Joelle tried on several dresses and decided on an emerald-colored shift with an A-line shape that flattered her figure. She also picked out a colorful pashmina that would compliment the dress and keep her warm if the restaurant were chilly.

She was checking out at the front counter when Rose walked in. The red-haired woman paused when she saw Joelle. Something flashed in the other woman's brown-eyed gaze before she put on a polite smile. "Hello, Joelle."

Deciding she needed to make friends with the woman who might one day become Mrs. Locke, Joelle returned the smile, putting in as much genuine pleasure as she could. "Hi, Rose. How are you today?"

"I'm good. You?"

"Good." And feeling awkward.

Rose stepped closer. "Oh, wow, I love your necklace." Her gaze lifted to Joelle's ears. "And matching earrings. Matt mentioned you were a talented craftswoman. He wasn't joking."

Pleased by both her compliment and the fact Matt had said she was talented, she fingered the necklace. "Yes, I made these."

The sales clerk came out from behind the counter. "They're lovely. Do you make jewelry only for personal wear or do you commission pieces?"

"I do both. I'm going to have some cards made up and I'll make sure you get one," Joelle said.

"That'd be fabulous," the sales lady said. "My name is Claire Tipton, I own the shop and I'd love to talk to you about carrying your designs. My customers love unique, one-of-a-kind things."

"And I bet Lisa Renee at Married in Marietta would be

interested, as well," Rose interjected. "Do you make wedding rings? Bridesmaid gifts?"

Joelle's mind exploded with possibilities. She shoved aside the stab of pain thinking about Matt and Rose's wedding rings. "I haven't, but I could. That's a good idea, Rose. Thank you."

Rose nodded. "I know you're planning on returning to New York, but you could easily make a workshop out on the ranch. The old red barn isn't being used for much."

A twinge of possessiveness hit Joelle. Of course Rose had been out to the ranch, she was dating Matt. But Joelle didn't like the idea of another woman being there. A fact she'd have to get over since she was selling her half. Matt was free to move anyone he wanted into the house. Her house. His house.

Conflicted and confused by her warring thoughts, she said, "The possibility has been brought up."

Rose's knowing look grated on Joelle. She and Matt had obviously discussed her. No doubt, soon Rose would become part of the family, so to speak. Because, Joelle realized with a little start, she did consider Matt family.

"Are you and Matt going to the football game tomorrow night?" Joelle asked. She wouldn't attend with them. She wouldn't want to be a third wheel. She'd go to the game with Callan or Eve. Or alone. She was used to doing things alone.

Rose stared at her for a moment, her gaze assessing. "No, we're not."

"Oh." Maybe she had to work. Her loss. Joelle's gain? She bit her lip trying not to be too happy at this turn of events. "Well, I best be getting back to the ranch. We had a new foal born this morning."

"Nice. It was good seeing you again." Rose stepped away. "I'm sure we'll run into each other soon."

Taking her packages, Joelle headed back to the ranch. Her thoughts dwelling on Rose's last remark. Joelle wasn't sure she could stomach seeing Matt and Rose together. Rose was nice enough and pretty but she didn't strike Joelle as the ranching type. But then again, what did Joelle know?

For the past seven years, she'd been telling herself she wasn't the ranching type but over the past few days, she'd begun to see the ranch and life in Marietta in a different light.

But even if she changed her mind and wanted to keep the ranch, she couldn't see herself living with Matt and his wife, whether that turned out to be Rose or some other woman. Not when Joelle was fighting an attraction to the kind, generous man Matt had become. She could see herself staying, helping to run the ranch, while creating her jewelry in the old red barn. But she also saw herself living in Manhattan, working side by side with her partners as they made jewelry to export all over the U.S. and possibly the world.

The dress shop owner's voice echoed what Matt had stated. If she branched out on her own instead of partnering with other designers, she could make the designs she wanted, create unique, one-of-a-kind pieces that would be special.

She was stuck between the life she thought she wanted and a life she was beginning to want. Why did life decisions have to be so hard?

∞ℭ

THE MARIETTA HIGH school stadium crackled with energy. Earlier in the evening a parade had marched through town, revving up the anticipation for the big game. Now the stands were filled with fans, most local from Marietta and a good portion from the visiting team of nearby Livingston High School. The two schools were huge rivals and that they were playing on the night of Homecoming upped the tension even more. Joelle let the excitement soak into her being as she and

Matt made their way through the throng of fans to find seats to the right of the spirit club. The teens were decked out in red and white, Marietta's school colors. They chanted a cheer led by the cheerleaders down on the track that circled the football field.

Cool, crisp fall air seeped through her jeans and jacket to penetrate the short sleeve shirt beneath. Joelle had brought a blanket in case she grew chilly but she figured her blood pressure would elevate with the game making her toasty enough and she would be fine in her jacket.

The kickoff started the game. Joelle's leg rubbed against Matt's leg as he shifted to watch the play on the field. He looked handsome in new jeans, a light green and white, checkered button-down beneath a close-fitting leather jacket that emphasized the width of his shoulders. His nearness distracted her and she missed the first touchdown by the visiting team. She forced her attention on the game, cheering on the Marietta Grizzlies.

At halftime, the score was even with two touchdowns each. The Homecoming court was presented, then local-hero-made-good, baseball player Chase Goodwin received an award from the town that loved him. Joelle's hands hurt from clapping so hard.

"Would you like something from the concessions?" Matt asked, rising to his feet.

"Popcorn and water." She stood and stretched. Even with the padded seat she'd brought, her backside wasn't happy sitting for so long. "I'm going to use the ladies' room."

They made their way down the staircase, separating at the bottom. Joelle joined the line for the women's restroom. With a start she realized the woman standing in front of her was Rose. She had her hair up in a topknot and a coat with the collar turned up. Interesting. She wasn't working at the diner. But why hadn't she come to the game with Matt?

"Hi, Rose."

Rose turned and smiled at Joelle. "Hello."

"I didn't think you were coming tonight," Joelle said, letting her curiosity get the better of her.

"I didn't say I wasn't coming, only that I wasn't attending with Matt. You have nothing to worry about from me. He's all yours."

Joelle couldn't have heard the woman correctly. "Excuse me? All mine? What does that mean?"

Rose's mouth pulled into a wry grin. "You best ask him that."

"I'd rather you told me," Joelle stated. Her heart beat an unsteady rhythm in her chest.

"He's not into me," Rose said. "Not the way he is with you."

Joelle let out a scoffing chuckle. "There's nothing going on between us."

"You sound like him." Rose shook her head. "You're both so stubborn you can't see what's right in front of you." A pensive look crossed her face. "Some people would give anything to be in your shoes."

Was she suggesting Matt had feelings—romantic feelings—for Joelle?

That was nuts. No way.

And Joelle certainly didn't carry those types of feelings for Matt.

Or was Rose seeing what Joelle was desperately trying to hide?

Joelle needed a moment alone to sort this out in her mind. "Excuse me."

She stepped out of line and headed toward the back of the bleachers where it was dark and relatively quiet. She searched her heart, finding that she did harbor feeling for Matt that surprised her and scared her. Adult feelings that went beyond friendship.

There was no denying she held a great deal of affection for him. Admiration and respect. Attraction, too.

But did she, could she, love him?

The thought rocked her back a step. She clung to the metal rung of the structure.

No. It was the close proximity. It was being home and the birthing of the foal and the comfortable way she and Matt had settled in that was making her feel all this emotion. None of it was sustainable. Being home was an interlude to the life she'd been working toward for seven years. She wasn't willing to give that up.

Not now, not ever.

ℴℙ

MATT SENSED A change in Joelle when they resumed their seats. She watched the game but without the enthusiasm she'd had for the first half. She also scooted away so their legs no longer touched. He missed the contact. He nudged her with his elbow. "Hey, what's up? Are you okay?"

"Yes," she replied with a wan smile. "All's good." She pumped her fist. "Go Grizzlies."

He turned his gaze back to the game but his mind was on the woman beside him. He shouldn't be so in tune to her moods. Or let her affect him in any way. She was leaving in a few days. And if everything worked out, he'd have ownership of the ranch.

He'd talked to Ren and the bank earlier this afternoon. The bank was willing to mortgage his half of the estate, whatever that amount might end up being once the appraisal came through next week. Until then, the bank was willing to extend a line of credit for the amount of money Joelle needed to fund her portion of the partnership she wanted to buy into. Ren said he'd have the entire paperwork ready to be signed by Monday. And then Joelle could leave, return to the life she wanted, far from Montana and the ranch and fulfill her father's promise. The rest of the documents could be taken care of long distance.

The thought shouldn't depress him so much.

He spotted Rose in the stands and wished he felt something more than friendship for her.

Maybe he was destined to be alone.

The game progressed, the tension among the fans rising as the ticking of the clock counted down the seconds until the timer ran out and the game would be over. A tied game wouldn't be satisfying.

In the last few seconds of the game, Flynn Goodwin, Chase's little brother, made the winning touchdown. The home crowd went wild. Matt jumped to his feet and whooped and hollered his approval. Even Joelle was pulled out of her morose mood to stand, clapping and cheering.

He glanced at her and met her sparkling gaze. For a moment the world receded. They were the only two people in the universe. He wasn't sure if he moved first or if she had, but suddenly, his arms slid around her waist, pulling her up against his chest. Her arms entwined around his neck and drew him closer until their lips met. Her mouth was soft and pliant. Her tongue rimmed his lips. He groaned and deepened the kiss, tasting, exploring. Sensations careened through him, heating his blood, rocking his world until he couldn't have said which way was up.

Slowly awareness filtered through the drug-like haze captivating his mind. Around them people stared. He could hear the whispered speculations.

He broke the kiss and dropped his forehead to hers.

For a moment, neither of them moved. Then she stepped back, extracting herself from his arms. The stricken look on her face pierced him like the sharp tip of a spear. Regrets flooded in. He shouldn't have done that, yet it had felt so good, so right and natural.

With a visibly shuddering breath, she squared her shoulders and turned to hurry down the stairs, nudging her way through the crowd. Matt watched her flee, his heart bleeding at his feet.

As far as mistakes went, kissing Joelle had been a doozy.

Chapter Eight

❧❦

THE HOUSE WAS dark when Joelle made her way from her room to the kitchen. She couldn't sleep. Not after what had happened at the football game.

Matt had kissed her!

Or she'd kissed him.

She wasn't sure which of them had moved first. The kiss had happened so fast and yet time had stood still, as if they were the only two people left on the planet. The roar of the crowd had faded to white noise, the stadium lights had bathed the world in a warm cocoon, and all she could see was Matt. All she had wanted in that moment was Matt.

He was everything she'd longed for in a man. Kind, considerate, respectful, compassionate, protective, honorable and generous. And that wasn't even counting his brooding good looks. She'd always been drawn to dark-haired men with smoldering dark eyes.

She put the kettle on for tea. While the water boiled, she sorted out her emotions. Or at least tried. She was stunned and delighted. Scared and yet her heart yearned for what she knew logically wasn't a good idea.

Her and Matt?

Rose's words came back to her. *You're both so stubborn you can't see what's right in front of you.*

Could Rose be right? Joelle hadn't thought so but after the past few days…

She grabbed the kettle before it could whistle. No. Rose was wrong. Wasn't she?

What if she wasn't wrong? A voice inside Joelle whispered. Then what?

Was Joelle willing to find out? Was she willing to change her life, to adjust her plans? Could she fulfill the promise she made to her father while staying in Marietta?

The questions rambled through her mind as she poured water into a mug and dipped a bag of chamomile tea until the liquid turned a golden color.

The only answer she came up with was she—just didn't know.

Needing a distraction from her upsetting thoughts, she put on her wool coat and with her mug of tea in hand, headed for the barn. Watching Daisy and her foal would take her mind off the turmoil kicking up anxiety to bubble inside of her.

A low light created shadows on the barn walls. The smell of fresh hay and warm horses soothed her more than chamomile tea ever could. She moved quietly through the stable of horses, pausing at Star's stall. The horse opened an eye and nickered softly. She reached through the slats of the gate with her free hand to pet his nose before moving away. Clutching her mug of tea, her steps faltered as she approached the large stall on the far end of the barn.

Matt leaned against the stall gate. He'd changed into his work jeans, boots and plaid shirt under a dusty wool and shearling coat. He wore no hat and his thick hair was unruly. A tingling in the pit of her stomach created waves of awareness cascading over her flesh, pricking her skin. She licked her lips, remembering the feel of his mouth on hers.

She should retreat before he realized she was there.

He glanced her way, his eyes widening then softening before returning his attention to the mare and her foal. A slight smile brought up the corners of his well-shaped mouth. Instead of retreating, her feet carried her forward as if pulled by some unseen thread to his side. Daisy stood patiently while the foal nursed.

"Couldn't sleep either, huh?" Matt asked in a low husky voice.

Was his reason for sleeplessness the same as hers? The thought made her throat feel parched. She quickly took a sip of tea.

"No," she replied, keeping her voice soft so as not to disturb the horses.

For a long moment, the sound of the foal sucking and the occasional nicker from one of the other horses filled the void between them.

"Have you named the foal?" she asked, giving in to her curiosity.

"The foal's new owners will do that when they come to see him next week," Matt said.

"But he won't leave the ranch until he's weaned. That's at least six months, right?" She didn't like thinking of someone else owning the foal. But that was part of the business. Probably part of why her father never let her witness the birth or get too close to the foals. He didn't want her getting attached. He had been protecting her from the heartache of seeing the animals leave the ranch.

Part of her appreciated his effort, yet another part of her wished he'd have let her face the realities of life.

"Yes, unless my loan doesn't go through and the ranch is

sold, in which case, I will offer to sell Daisy to the Conrads as well."

A knot lodged in her throat. If Matt couldn't come up with a way to buy her half the ranch could end up in the hands of strangers. Keeping the mare with her foal was practical, but knowing that Matt worried about the two horses filled her with a tenderness that bruised her heart.

"About earlier..." he said.

Her gut clenched. He was going to apologize for kissing her. It was just like him to taken on the burden of responsibility. She beat him to the punch. "I'm sorry."

He stared at her. "It was my fault."

"No." She wouldn't let him take the blame for something she had wanted.

She'd wanted him to kiss her.

The thought echoed in her head. She sucked in a quick breath. Maybe she always had? But the kiss hadn't meant anything. It couldn't. Could it?

He ran a hand through his hair. "Look, it was a mistake."

His words stung as if he'd slapped her. Ridiculous! She'd just decided the kiss hadn't meant anything and he confirmed it with his words, so why was she feeling rejected?

She needed sleep. She needed to leave the ranch, to put some distance between them. Squaring her shoulders, she sought for a congenial tone. "You're right. We got caught up in the moment. The Grizzlies won. A celebratory kiss. That's all it was. Nothing else."

The relief on his face pierced her heart.

"Okay, good. I don't want things to be awkward between us."

She laughed lightly to cover the bleeding of her heart. "Everything's fine."

But nothing was fine. Never would be. Her heart throbbed

with emotions better left unclaimed. When had she let down her guard? When had she given him power to hurt her?

Something she'd never allowed in her youth. Not when Matt had left her in the fun house alone, and it had taken her twenty minutes to find her way out. Nor later when she'd snuck into the hayloft to listen to Matt and RJ as they mucked out the stalls. Not when her father would clap Matt on the back and praise his B in math while barely acknowledging her A. Not when Matt had quietly picked up the broken pieces of the dishes she'd thrown at him after her father had left the room on the heels of telling her he was taking Matt on a fishing trip and she couldn't go.

That's how it had always been. Dad and Matt with her on the outside looking in.

She would have to shore up her defenses and keep Matt at a distance for the next three days or she'd find herself leaving the ranch not only with her inheritance but also with a broken heart.

છ૦૦રુ

DESPITE MATT'S MELANCHOLY, the next morning dawned bright with the promise of a clear sky. There would be much jubilation in town after last night's football win against Livingston.

The high school was holding another pancake breakfast to raise money to help the football team finish out the year. Ava would be working a grill, which left Matt and Joelle to fend for themselves at the ranch. Matt didn't mind cold cereal occasionally. He left the box of raisin bran out but put the milk back in the refrigerator when it became apparent Joelle was sleeping in.

Matt went about his morning chores of caring for the horses and tried not to let his mind think about Joelle. But that was impossible. She'd infiltrated all his thoughts.

A celebratory kiss.

If that was how she celebrated, he wanted to be with her on New Year's Eve.

A foolish notion on so many levels. He was sure when Clark asked him to watch out for Joelle, to make sure she had everything she needed, Clark hadn't meant for Matt to kiss his daughter. Besides, by New Year's she'd be in New York City, probably at some posh party with her friends and he'd...he had no idea where he'd be. He hoped and prayed he'd still be at the ranch. But the future was precarious and out of his control. The security he longed for seemed out of his reach. On Monday he'd have a better idea of what lay ahead. For now he needed to stay focused on doing what had to be done on the ranch.

And right now the Arabian, Domino, demanded his attention. The vet had returned to the ranch on Thursday afternoon to examine the horse, looking for further injury. None existed. The horse was either afraid to put weight on the leg or playing a game with Matt.

"Come on, baby, you can do it," he cooed to the beast.

Domino whinnied and tucked the leg up further.

Matt removed a carrot from his pocket. "How about a treat? Put your leg down."

He touched Domino's knee with a little pressure. The leg lowered but the hoof hovered over the ground. "Hmmm, almost there."

Keeping one hand on the horse's flank, he guided his other hand down the horse's foreleg, past the knee to the cannon bone and again applied pressure. With a snort, Domino set his hoof on the ground, then looked back at Matt as if to say, "Well?"

He laughed and handed him the carrot. The horse ate greedily, furthering Matt's suspicion that the animal was toying with him.

"That is such a beautiful horse."

Matt turned toward the sound of Joelle's voice. She'd climbed up on the railing of the gate. She wore a multi-colored vest over a white, gauzy-looking dress. The skirt billowed in the breeze. She wore the brown and turquoise boots, which warmed his heart. Her hair was loose and hung over her shoulders. Her lips were red and her eyes lit up from within, making him wonder what she was thinking, feeling. And he'd never seen a more beautiful sight. His pulse jumped and heat spread through him, making him feel as if the sun beat down directly on him.

"He is a rascal," he replied, tearing his gaze away from her pretty face. "He's milking his injury for all it's worth."

"Did Doctor Sullivan find anything wrong?"

"No. Nothing. Just stubbornness."

"A lot of that going around," she mumbled.

He gave her a sharp glance. "Is that directed at me?"

She laughed. A pretty sound that slid along his flesh, creating little goosebumps. "Maybe. Why didn't you tell me about Rose?"

He jammed his hands into his pant pockets. "What's to tell?"

Joelle's gaze narrowed. "She said you two aren't seeing each other anymore. Why not?"

No sparks. The words danced on the tip of his tongue but he bit them back. Instead he went with a more ambiguous answer. "We decided we're better as friends."

"Really?" Joelle's brow furrowed in obvious puzzlement.

"Yes, really." He needed to veer her away from the subject of Rose. He didn't want to discuss his private life with Joelle. Not when he was struggling to understand his feelings for her. "You going to the pancake breakfast?"

"Yes." She hesitated then asked, "Do you want to come?"

He hadn't, but now that she'd asked, he wished he could. He wanted to prove to himself, to her, they were okay. That what had happened last night at the game wouldn't change anything. Her thoughtfulness in asking soothed some of his anxiety. Things between them would go back to normal. Whatever normal was for them. "I can't. Tod Styles should be arriving soon to do the appraisal."

She wrinkled her nose. "I thought he wasn't coming until sometime next week."

"I asked Ren to light a fire under him. The sooner we can figure this all out the better." He wasn't holding any illusions that Joelle would change her mind.

A shuttered look crossed her face. He'd have thought she'd be happy to accelerate the proceedings. Why wasn't she?

"I see." She hopped off the fence. She gave him a tight smile. "I'll head out then. I would rather not encounter Tod again."

Matt watched her leave with an ache in his heart. Soon she'd be gone for good and he'd miss her.

ဆဝလ

TWENTY MINUTES LATER, Joelle arrived at Marietta high school. The front parking lot was full so she parked around the back where half of the spaces were taken up by floats from last night's parade. Each class did a float and at the end the town council voted on the best one. She couldn't remember which float won. They were all so good. Back in Joelle's day the winning class received a pizza party. She wondered if that was still the tradition.

She entered the school noting the hallways were lined with posters of a large round moon peeking over the horizon of a green field announcing the theme of Harvest Moon for the Homecoming dance to be held later that night. She took a detour on her way to the cafeteria to peek into the gym.

Several teenagers were busy arranging artfully made center-pieces of jewel-colored flowers and apples on sticks in tall vases on the sea of round tables covered in creamy cloth. Even the chairs were covered and tied with red ribbon. The retractable bleachers weren't visible amid the fall decorations of leaves, trees, pumpkins, a silly scarecrow and a large, round, yellow moon as a backdrop for pictures. Long strands of fall leaves in golds and reds and oranges hung from the ceiling.

The effect left Joelle breathless. The kids had gone all out. She remembered the many dances she'd attended while in high school. The excitement and anticipation of dancing with a guy. That thrilling moment when a boy would ask her to dance. And of course there were the times when she and her friends would gather in the center of the gym and dance together, not caring whether the boys joined in or not. Fun times. Easier times.

Leaving the gym, she made her way to the cafeteria. The folding tables were down and lined in rows. Along one wall a line of electric griddles and pancake makers waited. Picking up an empty plate, she headed to Ava for two fluffy pancakes and bacon. She spied Callan and Eve on the far side of the room. She smiled and said hello to several people as she made her way to their table.

"So what's up with you and Matt?" Eve asked as soon as Joelle sat down. "The whole town saw you two in a liplock last night."

Joelle's stomach churned. "It was nothing." Unexpected tears burned at the back of her eyes. She stared at her plate and fought to keep them from spilling.

"Hey, what's wrong?" Callan asked.

Joelle poked at the gooey mess of pancake swimming in syrup. "I'm fine."

Eve pointed her fork at her. "Your face says otherwise."

Joelle stared at her friends. The need to confide grew until she couldn't stop the words from flowing. She told her friends about her father's dying wish, about her business opportunity and about selling the ranch. And about her confusing emotions regarding Matt.

Callan sat back with a Cheshire grin on her face. "Sounds to me like you've fallen in love with Matt."

Joelle swallowed the lump in her throat. "No. No. I can't be in love with Matt."

"Why not?" Eve asked. She tucked her brown hair behind her ear. "He's dreamy."

Joelle stabbed at her pancake. "He said kissing me was a mistake. That he didn't want things to change between us."

"Do you want things between you to change?" Callan asked.

Did she? "I don't know," Joelle answered honestly. "Maybe."

Eve tsked. "I think you do."

"Me, too," Callan said. "And not just because I want you to come home to stay. Though that would be fabulous."

Joelle's heart twisted at the hopeful look on Callan's face.

"I think Matt's a good guy." Callan wagged her eyebrows. "And from the way he was getting all he-man possessive the other night, I think he feels more for you than he's letting on."

Joelle bit her lip. He had been surprisingly protective. "You think so?"

"I do." Callan leaned forward. "You're both coming to the alumni dinner tonight, right?"

"Yes." Her nerves fluttered at the thought.

"Good. Tonight will be the perfect opportunity for you to find out how he feels. And then you can decide if you're leaving or staying."

Leaving or staying. When had her choices come down to this?

The moment she'd let Matt into her heart.

She prayed she wasn't setting herself up for heartbreak.

Ⅎℴ

MATT WAITED IN the living room of the farmhouse later that night for Joelle. They were heading to town for the alumni dinner at the Graff Hotel. He hadn't seen her since this morning when she'd left to go into town for the pancake breakfast. While she'd been away Tod Styles had done his appraisal, keeping his thoughts to himself and promising Matt he'd have an official document prepared and sent to Ren on Monday morning.

Acid burned in Matt's gut. He paced a path along the back of the couch. He hated this unsettled feeling, not knowing how the future would shake out. He hadn't succeeded in changing Joelle's mind about leaving. He had no control over whether he would qualify for a loan big enough to buy her share and he dreaded the thought of losing the ranch. All in all depressing.

Joelle stepped into the room. Matt halted. His lungs forgot how to pump oxygen. Her tentative smile slammed into his midsection. She'd tamed her long, dark hair into a loose updo with curling tendrils framing her face. The emerald green dress showed off her figure to perfection and black heels emphasized her slim, shapely calves. The jewelry she wore caught his eye. Big and clunky yet elegant. She really did make interesting pieces. She was so artistic, gifted even. Clark was right in telling her to follow her dream. She needed to share her talent with others. But why couldn't she do so from the ranch?

He pushed aside his frustration to say, "Wow. You're beautiful."

"Thank you." She seemed pleased by his compliment as she glided toward him. "You clean up well, too."

"Thanks." He'd put on his navy suit. Clark had insisted he buy one for special occasions. Tonight seemed like such an occasion. He tugged at the blue and green striped tie circled around his neck like a noose. "I'm not used to this get-up."

"I never would have believed you'd be a fusser." She reached out to straighten the tie. "The suit fits you well."

He held her gaze, liking the swirl of blue in her eyes that now appeared more of a teal color. So pretty. "I like your dress."

Her mouth curved in a flirty smile. She stepped back and twirled. "Glad you approve."

Desire ran a ragged course through him. He swallowed. He didn't want to leave for the dinner. He wanted to pull her into his arms and kiss her.

But that would not be a good idea. Kissing Joelle again would only complicate things. He'd made the mistake of kissing her once already. He couldn't do it again because he was afraid kissing would lead to him asking her to stay and never leave him.

Life was hard enough right now without adding attraction and emotions that had nowhere to go to the mix. He needed to keep a distance between them. Both physically and emotionally. "We should get going."

Opening the front door, he followed her out to his truck. Once they were inside and headed toward town, he said, "Tod Styles said the appraisal would be finished Monday morning. Will you stick around long enough to see the numbers he quotes us?"

"Yes, I will."

She sounded so certain. He was glad but not hopeful that she would change her mind about selling. The thought tampered down his mood even more. He wasn't sure he should be attending this event. He wouldn't be good company.

The venue for the alumni dinner was one of the smaller ballrooms of the recently refurbished Graff Hotel. The alumni committee had decorated the chandeliered room with Marietta High School memorabilia. A large projection screen in the corner showed rotating yearbook pictures dating from way back to the most recent graduating class. A buffet style dinner had been set up at one end of the large space. Tables and chairs were positioned throughout the room and already the chairs were filling up. A large square space in the middle of the room had been set up for a dance floor. A sound box and DJ were set up discreetly in another corner. Music played in the background.

Matt saw RJ sitting with Lane. He led Joelle in that direction.

Both men stood as Joelle stopped by the table. "Hi, Lane, RJ. Good to see you both."

Lane touched the empty seat next to him. "You can sit here, Joelle."

Matt grabbed an empty chair across the large table and pulled it out. "Here. We'll sit here."

Joelle's gaze bounced from Matt to Lane and back again. A small smile played at the corners of her mouth. "Thank you." She sat so that she faced Lane and RJ. She leaned across to engage Lane in a conversation about billiards.

Matt sat next to her and met RJ's mocking gaze. Matt frowned. "What?"

RJ flashed him an uncharacteristic grin. "Nothing."

Joelle put her hand on Matt's arm. "Will you excuse me a moment, I see Callan."

Matt stood to hold out his hand and help her to her feet. He watched her walk away, along with every single male in the place.

"So you and Joelle, huh?"

Schooling his features into a neutral expression Matt turned to RJ. "We came together. That's it."

RJ's lips twisted into a wry smile. "If you say so. But from where I'm sitting it looks like a whole lot more. You decided to take my advice after all."

"What advice?" Lane asked.

Matt gritted his teeth. He'd like to punch RJ for bringing

that up again. "Nothing."

RJ snorted.

"It sure seems like you and Joelle have a thing going on," Lane stated. "Everyone saw you two kissing in the stands at last night's football game. Not that anyone would blame you. She's a keeper, that one. If you're not careful, Locke, someone else will come along and snatch her up."

The thought of Joelle with someone else grabbed Matt by the throat and squeezed until he couldn't draw in a breath. What did his reaction mean?

And what was he going to do about it?

Chapter Nine

∞♥∞

JOELLE WAS IMPRESSED with the Graff Hotel. Matt had told her that Troy Sheenan, another Marietta alum who'd done well for himself in the world away from Marietta, had returned to town. He'd bought and renovated the historical building last year. Apparently Troy had kept most of the original gold trim and sparkling chandeliers. The ballroom floor gleamed as people filled the space to dance to the tunes played by the DJ. The urge to be a part of the festivities seized Joelle.

She placed her hand over Matt's. "Dance with me?"

They sat across the white linen covered table from Lane and RJ. Callan and Eve had joined them. All through the dinner the conversation had been lively among the friends. Except for Matt. He answered if spoken directly to, but otherwise he'd remained mute. Sullen, even. Joelle hadn't missed the cagey looks being bandied about between Matt, Lane and RJ. Something was up and she wasn't sure she wanted to know but her curiosity was a strong driving force, one she had trouble curbing.

"I don't dance," Matt said.

She laughed. "That's not true. I've seen you dance. You have rhythm." She tugged on his hand as she stood. "Come on."

He narrowed his gaze but rose to his feet. "When did you see me dance?"

She grinned. "I watched you practicing in the barn before your senior prom."

He laughed. She liked the small crinkles around his eyes and the way his mouth curved. The remembered feel of his lips on hers sent heat flushing through her. His hand slid to her low back as he guided her toward the center of the dance floor. Sensations rippled over her flesh from the point of contact. Then he spun her to face him, one arm snaking around her waist and the other taking her hand. He pulled her close. She put her free hand on his shoulder. Her breathing caught, then sped up.

"I didn't know I was living with a spy," he commented, his dark eyes glinting with humor. "I hope you don't know all my secrets."

"Not all, I'm sure. A few though. But I'd like to know what's going on between you and Lane and RJ?"

He cleared his throat. "Nothing."

"*Pffft*. Something's up."

He swirled her around. "They were ribbing me about what happened at the game last night."

"Our kiss you mean?" She held his gaze. Her lips tingled with the memory of his kiss.

Red crept up his neck. "Yes."

Was he blushing? She stifled a giggle. "I took some ribbing from Callan and Eve, too."

He chuckled. "That's small town life for you in Marietta."

"Well, we weren't exactly discreet."

His hand on her back pressed her closer. "No, we weren't. I'm sure everyone thinks there's something going on between us because we're dancing."

"Is there something going on between us?" She held her breath.

"That depends on what other secrets you know," he quipped.

She swallowed back the temptation to rise on her tiptoes and kiss him. "I know you used to stash a bag of strawberry licorice in the bottom cupboard of the barn."

"Only so you wouldn't eat them." His brow wrinkled. "Hey, if you knew where they were why didn't you eat them?"

"It was more fun to badger you for a piece than to simply take one." Whenever she'd find him munching on a piece of candy, she'd harass him until he gave her some. It was the only way she could get his attention because most of the time he ignored her. Or tried to. She hadn't made his life easy. She'd let her hurt and anger drive her. Regret flushed through her. Regret and shame. Someday she'd make it up to him. She just didn't know how yet.

"Ha, I see how you are." His mouth quirked at the corner.

"How am I?" She wanted to know how he felt about her. Did he still wish she'd never come back to the ranch all those years ago? Did he resent having had to share her father with her, the way she'd resented sharing Dad with Matt? Did Matt feel the same attraction and pull to her that she felt toward him? She bit her lip to keep the questions from popping out.

His gaze held hers, his expression intense and unflinching. "Fiercely independent, talented and beautiful."

Each word fanned the flames glowing inside of her. He thought her beautiful and talented. She would have fallen over if he hadn't been holding her. "Thank you. That means a lot coming from you."

"I'm telling the truth." His fingertips rubbed little circles over her back, sending thrilling sparks shooting over her skin. "I admire you, Joelle."

She drew back slightly, stunned by his admission. She'd been nothing but trouble for him since they'd met. How could he admire her? And for what? "Me?"

"You. You have stayed true to your passion for creating art. You bravely went off to college not knowing anyone and succeeded."

"Daddy didn't think I would," she murmured, dropping her gaze.

"Hey, your dad was proud of you." Matt lifted her chin with the crook of his finger. The forceful look in his eyes drew her in, making her want to believe his words. "I'm proud of you, too."

Her heart expanded in her chest, crowding out the old hurts, the old anger, leaving only room for affection and...she shied away from labeling the tender emotion filling her heart, her soul. "Thanks," she murmured.

She laid her cheek against his shoulder and breathed in deeply, inhaling his masculine scent mingling with his spicy aftershave. She melted against him, relishing the hard strength of his body, the feeling of protection and care that seemed to wrap around her. They swayed to the music until the song ended. Joelle didn't want to move out of his arms but a faster-paced tune forced them apart. They stayed on the dance floor, moving to the rhythm of a Billy Joel song about Uptown Girls.

Though they no longer touched, each look they shared was a caress, an exciting invitation for things unspoken. At least she hoped the smoldering glances coming from Matt meant he shared the same attraction that set her body on fire as each new song played and they continued to dance. She preferred the slower songs when he'd take her in his arms, holding her tightly against him until their hearts beat as one.

As the night progressed, the crowd thinned as those with teenagers left to chaperone the high school Homecoming dance.

Much to Joelle's delight she and Matt danced until the very last song played. A slow number that sent her once again into his arms. A place she was finding extremely natural and exciting and comfortable all at the same time.

As the last notes of the tune drifted on the air, the room had cleared, leaving only a handful of people. Joelle was hot and sweaty, but feeling jubilant and alive. Her senses were hyper aware of Matt's every move, every breath as they said goodnight to the other stragglers and left town in Matt's truck.

Inside the cab, Joelle scooted close and leaned her head on his shoulder.

"Tired?" he asked.

"No, more like languid." She relaxed against his side, enjoying the feel of his thigh pressing into hers. It would be so easy to pretend she was his girl and they were heading home to be together. The thought made her breath hitch. She was letting her attraction to Matt mess with her good judgment. But at the moment she didn't care. There was nothing wrong in appreciating a handsome man. Even if that man was Matt. A man she'd never thought she'd feel such yearnings for.

"Languid? They teach you to use fancy words like that in college?"

She smiled at his teasing. "Yes, that and other big words—like magnanimous, which you are, and sesquipedalian, which I am doing right now."

"You think I'm noble. I'm blushing," he said in a husky tone. "The other word means..."

She lifted her head and grinned at him. "One who uses big words, of course."

His laugh filled her heart. "Of course it does."

When they arrived at the ranch, Matt opened her door and for a moment Joelle wished this outing had been a date and that Matt would ask for a good night kiss. She wasn't ready for the night to end. She captured Matt's hand before he opened the house door. "Let's not go in yet."

Though the porch light glowed softly in the wall fixture,

shadows fell across Matt's face blocking his expression. He remained silent and she feared she'd overstepped herself.

Then he squeezed her hand. "The back porch rocker."

Drawing her pashmina closer to ward of the cool night air, she followed him around to the back where her dad had bolted a wide porch rocker to the floorboards. During the day the view of Copper Mountain in the distance would be breathtaking. Tonight darkness obscured the mountain's face, leaving only a ragged outline against the moon hung low in the sky.

The rocker creaked as they sat together. A brisk wind whistled through the valley and made her shiver. Matt drew her to him, tucking her against his side, his arm settling around her shoulders. She burrowed closer, loving the feel of warmth, care, coming from him.

"This is nice." She never wanted to move from this spot.

"It is."

"I'll miss this when I leave." The thought made her ache in ways she'd never experienced before when she contemplated leaving the ranch. "I hadn't realized how much I missed the quiet serenity of the ranch or the friendly and open people of Marietta." *Or you.*

His fingertips drew little circles on her bare shoulder where the pashmina had slipped down. The roughened pads generated heat to warm her from the inside out. "We'll miss you, too."

She closed her eyes willing the agitated butterflies in her tummy to quiet down. But they wouldn't, nor could she fight back the need to know if this thing between her and Matt had a future. Did she dare hope?

Snuggled close to his chest, she could hear his heart beating, faster than it should. "And you, Matt? Will you miss me?"

He didn't move but she could feel tension radiating off him in waves that hit her with the force of a gale wind.

"I will." Though he didn't sound pleased by the admission.

She stared at the moon and blinked back the burn of tears. Maybe this attraction she felt was one-sided. She'd be a fool to push him for more no matter how much she wanted to.

"I'll miss you." The words burst from her before she could filter them.

He groaned and shifted, curling toward her at the same time drawing her flush against him. Her breath caught, trapped in her lungs as excitement revved in her veins. His free hand cupped her face, guiding her lips to his. His mouth captured hers, hard and searching as if he didn't want to give in to the attraction, the temptation of her kiss.

She opened her mouth and traced his lips with her tongue. He groaned again and softened, opening to her. She tasted the sweet chocolate from their dessert and the fire of desire as he claimed her with his kiss. His hands smoothed a path up and down her back.

The pashmina fell off her shoulders, but she didn't feel the cold. Only the heat. The heat of his kiss, his arms, his body. Her arms circled around him and she shifted closer, deepening the kiss.

Urgent, exploring, hungry. She wanted more.

More of him.

She pressed herself against the hard plane of his muscled chest. His touch roused a fiery passion in her that both shocked and excited her. She'd never felt so close to the edge of reason. Her thoughts spun out of control but she didn't feel afraid. She wanted this, wanted him.

Without breaking the kiss, she worked his tie loose and unfastened the buttons on his shirt. Frustrated by his t-shirt, she yanked at the edges of his shirts, pulling them loose until she could slide her hands over his skin, tracing the corded muscles and hard planes of his chest.

"I love you," she whispered against his mouth, the words

coming out of their own volition.

But she realized deep in her soul that it was true.

With the hurt and anger stripped away, there was only one emotion left and that was love. She loved Matt. The knowledge should have sent her running but instead she accepted the truth. Her heart nearly burst from her chest, it was so full of love for this man.

He stilled. His breath turn ragged, uneven. His heart beat wildly beneath her palms.

Then his hands slipped to her waist and tightened for a fraction of a second. Abruptly, he pulled back, breaking the connection.

She followed him placing a kiss on his chin, his cheek.

"Joelle, no," he murmured and set her aside.

A rush of cold air froze her heated skin and seeped into her heart. Her mind scrambled to understand what was happening. Why was he pushing her away? "Matt?"

He stood, facing away from her. "We can't do this. I can't do this to you."

Confused by his words, she retrieved the pashmina from the ground and wrapped the soft material around her freezing skin. "Uh, in case you didn't notice, I was a willing participant."

"I know. And that makes it even worse."

"Worse?" Anger lit a fire in her soul. She jumped to her feet. "I didn't realize kissing me was such a hardship."

Not to mention my love.

He turned toward her, but shadows obscured his expression. "No, that's not what I meant."

"Then what do you mean?"

"Us, together, is too complicated." His tortured tone plucked at her nerves. "There's too many reason why you and I can't happen."

She sucked in a sharp breath. He was rejecting her. "There's only one reason that I can think of," she ground out. Squaring her shoulders, she said, "You don't feel the same way about me that I do about you."

In the glow of the October moon she saw him run a hand through his hair. Her own fingers itched to do the same. She curled her hands into tight fists, crumpling the delicate silk and wool fabric of her wrap.

"Your father wanted me to watch out for you. This isn't what he had in mind."

"How do you know it isn't? He loved you like a son. He would want you to be happy. I know he wanted me to be happy. He wanted me to follow my dream. What if you're my dream?"

He sighed. "I know Clark wanted both of us to be happy."

She moved closer until she was right in front of him. "You know what, leave my father out of this. Right now it's only you and me. Could you, do you, love me?"

He groaned. "Joe, it's not that simple."

"Of course it is," she shot back, anger and hurt filling her until she thought she might drown. "Either you do or you don't."

"If I say yes, then what?" He barked out a bitter laugh. "You'll give up your dream, your once in a lifetime business opportunity, and stay on the ranch?"

The harsh tone of his voice set her back a step. She hadn't thought that far ahead. She'd been thinking only with her emotions, not her head. Was she willing to give up the chance to buy into a business for his love?

The question reverberated through her brain. Part of her knew the answer was yes. She would give up her life in New York to be here with him in a heartbeat. But part of her held back from saying those words, from committing herself, because… if she did say yes and he didn't love her…

"You said yourself I could make jewelry here," she pointed

out, hedging. "I could start a business here on the ranch."

"I did and you could. But not because of me. Never because of me."

She pressed a fist to her heart. "Because you don't love me."

"Because I don't want to be the reason you give up your dreams. You should follow your heart. Do as you promised your father. Follow your dream. And we both know your dream is not here."

"But what if it is?" For the first time in her life she felt like she belonged on the ranch and now he was telling her to leave.

She guessed some things never changed. Ice filled her veins, chilling her to the core.

"It's not. And I couldn't survive if I gave you my heart only to have you decide sometime down the road that you made a mistake."

"Whoa!" She couldn't believe what he was saying. "Wait a second. I am not my mother."

"I'm sure Clark never expected your mother to regret her choice either." He stepped past her. "Goodnight, Joelle."

Her heart shattered into a million tiny shards of ice as the lonely echo of his footsteps rang inside her head, reminding her of all the reasons she left the ranch in the first place.

෬෬

I LOVE YOU.

The whispered confession haunted Matt through the night. His heart felt like it had been fed into a meat grinder. Hearing those words had brought a wealth of joy flooding his system and an answering love filled his soul, shocking in its intensity. He'd danced on the edge of telling her that he felt the same when his mind finally kicked in gear and took over.

What he'd told Joelle had been the truth. He didn't want to

be the reason she stayed.

Because he didn't want to ever be her biggest regret.

If her love cooled and she'd passed up this opportunity to follow the dream she'd worked so hard for, she'd come to hate him.

And that was something he couldn't survive.

He'd rather loose the ranch than hurt her.

Though it was Sunday morning, he was up and on the phone before the sun had fully risen. The first call was to Tod Styles asking him to put out feelers for a buyer for the ranch. Despite the early morning intrusion, Tod had been enthusiastic about brokering the sale of the Winslow Estate. No doubt because there would be a hefty commission. Matt had given Tod the name and number of a few people who had approached Clark over the years about purchasing the ranch. Matt was sure one of them would jump at the opportunity to acquire the acreage, buildings and horseflesh.

The other call was to Ren Fletcher letting him know Matt's decision.

"Where will you and the rest of the staff go?" Ren had asked.

Matt had no idea. "I'm sure with my half of the money from the estate I can find a small place to purchase that could accommodate us all. I'm sure Tod will be happy to find something for me."

"And Joelle is okay with this?"

"She will be." Matt was sure once she thought through her options that she'd come to realize that returning to her life in New York was her best plan. Her only plan.

Because Matt would not use her love as a way to keep the ranch.

After hanging up from Ren, Matt made his way to the kitchen. Joelle's suitcases were sitting at the bottom of the stairs. The sight kicked him in the gut like a hoof, knocking the breath from his lungs. He hadn't expected her to leave today. But after rejecting her last night, he shouldn't be surprised. Regret tore a path through him, making him wish he could take last night back regardless how selfish it would be to ask her to stay.

He found Joelle and Ava in the kitchen. Ava, wearing her Sunday best—being a geometrical printed skirt and ruffled blouse—was at the sink washing dishes. Joelle sat on a stool, her legs covered by a long, clingy black skirt. Her shoulders drooping slightly, making guilt crawl through Matt like a spider on the hunt.

She turned to face him as he entered. The soft-looking pink sweater showed off her curves and dipped at the neckline just enough to make his mouth go dry. She was devastatingly beautiful.

The corners of her mouth pulled down slightly and dark circles bruised the tender skin beneath her blue eyes. There was no mistaking the sadness in her gaze before she turned away and sat up straight. Her chin jutted out in that way of hers that had once driven him nuts but now made him want to take her into his arms and comfort her.

He doubted she'd accept his offer. Not after last night.

"You're leaving today," he stated in as neutral a tone as he could.

"This afternoon."

The flat tone of her voice raked at his nerves. "I thought you wanted to be here when Tod gave us the results of the appraisal?"

"You can have Tod email the information." She folded her napkin and laid it on the counter.

Ava wiped her hands on a towel and gave him a searching look. "Joelle has agreed to attend church this morning."

"That's wonderful." And surprising. Joelle had attended as a kid and teen because Clark insisted they all go. Matt enjoyed the services and the community interaction. Joelle hadn't. "We can all ride together."

"We can't all fit in your truck." Joelle slipped off the stool and strode to the sink with her empty plate and cup. "Ava, would you like to drive in with me?"

"Of course, dear, I'd be delighted. Matt could ride in with us, right?"

Joelle's back visibly stiffened. "If he wants."

She walked out of the kitchen, her head held high, her gaze straight ahead, like a proud queen. For a moment he was struck with a sense of déjà vu. How many times had Joelle exited a room like that? Too many for him to count. Only before he'd always thought she was being snobby but now he realized her regal bearing hid her hurt and pain. Both of which he'd caused this time. And felt just as deeply. But it couldn't be helped. She needed to be free to follow her dream. And he had to protect his heart. The only way to do that was to deny his love.

To himself and to her.

He grimaced and met Ava's questioning gaze. He'd confide in the older woman eventually once the pain of loss lessened.

Though he had a feeling that wouldn't happen anytime soon.

Chapter Ten

∞∞

WITH MATT SITTING in the backseat and Ava beside her in the passenger seat, Joelle struggled to maintain her composure on the drive into Marietta. The ride had been silent and tense. Every time she glanced in the rearview mirror her gaze would lock with Matt's. Very distracting. Thankfully, the traffic was light going into town on this Sunday morning. The sky was overcast and gray. A storm was predicted for later in the afternoon, the first of the season. She hoped she would make it out of town by the first raindrop.

She slowed the rental sedan as the church she'd attended growing up came into view. The gothic-inspired St. James Methodist Church took up most of the block on the corner of Court and Church. She parked in the lot adjunct to the church building. The lot was nearly full. People milled around the entrance, waiting for the Sunday morning service to begin. She recognized most of the townsfolk. People who had known her since birth. People who had been friends with her, Ava, Matt and her father. A bout of anxiety attacked Joelle.

"I'm not sure I can go inside," she said to Ava, before the older woman could step out of the car.

Ava put a comforting hand on her arm. "What are you afraid of, honey?"

Good question. She didn't know. It had been a long time since she'd gone to a service. Not because she didn't believe in God. She did. But church had been something her father had insisted she attend. When she left Marietta, she'd wanted to leave everything that had to do with her father behind, including practicing her faith.

Now the thought of going inside where everything would be a reminder of her father set her nerves on edge. Matt had said she needed to make peace with her dad. She still didn't understand how to make peace with a dead man. Maybe the answers lay inside the church?

Matt's hand touched her shoulder. "Everyone here loves you, Joelle." *Everyone but you.* She shrugged off his hand, popped open the door and climbed out. Swallowing back her trepidation, she linked her arm through Ava's and headed toward the entrance, aware of Matt following close behind.

When they reached the large wooden doors, the minister, Reverend Jonathan Davis, and his wife greeted them.

Mrs. Davis, a tiny woman in her fifties, took Joelle's hand. "It's so good to see you, Joelle. We miss your father, as I'm sure you do."

Grief welled within Joelle and she smiled politely, hoping to hide her discomfort. She extracted her hand as graciously as she could. "That means a lot, thank you."

Mrs. Davis turned her attention to Ava, giving Joelle a chance to slip inside the church. It was larger than she remembered. The high ceiling and the tall, stained glass windows made her feel small and insignificant. A hand at her elbow sent ribbons of heat curling up her arm. She didn't need to look to know Matt was beside her. Not wanting to cause a scene in the middle of church she allowed him to guide her to a wooden pew. She slid in next to Carol Bingley. Of all people. Joelle didn't want to be grilled for gossip fodder today. She nodded a polite greeting to the older woman.

Matt leaned close, his breath tickled her ear as he whispered, "Want to trade seats?"

Grateful for his thoughtful offer, she nodded, rose and allowed him to slide over before she sat where he had. Now she sat wedged between Ava and Matt. Her family.

The thought touched a bruised and tender spot on her heart.

Matt may not love her the way she wanted him too, but he did care. And she would have to learn to be content with that, no matter how much her heart wanted his love.

꼶

THE SERVICE LET out an hour later. Joelle filed out of the church with Ava in front of her and Matt behind. A wind coming off the mountain whipped Joelle's hair, lifting the long wavy ends until she captured the mass in one hand and held on. She had enjoyed the sermon on giving of one's time. She didn't remember Reverend Davis being such a dynamic speaker. When she returned to New York, she'd find a place where she could volunteer her time. If she were staying in Marietta, she'd help at the recreation center with the teens.

And she'd wanted to help with the costumes for the church's Christmas pageant. There was no mistaking the anticipation in the pews when Reverend Davis talked about the upcoming Christmas season and all the activities that were being planned. She'd almost raised her hand when he'd asked for people to populate a committee to decorate the church.

But she wasn't staying. And no matter how much getting involved in the community of Marietta appealed to her, she had to be strong, stay the course and become a success in order to fulfill her promise to her father.

Because living in Marietta without Matt's love would be torture.

Ava tugged her over to meet a pretty brunette, dressed in a tailored pantsuit that looked expensive but not pretentious. "Taylor, I'd like you meet Joelle Winslow. She's in town for the Homecoming. Joelle, this is Taylor Sheenan. She married Troy and took over as the librarian when Margaret Houghton retired."

Joelle shook hands with the woman. "It's nice to meet you. I loved the library as a kid."

"You'll have to stop in sometime," Taylor said with a wide smile. "We've made some changes and upgrades."

"That's great. If I have time, I will." Heaviness settled in the pit of Joelle's tummy. There wouldn't be time because she was leaving. "Excuse me."

She hurried toward the car. She had to get out of here. It hurt too much to know she couldn't be a part of this anymore. Odd, considering there had been a time when she wanted nothing more than to escape this place.

"Joelle." Matt's voice called to her.

She turned to see Matt talking to Tod Styles. Hiding her dislike of Tod, she changed her direction and walked over to where the two men stood behind a brand-new Mercedes with the vanity plate that read TStyles.

"You're looking stunning," Tod said to her, his gaze raking over her and making her flesh crawl.

She gave him a tight smile then turned her gaze to Matt. It hurt to look at him, to know he wasn't in love with her. "Are you ready to go?"

Before Matt could answer, Tod spoke, "I was telling Matt I found a buyer for the ranch."

Shock pulsed through Joelle. "What do you mean, a buyer?" Her gaze whipped to Matt's. "I thought we were going to make a partnership and you were going to buy me out."

His expression shuttered. "That's not a feasible option for me. The best thing is to sell the ranch and then split the proceeds."

A week ago she'd have rejoiced at the news. Now it left her feeling hollow, scooped out and empty. Her heart plummeted. "You're okay with this?

"It's the only way we both get what we want."

She frowned, not understanding what he meant by that. "I thought you wanted to keep the ranch."

"I do. Did. But I realized I just want a place to belong. A home to call my own. Tod will find me a piece of property that I can build a new house on. Start a new life."

Pain as sharp as a knife's edge sliced deep into her heart. She hadn't thought she could hurt any worse, but hearing him talk of starting a new life, a life that didn't include her, seared her to the core.

"If you could both come to my office tomorrow at one we can get the ball rolling. The interested party would like to have this go through escrow quickly."

"How did you find someone so fast?" she asked as numbness flooded her veins.

"I gave him a list of names and numbers of people who have inquired about purchasing the ranch over the years," Matt said, his gaze hooded.

"I see." But she didn't see. None of what was happening made sense. Why would he give up the ranch now?

"Tomorrow at one?" Tod pressed.

She nodded, because she couldn't trust herself to speak. Her throat closed tight with emotion.

"Great." Tod opened the Mercedes door and climbed in. "See you tomorrow."

She and Matt moved out of the way so Tod could back out.

Joelle hurried to her rental and slid behind the wheel. Matt and Ava joined her a few seconds later.

By rote she drove out of the parking lot and down Court Avenue. Little drops of rain splattered the windshield. Looked like she wouldn't be leaving before the storm hit after all.

⁓⁔

MONDAY AT FIVE minutes past one o'clock, Matt stared out the front window of Styles Realty offices, feeling as if he were turning to stone. Rain poured from the sky as it had since late last night. Joelle had said she'd meet him here so they could sign the escrow papers to sell the ranch then she would head to Bozeman to catch her flight back to New York.

This was his choice. He clenched his jaw tight.

He could have accepted Joelle's love, kept the ranch and life would continue on pretty much as before, except he couldn't take advantage of Joelle. Nor could he risk having her decide she'd made a mistake, that he was a mistake.

RJ would laugh hysterically if he knew the position Matt was in. *Marry her*, RJ had said. Today the idea appealed more than Matt wanted to admit. Not because it would solve the problem of where he'd live but because he'd fallen in love with Joelle. He wanted nothing more than to ask her to spend the rest of their lives together. To have children together.

Then what are you going to do about it?

For a moment, Matt could have sworn he'd heard Clark's voice inside his head.

He rubbed a hand over his chin. If Matt wanted to marry Joelle, then he needed to be willing to leave Marietta and Montana to live wherever she wanted to live. If that meant New York City, then so be it. He was sure Ava would come with them, especially if she had the incentive of helping raise his and

Joelle's kids. And Matt could make it a condition of the sale that the hands were allowed to stay until they wanted to retire.

Giving himself a mental slap for not thinking of this solution sooner, he checked his watch. Twenty after. Where was Joelle? He called her cell phone. It went directly to voice mail. Most likely the device had died.

He called the ranch. Ava answered on the third ring. "Winslow Estate."

"Matt here. Is Joelle still there?"

"No, she left a little after you did. Is something wrong?" Ava's voice carried a note of concern.

"I hope not. She hasn't shown up at the realty office yet."

The long, low rumble of thunder rolled through the air. Lightning lit up the gray sky. Worry chomped a ragged path through him. He forced himself to stay calm.

"Maybe she stopped at the Circle C ranch to say goodbye to Callan," Ava suggested. "You should call there."

"Good idea." He hung up after promising to let Ava know when he found Joelle.

Hoping that was the case, he called the Carrigans' house and was disappointed and troubled to learn that Callan hadn't heard from Joelle since Saturday night.

He told Tod he'd be back and raced out to his truck. He headed back toward the ranch, fully expecting to come across Joelle's rental car. Maybe she'd had a flat tire? Maybe she was in a ditch, hurt and bleeding? Dread stole his breath. He forced back the dark thoughts. She had to be all right.

He concentrated on the road. The wipers couldn't keep up with the rain. Visibility was almost nil. He shouldn't be driving. No one should be out in this weather. He crawled along until he arrived back at the ranch. Joelle's rental wasn't there. His stomach sank. Distress filled his chest.

He hurried inside. "Have you heard from Joelle?" he asked

Ava.

Anxious lines creased her forehead. "No. Last I heard she was meeting you in town."

"She didn't show." He ran a hand through his hair, fighting the helpless feeling invading his chest. He shouldn't have rejected her. They belonged together. He loved her and he was a fool for not telling her.

Think, think. If she hadn't driven into town to meet him at Styles Realty, then where would she go?

Back to Bozeman? He grabbed the phone book and looked up the number for the car rental agency. Frustration and anxiety pounded at his temple. She hadn't returned the sedan. He made the girl on the other end of the line promise to tell Joelle to call him right away when she showed up there.

He checked the clock. Almost three. Her flight left at six. She had to be on her way to the airport.

Grabbing his raincoat, he said to Ava, "If you hear from her call me. I'm driving to Bozeman."

Worry clouded Ava's eyes. "You be careful. And find our girl and bring her home where she belongs."

"I will," he vowed, hoping he'd been able to keep his promise.

₧₧

JOELLE FULLY INTENDED to head into town to meet Matt at the Styles Realty offices, but instead, she exited the highway leading to Marietta and headed west. The rental car's windshield wipers worked hard to provide a clear line of sight out the front window. Rain tapped on the car's roof, the pace matching her heart rate. She felt drawn by an unseen force toward the Marietta Cemetery.

She passed a mini-mart and darted in for a bouquet of roses.

Ten minutes later, she arrived at the Marietta Cemetery. Rolling green grass dotted with white headstones and crosses stretched for a mile beneath the shadow of Copper Mountain. Joelle parked in the graveled lot. There were no other cars. Not surprising considering the downpour. But she was glad she wouldn't have to make small talk.

Pulling on the rain slicker she'd grabbed from the front hall closet as she'd left the ranch, she climbed out of the car and walked toward the Winslow family plot, her gaze zeroed on her path. A cold breeze nipped at her as if urging her on.

She found her father's grave. The headstone read, Beloved father to Joelle and Matt.

Tears welled in her eyes. Her heart ached, the agony so great she sank to her knees, not caring that the wet soil soaked through the material of her jeans.

Weeds poked through the lawn covering the parcel of land. She yanked one offending plant out and tossed it aside. Then another and another and another.

"Daddy, I miss you," she whispered. "I wish I'd told you that before. But we were never good at talking to each other, were we?"

The wind howled down off the tip of Copper Mountain and echoed inside her head.

"I've really made a mess of things. But don't I always?" She laughed, a hysterical sound that grated in her ears. "I love Matt."

The admission should have made her happy but saying the words aloud only fueled her misery. "How funny is that?"

She plucked more weeds. "But he doesn't love me." She snorted. "I told him you wanted me to follow my dream and so he's helping me do that. I am going to be a part owner in a business, making jewelry."

Tears slipped down her cheeks and landed in the soil. "Only thing is, Daddy, I don't want that dream anymore. My dream is right here in Marietta. I know I can make a success of my jewelry designs whether in New York or Montana. But what I really want is Matt's love. But I don't know how to win him over. I wish you were here to tell me what I should do."

She pressed a hand over her mouth, not minding the smell of earth coating her fingers, reminding her she was Montana born and bred. "Do you believe that, Daddy. I actually want your advice. Only it's too late now, isn't it." She buried her face in her hands. "Too late."

Even before he spoke, she knew Matt was there, she could feel his presence like a ray of sunlight breaking through the clouds.

"Joelle?"

She took a shuddering breath and wiped her tears away before lifting her gaze to meet his. Water dripped off the brim of his hat. His unzipped raincoat flapped in the wind. He held the bouquet of flowers she'd forgotten on the passenger seat of the rental. The sadness etched on his face twisted her up inside.

"I miss him," she confessed.

"I do, too." He knelt on one knee beside her and laid the flowers over the weeded patch of grass.

"He loved you," she said with the savage need to make Matt understand that truth. "I hope you know that."

His startled gaze jumped to hers. He swallowed. His eyes grew suspiciously misty. "I do know he loved me. And I know he loved his daughter more than anyone else."

His words were like a soft blanket swaddling her heart. She smiled through her tears. For the first time in her life she believed it. She wasn't sure what had changed. Maybe it was maturity or distance or the fact that she could look back through her life and see all the ways her father had shown his love, even though he couldn't tell her how he felt.

"How did you find me?" she asked.

He gave her a crooked smile. "I just had this feeling that you wouldn't leave town without saying goodbye. This was the only place I could think of that you might go." He plucked a clump of hair from her cheek and tucked it behind her ear. "What are you doing here?"

"Making peace with my father." Her heart felt halfway whole. There was still a part of it that was broken. She rose to her feet and brushed off her knees to give her a moment to compose the words she wanted, needed, to say.

Matt stood, his hands shoved into his jacket pockets, his shoulders hunched against the wind and rain. He was so handsome, caring, compassionate and loving.

She loved him. Fiercely.

Knowing she was taking a risk—he'd rejected her once already—she took a deep breath, exhaled and blurted out, "I love you, Matt Locke. I will never, could never, regret loving you. I know you don't feel the same. But maybe you could in time—" Matt placed a finger to her lips.

She swallowed back the devastation clawing its way up her throat. He didn't want to hear her declaration.

"Joe, I do feel the same."

Did she hear him correctly? "You feel the same?" Her heart hammered in her chest. Joy spread through her veins like liquid fire.

He cupped her cheek. His expression turned tender, his gaze full of love. "I love you, Joelle Winslow. And I'll follow you to the ends of the earth if that is what you want me to do."

"No, that's not what I want."

He tucked in his chin. "You don't want my love."

"No, that's—Yes, I want your love," she exclaimed and threw her arms around him. "I don't want to sell the ranch. I want to live here in Marietta with you."

He buried his hands in her hair beneath the hood of her

raincoat. "I love you." He dipped his head and kissed her lips.

Joelle kissed him back with all the love in her bursting heart. She was finally home. For good.

The End

Finding Home

A Montana Homecoming Story

Roxanne Snopek

For Cathie
Because you're awesome
and I love you!

Roxanne

Dedication

"For Ray. Anywhere you are is home for me."

Dear Reader,

Welcome to Marietta, Montana or, if you've visited before, welcome back! It's a great place to call home, even if it's just in our imaginations. In fact, that's how this story begins. My heroine, Samara, has had it rough her entire life and all she wants is to settle down somewhere quiet, where her little girl can grow up safe, secure and happy. She picks Marietta because the year she lived there during high school, was the happiest time she can remember, and she imagines she can recreate that for her daughter.

Of course, she fell in love for the first time in Marietta, which probably helped, right?

But nothing is ever exactly the same as we remember and that can be disappointing. Ah, yes, poor Samara. And poor Logan! Neither one of them was prepared for the shock and challenge of rediscovering each other. So they pretend that it's no big deal. They'll be friends; Logan will finish Samara's house so she and her little girl can move in. They'll wave at each other at the grocery store, and all will be well.

Ha! What was she thinking, trying to resist Logan, who's even sweeter and hotter than ever? Especially when her daughter and even the dog think he's the best thing since chocolate chip cookies.

I hope you enjoy following along as Marietta casts its spell on Samara and Logan, and even little Jade and her dog, Bob, who's a girl, by the way. (Jade named her that. No one knows why.) I think you will. I know I did!

Happy reading!
Roxanne

PS: Although I've visited Marietta many times as a reader, this is my first time here as a writer. I'm so grateful to the lovely Jane Porter for inviting me to join the party! This place – the imaginary world and real world it came from – is full of wonderful people who all understand the magic of coming home.

Chapter One

෨ඏ

O F COURSE IT had to be the underwear suitcase that slipped from her hands. The ancient hinges ruptured on impact with the sidewalk and it split open like a bale of fiberglass insulation. Except, instead of bright pink slabs, what burst forth was dull white, black and beige –

"Panties!"

Jade planted her little feet on the cobbled drive leading to the Bramble House bed and breakfast, and glared at her mother accusingly. "Panties are private, Mama."

Bob the dog cocked her homely one-up one-down ears, always alert to her little charge's ever-shifting emotions.

Some teenage boys leaving the park across the street paused in their roughhousing. One of them handed his football to the others and began loping over to her.

"Hey lady, need a hand?"

If there was anywhere on the planet where you could still find old-fashioned courtesy, even when you didn't exactly want it, it was Marietta, Montana.

Samara saw the instant he recognized the items flung about them.

He froze midway, seemingly paralyzed beneath the canopy of fall colors sheltering the street.

"It's okay, I've got it," she said. "Thanks anyway."

The boy rejoined his pals and they loped away, but not before she heard hoots of laughter.

Spare her from adolescent testosterone.

"Mama! Panties!" insisted Jade, agitation making her voice quiver.

"I know, honey." She squatted to shove the formerly neatly rolled items into the case, but it had been packed tightly and without hinges, the laws of physics just laughed at her.

"Stay here with Bob, sweetie," she said. "Bob, stay."

She popped the back of the mini-van and pushed and shoved stuff until she located a bungee cord. She could use it to hold the case shut. Naturally, it was underneath the spare tire and one of the s-hooks had become deeply attached, and resentful about being moved.

"You wanna fight?" she muttered. To herself or the stupid clingy s-hook, she wasn't sure. She yanked hard and, suitably chastised, the cord let go. Of course, being a *bungee* cord, it snapped back with great gusto and the metal hook, in an illustration of karma or retaliation or, more likely, that darn physics, grazed her chin.

She stumbled against the curb and landed on her butt in front of Jade, who was now clenching and unclenching her fists. Bob shoved her head under the girl's arm but it didn't have much effect.

"I wanna go home, I wanna go home, I wanna go home," Jade chanted, her voice rising with each repetition.

I know exactly how you feel, thought Sam, too weary to stand up.

Through tear-blurred eyes, she saw a pretty young woman burst out the door, a plastic garbage bag in her hand.

"Samara Davis, right? I'm Eliza Bramble. Welcome! I saw you arrive," she said somewhat breathlessly, hurrying toward them. "I was on my way down, but then I saw your suitcase break and I went to get a bag first."

"Thank you."

"Looks like your little one isn't very happy at the moment."

"It's been a long day." Samara got to her feet, one hand on her chin, the other reaching forward, hoping to distract Eliza with a handshake.

Too late.

She squatted down in front of Sam's quickly dissolving daughter, her voice friendly, her face open and helpful. "I'm Eliza. And you must be Jade."

Instantly, the dog moved to stand between Jade and the new person. Eliza looked at Sam, eyebrows raised.

"That's Bob. Don't worry, she's friendly, but Jade is… wary of strangers."

Sam shoved her underwear into the bag, heedless of order or anything other than getting them out of public view, making a mental note to get rid of every single piece, as soon as she had a chance to buy new ones.

A whole drawer-full of new undies.

Starting over from the bottom up. Literally.

Eliza moved to touch Jade's hair. Sam knew it was a well-intended gesture but Jade shrank away. Before she could begin crying, Sam scooped her up, the bag dangling from her arm.

"She's very shy," said Sam. "It's been a really long day."

"Then let's get you to your room." The woman stepped back, her smile less sure now. "Don't worry. I'll get your luggage. You take care of your little one. There's some supper in the warming oven, for whenever you're ready. We'll get better acquainted then."

As Samara hurried up the weathered stone path to the front

door of Bramble House, her chin throbbing, her arms shaking, her heart broke again for her little girl. It was too much. It was all too much.

Just a few more days, she reminded herself, as she'd been telling herself every day for the past few weeks. A few more days and they'd be in their very own home, finally.

Shelter. Privacy. A place where she and Jade could finally rest and recover. Where she could hear herself think and be alone long enough to grieve the life she'd lost and maybe figure out a way to stop dreading each new day and embrace their future.

She stepped over the threshold, surveying the vaulted ceiling, richly textured walls and elaborate chandeliers. But what must have been a beautiful home at one time now had an air of faded gentility, unspoken and unacknowledged decay.

"Samara Kim."

She jumped and turned to see an elderly woman who could only be Mabel Bramble. Tall and unbent by age, she stood motionless at the railing, her thin veined hands resting as if posed for a portrait.

Samara flushed, acutely aware of her travel-wrinkled, sweaty attire. Not to mention the unhappy child in her arms and their dog of questionable parentage that was no doubt already shedding all over the well-polished marble.

"I'm sorry we're later than expected," began Sam, desperate to break the silence.

"Never introduce yourself with an apology." Mabel Bramble descended the grand staircase, no smile to soften her words.

Her real estate agent had given Sam an oblique warning about Mabel. Great-aunt to the Carrigan girls of Circle C Ranch, as well as one of the original founders of Marietta, Mabel had strong opinions on how her town had deteriorated, and who was to blame.

But great-aunt Mabel's lack of lifetime achievement awards wasn't *her* problem.

"My name is Samara Davis, actually. This is my daughter, Jade Davis-Kim."

Mabel sniffed, as if rejecting a husband's surname was a mark of ill repute never spoken of in polite society. But she stopped in front of Sam and extended her hand.

"Welcome to Bramble House."

The older woman's grip was surprisingly strong and instead of letting go, she held Sam's hand, her eyebrows raised. Waiting.

"I'm very pleased to meet you, Ms. Bramble," said Sam, feeling her face burn.

"You may call me Mabel." She nodded once, then released Sam's hand. "And your child is called Jade, you say. Hello, Jade."

Oh dear. If Aunt Mabel disapproved of Sam's manners, things were about to take a sharp downward turn.

But Jade turned her dark gaze in the direction of this older woman who was keeping her distance and therefore safe to check out.

"Hello, tall lady. Are you mad at me?"

A bark of laughter shocked them all. Mabel lifted an elegant hand to her mouth.

"Gracious, child. You are an impertinent one. You may call me Aunt Mabel. Can you do that?"

Jade cocked her head in that particular way that told Samara she was uncomfortable but holding it together.

"Hello, Aunt Mabel."

"Well done. Now, tell me, Jade, who is this creature with you?"

In their email communications, Sam had been careful to ensure that dogs were welcome at Bramble House. Eliza had been understandably cautious, but once Sam explained that the dog was very well-trained, and part of Jade's coping mechanism after her father's death, Bob had been approved.

"This is Bob," said Jade, making the briefest eye contact with Aunt Mabel. "She is part Labrador Retriever, part Border Collie, part luck of the draw. Bob is my best friend. She is five. I am four."

Samara felt a flush of pride. Jade had recited the explanation just as they'd practiced!

Aunt Mabel was unimpressed. "I'm not accustomed to bringing farm animals inside the house but I've agreed to allow it during your stay. I trust she will not be a nuisance."

Thankfully, Eliza entered the room during Jade's introduction and heard the veiled insult in her aunt's response.

"Bob is simply lovely, isn't she? And smart, too. Now, if you'll excuse us, Aunt Mabel, I'll show our guests to their rooms."

Eliza herded them toward the hallway.

"Don't mind my great-aunt. I think you're going to love your stay with us. You've got a Jack-and-Jill bathroom connecting your bedrooms and there's a sliding door to a patio off your room, Samara. Now, let's get you settled, shall we?"

As she followed Eliza through the once-opulent hallway, Samara felt Aunt Mabel's keen eyes boring into her back.

She feared they hadn't made the best first impression on Aunt Mabel.

And that was before she remembered the display of underwear in the street.

&oes;

AN HOUR LATER, lying on the bed beside her exhausted, maxed-out, melted-down-to-a-puddle little girl, despair threatened to overwhelm her, as it had so often in the bleak months since Michael's death. To her shame, Sam barely remembered the grief, because of the devastating rush of tasks involved at the time. The mountain of paperwork at the hospital. Calling Michael's family in Taiwan. Talking with the funeral director.

And the fear that chewed relentlessly beneath everything, of how she would raise the child screaming on her hip, without him.

Samara stroked her daughter's damp forehead, sad again that this child had no one but her.

Then she elbowed up off the bed. There was nothing to be gained from self-pity.

She went to the window and pulled the drapes tighter, but a small ray of soft evening gold shone through, illuminating her sleeping daughter. Bob lifted her head watchfully, then sighed and tucked her muzzle up against Jade's arm again.

Sam's heart caught in her throat. For a moment, the fatigue and worry slipped away as she watched Jade breathe, slow and smooth, her face relaxed, her body loose as a rag doll.

This is what kept her going.

Chapter Two

৪৩ঙ্গ

SAMARA SHIVERED AS she and Jade walked through the park the next morning. The late summer sunshine slanting through the trees wasn't warm enough for her to go without a sweater in the morning.

"You excited to see our new house, sweetie?" Samara squeezed her daughter's hand, hoping her mood had improved after a good night's sleep. They turned onto Collier Avenue. Bob paced evenly beside them, her tongue lolling happily.

"We're going home?" said Jade, hopefully.

Sam sighed. It was like beating her head against a brick wall some days.

Change was not a welcome event, in Jade's world. Switching from her favorite brand of breakfast cereal to the store version ignited a three-day hunger strike that only ended when Jade decided she preferred eggs and toast anyway.

The first day of pre-school had become the last day of pre-school when the teacher took Sam aside and suggested that Jade needed "a bit more time to prepare." Or a one-on-one aide. Which Sam knew would be a waste of time even if she could afford it.

Michael had left them well provided for, buying her some much-needed time. Leaving their tiny but expensive Upper West Side apartment had been a bad day for both of them, but there was no choice. She should have done it sooner.

However, seeing all her toys put into boxes, the walls cleared of her pictures and posters, had sent Jade spinning out of control.

And now, Samara had brought her daughter to this new strange place they'd be calling home.

Before she'd seen the ad, she hadn't thought of Marietta in years. Then, memories of that one good school year flooded back.

The first place she'd belonged. The first school she'd enjoyed.

The first boy she'd loved.

Her house was part of a new high-school project in which the town of Marietta partnered with the local schools to provide work experience for underprivileged or challenged students, using derelict heritage houses owned by the city.

The houses would then be sold at below-market prices, the proceeds used to fund the next project.

She paused at Second. "What do we do here, Jade?"

"Look to the left. Look to the right. No cars? Cross. We're going home now?"

It was a treat to cross two lanes with no cars, instead of being part of a sea of pedestrians navigating over six or eight lanes, at a light-controlled intersection.

"Not New York home. Montana home. Remember?"

"I wanna go home."

Her voice was forlorn, little, hopeless, and Samara's heart broke. Buying this place was a risk, certainly, a pig-in-a-poke sort of situation. But it was the only way she could afford a decent house in a nice town.

She wanted so badly for her baby girl to be happy, healthy, to give her the world.

But no matter your intentions when they first place that warm, wrapped, squirming bundle in your lap, you're going to fall short. There are no super-moms. Eventually, you just have to hope your kid survives all your parental screw-ups.

At least here Jade would grow up safe, play outdoors, go to school with the same kids from kindergarten to graduation.

"This is our forever home now, sweetie," said Samara, squeezing her daughter's hand.

Once they'd crossed Third Street, she could see the old brick of the elementary school off in the distance. Their house was just ahead. She picked up the pace and then, she scanned the number – there it was.

She tugged Jade closer to her side.

"Look at the pretty house, honey," she breathed.

Photos hadn't done the place justice. All the homes on Collier were on oversized lots, as was typical at the time Marietta was established. Their half-acre was tiny by the standards of the day. But today? It was like having her own kingdom.

The butter-yellow Queen Anne style cottage had a small front veranda with white picket rails and gingerbread touches at the corners. The red roof was steeply pitched over what she knew would be Jade's room. The windows had been replaced but their deep-framed casings remained true to the period.

Lattice-work enclosed the three steps leading to the front door. From the street, a gold-leafed shrub and soaring red maple accentuated the colors, dappling the sunlight and making her feel as if they were about to enter a fairy tale turned real.

Except that Samara didn't believe in fairy tales.

"Mama!" Jade tugged her hand away. "You're squishing."

"Sorry, honey." She squeezed her own hands together as nervous excitement bubbled through her.

For better or worse, she was a property owner now, a *have* finally instead of the *have-not* girl she'd been for so long.

A man stepped out of the sleek black sports car parked at the curb. A flash on the door read *Tod Styles Real Estate. Getting YOU Home!*

"Hello!" he called. "You must be Samara and Jade."

She was surprised to see him. Due to the reduced price and the unusual nature of the deal, Tod was only getting a fraction of his commission. As a result, she'd received a fraction of service. Her search had brought up two Styles realtors; she wondered if she'd have had better luck with the other one.

Tod glanced at the truck across the street.

"Foreman's here. Let's go see what you bought."

"I can't tell you how long I've been waiting for this moment," she said.

Samara hadn't been involved with any of the design or restoration; she had no idea who the workers were. But surely having the foreman stop by, even now that the work was completed, was a good sign. He must be conscientious.

The door complained noisily when she pushed it open.

At triple the space of their Manhattan suite, even the relatively modest front room of this house yawned before them.

"Mama?" whispered Jade. "I wanna go home."

Samara lifted her up onto her hip, unease creeping over her.

"It's pretty, isn't it?" she repeated, to convince herself or Jade, she wasn't sure.

"No. It's dirty."

Bob trotted over the threshold into the front room, leaving paw prints in the thick layer of sawdust on the hardwood. A beam of sunshine slanted through the chilly room, highlighting the dust motes hanging in the air, waiting.

Jade had a point. But she knew it wasn't the dust that bothered her child as much as the chaos. She craved routine, predictability and order; this was anything but.

"Looks like things are coming along," said Tod. He brushed something off his tailored sleeve and walked ahead of her to the next room.

"Wait." They weren't supposed to be *coming along*. They were supposed to be *already there*. "You told me it was complete."

"Yeah, today's the date they gave me."

She stepped into the small front room, with its wide windows overlooking Collier Avenue to the north. Samara ran the toe of her sneaker over the hardwood, to see the grain beneath, telling herself to stay calm. Polished up, it would be beautiful.

But on top of it, against the walls, baseboards lay in piles, ready to be nailed into place.

"This isn't ready, Tod." She bit back the stronger words clinging to the tip of her tongue. How long did it take to install baseboards? They still had a couple of days. She was probably overreacting.

Think positive, Samara. Don't borrow trouble.

She imagined a lushly textured carpet being rolled up, so people could dance on that warm, dark wood. Jane Austen, the country-western version.

It didn't work.

The central feature wall should be the proud home of numerous ancestral portraits, she thought with a pang, not their meager family photo collection.

And she shouldn't be able to see the drywall tape.

The ceiling – painted at least – loomed above them, a single bulb dangling from a cord, shining down like a searchlight.

The brand-new windows still wore their factory stickers, jarring against the old, stripped and as yet unpainted trim.

These walls, so long neglected, wanted to be filled with friends and family, laughter and love and life and who were they getting? A lonely woman and her odd little girl.

Samara felt suddenly like she was trying on a princess gown, hoping it would transform her, knowing the whole time that no matter how she stuck out her chest, she couldn't fill it.

She pushed away those thoughts and went to find Tod. Whether or not she had second thoughts, the deal had closed. She'd made furniture delivery arrangements based on Tod's assurances that everything was on track.

And from what she could see, there was a month of work left.

℘℩℺

LOGAN STAFFORD SURVEYED the mess in the master suite bathroom, shaking his head. His students were in class all morning, giving him time to examine their work and do any necessary fix-ups.

There were always fix-ups.

This time, someone had dripped blobs of spackle into the luxurious clawfoot bathtub, then tried to scrape it off. He'd have to get someone in to refinish the surface.

He guessed the new owners would be arriving soon – the real estate agent's communication left much to be desired – but everyone knew that house construction rarely came in on time or under budget. His original estimation of being ready for final inspection in a week was off by at least two weeks, probably three. The chances of moving in on schedule were slim to none.

He examined the millwork on the bathroom cabinets. Original maple, over a hundred years old, and more beautiful than ever. His students had stripped and refinished them, installed new hardware and assisted in the reinstallation.

Time-line aside, the kids were doing a great job. They'd done their assigned tasks with care and precision, eager to get their shop credit, determined to finish high school with a leg up toward a career in construction. Their enthusiasm was a joy to behold.

Helping struggling students succeed was the best part of his job.

But if they couldn't meet their deadline, if the new owners weren't flexible, he'd have to bring in outside help. His students would still get their credit, but his hard-won project might not be renewed for next year.

Education politics was the worst part of his job.

Footsteps sounded from below.

"Stafford, you here?"

Tod Styles. *Getting YOU Home!*

He didn't dislike the man, exactly, but Tod hadn't made his opinion of this project a secret. He clearly considered his time a precious gift he couldn't afford, rather than a partial donation to a worthy cause.

The other Styles real estate agent – Tod's brother or cousin, maybe? – had a similar reputation. Rick, that was his name. He couldn't imagine how they survived, splitting Marietta's flat housing market between them.

"Hey, Tod," he said, descending the stairs.

"There must be a mistake." He heard a voice from around the corner.

A woman's voice, melodious, modulated.

Familiar.

A black and white dog bounded up to him then, wagging her tail and slipping on the hardwood steps. "Whoa. Who are you?"

"Bob?" called the woman. "Come on back, girl."

His mind raced as he walked toward the voice, unable to place her, but aware of a desperate urgency to do so.

Then he rounded the corner to the kitchen and came face to face with her. She stopped short, one arm tightening on a child who clung to her back like a limpet, the other gripping the doorframe so tightly her knuckles were white.

A child.

Then memory snapped into clear focus, shutting down rational thought for an endless split second, allowing emotion to flood in and take over.

Years fell away and he was back in high school, waiting for his calculus class to end so he could run out to their spot, under the bleachers. She would already be there, waiting, her slender form poised with eagerness. He'd watch the tension fall from her face as she broke into a smile. How he'd loved that, being the one who made the new girl smile and laugh.

It couldn't be her.

It couldn't be anyone *but* her.

Apparently she was having a similar reaction. She shifted the kid – a little girl with Asian features – onto her hip, holding her close with both arms.

He shouldn't be surprised she had a child. But children come with daddies and that thought carried a surprising amount of distaste.

"Logan?" she said, finally, the bell in her voice cracked.

Her face was paler than he remembered, her dark eyes huge. Her slenderness had progressed to the hard thinness he associated with long distance runners. He could see tendons stretching between clavicle and throat and small lines bracketed her mouth.

"Samara."

He reached back for the teenage agony that had sliced through him when she'd disappeared from his life, wondering if it was still there. It wasn't.

The only movement she'd made was to blink but he could see a muscle flicker in her jaw. Whatever life had handed her hadn't been easy. She was still Sam. Guarded, careful, trying to hide her vulnerability. Failing.

He took her hand, pressing it between his like a damn politician, unable to resist touching her more. Her skin, against his. Her small bones, as he remembered.

Then he stepped in for a quick hug, a kiss on the cheek, and then another squeeze. The smell of her hair caught him like a right hook to the jaw, staggering him with a rush of memories.

The new girl, books held tightly against her chest, dark eyes wide and cautious. The first time their eyes met, the flare of recognition that lit up inside him. The sensation of her lips opening against his, yielding, giving, so, so sweet —

The kid in her arms squirmed as if frightened and Sam shifted away.

"I can't believe it," she said, her voice steady and impersonal once more. "Is it really you?"

How quickly she'd collected herself, put up her shield and donned the guarded face she presented to her unknown and potentially hostile world.

"In the flesh," he answered. He forced himself to smile. "And in shock. You're not about to turn into a totally traumatized Girl Guide selling cookies to a man who's seeing things, are you?"

Her cheeks colored and a smile, an authentic one, broke through the mask.

Tod appeared then, clicking off his cell phone and slipping it into the breast pocket of his monkey suit. As usual, he seemed oblivious.

"Good, you're both here. Logan Stafford, general contractor, meet Samara Davis, purchaser. Nice job, Staff."

Staff. As if they were friends. As if Tod Styles knew plywood from cork board.

He wasn't just the general, either.

"Listen," said Tod, "I've got to run. Lock up when you leave, Staff."

"I will, Tod."

Like he did every single day.

Sam turned to the door then, as if remembering something. "Tod, hang on a second."

But it was too late.

Then the penny dropped for Logan.

"Wait. *You're* the purchaser?"

"Me, my daughter, Jade and her dog, Bob."

"*You're* S. Kim? You bought this house?"

He recalled the name on the transfer papers, the new owner purchasing this neglected beauty from the city.

She nodded, as if unsure how to react to his shock. "Kim's my married name."

Of course she was married. A woman like her would hardly have stayed single.

And of course, Samara's marital status was absolutely none of his business.

"Good," he said, like she needed his permission or something. "Lucky guy! Can't wait to meet him."

Shut up, Logan!

"You won't," she said, stepping around him. "He passed away."

A widow. *That's* how a woman like her would be single.

Chapter Three

ഇറ

NOT MARRIED. NO daddy. Relief surged through him, followed immediately by shame. What kind of a selfish jerk was he?

He could feel his mouth opening and closing. Thank goodness no sound was coming out.

The kid squirmed and Sam put her on the floor.

"Stay with me, honey," said Sam, gesturing to her daughter. "What do you think of our new old house?"

"I wanna go home." The little girl plunked herself down on the hardwood and crossed her arms. The dog promptly flopped down beside her, as if her sole purpose in life was to hang with this kid.

"So, let me get this straight," said Logan, brushing over the whole widow-situation, "you're S. Kim and you're moving to Marietta? Coming back, with your daughter and your dog. After all this time?"

She nodded. "Long story. Anyway, I'm back and moving in next Friday. I wanted to check in."

She straightened up and began moving down the hallway to the kitchen.

"This is the first time I'm seeing it in person," she continued. "I found out about it from my agent in New York. I'm a teacher myself – well, I was before Jade – so I'm thrilled to be part of a project like this."

There was pride and excitement in her voice.

"Yeah," said Logan, as his heart sank.

He heard her footsteps stop abruptly. She'd found the kitchen, then. The kitchen, where the plumbers were still working to connect the original iron sink to modern up-to-code pipes. The kitchen, where his students were slowly and painstakingly installing the slate flooring. The kitchen, which was still at least a week away from completion.

She turned to him. "How long will that take? It's supposed to be approved for occupancy by now. I'm moving in next week."

They'd managed to stick to the budget, because of the free labor, but the free labor had, yeah, put them behind schedule.

Then she frowned, as if remembering that Tod Styles had referred to him as the general contractor.

"If you're in charge, then you can speed things up, right?"

Logan ran a hand over his face. "I am in charge. I'm the curriculum designer, teaching out of Livingston High. The sub trades go through me but my main focus is educational."

"Okay." She lifted her eyebrows and drew out the last syllable, making it into a question. Teacher-Sam was impressed; home-buyer-Sam was not.

"The students work with the tradesmen, under my supervision and we work to our students' abilities. That's why we're behind schedule. Having never done it before, delivery dates are subject to change. Didn't Tod Styles tell you?"

Obviously not. No wonder the guy disappeared so fast.

Samara blinked. Confusion and anger washed over her features. She crossed her arms, then raised her fist to her chin, shaking her head.

"We're moving in next Friday. My furniture is heading out tomorrow, the last eighth of the truck. It's a milk run and the schedule is tight."

Thanks for nothing, Styles.

"I don't know what to tell you, Sam."

Logan looked around him. No wonder she was upset. There had to be something he could do to push the project and meet her deadline.

Something. Anything to take away the disappointment on her lovely face.

"I'll see what I can do to speed things up, okay? Now, let me show you the rest of it."

She took a deep breath. "Might as well. Jade? Come on, honey."

"No!" said the kid, still sitting in the corner. "I wanna go home."

Despite her sulky tone, Logan sensed that the kid was more scared than anything.

"There's a perfect little girl's room up there," offered Logan, grateful that they'd put the bedroom closet doors on yesterday. But Jade wouldn't be moved. She clung to that dog like a life-preserver, rocking back and forth.

Samara looked torn.

"We'll just be upstairs," he said. "She'll be fine."

"I'll be right back, okay, honey? Bob, stay." She dropped a kiss onto the kid's head.

"Upstairs, Sam. Not off planet, I promise."

Samara lifted an eyebrow at him. "She's my child."

"My bad." He lifted both hands in apology, then turned to Jade. "I'll bring your mama right back, okay kiddo? Don't grow up and start driving in the meantime."

Sam's lip twitched. She walked past him to the staircase, her eyes on the reclaimed hardwood stretching across the great room.

"Beautiful, isn't it?" he said. "My boys did a great job on the flooring. It would have been much easier to buy a package from Costco, but this floor is unique and in keeping with the character of the home."

"It's lovely."

She looked up and down the staircase. It was the original structure, with only a few risers replaced, plus a total refinish. These stairs were a particular point of pride for his boys and he found himself exhaling in relief at her nod of approval.

She trailed her hand over the banister, then continued up to the bedrooms, feeling the texture of the carpet, running her hands along doorframes, windowsills, even the walls, as if she was blind.

"It's going to be just lovely." Uh-oh. Her voice was crackly, like she had a cold.

"Painting is next." He spoke quickly, hoping to sidestep the threat of tears, recognizing how far from done everything must appear to her. "The swatches are on the paint cans. A professional decorator handled the color choices."

She barely glanced at them.

"They're fine."

She pushed open the door to Jade's room. A small squeak sounded.

"I'll oil that tomorrow," said Logan, before she could ask. "And the front door, too."

"Thank you."

"And we'll have the cleaning crew in once we're finished creating dust," he said as she brushed her hands together.

"Of course." She walked through the bathroom, touching the surfaces and checking doors without comment, then went toward the master bedroom.

And stopped abruptly in the doorway. She cupped one elbow tightly against her stomach and her other arm crept between her breasts, her fingers against her throat.

Logan couldn't help but stare.

Damn. Those fingers, that throat. Those breasts.

But even after all those years, he recognized the defensiveness in the gesture, her need to guard herself.

Against what? Disappointment?

"This is the best room in the house," he said, touching her back lightly. They'd combined two small rooms into one to allow for the ensuite bathroom. They'd salvaged the original tin-tile ceiling. They'd installed a much larger window, complete with a hinged window seat running the length of it, and flanked on either side by built-in bookcases.

It couldn't have been designed better, even if they'd known it was for her.

"You always were such a bookworm-"

She waved away his words, her fingers now pressed against her mouth, holding herself very, very still. She hadn't stepped forward, and now they were standing close enough that Logan could feel the warmth coming from her body.

"I'm sorry we're behind schedule," he began desperately. "I'll get everyone in first thing in the morning. We'll work night and day to make sure it's ready for you. And if you don't like the bedroom-"

"I love it." Her voice was hoarse. She walked into the room, finally, as if entering a cathedral.

He had no idea what was going on. Was she mad? Happy? Disappointed?

Ten minutes with her, and he felt like the only task that had any importance in his life was to make her smile. To hear her laugh. To see the tension ease from her body. To feel her soften against him. To earn her trust.

"Anything you want changed, we can change. I'll do whatever you want, Samara."

She gave her head a little shake. "It's perfect, Logan. I'm thrilled with the house. I'm overwhelmed, to tell the truth. I'm just disappointed it's not ready. It's been a long week."

Relief flooded through him. She did, in fact, look exhausted. Perhaps it was the hollowness of her cheeks. A thought occurred to him suddenly.

"I know it's early, but have lunch with me."

His kids would be working here all afternoon but right now, he had time.

She lifted her eyebrows and glanced pointedly at his left hand. "Surely your wife or girlfriend would object."

Surely the fact that she wanted to know meant something.

"I'm divorced." He swallowed. But for once, the bite of the hated word, metallic on his tongue like rusted chain, wasn't so strong.

"Oh. Well," she said, pulling her hand back. She checked the time on her cell phone. "I can't anyway. Jade's going to need a nap soon. She was up late last night."

"A quick burger, that's all." He wanted to get to know her again, a desire that now he'd recognized it, was surprisingly strong. "Surely the chipmunk could eat?"

He gave himself a mental slap against the hope that leaped up at the thought. *What are you doing, dude? You think you can just pick up where you left off? She's not the same person.*

How she must have suffered, to be a widow so young, left with a child to raise on her own. The long-ago months they'd spent together, in such an agony of young love, were so far gone that they may as well be strangers to each other.

Yet, when her eyes met his, he felt as if a deep thirst he hadn't even been aware of was finally being slaked. Perhaps this unexpected overlap in their lives was a gift, an olive branch, an opportunity to rebuild their friendship, if nothing else.

Perhaps they were being given a second chance.

"Come on, Sam. You look like you could use a good meal."

She appraised him slowly, her hand on the doorknob. Fatigue and sadness etched her face. "I'm fine, Logan. I appreciate the sentiment, but I'm not the same person you used to know."

"Of course you're not."

Did she sound disappointed? Or was it his imagination?

"I mean," she clarified, "you don't have to feel sorry for me. I don't need rescuing. All I need is to have my house ready for move-in next Friday."

She reached out and touched his arm. "I am glad to know someone here though, after all these years. I hope we can be friends."

She walked away, her back straight, her head held high, as if they'd never been anything to each other. She had her life under control, tightly contained.

If this was a second chance, it was pretty damn slim.

A sharp woof sounded from below. Samara's head jerked, then she hurried down the stairs.

The front door, that Logan knew he had closed behind him when they'd entered, was standing wide open. Bob was hovering on the threshold. At their arrival, she barked sharply, then dashed down the front steps to where Sam's daughter was hunched over a patch of dandelions on the lawn.

"Jade!"

There was little traffic on Collier Avenue, but Samara leaped in as if the kid was playing hopscotch on the interstate.

She tugged her child toward the front door, but the kid started kicking and screaming, bludgeoning Sam's arms and legs. Logan sympathized with the girl, but Sam was taking a beating for it.

"Hey, hey now," he said. He stepped in and gently scooped

Jade around her waist.

For a second, she stopped. Then a fresh spate of screaming began, wilder, higher and more frantic than the first.

"It's okay, I can handle her," said Sam, reaching for her daughter.

Bob barked wildly at his feet, as if to emphasize the point.

"I've got her." Logan collected all four limbs and brought them in tight to his body, holding them immobile, understanding now the wiry leanness of Sam's arms.

"It's okay, little one," he crooned, watching Sam as the girl's shrieks turned to sobs. "She packs a good punch, doesn't she?"

"Give her to me," Sam said, her arms open and waiting.

"She's settling down," said Logan, continuing to hold and rock the distraught child. "I guess you were right about that nap."

"I shouldn't have left her," muttered Sam, holding her elbows in her hands, bouncing from foot to foot. "I got distracted. I know better than that."

"She's a kid, Sam." Logan continued stroking the girl's hair. Her small body was relaxing. "Kids like to play outside. It's a safe neighborhood, I promise."

"We definitely need a flip lock on that door." Sam took a deep breath. "Way up high so she can't reach it."

Then she squatted down and gathered the dog into her arms. "Good girl, Bob. You're such a good girl." She dug around in her pocket and brought out a small square treat, which Bob took politely, while keeping her eye on the damp bundle in Logan's arms.

Samara had always been wound a little tightly, but the screw had tightened dramatically over the years. Looking at her now, feeling the tension slide out of her almost-sleeping child, Logan sensed she was only a turn or two away from the breaking point.

And that this interaction with him had made it worse, not better.

Chapter Four

ಹಿಂ

S ECOND VERSE, SAME *as the first.*
A little bit louder, a little bit worse.

The old cheering song popped into Samara's head as she and Jade walked back to the house on Collier Avenue that afternoon. No big surprise, considering the weeks she'd spent rah-rahing in the bleachers with the rest of the students.

Way back.

When she and Logan were a couple of kids, imagining themselves in love.

Her legs felt wooden, yet weak. Logan Stafford! Not just still in Marietta, but working on her house. She hoped her face hadn't revealed the shock and, yes, the thrill, of seeing him again after all this time but she suspected it had been clear as a billboard.

Their love story had ended long ago, and yet one smile from him brought it all back, the joy, the heartache, everything.

True love stories never have endings.

The line from a book on their junior year reading list popped into her head, instantly transporting her back to the sun-dappled lawn behind the school, where she and Logan were cramming for their lit exam, deciding that the author had written the words just for them.

For a few months, she'd believed that.

Well. Theirs had been a short story, as it turned out, with an abrupt and very clear ending.

She glanced down at Jade, holding onto Bob's harness like it was her mission in life. Samara was done with short, tragic stories. She'd never survive another one.

As they rounded the corner, the house came into view, lifting her thoughts out of the past. This was their future, building a home for her daughter. So Logan happened to be there; so he happened to be single; so he happened to still have the ability to stir her flagging heart like a sweet autumn breeze.

Their love story was long over. But that didn't mean they couldn't be friends.

He'd always been a great guy.

After the meltdown, Logan had driven them back to Bramble House so Jade could take her nap. Samara was determined to create a positive association in Jade's mind about the house, so here they were again.

This time, as they walked up the sidewalk, she could hear voices and banging sounds. A saw revved up, chewed through something, and faded.

It was no surprise when Jade lifted her arms.

Samara swung her onto her hip, and went around to enter by the kitchen door. "One day soon, kiddo, you're going to be too heavy for this. Maybe you'll have to carry me then. What do you say?"

"Nuh-uh."

Jade's grip on her neck grew tighter and Sam steeled herself for optimism. Maybe the house was closer to ready than it had appeared in the morning.

This time, the first thing she saw was the oversized, cast-iron kitchen sink, situated beneath a large window overlooking the garden.

Instantly, she imagined Jade and Bob playing outside while she washed dishes. It was perfect!

Or it would be, when the sink was connected to that big pipe lying on the slate floor. Beside a pair of denim-clad legs ending in work-boots.

The legs pushed out, revealing a young man with a shock of wavy hair and a dark smear on his cheek. He was wearing gloves and a mask.

Jade buried her head in Sam's shoulder.

Logan came around the corner just then, wiping his hands on a towel. His eyes lit up when he saw them and her heart gave an answering leap.

"I was hoping you'd be back," he said, his smile big and warm. "Come on in so I can introduce you around."

He gathered his crew, a small cast of characters, some of them appearing almost as uncomfortable as Jade in the sudden social arena.

"Guys and gal," he said, nodding to the lone girl in the group, "this is Samara Davis and she's the one who'll be living here when we're done."

Samara's irritation at the delays evaporated. The students before her were kids who needed encouragement, not criticism, she could see that immediately.

And it was clear they admired Logan. He'd always had a way of bringing people together, of making them feel included, on the same team. He'd done it with these kids, some of whom had likely experienced more than their share of ostracism.

He lowered his voice. "Now, you can't tell, but there's an invisible chipmunk on her back. This chipmunk will materialize when she's ready but until then, she's not here. Got it?"

Sam felt Jade's head lift. Gratitude rushed through her. She could just kiss Logan for understanding Jade's discomfort. People tended to either want to jolly her out of it – definitely not a good plan – or comment on her immaturity, implying or outright stating that Samara should be tougher with her.

"As it happens, Ms. Davis is an old friend of mine, so treat her right, okay?" Logan's smile was like a ray of sunshine peeking through a cloud.

"Mr. S," said a handsome boy leaning against the doorframe. "Good job!"

To her surprise, Logan colored, ever-so-slightly. "That's Flynn," he said, pointing to the boy. "That's Robbie, that's Josh, James is under the sink and Carter's the one in the red coveralls."

There were several more, but after seeing Robbie and James, she lost track. They'd been part of the group across the street that witnessed her panty-drop. But if their red faces and shuffling feet were any indication, they felt worse about it than she did.

"And this is Gabi." Logan gestured to a short blonde girl who had a carpenter's square slung over her shoulder.

"Pleased to meet you," said Gabi, reaching forward to take her hand. "Finally, I'm not the only girl in the group."

"I'm happy to meet you all," said Samara.

But would this crew be able to get everything done in time?

Finally, he gestured to the tow-headed boy in red coveralls. "Carter, show Ms. Davis the powder room, where you helped put in the linoleum. You did a great job."

As Samara passed Logan, she whispered, "Invisible chipmunk thanks you."

He touched her arm, being careful to avoid Jade's leg. "You're welcome."

The casual touch sent more warmth streaking through her and she smiled.

৪৩৫৪

IF HE DIDN'T already know how anxious Samara was about moving in on time, he'd never be able to tell from her behavior among his students.

Logan watched with amazement as she wandered among them, Jade clinging to her like a little monkey.

"You're doing a lovely job on this," she said, patting James on the shoulder. "You should be very proud."

The boy's face, still softened with baby fat, went incandescent. He ducked his head, mumbled a *thank you*, and nearly impaled himself on a length of baseboard.

Huh. Logan's praise had never affected him that way.

Then again, Samara wasn't being paid to encourage him. She'd be dynamite in the classroom. There was a quiet nurturing sincerity about her. It wasn't motherliness, exactly. More like a kind and very hot aunt.

Frighteningly hot.

She needed a bit more weight on her bones, but every pound she had was in exactly the right place. His fingers tingled. He could still remember how she felt in his arms, that silky skin pressed against him, their awkward, urgent, desperate high school fumbling.

How they'd managed not to go all the way, he couldn't imagine.

What would happen, if they got another chance?

Chapter Five

ℰℭ

"YOU'RE THE ONE who designed the project in the first place, Logan."

Frank Stern had been the principal of Livingston High School for twelve years, during which time he'd lost his smile and his marriage, replacing them with forty pounds and a jaundiced attitude.

"If you change the rules now," he continued, "forget about getting approved for next year."

Frank considered Logan impassively from across his government-issued desk. Except for a pen, a single sheet of paper and an oversized computer monitor, the desk was empty. No photos of his kids, no potted plant, no coffee mug, nothing. He'd once done great things for the school. But he'd had concerns about Logan's pet project from the start.

"It's an administrative hoop, Frank. I'm simply asking that we request parental approval for extracurricular work hours. The kids know that completing a job within an owner's time frame is essential in this business; so do their parents. Rubber stamp it and let's go."

Frank went on as if Logan hadn't even spoken.

"I'm surprised you'd jeopardize this after you lobbied so hard to get it in the first place. You ran the fundraisers. You're the one who secured the arrangement with the city. You're the one who talked to the local Trade Association about taking these boys on after graduation. You promised that the students would fulfill the tasks laid out as stipulated."

"Which they have," said Logan. "But since we are running behind schedule, and this is causing the purchaser great inconvenience, it's reasonable to have them work extended hours to make up the shortfall."

Frank shook his head. "As long as they're working under the LHS umbrella, we stick to school hours. That's non-negotiable. I'm sorry, Logan. I'm sure you can work something out with the purchaser."

He turned back to his laptop and Logan understood he was dismissed.

"I'll make it work." He got to his feet, extending his hand. "I appreciate your time, Frank."

The principal glanced up, as if mildly surprised. "Of course. Of course."

The man had engaged the cooperation of his staff, but not their love, and it saddened Logan that the ordinary niceties of social interaction were unexpected.

He walked down the hallway, taking a moment to enjoy the quiet. The shiny floors, the walls full of colorful notices, posters, art projects, murals, trophy cases. So much pride here.

The upcoming football game between Livingston and Marietta high schools featured heavily on the walls. Working in Livingston while living in Marietta had never been a problem for him. He cheered until he was hoarse for his school team. Then, when he went home at the end of the day, he lifted a glass in congratulations or commiseration or defeat with whoever happened to be at the bar. He had good friends on both sides of the rivalry and he liked it that way.

Now, however, he had to find a way not to let one house in Marietta ruin a Livingston project that spanned both towns.

He wouldn't let his students down.

But he couldn't let Samara down, either.

 ∓

EARLY THAT EVENING, Samara lifted the key to her new house with shaking fingers. She was already feeling anxious about leaving Jade asleep in her room at Bramble House, under Mabel's crusty supervision. Now, finally able to make an undistracted progress check, alone, she was anxious about what she'd find.

But as she unlocked the kitchen door, she noticed the scent of something tangy wafting up. Looking down, she saw a hose attached to the side of the house, and on either side of it, herbs.

An herb garden, gone wild!

She'd grown basil in her Manhattan windowsill, but this, oh this was the real thing. Dill grown tall nodded at her and thyme crept between the broken paving stones at her feet. She bent forward and let her fingers drift over the soft spikes of fragrant rosemary and on to a stand of leafy bee balm, inhaling the scent of tea and sweet spices.

Her mother had grown herbs the summer they'd lived in Marietta, and the luxurious aromas brought with them images of the greenery she'd tended in hopes of brightening up their dumpy shack.

Samara straightened up, shaking off the bittersweet memories.

She stepped over the threshold, forcing her thoughts back to the present. She and Jade had spent enough time in limbo; they needed to be settled. Time was ticking! They couldn't afford to waste a single minute, yet when she surveyed the kitchen, it appeared as if no one had been inside all day. If anything had changed, Samara couldn't tell.

But when she flicked the switch in the front room, the light shone soft and warm over the room. A beautiful light fixture now covered the bare bulb, and surrounding it was a sparkling panel made of the same beautiful embossed tin as in the master suite.

Her annoyance dissolved. Clearly Logan had been here.

Of course he had. He promised he'd get it done and he was a guy who kept his word. It wasn't Logan's fault that the house was behind schedule, she understood that. She didn't want him to jeopardize a project so long in the making, and something that would do so much good to students who needed the hand up.

Samara hugged her elbows, surveying the big empty walls. This time, they didn't loom as much as they waited, patient and expectant, for her and Jade to bring them back to life.

She bit back a grin. This was her house!

However, in the meantime, she still had a truckload of furniture arriving in less than a week, and an unfinished house full of workers, sawdust and equipment.

Samara took inventory of the remaining tasks: the technically challenging work was mostly in the kitchen. The upstairs trim needed to be installed. Most of the painting was yet to be done. Everything needed cleaning.

His students couldn't work overtime, and they needed the plumbing credit, she understood that.

But *she* could paint. *She* could clean.

And after forming a wholly unexpected and somewhat uneasy alliance with Mabel, Jade's preference was to remain at Bramble House rather than accompany her mother to "the boring place."

Hope lifted her spirits.

They had six days left.

She pulled out her cell phone.

"Logan?" she said. "I have an idea."

ও৩শ্ব

IT WAS THE sort of hair-splitting Logan hated.

"You're not covered by the school's insurance," he told Sam. "Until the house is approved for occupancy, you're allowed in only to assess the progress."

"I'll get extra insurance," she countered. "I'd never put the school at risk, or put you in a position that could damage your job or the project."

Even over the phone, he couldn't help but be drawn to her. The silky voice.

The word *position*.

In the space of thirty-six hours, he'd lost his mind. Just like high school.

He was actually considering altering his professional *raison d'etre* to fit her needs.

A sliver of resentment, long forgotten, quivered to life. He thought he'd burned that thing out but apparently not.

She hadn't wanted him to run for student council, either, way back. After she left, he revelled in his triumph as president, all the while knowing that his campaigning had taken time away from what would turn out to be their last month together.

But if he'd withdrawn his name for her, he'd have done it for nothing.

At seventeen, everything seems an impossible, heart-breaking, life-changing crisis. Only years later would you recall it with fond, head-patting maturity, tinged with embarrassment, perhaps. In the moment it was everything.

It was your life.

He dealt with such drama on a daily basis, after all.

But he hadn't expected to still harbor, at thirty-three years of age, remnants of the essential human conflict: wanting someone else's happiness so, so badly – but not at the expense of your own happiness.

And he desperately wanted Sam to be happy.

"We might have to do it on the down-low," he said.

She chuckled, a throaty sound that made his inner teenage boy spring to life.

"We can manage that, don't you think?"

Chapter Six

೫೮೦೦೩

S AMARA BENT HER head as the minister began his closing prayer. It had been years since she'd been to church. After an hour with Logan last night, during which they negotiated what could and could not be done by her, he convinced her to attend the worship service.

If she wanted to be part of the community, she had to start joining in things, he said. Bob would be welcome, too, he assured them.

She'd refused to let him escort them, but she and Jade and Bob had slipped into the back pew, after everyone else had entered. Jade was happily doodling pictures of dogs while Bob snoozed, her white-tipped tail flapping gently against the ancient hardwood floor whenever Jade touched her.

It was actually rather soothing.

"Do we have any announcements from the congregation?" asked the minister.

From a pew near the front, Logan stood up. Her pulse quickened. Even from a distance, Samara could see the kindness in his eyes.

"I'd like to remind everyone of the pancake breakfast to

raise funds for Homecoming this year." He turned around, scanning the crowd to address everyone. "I know I'm officially on the wrong side, but I'm on my own time right now. And you all know I'm a Marietta boy at heart."

Titters floated over the room. Logan seemed to have the ability to throw himself fully into his job in Livingston, while remaining a loyal home-town boy. Apparently, even the upcoming Livingston-Marietta high school football game didn't cause any awkwardness.

"Volunteers are still welcome and remember, all the money raised goes to purchasing more and better equipment for the students of Marietta High School. I hope to see you all at the school gym on Saturday, October fourth. Don't forget your appetites – or your wallets. Thank you."

Samara remembered when Logan had been running for school council way back when they were students. His passionate campaigning even managed to garner support from the grumpy drive-in theater owner, who donated a bunch of midnight matinee tickets.

Despite her fear of losing his attention, she had known he deserved to win.

It was tough to resist Logan's enthusiasm.

It was seductive.

A shiver ran over Samara's body.

His enthusiasm ran to everything. She'd never felt so completely cherished as she had those months when she was Logan's girlfriend.

And unlike some of the boys she met later, Logan's adoration wasn't simply a ploy to get into her pants.

He'd touched her as if she was the most perfect thing in the world. He electrified her, made her come alive, made her burn, made her want to spend every waking moment with him and be as close as she could, whenever they were together.

She shifted in her pew. It had gotten hot in the church.

And her thoughts were moving in a direction that would probably get her kicked out, if any of them happened to show on her face.

The minister made his closing remarks and the service ended. As the postlude began, sending chimes of organ music swelling around them, people got to their feet, collecting their bulletins and notices and replacing hymnals.

A very properly attired woman a few rows ahead turned and stared directly at her, as if waiting for this moment. Samara's cheeks prickled with heat. Oh dear. With her luck, she was sitting in church, fantasizing about Logan, right behind a bona fide psychic, with a puritanical bent.

The church lady elbowed her way in closer, making a beeline for them as the congregation drifted past them out of the sanctuary.

"What a darling little girl," she said when she reached them.

The comment sounded less like a compliment and more like a cue for *what big teeth you have, granny.*

Samara leaned closer to Jade. "Thank you."

"I'm Carol Bingley." Granny-wolf paused expectantly.

Samara forced herself to smile. "I'm Samara Davis, this is my daughter, Jade and this is her dog, Bob. Nice to meet you."

"Yes, I see. A dog. In church. Your child doesn't appear disabled."

Carol Bingley had set her trap and now she waited.

Bob was a service-dog reject, which sounded harsh but made her perfect for them: more skilled than the average canine, but without the price tag..

Of course, official service-dog status or not, Bob stirred curiosity and Samara hated all the questioning that followed when she tried to explain.

"I was told-"

"Don't worry about it. I'm close friends with the minister," said Carol Bingley. "I'll be sure to speak to him for you."

I'll be sure to let him know you broke the rules.

Message received, thought Samara.

Then the woman leaned over the pew and peered down at Jade. Sam felt her daughter grow still and withdraw into herself, growing smaller, tighter, tenser. Bob got to her feet and pushed herself between Jade and the woman leaning over the pew, but the angles were wrong and it did nothing to reassure the girl.

"Hello, sweetheart." She used that slightly too loud, slightly too high voice that Samara hated.

Jade flinched, hating it even more. Bob whined, sensing her girl's growing agitation. It was one of those short slice-of-time moments in which the differences in tiny family stood out so acutely that it triggered a terrible sense of loneliness.

Jade wasn't like other little girls. She wasn't the kind of child who took to well-meant, cheek-pinching familiarity, and if Ms. Bingley didn't get out of Jade's face she'd get a first-hand illustration of what that meant.

"Carol Bingley," came a familiar voice behind them. "Aren't you a lovely sight this fine morning?"

Logan put one hand softly on Samara's shoulder as he eased into the pew, extending his other hand to Ms. Bingley. When she turned away from Jade to return the greeting, Logan subtly leaned in, making the woman take a step back.

Jade swallowed and her breathing lost the pre-panic quickness.

"Are you working on the pancake breakfast?" His smile was warm and crackly at the corners. "I know the committee was hoping you'd join the cooking team. Everyone remembers your contributions to the bake sales, after all."

Carol blushed. "Well, I hadn't been planning on it-"

"And I'm so embarrassed to admit that it's my fault you

haven't been asked until now." He shook his head with a self-deprecating grimace. "I asked for the privilege of contacting our more prominent community members to assist with various tasks, and then immediately lost my list. Thank goodness I saw you standing here today. So save me from my own inadequacies, please? Tell me you'll lend your talents to the pancake breakfast?"

The entire time, he'd been gently drawing her into the aisle, where he managed to insert himself between her and the little family behind him. Samara marvelled at his timing, gratitude flooding over her.

How did he *do* that?

As Logan escorted Carol Bingley to the foyer, he cut a quick glance at Samara. He hadn't addressed either her or Jade during the brief interchange, but if Sam had any doubts as to his true intention, they disappeared. The jocular smile faded, as if it was a mask, bumped askew momentarily. The lines on his face slipped into concern, maybe apology, maybe even uncertainty. He lifted his eyebrows in a "you okay?" expression.

Sam nodded, feeling warmth flush into her cheeks. Then Bob nudged her leg. Jade was standing, her restless feet indicating their next stop should be a ladies' room and quick. She picked Jade up, knowing she'd rather walk, but unwilling to risk another close encounter. When they made their way through the foyer, to find the washrooms, Logan was nowhere in sight.

⁞

DURING THE SHAKING of what seemed like a hundred hands, Logan lost sight of Sam and Jade.

"Hey buddy."

"Dawson!" chided the pretty red head beside him. "How are you, Logan?"

Logan rubbed his arm. A good-natured punch from a champion bullrider wasn't something you ignored.

Logan and Sage Carrigan had both grown up in Marietta, but she was a few years behind him. A former barrel racer, she'd left competition to open Copper Mountain Chocolate, but it had been through rodeo that she'd first met Dawson O'Dell. Now it appeared that Dawson and his daughter, Savannah, had settled in Marietta for good. Since he understood wedding bells were in their future, Logan guessed that Sage was the reason.

"Did I see you chatting with a cute brunette a moment ago?" continued Sage. "Who is she?"

He explained, then added, "Her daughter, Jade, is a little younger than Savannah here. You might want to introduce them sometime."

"Absolutely," said Dawson, ruffling his daughter's hair. "This one's always ready to expand her social circle."

Maybe precocious Savannah was just the thing to bring Jade out of her shell.

"And," said Sage, "you should stop by the shop. I'll make you up a special Welcome-to-Marietta chocolate basket for Samara. She'll love it."

Of course. He should have thought of it himself.

"She's got this salted caramel thing that will earn you major points," said Dawson. "The ladies love it."

"I shouldn't say this in church." Sage looked down, and dropped her voice to a whisper. "But it's been called orgasmic."

With that word, for a split second, everyone around him disappeared. Logan imagined putting a tiny square of rich, smooth candy onto Samara's tongue, watching her lips move as she savored it, kissing her, sharing the sweet, silky heat. What sound would she make when the flavor hit the back of her mouth? Would she moan? Would she ask for more?

"It's a gift that keeps on giving," added Dawson, waggling

his eyebrows.

Logan swallowed hard, and forced himself back to reality. What was wrong with him, having thoughts like this in church?

A lot of assumptions were being made, he realized suddenly. Premature assumptions. Way premature.

"Uh, actually, Samara and I are just friends."

"Okay." Sage laughed. "If you say so."

"Did you hear yourself?" Dawson shook his head. "I hope you don't play poker."

Yeah, he had heard himself. Pathetic. Completely unconvincing.

Because he himself wasn't convinced, and wasn't even trying.

How could he and Samara ever be just friends?

Sage and Dawson left, just as another shoulder brushed against his.

"Good to see you, Logan," said Skye, secretary at Marietta High. "You'll be cheering for Marietta, I hear."

"Of course," he answered with a broad wink.

He and Skye weren't close but they'd known each other forever and saw each other frequently at school events. It was a relief to have the spotlight shift from Samara to the all-encompassing start to football season.

Like everyone associated with the schools, he was eagerly anticipating Homecoming. With two players in his student group – Flynn playing for Marietta and Josh for Livingston – he had to watch the trash talking. Mostly, he deflected it to himself, the traitor-teacher or, as he liked to say, Switzerland. All in good fun, and at game time it certainly got the crowd going.

But it occurred to him that Samara's arrival during this time made it tough to focus on football. If she moved in on Friday – *when* she moved in on Friday, he amended – he wouldn't be able to attend the game, knowing she was buried under a mountain of boxes.

The crowd was thinning and still, he hadn't found Sam. Maybe she'd gotten away without him noticing.

He heard a child's angry shriek, cut off sharply. Then a dog barked and he saw them, huddled on the ground next to Samara's car in the church parking lot.

He jogged closer. "Everything okay?" he asked.

Jade was sitting on the ground, digging a hole in the gravel with her feet, her face set stubbornly. Samara squatted on her heels, distraught.

"She thought there was a playground here." She grimaced. "Probably because I said there was. I keep expecting things to be like they were fourteen years ago."

The dog was stretched out between them, halfway lying on the little girl's lap. Samara sighed and stroked the glossy fur.

It must be hard, thought Logan, to be the agent of your child's disappointment. Good cop and bad cop rolled into one. And given that kids always wanted more than they could have, bad cop always got the most air-time.

Logan helped her to her feet, hoping he could help instead of making things worse.

"I wonder if you could do me a favor," he said, angling his body away from Jade. From the corner of his eye, he saw her tip her head watchfully.

"What's that?" said Samara with a frown.

"There's a park across town that's perfect for walking dogs. I love to go there on Sunday afternoons but, well, as it happens, I don't have a dog."

A slow smile spread across Samara's face. "You want to borrow Bob."

"I understand it's a lot to ask. Dogs being as precious as they are and all. I know Jade could never part with Bob, even for a little while." Then, he put his finger to his chin, as if the idea had just occurred to him. "You could join me if you wanted to. I guess."

"I wouldn't mind," said Samara, as if it didn't much matter one way or the other.

"She is my dog," said a little voice, most definitely. "She is part Labrador, part Border Collie and she's my dog."

"Oh!" said Logan, feigning surprise. "I beg your pardon. Then I'll ask you. Would you and Bob and your mom come with me to the park?"

"No."

"Oh." He sighed deeply. "Too bad. I really love that park. There's chipmunks to feed. Not the Jade-kind, but the ones you can see. And did I mention the playground?"

"You heard Jade," said Sam. "She said no, so that's it."

Jade's face was a study in conflict.

"You're absolutely right," said Logan. "I understand completely."

"Wait," said Jade, scrambling to her feet. "Playground?"

"You have a nice day, ladies," said Logan, turning to leave.

"Mama!" cried Jade. "Let's go to the park with him!"

"Really?" said Samara. "But I thought you didn't want to."

Logan took a couple of steps away, then stopped to check his watch, pretending not to hear them.

"Please, Mama, please!" She was dancing from foot to foot, tugging at Samara's shirt.

"I'll have to ask Mr. S. Or," she paused here, as if an idea had just struck her. "Perhaps you could ask him."

"Mama!" pleaded Jade.

"Quick, I think he's going!"

Jade made a tortured sound. "Mister S? I changed my mind."

Logan figured that's as close as they were going to get, but he couldn't resist playing it out.

"Did you say something, Samara?"

"Me!" said Jade, stamping her foot. "I changed my mind."

"So," said Logan. "Are you saying that you and Bob and your mom would like to come to the park with me, after all?"

"Yes. Yes!" Jade groaned. "Mama?"

Logan grinned. "It's up to you, Mama."

Jade sent pleading eyes up to her mother.

"All right, honey, we'll go."

Jade jumped and down, then threw herself against Samara's knees. "Yay!"

"Thank you," mouthed Samara, while her daughter squeezed so tightly, her little face turned red.

"You're welcome," he murmured back.

If this playground wasn't up to Jade's standards, he'd drive them to Livingston. Hell, he'd drive them to Billings if he had to.

Whatever it took to keep that smile on Samara's face.

§✵♋

THE COMMUNITY PARK was a stone's throw from the elementary school Jade would be attending as soon as they were settled.

She should be there now, but Samara couldn't add that to Jade's already overloaded life. Soon.

Though from the look of it, Jade might be more prepared than Samara gave her credit for.

With her mother's permission, she'd unclipped Bob's leash, and the two of them had raced across the park, straight to the playground equipment, birds and squirrels dashing away at the commotion.

What was taking Logan, she wondered? They'd each taken their own cars; had he made a stop on the way?

There he was and yes, he was carrying a box in his hands.

"I stopped at the deli," he called. "I hope you still like Reuben sandwiches. I got ham and cheese for the rug-rat."

He sat down at the picnic table beside her, where they could both see Jade and Bob.

"You didn't have to do that," said Samara. She opened the box. He'd gotten more than sandwiches; pickles, potato chips, bottles of iced tea, three chocolate cupcakes, he'd even thrown in some roast beef slices for the dog.

"I wanted to," said Logan. "Mustard?"

She shook her head, took a bite of her Reuben and nearly moaned.

"Good?" asked Logan hopefully.

She closed her eyes and nodded. Better than good. The sauerkraut was crunchy but not overpowering, the meat was thinly sliced, but thickly layered, the Swiss cheese soft but not gooey.

She glanced up and caught him contemplating her, a strange expression on his face.

"They certainly know how to slap a sandwich together," he said, turning away.

But she'd seen it, a mixture of longing and desire and fascination that left him mystified, uncertain. She recognized it because it was the same expression she'd seen on his face in algebra class, the day he'd first spoken to her.

The memory was clear as a photograph.

Logan Stafford, captain of the football team, student council representative, handsome, popular, smart and talented, didn't know what to make of her. Couldn't talk to her, not for days, but couldn't quit watching her either.

"Delicious," she said.

He looked back at her sharply, as if he'd heard more than she intended. Samara reached for her drink, but in her haste, bumped it, spilling it on the table.

"Here, let me," said Logan, grabbing some paper napkins.

"I'm so sorry," said Samara, feeling her face flame. Together they patted the weathered boards dry without getting drenched in the process.

Somehow, after, they seemed to be sitting a lot closer than they'd been before.

Chapter Seven

℘℧

BEFORE COMING DOWN from her room Monday morning, Samara had an interruption-filled but ultimately successful conversation with A-1 Movers. She clicked off her cell, feeling that maybe, just maybe, things would work out after all.

And hungry.

That wonderful al fresco lunch with Logan had apparently turned her appetite back on. The food had been so good; the company so easy.

As she walked through the bathroom to Jade's room, the smell of bacon wafted up faintly from the kitchen below and sent her stomach rumbling even more.

She pulled a still-clean top from the diminishing pile in Jade's suitcase and held it briefly to her nose.

If she closed her eyes, she could still smell the sunshiny-fresh scent of Logan's clean church shirt, and see the tanned skin of his forearms, where the sleeves were rolled up.

When they sat side by side at the picnic table eating their sandwiches, and his bare arms occasionally brushed against hers, he may as well have had her stretched out naked under the afternoon sky, for the effect it had on her body.

"Mama, I'm cold."

Jade had taken her pajamas off and was waiting impatiently for the clothes Samara was day-dreaming over.

"Sorry, sweetie," she said, hastily completing the task.

When they got to the kitchen, Eliza was tending a sizzling pan at the stove.

"Good morning, everyone," she said. "I've got scrambled eggs in the warming oven and the bacon's on the way."

Mabel sat at the small table, doing her crossword in a patch of sunshine. "Samara, you look like the cat that ate the canary."

"My delivery date's been extended." Samara smiled as she fixed Jade's breakfast, eggs in the center, toast cut diagonally, framing but not touching the eggs. "Turns out they had a breakdown or something; my things won't be here until Wednesday, the twenty-fourth. We'll need to stay here a little longer; I hope that won't be a problem."

Eliza set the platter of bacon in the sideboard. "That's wonderful news, Samara; you must be so relieved. Of course you can keep the rooms. If you haven't noticed, you're our only booking. Besides, we're enjoying the company."

Mabel lifted her eyebrows but didn't speak.

Jade took the plate Samara handed her and set it on the table next to Mabel. Then she dragged the chair a little closer and climbed up, settling in for her breakfast.

"Bob is my dog," she informed her tablemate. "She is part Labrador Retriever, part Border Collie."

"Yes, Jade," said Mabel. "So you've said."

Jade observed her meal for a moment, then made a minute adjustment, lining the bacon up with the toast points.

"Aunt Mabel, are you mad at Bob?" she asked, without lifting her head.

A wave of discomfort rippled over Mabel's face. "Don't be silly. Your dog is… quiet. And she seems devoted to you. I have no quarrel with her."

"Mama says she is part luck-of-the-draw. That means she doesn't have a family. Like me."

The room went silent, except for the sound of Jade's utensils on her plate. Jade's matter-of-fact words cut Samara to the heart. With the Kims in Asia, her dad gone and her mom busy with her new husband, it was the two of them, that's it.

She poured herself a cup of coffee, and got a slice of toast. The bacon and eggs had lost their appeal.

"Everyone has a family," said Mabel, her voice rough.

"We don't." Samara spoke briskly. "Jade, sweetie, finish your breakfast."

Mabel waved away Samara's words as if irritated by the interruption. "Jade, tell me something else about, er, Bob."

Jade glanced at her mother with a frown, but not like she was becoming agitated. More like, she was... intrigued.

Some strange magic was brewing here.

"You could tell Aunt Mabel how old she is," suggested Samara.

Jade's expression cleared. "Bob is five years old. I'm four years old."

"We established that upon your arrival," said Mabel with a scowl. "What activities does your Bob enjoy?"

Jade thought for a moment. "She likes to eat and she likes to chase squirrels and she likes it when I rub her belly. She likes car rides."

"Does she like to play with other children?"

Jade thought again. "Other children?"

Guilt twisted Samara's gut again. Their post-Michael socializing had shrunk to the grocery store and the doctor's office. When she could bear to re-join the happy wives and nannies at playground, the ranks had closed around them, as if their tragedy was contagious. Any play-dates she managed to arrange for Jade weren't reciprocated. Not that they'd been wildly successful beforehand.

"Does Bob like other people?" Mabel repeated. "Friends or playmates or neighbors, perhaps."

"She likes Mama," said Jade. "She likes Mr. S. And lookit – she likes you too!"

Bob leaned against Mabel's chair, staring up at the woman in adoration.

The old lady had put a spell on both of them.

"Jade, eat your eggs. We need to leave soon."

Mabel arched an eyebrow at the expression on Samara's face. "Don't rush us. We're having a lovely conversation, the tadpole and I."

"I'm a *chipmunk*," said Jade, around a mouthful of eggs.

"You're a tadpole with me." Aunt Mabel went back to her crossword without looking at Jade and Jade continued eating, her gaze stuck on the food in front of her.

"Perhaps the tadpole might help me sort through some pictures today," said Aunt Mabel casually. "If you can spare her, that is."

"Pictures?" said Jade.

Sam thought of the mess that still remained in her kitchen. She desperately wanted to get working. Her extra time was a welcome reprieve, but they still needed every possible minute.

But she hated to leave Jade.

"I don't know," she said.

"I have pictures," said Jade. She scrambled down from her chair and ran to fetch them from her room.

"I couldn't ask that of you," said Samara quickly.

"You didn't ask."

"She's not like most children."

Mabel sniffed again. "Most children are irritating. Leave her here. It will be good for the child. And I need a break from

Eliza's relentless toadying."

"My pictures are of dogs," said Jade, breathlessly. She opened up the flashcard box and spread out her collection. "Labrador Retrievers and Border Collies are my favorites."

"Do you want to stay with Aunt Mabel, honey?"

Jade hesitated. "I want to put my pictures in piles."

"The tadpole will be fine," said Aunt Mabel.

"I'm a chipmunk. Bye Mama."

So Samara left.

₠ℂℂ

THE STUDENTS WERE in the kitchen with the tradesmen, getting a lecture on proper grout sealant, when Logan saw Sam slip in the front door.

Blue jeans emphasized her long, lean legs and the simple t-shirt hugged her curves just right.

He'd have to be careful to keep an eye on the horn dogs in his group.

"You're an early bird," he said. For the first time since her return, she appeared relaxed. "Where's the chipmunk?"

Sam's smile lit up his insides, like turning on a light in an abandoned basement.

"At Bramble House with Mabel, where apparently, she's a tadpole. But Jade's arguing the point." She shook her head in wonder. "Seems the two of them have taken to each other."

"Mabel and Jade?"

"I know." Sam grinned at his expression. "But I promised I'd be back in a couple of hours, before the spell is broken and everything goes back to pumpkins and chaos. So, what's on the agenda for today?"

Sam put her hands in the back pockets of her jeans, a movement that made her breasts jut out. He wondered if she was aware of it.

Decide to enjoy it, regardless.

"Painting crown molding," he said, lifting his eyes to meet hers. She twinkled knowingly at him. She knew exactly what she was doing. "Come on up. I'll show you."

He led her to the master bedroom where the lovely curved lines between ceiling and wall were already taped off, ready for white paint that would off-set the lavender.

He wondered if she felt the charge between them too. With everyone else working in the kitchen, they were alone. The room was warm, and Logan was pretty sure it wasn't due to the autumn sunshine.

"Between the two of us, it shouldn't take long," he said. "You okay on a ladder?"

"Of course."

She climbed her ladder, giving him an even lovelier view of her legs, the graceful curves from knee, to hip and waist. She quickly got to work, loading her brush, then reaching out to stroke the paint smoothly onto the waiting board.

Her t-shirt rode up and he got a glimpse of the smooth tan skin beneath, that dip of belly button, the little gap between waistband and hipbone, just enough for a finger –

"So we'll start on opposite ends and meet in the middle?" She looked down at him, the paintbrush dripping into the tray. Her smile faded. Caution rushed in. "Logan?"

"Yeah, exactly." He fumbled and nearly dropped his brush. "I'll be over here."

He worked in the opposite corner and for a while, the only thing breaking the silence was the soothing sound of brushstrokes.

I hope we can be friends, she'd told him.

Friends.

Could he do that? Was that even possible between them?

They both worked to the extent of their reach, then got down, moved their ladders, and started on a fresh section. Before he knew it, they were only a foot apart, working towards the same unpainted spot.

"Hey, stranger," she said, as if surprised.

He could have set her on a different task, in a different room but then they'd be circling each other, as they had been since her arrival. He was tired of that.

"Remember that old Disney movie, the cartoon with the dogs, Lady and the Tramp?" she said with a jerky laugh. "It's Jade's favorite of course. We've watched it a million times. This reminds me of that scene where they're eating spaghetti."

He raised his eyebrows. He knew exactly the scene. Both dogs both slurped the same piece and ended up kissing.

He stepped down from his ladder and held hers so she could do the same. When she got to the bottom, she was facing him, so close he could smell the peppermint of her toothpaste.

Logan put his arm around her back. She stepped into the embrace as if it was the most natural thing in the world.

"Hey," she said, her voice husky.

"Hey." He tipped her chin up so he could stare into that beautiful mahogany gaze. "Let's take a break. Have lunch with me. We can run over to Bramble House first and check on Jade, if it makes you feel better."

"I couldn't," she said. But she didn't move.

"Lunch, Sam. You have to eat anyway."

"We shouldn't. It's not… it's too complicated."

"You really think we can be just friends?" He ran a finger along her cheekbone, feeling the shudder that ran through her.

"I don't know, Logan." Her voice was husky. "It's like we've stepped through a portal or something. It feels like the past is gone and I'm sixteen again, only we're grown-ups this time."

He could hear her ramping up and rather than letting it

happen, he silenced her the best way he knew how.

He lowered his head to hers, slowly, so she could see him coming. Her lips parted, in anticipation, in fear, out of breathlessness or a need to speak, he didn't care. He pressed his against them and heard her quick intake of breath.

Her hands went up to his neck and she pulled herself closer, her mouth softening against his, opening, until they were necking like the pair of teenagers they had been, urgently, desperately, the rest of the world falling away until it was only them, no one else mattering, nothing necessary to their survival but that they hold on, hold on, hold on to each other and never let go.

Until, of course, they did let go.

ಐಲ

SAMARA GRIPPED THE door handle of Logan's truck, anxious to get back to Jade, fighting irritation at Eliza's undoubtedly well-intentioned gesture of arranging a spontaneous play date for Jade.

Eliza had invited strangers to Bramble House, while her daughter was there without her.

And casually informed her by voice-mail.

A play date. For Jade.

Mothers arranged play dates. Not acquaintances.

The fact that Jade's mother no longer arranged play dates was beside the point. It wasn't Eliza's place to do it.

"Sage is Eliza's cousin," said Logan. "Another of Mabel's great-nieces. Sage and her sisters don't come around much, but that's Mabel's doing, not theirs. Who knows why? That generation is famous for their feuds. But you'll love Sage. And Savannah is a great kid. Sage already sees herself as her step-mom."

"That's not the point," said Samara. "I'm sure Sage and Savannah are very nice. It's just..."

It's just that Jade was *her* daughter. Eliza should have asked her, that's all.

She winced, inwardly. Was she really that insecure? That controlling?

Yeah, she was.

"Jade'll be too busy playing to even notice when we stop by," continued Logan. "Then we'll go out and have a nice, relaxed lunch together."

Samara gripped her hands together. Of course she wanted her daughter to make new friends. Of course she hoped they were having fun.

But what did it say about her mothering skills if Eliza, practically a stranger, could achieve something with Jade that she herself could not?

Logan reached across the bench seat, peeled her hands apart and trapped one in his steady, warm grip.

"Don't worry, honey."

The endearment landed like gentle rain on her parched heart, a painful and dangerous relief. A little rain was worse than none at all, bringing life to dormant roots, sending tender sprouts through hot, cracked earth, only to wither when the rain stopped.

"Samara."

Logan turned off the engine without letting go of her hand. He waited until she met his gaze, simply holding her.

Calm flowed from him like a river, clear and smooth and unending, catching her up like a fallen leaf.

"You'll meet Sage and Savannah," he said. "You'll talk to Jade. If she's happy, you'll have lunch with me. If not, you'll stay there."

ℰᘐᘉℭℛ

IT WASN'T LUNCH, thought Samara, as Logan held the door of Grey's Saloon open for her.

It was dinner.

Which was much, much worse.

Hours earlier, when she and Logan had arrived at Bramble House, she'd found Savannah and Jade in the garden, surrounded by a collection of dolls. Sage and Eliza had convinced her not to rush down to Jade, but to observe the girls from the window for a bit.

Mabel, more irritable than usual, had snapped at her to stop hovering but Samara had been too fascinated to feel scolded.

They were having a tea party. Savannah was chattering away and while Jade didn't appear to be responding much, she was clearly engaged. In fact, it appeared that Jade was studying the older girl. When Savannah straightened up a slouching doll, Jade adjusted her own doll's posture. When Savannah added imaginary sugar to a cup, Jade did the same.

Normal play behavior, thought Samara, pressing her fingers against her lips. A few years late, perhaps, but it was coming.

"Smells good, doesn't it?" Logan said, breaking into her thoughts.

He'd agreed to give her the afternoon, if she'd come to Grey's with him later on.

Sage, Eliza and even Mabel had insisted she accept. Well, Mabel insisted she unknot the stranglehold of her apron ties and give her child a chance to breathe, but it meant the same thing.

Logan's hand rested lightly at the small of her back, a touch she felt all the way to her toes.

It was just a casual pub meal. They wouldn't be here long. And it did smell fantastic.

"My stomach's growling," she confessed.

"Good." Logan gave her the private smile she remembered, the one that made her feel like she was the only one that mattered. "I can't wait to feed you."

Heads turned as they entered and several calls of "Hey, Staff," drifted toward them. A small group of men were watching football on the big screen mounted in the corner, feet propped on chairs, arms loose, comfortable.

Logan's expression changed from the smile he gave her to his everyone-else smile, but he tightened his arm around her.

A couple of women sitting at the bar preened, their hungry eyes traveling up and down. When he ignored them, they took momentary measure of her before turning back to their drinks.

She'd seen that desire aimed at him before. Logan was the cutest boy in high school. The intervening years had added height and bulk, a touch of silver in his hair, a few lines around that easy grin, until that cute boy had turned into the full-grown, hard-bodied, breathtaking male who was standing in front of her, holding out a chair.

And he was with her.

"Don't worry about those two. They're buckle-bunnies, on the hunt for cowboys."

"I'm not worried," she said, quickly taking her seat.

Besides the football fans and the cougars at the bar, the place was full of couples.

"You probably don't remember Skye Wolcott." He gestured discreetly. "She was a year behind us. She's the secretary at Marietta High. But I'm sure you recognize Chase Goodwin, the guy she's with. Every girl in school was after him."

"I wasn't. I don't recall him at all."

There were no other guys in school, where she was concerned.

"Well, don't you just know the right thing to say?" The private smile was back. "Goodwin played pro ball until, oh, not long ago, I guess. Baseball, though, not football. His kid brother, Flynn, plays for the Marietta Grizzlies. Flynn's also working on your house. You met him earlier."

The bell over the door tinkled and a woman came in, headed straight for the bar where she grabbed the man behind it and planted a big kiss on him.

"Hey, Lorelai," called Logan. "Let the man work."

Lorelai Grey, he explained, and the bar owner, Reese Kendrick.

"He owns the place, inherited it from her father. Long story."

With an obviously happy ending, thought Samara.

Logan pointed out other Marietta residents.

So many couples.

Some new hopefuls, their faces shining with anticipation, holding hands across the table, heat smoldering between them. Others obviously established, deep in conversation, comfortable enough to spear tastes from the other's plate.

One couple in a booth cast only tight-lipped, careful glances at each other. He had two empty beer glasses in front of him.

"Who are those two?"

"Noelle Winslow, from a big spread north of town. Her father passed away recently. That's Matthew Locke, who managed the place. She never much liked him, but she's going to need him now."

Sam wondered if there was more tension between them than a simple like or dislike relationship would warrant. They looked deeply connected but deeply conflicted about it.

Or maybe she was imagining things.

Loneliness struck hard and fast, as if she hadn't had years to adjust. She missed it, all of it. The heady excitement, the comfortable togetherness, even those horrible times of feeling so far away from each other you don't know how, or even if, you can find your way back.

Practically, she missed having someone at her back, knowing that it didn't all fall on her, every hour, every day, every month, every task.

But it was the everyday intimacy that left a gaping hole. The teasing you-wear-the-black-teddy-I'll-kill-the-giant-arachnid and the I'll-clean-the-shower-drain-if-you-drape-your-hair-over-my-belly negotiations. Samara swallowed hard against the thickness in her throat.

The Spider-Killing Factor. You didn't appreciate it until it was gone.

She bet Logan would be a great spider-killer.

"You okay?" He looked at her quizzically.

She dragged her attention back. "Yeah. Just trying to re-member all the names."

"You've got lots of time for that," said Logan. "We should order. And before you ask, everything's good here. I have a weakness for the meatloaf but you would love the chicken pot pie. It's crammed with vegetables, and I'm guessing you like your veggies."

A waitress walked past then, leaving a wake of aromas drift-ing over their table. Oh, sweet merciful heaven, that was *food*.

Maybe she was getting emotional simply because it had been so long since she'd eaten in a public place, or with anyone other than Jade. Or dined on anything other than Jade's ever-so-slowly-widening list of acceptable foods.

Maybe it had nothing to do with being here with Logan, or the air of coupledom surrounding them.

Right.

Suddenly her stomach was filled with butterflies.

"Soup and salad will be lots for me."

"Please." Logan shook his head at her. "I can hear your stomach growling from across the table. And you've been licking your lips, did you know that?"

She jerked her head. "I have?"

"You have. Enough to draw attention from the football corner over there; keep that lip thing going and they'll be lining up for your phone number."

Samara laughed, surprising herself. "I highly doubt that."

But even hypothetical attention felt so good.

"Hey Logan," said the waitress with a smile. "Haven't seen you in a while. Who's your new friend?"

The young woman turned to her, bright-faced with curiosity.

"Hey Mardie, meet Samara," said Logan. "Sam's actually an old friend. And I'm happy to say that after a long absence, she's made her way back to... Marietta."

He held Sam's gaze the whole time he was talking and beneath his polite words ran a powerful undercurrent, a warm, intimate subtext meant only for her. He *said* Marietta. But she'd swear that he almost said *me*.

Mardie and Logan began chatting about Homecoming and the rivalry between the Marietta and Livingston football teams.

She hadn't come back for Logan. She hadn't even thought of him.

Had she?

Her good memories of this place were tied up with Logan, of course, but that's not why she returned. She wanted to walk down the street and say hi to people, by name. She wanted to know her child would grow up without sirens at night, or neighbors screaming through the walls, or being in a classroom with different kids each year. She wanted that sense of calm and stability that came with an old town that held onto its heritage without getting stuck in the past.

She came here to find a home and make a life.

She'd never even thought of Logan.

Except that Logan was part of everything she loved about

Marietta.

"I'll be right back with your drinks," said Mardie.

"Um. Drinks?" Sam's cheeks grew hot.

Logan grinned. "You jumped time zones briefly, so I ordered for you."

"You did not!" Shock at his presumption was accompanied by an unexpected sense of relief. Presumption was a privilege of coupledom, but it was so luxurious to let someone else take the wheel, even briefly, in something as small as a pub order, she couldn't be annoyed.

Plus, they were here together, weren't they?

"You need more than soup and salad. Plus, I want to see if I still know what you like."

Logan's eyes drifted down over her body, and the little hairs on her arms lifted, as if he'd drawn a line down them with his finger.

"And here we are." Mardie swooped in and set a frosty sleeve in front of her. "For the lady. And for you, Logan. Enjoy!"

"Wait," protested Samara. "I'm sorry, I didn't order beer."

With one hand, Logan sent Mardie off to handle a fresh wave of customers.

"Come on. Surely New Yorkers drink beer."

"Of course," said Sam. "But I haven't had alcohol since-"

Since Michael died. No, before that. Since Jade was born. Actually, since their honeymoon, when she couldn't figure out why she was so queasy.

But Logan wasn't listening to her protest.

"I'm sticking to soda so you don't have to worry about my driving, and you're going to enjoy this golden ale guilt-free. With any luck, by the time we leave, those tight shoulders of yours may have loosened their stranglehold grip on your ears."

She punched him lightly across the table, annoyed and delighted in equal measure. "That's a horrible image!"

He shrugged, his eyes dancing. "Truth hurts, lady. Drink up."

She took a tentative sip. The chilled liquid slipped over her tongue, smooth with a slight bite. She took a second sip, feeling the cool drift down to her stomach, then turn to the tiniest whisper of warmth.

She heard a little moan of appreciation from the back of her throat.

"Good, huh?"

She looked up from her glass to find Logan watching her intently. His smile was gone and in its place was an expression of such longing, such sadness, such concern that she was instantly back in high school, telling him that her father had lost yet another job. That she was moving away. Again.

"Yeah," she answered, her voice hoarse. "Logan, are you okay?"

With one quick gesture, he shook off whatever he'd been feeling and his face settled back into his usual comfortable, friendly expression.

"Apparently not, if I'm out with a beautiful woman and not following the conversation."

She flushed at the compliment but wondered what had triggered that brief moment of emotional nakedness.

Their food arrived just then.

Samara watched with amazement as Mardie set a heaping plate of chicken pot pie in front of her, the gravy still bubbling through the top of the pastry. The aroma, rich and comforting, hit her nose and instantly, her stomach growled so loudly that she pressed her hand into it, certain that the whole room must have heard it.

Mardie wasn't done. She set down a second plate with salad, then a basket of bread for them to share, then pickles and finally,

Logan's plate.

"Make sure he gives you a taste of his meatloaf," said Mardie. "It's to die for." She winked at Logan and left before Sam could even respond.

"Eat up, honey," he said, gesturing to her plate. "We'll talk more once your plate's clean."

Honey? Warmth stole over her, completely unrelated to the oven-hot food in front of her.

"This is far too much," she said.

He looked at her thoughtfully, then speared a small piece of meatloaf and held it out to her across the table.

"Try this."

She shook her head. "No, no, I'll have enough trouble eating my own."

His eyes dropped to her neck, then lower, ranging over everything visible above the table top. Again, like a fiery finger, his gaze scorched every cold part of her.

"Eat."

She opened her mouth and he put the bite of meat onto her tongue, then sat back and watched, his eyes hooded and dusky, as if anticipating her pleasure gave him even greater pleasure.

Flavor burst onto her tongue. She moaned as the tiny tease of satisfaction made her hunger roar to life. She wanted more, much more.

"Oh my God," she said when she could speak. "We should trade."

"I knew you'd like it." He grinned. "Now try your pot pie. If you still want to trade, fine. Otherwise, we'll switch orders next time."

Next time?

"You seem pretty sure of yourself, Logan Stafford."

He enjoyed another forkful of meatloaf, a satisfied smile on his face.

Samara gaped at the mouth-watering abundance before her, then pierced the flaky crust with her fork and took her first small bite.

And moaned again.

"Don't tell the meatloaf," she said, speaking through her food and not caring, "but this is the best thing I've ever tasted."

"Good. I'm making it my personal challenge to get some weight back on your bones."

She raised her eyebrows. "Who died and made you king?"

"Don't you mean to say 'You're not the boss of me'?"

It had always been so easy to be with Logan, she remembered. Years ago at school, he found a way to bring her out of her shell and here he was again, helping her feel comfortable again, making her feel special.

Loved.

She remembered kissing him under the bleachers.

"Getting warm?" asked Logan. "A good meal will do that."

She nodded, but it wasn't only the food. He was the first boy she'd ever explored physical intimacy with. They talked about going all the way, but both being virgins, agreed to wait until their one-year anniversary. To make it really special, a night to remember.

Only she was gone by then.

Logan waved down their waitress. "Another beer for the lady, when you have a moment."

With shock, Samara noticed that her glass was empty.

"Did you drink my beer?"

He smiled and shook his head. "You did it all by your sweet lonesome. Just like you polished off the pot pie."

He was right. The chicken pie was gone. A single piece of lettuce lay wilting on the salad plate. There was a breadstick in her hand and the most wonderful feeling of satiation in her belly.

"My goodness, I'm like a hog at a trough!"

"Now, don't even start with that," said Logan, reaching across to touch her hand. "I enjoyed watching you eat almost as much as you enjoyed eating. There's nothing a man likes more than to see a woman happy. Especially if he can take the credit."

** හ**ග

LOGAN WATCHED SAM stack their empty plates, nestling the knives and forks, folding the crumpled napkins. Her fingers were long and elegant, the nails unpolished, short and smooth. She'd been organized and tidy as a teen, a way of coping with a life filled with upheaval and uncertainty.

But there was more to it now, and he had a feeling he knew why. He remembered the way she touched the carpet, how she checked for parallel lines and right angles, her distress at finding a rough patch on the banister.

"Don't take this the wrong way," he began, "but what's the deal with Jade?"

She jumped. "Nothing. She's fine. She's unique. There's nothing wrong with her."

"Whoa, there," said Logan. "No offence intended. I'm just trying to figure things out. You have to admit, you're a little overprotective."

He waited. Parents of special needs kids had to be highly organized and schedule-oriented. They were often frustrated and highly-defensive, too. Sadly, the desire to do the best for their children often pitted mother against father when they needed each other the most.

But then, he'd seen that in parents of ordinary kids, as well.

A muscle in her jaw flickered. "I don't like labels."

"Has she been assessed?"

Samara sighed heavily. "Over and over and over. She cried so much, you see. Some days it seemed like that's all she did. We weren't prepared, especially Michael. As she got older, the crying stopped, but they still never bonded. I was the only one who could hold her. He thought something must be wrong with her. So we went from doctor to doctor. But they all said she tested 'within normal limits.' We were told to take parenting classes."

He heard the humiliation behind the words.

"Rough start."

"Michael wouldn't take them without me, and we'd already scared off every sitter we could find, and then suddenly," she paused for a shaky breath, "he was gone."

"How old was she when Michael passed away?" he asked, as gently as he could.

"Not quite three." She looked down at the breadstick in her hand. "I pretty much shut down for a while after that. My poor baby."

Poor Sam, he thought, knowing how much she despised pity.

"Bob's trained for autistic kids, isn't she?"

She froze. Had he gone too far?

Then she began pulling off crumbs and putting them in rows.

"She's not certified," she answered finally. "But, yeah. She's had some training."

Jade seemed immature in some ways, and she had definite socialization issues, but that could be said about some of his students, too. And none of them were autistic.

"Seems to me she's everything Jade needs."

He suddenly remembered a day from that one summer they had together. He'd convinced her to join a group of them who were hanging out by the cookhouse on Yellowstone River, swimming, sunning, sharing a few purloined beers. She was excited until they insisted – not unkindly – that they drive across town so she could grab her contribution to the snack pool.

A buzz sounded from Sam's bag.

She pulled out her smart phone and scanned the screen, her eyebrows furrowed.

On that long-ago day, when they bumped over the tracks to the tumble-down rented cracker-box where she lived with her parents, the truck grew quiet. Two men sat on the concrete steps leading to her front door, a couple of empty six-packs littering the dead grass around them. Her father, he knew without being told, and old man Goodwin, Flynn's dad and the town drunk.

Samara returned, stepping over the intoxicated men with an opened box of saltines and three soda cans in her hands. As she walked between house and truck, her flaming face tight and hard, she'd been more alone than anyone he'd ever seen. His friends adjusted their smiles, tucking her into the not-our-kind-but-we'll-be-nice-for-Logan's-sake category.

An almost-forgotten guilt twisted hotly in his gut. He should have leapt off the back of the truck and walked beside her, proudly, to the truck full of shallow, immature, self-absorbed people he'd thought were his friends.

He'd loved her then, or thought he did, but he'd been a shallow, immature, self-absorbed boy, himself.

A boy with a boy's love.

All Sam had wanted was to be included. To fit in.

No wonder her daughter's uniqueness triggered such fear. By definition, unique meant alone.

"I have to go," said Samara, stuffing the phone back into her purse. "Jade's tired. She needs me."

Logan held out his hand. "Can I read the text?"

It was from Eliza.

Jade said Bob needed to go to bed. Figured it meant she was tired herself. :) Aunt Mabel just tucked her in. All fine. No need to rush back.

"No need to rush back?" He raised his eyebrows at Samara. "I'm not sure what subtext you read into it, but to me, it sounds like there's no need to rush back."

"You don't understand-," she began.

"Here you go," said Mardie, writing up their check.

"False alarm," said Logan. "In fact, can we see a dessert menu?"

"Logan," said Sam, getting to her feet, "this isn't your decision. I need to go and thanks to the beer, you need to drive me. No dessert, thank you, Mardie."

The waitress looked between them.

"Give us a minute, will you?" he said gently. Mardie left, shaking her head.

Their interaction had drawn a few eyes, which wasn't helping calm her.

Logan touched her arm and she grew still. "Samara."

Tension like steel wires ran just beneath her skin. He remembered sixteen-year-old Sam's determination to stay with him at that party, despite the thinly-veiled pity from the other girls, the special voice they spoke to her with, different from how they spoke to each other. How the boys followed her with a bit more familiarity, winking at Logan as if the fact that she was a pretty girl from the wrong side of the tracks, poor as dirt, automatically made her an easy lay.

He tugged her back into her seat, gently.

"If Eliza says Jade is fine, then Jade is fine. Hell, Mabel tucking her in is the headline here."

That tendon in her neck was jumping again, and she didn't return his smile. But now she looked torn.

"I think the only one who's not fine, who hasn't been fine in a very long time," he said softly, "is you. But if you need to go, we'll go."

He kept his hand on hers, stroking lightly.

"I'm enjoying getting acquainted with you all over again. How about you?"

Her head dropped forward then, just slightly, and Logan knew he'd won.

"A half-hour longer," she said. "That's it."

He grinned and stuck his hand up in the air. "There's a chocolate volcano cake here that will make you think you've died and gone to heaven. And I, for one, don't share dessert, so you'll have to order your own."

"You don't play fair, do you?" she said.

"I do whatever it takes, honey."

ഈൽ

SAM BEHELD THE empty plate in front of her with disbelief, marvelling that somehow, she'd managed to put away that entire, huge, luscious chocolate volcano cake. And after everything she'd already eaten.

"I think I just gained five pounds," she said, putting her hand on her stomach. She felt sated, as if a long-term deficiency had been filled.

But it wasn't just the food; it was Logan. Who else could make her leave her daughter with near-strangers just so she could spend an hour or two with him?

"Five pounds? Then we'll have to do this at least four more times," said Logan. He'd had the cheesecake and it was fantastic too. She knew because he'd insisted on giving her a taste.

"Twenty pounds?" She tossed a paper napkin at him.

"At least." He stood up. "Half-hour's up. Time to go."

"Right. Of course." She shook her head. It was as if she became someone else in his presence. Someone who was more than a mother.

She took out a couple of twenties. "Here, this should cover

my portion."

"When you ask me out," he said, pushing them back into her bag, "you can pay. When I ask, I pay."

He lifted her sweater off the back of her chair and held it out for her. "Besides, I never got to treat you the way I wanted to, way back when. Let me do this now."

He looked regretful, she thought, though for what she couldn't imagine. He'd been such a wonderful boyfriend. Her first, which may have colored her memory, of course. But still. He'd been sweet, funny, courteous… and the chemistry between them.

Well.

It had been ferocious. The kind of heat you look back on years later with fondness, knowing it was wrapped up in hormones and youth, nothing that could last.

Nothing real.

He unlocked the passenger door of his truck and held out his hand.

She needed his help like ducks need a map to the lake, but she couldn't resist the chance to touch him again. She'd always loved his big hands, his long fingers, the elegant curve of his thumb. Even though he spent his days working with wood, there was nothing rough or crude about his hands. If anything, he had the touch of an artist.

The solid warmth flowed from his skin to hers and it felt… right. Familiar. Comfortable.

Hands didn't change, she thought.

Logan walked her to the door. For a moment, they stood on the porch, the last golden streaks from the dying sun slanting through the trees.

"Thank you," she said. "For making me have dinner with you."

He laughed. "Next time maybe I'll really torture you and

take you to a movie."

Next time.

Then he took a step closer to her. She backed up but the rough stone façade stopped her.

"Goodnight, Sam," he murmured. Then he lowered his head and covered her mouth with his. Her hands went to his chest, as if to push him away, but when he deepened the kiss, they crept up, up to his neck until she was clinging to him, dragging him closer, unaware of anything but the need to be touching, every bit of them, with no stopping, no barriers.

Logan chuckled, breaking the kiss. He leaned his forehead against hers. They were both breathing hard.

"Wow," she said. Her voice shook. And she thought the kiss this morning had been crazy.

"Yeah." His eyes met hers and a current charged between them, sizzling and dangerous, jolting, binding and unbreakable.

"I guess," he said, "some things never change."

Chapter Eight

On Tuesday morning, as Sam walked up to the house, nerves tightened all her movements. But for once, it wasn't because she was worried about Jade, or moving, or her house.

This jumpiness was entirely due to that mind-bending kiss they'd shared yesterday. It was amazing how her lips recognized his, how his chest and shoulders and back were still familiar to her fingers, even though he was broader and thicker everywhere now.

What did it mean? Did he still have feelings for her?

Did she still have feelings for him?

In truth, she'd locked her memories of him down so tight, that she didn't even know.

Though it appeared her body had no such reservations.

Her face burned at the memory of her response. She'd responded like a cat in heat, rubbing against him as she had. Only later had she remembered she hadn't yet addressed the granny-panties situation, so first thing this morning she and Jade had driven into Livingston and found a department store. She smoothed her hand over her hip. Jade had enthusiastically approved of the "pretty, pretty panties" and she had to admit, it was fun to dress like it mattered again.

She wasn't doing this for Logan, she told herself.

She was doing this because it was time to stop mourning. That phase of her life was over. Time to start anew.

And if it so happened that Logan ended up seeing them, well, hopefully he'd approve as well.

Samara! She heard her mother's voice. *Have you no shame?*

It appeared she did not. At least, it wasn't slowing her feet. She pushed open the door, her heart skipping a beat as Logan's eyes met hers.

"Good morning," she said, feeling a grin spread across her cheeks.

The answering smile didn't last long, though.

"Small glitch," he said, brushing his gloves on his jeans.

"A glitch?"

It took her a moment to change gears. There was no time for glitches, of any size.

"We had to open up a couple of walls upstairs, around the outlets, to check the electrical. There's no problem, the wiring is great," he hastened to assure her. "And the holes are small. We could even fix them after move-in. But if it was me-"

"It is you. You're the project manager." Sam swallowed. It wouldn't do any good to snap at him.

"If Jade was my daughter," he corrected, "I'd want it done."

And with those words, her annoyance slipped away. He knew exactly where her priorities lay and he was working to make sure her daughter was cared for, even when she didn't realize it.

"My guys have already been evaluated on drywall," he continued. "I need them with the plumber now, to finish the sink and dishwasher install. But there's no reason you and I can't fix the holes."

The two of them, working upstairs again, just like yesterday. With the painting. And the kissing.

The kissing, which had led to dinner and dessert and more kissing.

Which had led to a sleepless night.

"I know nothing about drywall," she said.

"Prepare yourself, then, sweetheart." Logan slung an arm over her shoulder. "Do I know how to show a girl a good time, or what?"

₧₧

NO POINT BEMOANING the set-back, thought Logan. But when your high-school sweetheart comes home and kisses him the way Sam did, and you give her bad news in return, a guy can't help but want to punch something.

Her house was supposed to be ready. He was supposed to have made that happen. She had every right to be upset with him.

And she had been upset, he'd seen it. But then she shuffled it off and threw herself into the tasks he gave her. You had to admire that.

"What do you think?" she asked, snapping him out of his reverie. "How am I doing?"

She was crouched on her knees in front of the outlet, focusing intently on smoothing just the right amount of plaster onto the seam patching the sheetrock. Her bottom lip caught in her teeth, making it impossible for him to look at anything else.

"Logan?" She raised her eyebrows innocently.

He squatted down beside her. "You did a good job."

Their knees touched but instead of pulling away, Sam held her position, pressing ever so slightly against him.

"Really." Her voice took on a teasing tone. "Or are you just saying that because I'm a drywall virgin and you want me to have good memories about my first time?"

A very teasing tone. His pulse quickened.

"A drywall virgin, huh? I wouldn't have known if you hadn't told me."

"Is that so?" She sat back against the wall, her knees bent, her hands resting lightly on them. She watched him, a small smile on her lips. "I thought my work would give me away. I must be a natural."

He sat on the floor and stretched one leg out until it reached her foot. He gave it a nudge.

"Or you had a great teacher."

She nudged back.

"Or you're just so grateful that someone's doing it with you, you're overlooking my deficiencies."

He tipped his head. "Gratitude plays a role, true. But on second thought, you could use a little more practice."

She scrambled to her hands and knees, mock outrage on her face.

"Oh!"

Laughing, she pushed him until he fell over halfway and before he knew it, she was straddling him, arms up as if she was about to give him a pounding.

Without thinking, he flipped her over. She shrieked as he pinned her arms to the ground.

"No back talk," he growled. "Or I'll have to keep you after school."

Her pupils were so big her eyes looked black, and her cheeks were flushed. Her breasts rose and fell quickly and her t-shirt slipped up just enough to see a strip of creamy skin above her jeans.

He'd never seen anything so completely sexy in his life. He pressed his pelvis against her to let her know that her little game had consequences.

"What will you do with me?" she said in a breathy whisper.

But before he could answer, footsteps sounded on the stairs.

They sprang apart, fumbling to rearrange their clothing.

Flynn Goodwin stuck his head in the doorway. "Plumber wants you to go over the sink installation with us, Mr. S."

"Of course." Logan put down the trowel. He'd just slapped a pile of spackle on a perfectly fine section of wall. *Idiot.* "Right. Sam, you can keep working on, uh, what we were... working on."

She blinked at him, wide-eyed. "Absolutely. It's harder than I expected, though. I'll need your help to finish."

The twitch of that full lower lip sent a rush of blood straight to his groin. She was killing him.

He turned Flynn around and sent him back downstairs. Then he stuck his head around the corner.

"We're not quitting until I'm satisfied you know what you're doing," he said in a low voice.

"Until we're both satisfied," she corrected.

Killing. Him.

ⅎ℻

LOGAN WAS GONE longer than she expected. Which was good, gave her a chance to let her brain start working again. What was she thinking, flirting with Logan like this, while his students were steps away, and so much work for each of them that they barely had time for lunch, let alone fooling around like kids.

Samara heard hurried footsteps approaching, and composed herself.

One look at her and Logan's face fell. He walked to her side and took both her hands in his. She shook her head, unable to meet his gaze.

"Sam, you're overthinking this," he said. "It feels like it was just yesterday we were necking out under the bleachers. I want to be with you like that again."

He drew her in and put his arms around her. No teasing this time, no pushing the boundaries little bit by little bit, in that irresistible and inevitable dance.

"No you don't," she whispered. "I'm still the new girl from the wrong side of the tracks, Logan. I've got better clothes now but inside, I'm even more broken than before. You're still the hometown hero, the guy everyone loves. Don't let me mess that up for you. Not again."

She waited for his reaction. He had every right to be angry. Hurt. Disappointed.

The heat was still there, ready to flare up at a moment's notice, but banked for now, comforting, soothing and soft.

But to her surprise, he chuckled.

"You've just spent way too much time alone, is what I think," he said. "Stop analyzing everything, Sam. Just for a moment."

Then he leaned down and kissed her, soft and sweet and lingering, his tongue running lightly against her lips, the kind of kiss that made a girl believe she was good and beautiful, worth loving, and that everything would be okay.

She couldn't help herself, she clung to him as if he was the only thing that might keep her from disappearing, resisting his love with everything in her.

His *love*.

"You feel it, too. I know you do," Logan murmured against her hair.

"Don't, Logan," she whispered.

"Getting a second chance together is a miracle, Sam. It's a gift."

It took all the strength she had to turn her face away from

his. They'd loved once already – and lost.

"It's not a gift, Logan. It's a gamble." A tear dripped onto his shirt, a small, spreading mark. "And I can't afford to gamble."

His breath came out in a hiss, but he tightened his grip around her.

"So we'll take it slow then," he said. "I won't push you beyond what you want, Sam. But fair warning: I will push you. When this happens, it'll be on your terms, because you want it as much as I do."

Not *if*, but *when*.

She tried to pull away. "I can't deny there's something between us. And I'm so grateful that you're here, when I really need a friend-"

"We were never just *friends*," he bit out, refusing to let her go. "And we're not going to start now."

"But that's all we should have been. I should never have let you think it could be something more. Dad couldn't hang onto a job, so we always moved, just when I got settled into a school. I'd hoped...But I always knew we'd break up in the end."

"We never broke up, Sam," said Logan, enunciating precisely. "You left."

"You knew I was leaving."

"I knew you were leaving sometime that weekend! I didn't know you'd disappear after final period on Friday!"

"I didn't know either!" She finally broke away from his embrace. She bent down to put the lid on her paint can, grateful for a task that hid her face. "Turns out my dad had skipped out on the rent. My stuff was in boxes in the car. I had to go, right then and there."

Years later, once she was finally earning a salary, she located the owner and paid the bill; he was gone now, but the man's understanding had reminded her of all the good in Marietta.

"I searched for you at lunch that day," she continued, quieter now, "but you were off campaigning for student council president, even though you knew it was our last week together. You chose to spend your time on that."

"That was a mistake," Logan responded. "But it was good that I won. It kept me too busy to miss you."

Silence fell between them. Samara looked up.

"You really missed me?" she said in a small voice.

Friends always said they'd keep in touch, but they never did.

"Of course I missed you!" He paused. "Didn't you miss me?"

She stood up and took a deep, shuddering breath. "I thought I'd die, it hurt so bad."

"So why didn't you write? I had no idea where you were. The post office told me you left no forwarding address, and that I wasn't the only one asking."

Sam squeezed her eyes shut at the memories of that year.

"I nearly went out of my mind." Logan gripped her shoulders and gave her a little shake. "I didn't know if you were okay, if your dad was back in jail, if you and your mom were in a homeless shelter somewhere."

The old familiar shame welled up, making her squirm.

"I never meant to hurt you, Logan," she said. "But it was just as well that things happened as they did. You were going places, your future was set. You needed the head cheerleader, or that girl who aced all the science awards, or that one who ran fundraisers for needy children. You didn't need the welfare girl."

"I married the head cheerleader," said Logan through gritted teeth. "Six months of great sex, followed by four years of insecurity, accusations and way too much hairspray. She was runner-up to the welfare girl, and she knew it."

That couldn't be possible. He couldn't have had such deep feelings. Could he?

"Logan." She picked her jacket up off the floor and held it against her chest. Tentatively, she took a step toward him.

But before she could think of what to say – what could she say? – her phone buzzed.

When she pulled it out, she saw message notifications, both voice and text. She'd forgotten her phone was on mute. Her fingers started shaking.

"It was real then, and it's real now," said Logan.

But Samara barely heard him.

Every message was from Eliza.

Jade! My baby!

She fumbled and nearly dropped the device.

"Sam! One way or another, we're going to deal with this!"

She scrolled to the most recent text.

Don't worry. Minor fracture only. In casting room now.

The breath left her lungs.

Minor fracture?

Her pulse was thudding in her ears, drowning out all other sounds.

Don't worry?

She shoved the phone back into her bag, without reading the earlier messages. Jade was hurt. Bad enough to need a cast!

"What's going on?" said Logan, stepping in front of her.

"Something happened to Jade!" She brushed past him.

"What? What happened? Where is she?"

He reached for her but she shook him off.

"At the hospital, Logan. I don't know why! But this is why we can't be together. I'll always choose her. Do you understand? You'd never be first in my heart."

She ran down the sidewalk and leaped into her car. As she squealed out into the quiet street, she caught a glimpse of him in her rear view mirror, Logan, getting smaller and smaller.

Chapter Nine

୫୦୦ଃ

"EXCUSE ME," SAID Samara, elbowing her way through the small group just inside the sliding doors of the emergency room.

Don't worry, Eliza's message said.

Right.

A middle-aged man was seated at the chair at the triage window talking to the clerk.

She leaned over him. "Excuse me. I'm looking for my daughter."

The clerk's face tightened at the interruption. "Take a number," she said, pointing to the dispenser.

"Jade," said Samara desperately. "My daughter. I'm her mother, Samara Davis. She's four years old. I'm not sure what happened but I know she went for x-rays and something's broken. She was in casting! Please!"

The clerk's expression changed. "One moment," she said, but whether she was talking to the man in the chair or Samara, it was hard to tell.

Don't worry.

Eliza wouldn't have texted *Don't worry* if it had been serious, right?

Except she wasn't a doctor. How would she know? People always said that, *Don't worry, everything will be fine, calm down, he's okay, don't worry, don't worry, don't worry!*

The officer who called after Michael's accident had said the same thing.

Minor injuries, they said. Lucky to be alive. Overnight observation, home tomorrow, they said. *Don't worry.*

Then there was a team of people clustered around his bed, machines and tubes everywhere, all practiced speed and efficiency, while the latte slipped from her fingers.

Panic clawed at Samara's throat and she fought it down. That was different.

Don't worry. Don't worry.

The clerk kicked her rolling chair to a different desk, tapped the keys in rapid fire, then called to a nurse wearing green scrubs. Samara couldn't hear the conversation, but she saw the young man frown and shake his head, before bustling away.

The chair clattered loudly on the tile floor. The room had gone quiet around them. Time slowed and a heavy stillness descended on Samara, that infinitesimal, endless moment that cuts a life into Before and After.

"I'm sorry," said the clerk. She looked nicer now, concerned, wishing she had better news.

Samara's knees buckled. She grabbed for the edge of the counter. She'd seen the same discomfort before, when they realized she was in the doorway, too late, the widow, clutching her child, milk and coffee splattered on her pants.

"No, no, no, no!" cried a voice that seemed to be coming from her but didn't sound at all like her.

I'm sorry, the clerk said.

Nothing good ever came after those words.

She couldn't breathe. She had to find Jade!

The clerk's face paled. "I don't mean that! We haven't admitted a child by that name tonight. That's all. I didn't mean…"

Behind her, Samara saw the young nurse calling, his lips moving as if in slow motion, his voice muffled, like it was under water.

An automatic door whooshed open and the young nurse came sprinting through, pushing a wheelchair, still calling out something.

Don't worry.

This is why she worried! Catastrophe was always just around the corner. She had to be on high-alert at all times because it struck when you least expected it and who else was going to take care of Jade but her, that was her job, her responsibility because there was no one else now!

The nurse, Dave, according to his tag, caught Samara by the elbow and eased her into the chair.

"Breathe, Ms. Davis."

Dave. Davis. Davis and Dave.

"Your daughter's fine," he repeated, wheeling her quickly through the doors into a quiet exam room. He pulled a chair up so they were knee to knee and clipped something to her index finger.

"Jade's here, and she's fine. She came in with Eliza and Mabel Bramble. Eliza left a note with triage that you'd be coming, but the admitting clerks just changed shift and someone missed the memo."

He slipped a blood pressure cuff on her arm while he talked but she barely noticed.

Jade's here. She's fine. Don't worry.

"Why is she here if she's fine? What aren't you telling me?" She tried to stand up but Dave held her firmly in the chair.

"Ms. Davis, if you stand up now, you'll probably faint. You don't want that, right? It'll scare Jade if her mama gets all banged up."

He was right. She had to keep her head. She forced herself to speak more slowly.

"Where is she?"

She couldn't catch her breath. She felt as if she was spinning under a spotlight, going faster and faster, until soon, she'd spin off into the darkness.

The clerk popped her head in, handed Dave a sheet of paper and gestured to the triage desk.

"Buzz him in," Dave told her, before turning his attention back to Samara.

"Jade is in the family room with Eliza." Dave spoke deliberately, as if she was a child. "Mabel Bramble had a fall; Eliza was worried so she brought her in. Jade came along for the ride."

Never ride with strangers.

But strangers were everywhere. She'd only known Mabel and Eliza for what, six days? Not even a week!

Don't take candy from strangers. Don't talk to strangers on the street.

Everyone was a stranger.

"Take me to her!" She was gasping and crying, clutching at Dave, trying to make him understand. "She'll be so frightened!"

Dave slipped something over her face and put prongs into her nostrils. Immediately delicious cool air flowed into her airway. She closed her eyes.

From somewhere far away, a buzzing noise sounded.

"Ms. Davis. Samara. Listen to me. Your heart rate's too high and your BP's too low. As soon as your vitals are stable, your friend will take you to the family room, okay?"

Her friend?

She had no friends. She barely knew anyone here. Then a hand touched her shoulder. She jumped, then wilted with gratitude.

Logan.

He stroked her cheek and she leaned into it, feeling the dampness under his fingers.

Of course it was Logan.

The spinning slowed, just enough for her to catch a breath.

"Hey, babe, how are you doing?"

"Fine." She swallowed, hard. "I thought we weren't friends."

He kissed her forehead. "It's a grey area."

"She's pretty shook up," said Dave, as if she wasn't there. "More than I'd expect, under the circumstances. Samara, do you have a history of panic attacks?"

She thought of that young widow, screaming, with coffee-splattered pants and a hysterical toddler on her hip.

The disco ball sped up again, spangly and bright.

"Panic attacks, no, I don't know. I get anxious, but you would too if your daughter was in the hospital with strangers and you couldn't get to her."

Tears flooded in. She pressed her hands over her face. The spangly lights were blinding. She was dizzy and her stomach didn't feel well.

"You're exhibiting all the signs-," began Dave, but Sam couldn't stop talking.

"People say don't worry, don't worry, and hospitals are the worst. You want to believe them, so badly, and why not? Why wouldn't you trust them?"

She heard the words running together but she couldn't stop.

"They keep saying everything's fine, like you're a paranoid idiot or a kid who just doesn't get it. But then they change their minds and say things like *subdural hematoma* and *we did everything we could* and *would you like some water*, because that'll help when you've just lost your husband and you don't know what to do and your baby's crying and you've got no one and you shouldn't be hearing this because they told you and told you that everything was fine, that you shouldn't worry!"

Sometime during her rant, she'd yanked off the nasal cannula. She started to get out of the wheelchair but the spangly lights swirled above her.

"Sam!" Logan grabbed her and pushed her back into the chair. He held her while Dave replaced the devices.

"Look at me," he commanded. "Breathe in. And out. Sam, focus! Watch me. Breathe when I breathe. In. Out. Again."

Gradually the terror slipped away. In its place came fatigue, embarrassment and still that fear that wouldn't ease until she had Jade in her arms.

Dave checked the monitors and finally satisfied, took them off. He left for a moment, then returned with a slip of paper. "I'm guessing you don't have a family physician yet. Here's Dr. Gallagher's card. He's a great guy, very understanding. I think you'd like him. You should get set up with him, okay? Other than that, you're good to go."

He gave Logan a meaningful look.

"I'll make sure it happens," said Logan. "Thanks, Dave."

"He thinks I'm crazy," said Sam, unable to care.

"No he doesn't, honey," said Logan. "Can you walk?"

She got to her feet. "Of course I can walk."

He put an arm around her waist, supporting her, and she leaned on him, appreciating his comforting solidness, the strong, hard body beneath the soft cotton of his shirt.

She was still sniffling, feeling foolish but unable to stop and unable to explain. Logan didn't ask questions, or say anything at all. He just aimed her in the right direction, held her up and kept her going, his steady heartbeat next to hers, lending her the courage she didn't even know she needed.

๛

LOGAN PUT ONE foot in front of the other, holding tightly to the bundle of bones and nerves and sheer panic that was Samara. She trembled in his arms like a wild bird, captured, terrified, exhausted.

He'd known, the second she opened her phone and the color bled from her face, that it was about Jade. Nothing but maternal instinct could possibly have triggered such a primal, gut-level reaction.

But he had no idea of the trauma she'd experienced when her husband passed away.

Logan's heart slipped sideways.

A critical error, Staff.

"Where is she?" asked Sam. Her voice wasn't hitching any more but it was still tight and higher than normal.

Logan pointed to a sign at the end of the hallway. "Right there."

Samara broke out of his grasp and began running toward the room, and he let her, hurrying behind her, feeling a sinking sense of deja vu.

He still wasn't sure of the details, but the clerk had assured him – once Dave had vouched for him at least – that Jade was uninjured. Aunt Mabel was the one who'd been hurt, a minor hand or wrist fracture, something like that. When Eliza couldn't find Samara, she'd simply taken Jade along with them to the hospital.

When he entered the room, Samara was on her knees in front of Jade, hugging her and stroking her hair.

Eliza watched, clearly taken aback at Sam's reaction. Jade wasn't impressed, either.

"Mama," she complained, pushing out of her mother's grasp. "My pictures!"

"I think Mama was a little worried," said Eliza. "I told you she was fine, Samara."

Logan watched as Sam composed herself, straightening her shoulders, easing herself onto the couch beside Jade, holding her fluttery hands together tightly in her lap.

"Thank you for watching my daughter," said Sam, her words clipped. "I appreciate it, I do. But you should have found me. You knew where I was. You shouldn't have taken Jade in your car. You don't have a car seat. And you didn't bring Bob."

Eliza's mouth fell open.

"Sam," murmured Logan.

"No." She lifted her chin. "She's my daughter and I make the rules. Me."

Eliza glanced between him and Sam, bewildered and horrified. "I tried to call you, Samara. Several times. But you didn't answer and we couldn't wait."

Samara stood up and paced to the far side of the room, to the window overlooking a small courtyard. After a moment, she said, "I don't blame you. It's my fault. I didn't get your message until too late. I should have left you with my vehicle. Or I shouldn't have left her with you at all."

Silence descended on the room. Samara was clearly distraught but this was entirely unfair. She was simply taking it out on whoever happened to be within striking distance.

He moved closer to Sam. If anyone should be taking her anger, it was him.

Sam stopped and he could feel electricity flowing off her. She was practically vibrating, all her defences on high alert, all her weapons at the ready.

Then Jade pushed a pile of pictures toward Eliza. "Do yours."

Eliza blinked, then swallowed. "Of course, sweetie."

She turned her attention back to Jade's game, but Logan could see her lips trembling.

An orderly appeared at the door. "I've got a lovely lady here who needs a ride home. Any volunteers?"

Behind him sat Aunt Mabel, regal in her wheelchair, her left arm plastered from fingertip to elbow.

Eliza leaped to her feet. "Yes! I'm right here."

She paused awkwardly at the door. "We'll finish your pictures at home, okay, Jade?"

"Uh-huh." Jade, engrossed in her project, didn't look up.

Samara remained at the window, her hands twisted tightly together. The tension in the room was palpable. As Logan watched, she made a concerted effort to compose herself.

"I'm sorry you were hurt, Aunt Mabel. Are you all right?"

"I broke my wrist!" snapped Mabel. "Of course I'm not all right. But Eliza and the tadpole took care of me."

She shot Sam a pointed glare and Sam turned away, her shoulders tight, her hands gripping her elbows.

"I'm sorry, Logan," whispered Eliza as she passed him. She was near tears. "I never meant to scare her. I don't quite know what happened here."

He squeezed her arm. "You look after your great-aunt, okay? I'll take care of Sam and the chipmunk. Everything will be fine."

But from the tempest on Samara's face, he had a feeling that he might be wrong about that.

෨෬

THERE WAS NO longer any need for it, but the adrenaline powering Samara continued to race through her system. And now, it was joined by guilt.

As soon as Eliza and Mabel left, she pulled her cell phone from her pocket with shaking hands and checked her text messages again.

Don't worry. Minor fracture only. In casting room.

But before that:

Taking forever. See you here or at home.

Then:

Aunt M getting x-rays. J fine. Waiting in family room.

A missed call, then:

Sorry, must leave now, bringing J. Call when you get these msgs!

Another missed call, followed by:

Samara? Wrist swelling badly, must go now. Happy to bring J but no car seat!

And finally, after two missed calls, the first message:

Sorry to interrupt! Can you come home? Aunt M slipped, hurt wrist. Nothing serious but should go to ER.

Eliza was right; she'd tried to contact Sam. She'd done everything right and how had Sam reacted? Leaped down her throat, blaming her when it was all Sam's fault. She's the one who accidentally muted her phone. She's the one who didn't check for messages.

She's the one who was too busy fooling around with Logan that she'd forgotten all about her daughter, the most precious thing in her life.

How could she have done this?

"Sam?" said Logan.

She whirled around. He's the one who distracted her, made her think of herself as a woman again, stirred up desires she hadn't allowed herself to feel for so long. He knew that Jade was her one and only priority, and still he pulled at her, selfishly.

And then there was the episode in the ER exam room. That was a bell she wished she could un-ring.

But maybe if Logan knew just how messed up she was, he'd finally understand that getting involved with her wasn't worth it.

Then she noticed Jade, her dark eyes wide, following them closely.

Sam clenched her fists and took a deep breath, willing the storm of emotions to stay inside, instead of spilling out where it could frighten her child and probably destroy any chances of whatever friendship she and Logan might still have.

"We need to get home, honey," she said. "Get your pictures together, okay?"

"No," said Jade. "I'm not done."

"Let me drive you two home," said Logan. "You've had a bad scare and shouldn't be behind the wheel."

"It's five blocks," Sam said tightly. "I'm fine."

He tipped his head pointedly at Jade and pasted a smile on his face. She could see the muscles in his jaw twitching.

"Sam, if she rides with you now, while you're this upset, she could end up actually hurt, instead of imagined-hurt. Don't put her at risk just because you're too proud to admit you were wrong."

Sam stepped back as if slapped, but before she could react, he turned to Jade, squatting down by the coffee table where her pictures were in careful piles.

"Time to go, chipmunk," he said. He made no move to touch her things, or make eye contact. Jade frowned, her fingers tightening on the card in her hand, and Sam braced herself for a fight.

Good, she thought, knowing it was petty of her but unable to stop the feelings. It's easy to be a hero when it's all piggybacks and ice cream. It's not so much fun when you have to be the tough guy.

"Eliza and Aunt Mabel are waiting for you at the house," he said, more firmly this time. "Shall I collect your cards, or will you?"

"I'm not done!" said Jade, her body tensing protectively over her collection.

Samara crossed her arms. This was going to be quite the show. She'd been through this too many times, herself.

Before Jade knew what was happening, Logan swept the cards up into a neat pile, wrapped the elastic band around them and slipped them into his pocket.

"No! No! No!" shrieked Jade.

Samara stepped forward. Logan was way out of his depth. Jade lashed out, knocking one small fist against her mother's chin, where it was still bruised from the bungee cord.

"That's it," said Logan. Calmly, but with complete authority, he gathered her screaming child in his arms, pinning the flailing limbs as best he could. "Let's go."

She had no choice but to follow. They garnered much attention as they made their way through the corridors and out the front doors, but as they walked to the parking lot, Jade's cries had begun to fade.

By the time they reached her car, and Logan lowered her into her car seat, she was down to hiccupping sobs.

By the time Samara had her properly buckled in, she was asleep.

"Get in," said Logan, pointing to the passenger seat.

"Logan," she began.

"That wasn't a suggestion, Sam."

He slid awkwardly behind the wheel, then adjusted the seat to fit his frame. She got in and immediately turned around to check on Jade.

"She's fine." Logan started the engine and moved the mirrors. "Just like she was two seconds ago."

"You're way out of line, Logan," she said quietly.

"Maybe," he said, turning onto the road. "But so are you. You had no right to go off on them like that."

Guilt squirmed hot and uncomfortable inside. She had no response and they traveled the short trip to Bramble House in silence.

She was suddenly exhausted beyond measure. Logan shut off the engine and got out, closing his door carefully. Before she could get to Jade's door, he was already there, undoing the buckles and gathering her into his arms.

"I can take it from here, Logan."

He ignored her weak protest. "Get your things."

With one big hand stroking her hair, Logan cradled Jade's head gently against his shoulder and strode down the walkway ahead of her.

The image triggered something in Samara, a yearning so powerful, so unexpected, that it nearly felled her.

Logan had no right to take over the way he had.

But the sense of having someone else to rely on, to let herself feel tired, without feeling either guilty or terrified that she was indulging herself at her daughter's expense...

Tears choked her throat. The rush of emotions that had flooded over her in the space of a single day left her feeling weak and off kilter. And through those doors, were two women who'd befriended her, and were now undoubtedly regretting it.

She'd barely remembered to ask after Mabel.

She'd come to Marietta to find a forever home, to hopefully join a community and learn what it meant to be a part of something.

And within a week, she'd alienated the first people to be nice to her.

"Come on in, honey." Logan stood under the porch light,

holding the door open for her. He held Jade against him with one arm, managing the weight far more easily than Sam herself could.

"Sam," he said gently. That beautiful blue-green gaze was so soft, so full of compassion. She walked forward, hardly feeling her legs, bypassing the kitchen and leading Logan to her suite.

Bob greeted them with quiet concern, snuffling insistently at whatever part of Jade she could access. The dog had probably been almost as worried as she'd been herself.

At Jade's doorway Samara stopped. "You can put her down on the bed. I'll get her into her pajamas."

But Logan pushed past her. He flipped back the coverlet, lowered Jade onto the sheets and slipped off her shoes. "She can sleep in her clothes."

She didn't have energy to argue. She could always get Jade settled properly once he was gone.

But Logan turned off the light, pulled the door almost but not completely closed, and turned to her.

"Now," he said, his eyes glittering. "Your turn."

୫୬ଓ୨

HE WANTED HER.

Logan looked down at Sam, standing in the dim hallway light, her posture still tight and determined, despite the mixture of emotions he knew she was feeling.

Almost a decade and a half since high school, and she was as beautiful as ever.

More, in fact.

Back then, he'd wanted to gather her under his arm and be her shield against the world, or her entry ticket into it. He was the big-man-on-campus and he wanted to prove it to her. He was the guy who got the new girl. The ice queen who wouldn't give any of them a second glance hadn't been able to resist him and oh, how he'd loved that.

Shame rippled through him.

He thought he'd loved *her*, but it had all been about him.

"Thank you, Logan." Sam took his arm as if to lead him away from their rooms. "It probably doesn't seem like it, but I appreciate what you've done tonight."

"I know." He stood still. "But I'm not finished."

"I'm exhausted, Logan," she said. Her eyes, black in the soft lighting, were wide, not frightened, but wary, watchful.

He touched the back of her neck and felt a shudder run through her. Electricity arced between them, as if her neck and his hand were charged, waiting for connection. Whatever had been stirred up mere hours ago, alone in that house, flared to life, as if the intervening years, and the recent hospital scene, hadn't even happened.

"Your muscles are like concrete," he said, moving his fingers over them lightly. "Let me give you a massage."

"Logan." She turned her head. But she did not step away. "I can't. We can't."

Was it his imagination, or did she lean into his touch?

"A massage," he said. He swallowed to moisten his dry throat. "That's it."

She wilted against him then, letting him put his arms around her slight frame. Lust roared through him, but he tamped it down. If they ever went there, it would not be now and it certainly would not be here.

And it definitely would not be until she wanted it as much as he did.

He swooped her into his arms and held her tightly. "In here?"

She nodded against his chest and he carried her into her bedroom.

"Give me a minute," she said, slipping out of his arms. Without looking at him, she hurried into the bathroom connecting her room to Jade's.

He stood awkwardly in Sam's rented bedroom, wondering what exactly he thought he was doing. A lamp in the corner made shadows flicker and dance, concealing, then revealing, then transforming.

He'd let this woman tear out his heart once. Was he letting himself in for that same pain, all over again?

She bought a house. This time, she won't disappear.

But would that make it better or worse? If they were in the same town, and he had to see her at the grocery store, or the theater, or the school, without ever getting close to her again, would he be able to stand it?

The bathroom door opened and Sam stood there, in baggy pajama bottoms and a snug tank top. Nothing the least bit sexy or seductive, yet she might have been wearing a black silk teddy, for the effect it had on him.

She was ready for bed.

And he was there, poised to touch her... without *touching* her.

"Logan," she began, her voice unsteady. "Maybe you should go."

Maybe.

"Yeah," he said. "I probably should."

But neither of them made a move.

"We're not kids anymore." She crossed her arms over her chest, without taking her eyes off him. His gaze slipped. Her nipples were clearly visible beneath the thin fabric.

"I'll go if you want me to."

She swallowed, then took a step toward him. "Do you want me on the floor or the bed?"

His knees nearly buckled.

"Never mind," she said, pulling the blankets back. "I'm not sleeping on the floor."

She stretched out, face-down, and tucked a pillow under her. The loose pants stretched tight against her bottom, round in spite of her thinness, and when she wiggled to get comfortable and gathered her hair away to expose her neck, he knew he was in serious trouble.

He perched on the edge of the bed, not touching her.

"You want to give me a massage," she mumbled against the sheet. "So climb on and give me a proper one."

Lord have mercy.

But he straddled that round bottom, felt it rub up against his thighs, and higher. He leaned forward, feeling that exquisite flesh against his aching body and put his hands on her upper back.

She moaned. The sound sent a vibration through her body, straight into his groin.

"There's lotion on my bedside table," she added, then tugged the sleeves of her tank top down, just enough so he could touch her whole upper back.

He was going to die.

He forced himself to think clinically, focusing on anatomical structures, then rubbed lotion on his hands, pressed his fingers into the tight, rock-hard muscles.

Trapezius, locked up like a vault. The deltoids, knitted and knotted, the little muscles running along her spine jumping in protest beneath his fingers.

He rubbed in long, slow movements, giving them time to recognize what was happening. Up, down, then across and back, picking out the worst spots and applying gentle, relentless pressure, feeling her body warm and soften beneath his hands.

"Oh, Logan."

Sam arched herself up, pulled her arms out of the tank top and shoved it further down, still on, but exposing that whole, lovely expanse of creamy flesh.

So much for clinical.

He flattened his hands now, using his palms in wide, spreading motions. Even in the dim light, he could see her skin becoming rosy. His hands felt like they were on fire.

But still, he kept them moving.

"That feels so good," she mumbled. "Don't stop."

As if he could.

"You needed this." He struggled to find words. "You're really tight."

God. Someone, please shoot him.

But Sam didn't seem to hear. He moved his hands lower, his palms spanning her ribcage, his thumbs working into latissimus dorsi muscles narrowing toward her lower spine.

Traps, delta, lats. What else could he remember?

His hands were mere inches from that round bottom. She shifted to give him better access. He slipped his fingers beneath the tank top bunched at her waist, to get at the small of her back. She was so slender that when he opened both hands, his fingers crept around the curve, touching that delicious dip beneath the ridge of hip bone.

She quivered.

Gluteus maximus. Pelvis.

He pressed his thumbs into the tiny divots at the base of her spine, moving them just under the waistband of her pants.

She'd softened under his touch, her muscles were loose and long now. He could go now. He should go now.

He should lift himself away, climb off her bed and leave. That's what he should do. Instead, as if disconnected from his brain, his fingers crept lower, ever so slightly further beneath the elastic, feeling that rise of firm, yielding flesh, mere inches and a few thin layers of fabric away from the contact he craved.

Then Sam shifted, nudging him off and spooning against

him.

So much for the inches. Now it was just fabric.

"Sam," he croaked.

"Shh. Don't stop."

His hands were still on her hips, his fingers now further into the dip of her pelvis, his thumbs on the other side. He held her tight against him, making sure she could feel the length of him against her, know what she was doing to him.

She reached behind herself, feeling for him, but he caught her hand.

"No." He ground out the word.

"Logan."

Everything inside him was at war, screaming at him to take this, lose himself, grab the pleasure she offered, to hell with the consequences.

Only he'd promised.

Not here. Not now. Not like this.

But.

His fingers crept lower. Another shudder rolled over her. He could feel her heart thudding almost as hard as his own.

He shifted until he could touch her bare breasts, so warm, so soft. When he stroked first one, then the other, he felt the tight nipples scrape against the rougher skin of his palm, heard a short, sharp intake of breath.

He edged his fingers beneath a thin bit of elastic, until he touched silky hair, then crept lower still, and lower.

Again, she moved to give him access. He continued his relentless probing until he found her hot, slick center and the tight bud hidden inside.

He circled it with a fingertip and she arched against him. He stroked deeper, finding a well of liquid heat at her core.

She was making tiny mewling sounds now. Slowly and lightly, he moved his finger over the slippery folds, feeling that bud swell and open.

Then, she was thrusting against his hand, and the sounds coming from her muffled by the hand she held against her mouth.

Harder and harder she bucked and higher and higher her small cries until she clamped her thighs tight on his hand, quaking as the climax rolled over her.

She collapsed, letting her hand fall away from her face, her body limp against his. For a few moments, she lay there, gasping as her breath returned to normal.

Logan's was nowhere near normal.

Then she shifted onto her back and threw one arm up, her elbow over her eyes.

"Logan," she said.

But whatever she intended to say, he didn't know because right at that moment, a scratch sounded at the door, followed by a whine.

Samara tensed, then sat up abruptly.

Over the baby monitor came a small voice.

"Mama?"

ℰᏮ

SAM LEAPED OUT of bed and adjusted her clothing with shaking hands, relieved that she'd put on the good underwear that morning.

Because that's *what's important right now.*

Every cell in her body screamed at her to strip off the new panties and everything else and climb back into bed with Logan but that wasn't an option.

Still, she paused at the door and looked back at him. He remained on his side, one elbow beneath his head, the other arm lying on the empty sheets beside him.

Desire, a silent entreaty, patient and relentless simmered off him in waves, catching her in the solar plexus, nearly bringing her to her knees.

This was unfair to him, to both of them, but it was Logan her heart broke for. What was she doing, getting lost in his arms when her child was in the next room, suffering through a nightmare alone? How could she let him think that this could work?

"I'm sorry," she began.

"No." He eased off the bed. "Do not be sorry."

Sam grabbed a hoodie and yanked it on. "This should never have happened. I have to go."

She whirled around and reached for the door, but Logan got there before her.

"You needed that." He leaned down and kissed her, his tongue grazing her lip, sending her flames even higher.

"You should go. I can't... we can't... we just can't."

Another cry sounded over the monitor, small but distinct.

"She's fine, Sam," he said softly.

"I have to go!" She was having trouble breathing. "This was a mistake."

Logan touched her cheek, eased a strand of hair away from her face, his laser-like gaze drinking in every freckle and line.

"You're crying, Sam. You're going to scare her." He kissed away a tear. "Let me check on Jade."

He took her hand and before she knew it, they were following an anxious Bob to Jade's doorway.

The dog looked between the two of them for a moment, as if thinking. Would Bob even allow someone else in Jade's room?

"Mama." Faint hiccupping sobs shuddered over the small form in the bed. She wasn't even awake.

Logan stepped forward, Bob at his side, apparently giving full approval.

Samara clung to the door, watching in the dim light, as Logan perched on the edge of Jade's bed and lightly stroked the hair off her forehead.

"Hey, chipmunk, you're okay. You're safe."

Jade frowned and her eyes fluttered open. "Mr. S?" she mumbled, her lisp more pronounced in sleep.

"I'm here, honey. Your mama's here too. Go back to sleep."

Samara held her breath. This is where Jade would typically panic, searching for the one constant in her ever-changing life.

But after a moment or two of blinking blearily, Jade simply said, "Okay. C'mon, Bob."

That was it? She was just going back to sleep?

A strange mix of confused relief struck Sam. It was another milestone for Jade, to be sure. And a tiny bit of freedom for Sam, a little step toward letting go.

And the realization that maybe she wasn't indispensable, after all.

But isn't that what you wanted?

Wasn't this part of living in community? Being able to share responsibility? It takes a village to raise a child, and all that?

Sharing her child with a man, however, was different.

Samara swallowed hard, memories rushing over her. From the beginning, she admitted to herself, she'd cut Michael out of the circle. In her determination to do the best job possible, she'd done it all. No wonder he'd had trouble bonding with Jade.

No wonder he'd resented the baby and wondered if there was something wrong with her. No wonder he'd found fault with everything Samara did. Instead of gaining a daughter, he'd lost his wife, left out in the cold, with no role to play.

Grief revisited her but for the first time, it came without stirring up bitterness.

I'm sorry, Michael.

Bob hopped back onto the bed and curled up tightly next to

Jade, resting her head on the little pink-clad shoulders.

"Good girls," murmured Logan. The dog thumped the bed with her tail.

Quietly, he backed out and shut the door. In the dim glow of the nightlight, he looked down at Sam, his expression unreadable.

Logan had slipped so easily into a place of comfort and ease with Jade. And she was letting him.

Why?

Sam bowed her head. She'd made so many mistakes. She and Michael hadn't had enough time to learn how to be a family. They had failed each other and they'd loved each other and they'd kept on until death parted them.

"Hey, hey," whispered Logan. He drew her against his chest. "What's all this about?"

She shook her head, unable to speak and after a while, her silent sobs abated.

He held her away, examining her face.

She still read desire in his gaze, but it was tempered with caution. As well it should. She was a mess, thinking about her daughter and her late husband, only minutes after being intimate with Logan. She didn't know if she should invite him back to her room now or not. Away from the heat of the moment, she didn't know how to feel about her earlier wantonness.

"You should get some rest," he said, finally.

"Logan-"

"Shh." He touched a finger to her lips. "Go to bed. I'll see you tomorrow."

He kissed her again, a sweet, lingering kiss full of gentleness and promise that left her aching with longing.

When she tiptoed back into her room alone, she saw the bed, covers rumpled, both pillows indented.

It wouldn't have surprised her to see smoke rising from the

sheets.

Logan's touch had been a match to long-forgotten kindling lying hidden among the ashes in the cold hearth of her heart. She turned out the light and slid back underneath the sheets, where the ghost of his cologne still lingered. Now, with her head clear for the first time in hours, she lay back and thought about what exactly she was doing.

She was preparing to move into her new house, that's what she was supposed to be preoccupied with.

But even as she pushed Logan from her mind, she traced a path over her breasts and ribs, and lower, remembering what he'd done to her, the life he'd breathed into her with his touch, the pleasure he'd brought, with her giving nothing in return.

What would have happened if they hadn't been interrupted?

She knew the answer to that. They were no longer teenagers, hiding out from their parents, sneaking off for clandestine meetings under the bleachers.

She remembered the sound of his voice in the emergency room. How her heart had leapt when he strode to her side and put his arm around her and supported her, when she believed she had no one.

She hadn't asked him to come. In fact, she had an uneasy recollection of throwing some harsh words his way.

Why had he followed her? Was it possible that that long-ago, tender, immature passion had carried over to adulthood, for both of them?

She'd barely thought of him over the years. What was the point? She didn't know where she'd be from one month to the next, it seemed, and what teenage guy wants a long-distance relationship?

And once she was on her own, squeezing each dime, working days and studying nights for those life-changing scholarships, there was no time.

Besides, he'd probably forgotten all about her anyway. They'd moved on. He made his life, she made hers. They shared a brief, wonderful time together, then it was over.

Hot tears trickled down her cheeks.

Who was she kidding? She'd never stopped thinking about Logan; the spaces in between lengthened, that's all. Then there was Michael and the sweet, whirlwind honeymoon rush, and then right away, too soon, there was Jade and the honeymoon was over and then it was tragedy and black days when it was all she could do to put one foot in front of the other.

She'd never, in a million years, expected Logan to still be in Marietta. He'd been a mover and shaker, destined for more than a small-town life.

She certainly hadn't expected him to be single.

Knock, knock.

Samara jumped, then scrambled out of bed and reached for her robe.

"Yes?"

She opened the door to find Aunt Mabel standing there, holding her casted arm.

"Good, you're awake." She tilted her head toward the kitchen. "I need someone to make me a cup of tea."

"Shouldn't you be resting?" said Samara, following hesitantly. The way Aunt Mabel walked suggested she was in more pain than she let was willing to admit.

"I'll rest when I'm ready." She gestured rather imperiously to the cups and saucers on the table. "I don't like to go to bed with tasks undone."

Sam heated up the water and poured it steaming over the tea bags, feeling as if she'd just been called into the principal's office.

"You, Samara Kim, or Davis or whatever name you're using, are more work than I was expecting." Aunt Mabel observed her over the rim of her teacup, her expression steady, waiting.

Instantly, Sam's defences rose. "I know we're staying longer than originally planned. I'm sorry. And I shouldn't have left Jade with you. I expected my house to be ready by now and-"

"You're apologizing for the wrong things, child."

Aunt Mabel's eyes sparked. She set down her cup.

"If I had my way, Bramble House would never have been opened to strangers. Always in and out, with their muddy shoes and their noise and clutter. But there's nothing for it and I will not complain. However. Some behavior I cannot abide."

Sam looked down, feeling her face flame, like the teenage version of herself she'd just been thinking of.

But Mabel held up her good hand. "I'm referring to your treatment of Eliza."

Eliza.

Mabel was absolutely right. Sam winced, remembering her outburst at the hospital. She'd acted badly out of fear for her daughter and had hurt her hosts in the process. But she hadn't expected to be called onto the carpet for it.

"Eliza is my great-niece." Mabel sighed and shook her head. "The Bramble blood is thin in her, but nevertheless, she is family and I cannot stand by and see her misjudged. It is Eliza to whom you must apologize."

"Of, of course," stammered Samara. She recalled the tight smiles of women who would chat with her at the park, but raise their eyebrows when she needed an emergency contact name. And somehow forget to invite her to their book club.

This straightforward scolding was a shock, but refreshing too, in a way. So much better than always wondering if the other mothers avoided her because her daughter didn't always play well with others, or if her tragic loss had marked her in some way, made her defective.

"You're a tough nut to crack. That's what I meant by you being work." Aunt Mabel took a sip of tea. "I believe in being honest. And so I confess, for some unaccountable reason, I find you less… unpleasant than our usual guests."

Samara looked up from her tea. "What?"

"Now don't go reading all sorts of things into it. I'll enjoy the quiet just fine, once you're gone. Perhaps I've spent too much time with Eliza, but you and Jade intrigue me."

Mabel frowned as if annoyed at the confession.

"We intrigue you?"

"Yes. You irritate me as well and I'll tell you why." Mabel pursed her lips. "My family founded Marietta. Good people have come and gone. Many have stayed. Now outsiders seem to be flocking in, which is unavoidable, I suppose, but when people like you decide to settle in my town, you could have the decency to recognize how lucky you are."

"I am lucky. I'd never have been able to purchase a home like this in the city."

"I'm not talking about real estate!" snapped Mabel. "Marietta is full of people who'd like to be your friends if you would unbend long enough to give them a chance."

Sam thought about Sage Carrigan and the little girl – Savannah? – that Jade had played with.

Being needy scared people away.

But being walled off was worse.

"And for heaven's sake, would you put Logan out of his misery? The poor man is turning himself inside out for you."

Samara's head snapped up at that.

Aunt Mabel snorted delicately. "He's been one of Marietta's most eligible bachelors for too long. Ever since divorcing that useless ditz of a wife, we've all been watching and waiting for him to dip his toes into the dating pool again. Nothing. Then, you show up and what happens? He dives straight into the deep end, without taking off his shoes."

An image of the two of them, twined together on her bed,

flashed into Sam's mind.

"I don't wish to know details," emphasized Aunt Mabel, "but I know a man in love when I see one."

In *love*.

Samara set down her cup, sloshing tea into the saucer. "We were in love once, a long time ago. Seeing each other again has brought back a lot of memories, that's all."

Aunt Mabel regarded her steadily across the table, but didn't speak.

"He's been great with Jade, and that caught me off guard," continued Samara, feeling desperate. "I've seen him with his students, so I know he's got a gift for kids. And he's been working day and night to get my house ready because it's his job. He'd do it for anyone, I'm sure."

But would he follow just anyone to the hospital, hold her when she was fighting him off, support her despite her craziness, challenge her to try trusting people again? Ease past her defences and touch her with such gentle passion she couldn't help but –

"Oh God," she said with a gasp.

"There you go." Aunt Mabel smiled and lifted her cup. "Now we're cooking with gas."

Samara was in love with Logan.

All over again.

Chapter Ten

THE PERSISTENT TINKLING of her cell phone hauled Samara from a deep sleep the next morning. It had taken a long time to settle down last night.

She grabbed it off the night table, just as it went to voice mail. The notification screen read *A-1 Movers.*

Good. She'd been trying to get a status report from them.

She clicked the recording, and rubbed her eyes while waiting for it to play.

She felt awful for Mabel's injury, and worse for the way she'd spoken to Eliza. But Jade was fine. As self-centered as it seemed, that was the main thing.

As for Logan… knotted emotions writhed eel-like inside her. She ran a hand through her hair.

They'd crossed a line last night. Part of her was grateful that Jade had awakened when she did; part of her wanted desperately to know what it would feel like to have Logan inside her, to finally have that ache eased, to let their bodies connect the way their minds and hearts already had.

"This is A-1 Movers," said a chipper voice on the other end. "We're pleased to inform you that the truck containing your belongings is scheduled to arrive at the address you provided at 1 pm today. We're happy we were able to accommodate your adjusted date. Thank you for choosing A-1 Movers. Have a great day!"

Sam looked at the small screen in confusion.

Today?

"No, no, no," she muttered, her fingers flying over the keys. Surely this was a mistake. She'd been crystal clear that she needed *more* time, not less time! This was even worse than the original date!

"This is A-1 Movers," said the same chipper voice.

"This is Samara Davis," she began.

"Your call is important to us," interrupted the voice. And then her phone died.

"Argh!" Sam threw the device against her pillow, where it bounced harmlessly. In all the activity last night, she'd forgotten to charge it.

Activity involving Logan, in her bed, massaging her, caring for her, giving her the best-

She leaped out of bed and quickly yanked on the first outfit that came to hand. Her furniture was arriving soon, but her house wasn't ready.

She needed Logan.

Low in her belly, something fluttered. He'd know what to do. He'd help figure it out.

Mabel and Eliza were already up, sipping tea, when Samara entered the kitchen. The fresh white cast on Aunt Mabel's left hand beamed brightly in the morning sunshine, but there were heavy, bruised circles under her eyes. Had she stayed up late just for their talk?

"Good morning," said Eliza quietly. "You're just in time for French toast. Coffee's fresh, too, if you want."

Remembering the point of Mabel's speech, Sam forced

herself to slow down. She went directly to Eliza. "I'm so sorry for how I spoke to you yesterday, Eliza. You've been so wonderful with Jade. You've been kind and welcoming and I treated you abominably. I hope you can forgive me. And I hope we can be friends."

Eliza's face broke open with a smile as she pulled Samara into a hug. "It's forgotten. And of course we can be friends. We already are."

"I'm so glad." Until that moment, Sam hadn't realized how important it was to mend that bridge. "I'm so glad!"

"Perhaps," said Mabel, "I could trouble one of you to refill my cup before I perish of dehydration."

"Absolutely," said Sam. "I just have to use the house phone briefly. Is that okay?"

Dull red rose in Eliza's cheeks. "It would be, except the company is, um, doing maintenance in our area right now. A tree down or something."

"Or you forgot to pay the bill again," suggested Mabel, waspishly.

Eliza's cell phone buzzed. "Excuse me, I have to take this." She practically ran from the room, frowning at the device.

Great, thought Samara. No phone. Maybe she could borrow Eliza's cell, once she was done.

"How are you feeling this morning, Aunt Mabel?"

"Thirsty," said Mabel.

Samara dropped a kiss onto the old woman's papery cheek. Mabel shrank back and pulled the knitted throw in her lap over her shoulder, padding her bad arm. Her skin felt cool and even clammy beneath Sam's lips and she was paler than usual.

Eliza came back into the room, her phone to her ear. "I have to run. Aunt Mabel, will you be all right on your own for a few hours?"

"For heaven's sake, I don't need babysitting." Mabel looked

away, as if offended.

Before Sam could speak, Eliza scurried out the door.

"All secrets and mystery, that one," said Mabel. "That's not how Brambles behave."

The flippancy sounded forced. Sam quickly poured a cup and set it next to Mabel. The woman's hand trembled when she lifted it and after one sip, she abandoned it, cradling her casted arm again.

Were those lines of pain around her eyes?

Eliza wouldn't leave if Mabel wasn't feeling well, would she?

Sam wished she didn't have to go. But the movers were on the way. She had to tell Logan. She'd make a quick breakfast for Jade and Bob, and then head out to the house. She'd check in with Eliza on Logan's phone and as soon as they'd come up with a plan for the furniture, she'd return to Mabel.

Unable to sit, she went to the counter to fix Jade's breakfast.

Wait. She hadn't had her coffee yet. If ever she needed caffeine, it was this morning. She sloshed some into a mug and added a dollop of low-fat milk.

"Sit, Samara. Your jitterbugging is giving me a headache."

"Oh." Sam grabbed a paper towel to clean up the coffee drips she'd left behind. "Sorry."

Mabel lifted her cup, then she set it down again without taking a sip. The china clattered against the saucer.

"Are you sure you're feeling okay, Mabel?" asked Samara, sliding into a chair.

"You're the fidgety one," she complained. "Now, what's wrong? You're exhausting me."

Mabel didn't need any more trouble, but she wasn't going to rest until Sam explained.

She sighed.

"The moving company screwed up. My furniture is arriving today. Not next Wednesday. Today. We don't even have an occupancy permit yet."

In her mind, she replayed her conversations with the moving company but could find nothing to explain it other than simple human error. Hers or theirs, it didn't much matter; if she couldn't fix this in a hurry, her entire life was about to be delivered onto the Collier Avenue sidewalk.

Breathe, Sam reminded herself.

"Use the garage." Mabel sounded like Jade when she had a fever.

"The garage is full of tools."

"Storage then. Logan will be happy to arrange it, I'm sure."

Sam's cheeks warmed. "I'm sure he would, but I have to tell him first and there seems to be an epidemic of dead phones around here."

"Well, fretting won't help."

Little footsteps and the unmistakable click of claws sounded on the steps.

"Mama?" said Jade, rubbing her eyes. "Are you mad?"

"Of course not." Samara took another deep breath and forced herself to smile. She squatted next to her rumpled little girl and gave her a hug. "You sleep okay?"

Jade nodded, as if she'd forgotten her earlier nightmare. "Is that French toast, Auntie M?"

"It is." Aunt Mabel attempted a smile. "But you've got to sit beside me to eat it. Can you do that?"

"Yeah!" said Jade, clapping her hands. Before Sam could object, she hopped over to the table, inadvertently brushing Mabel's left elbow, just above the cast.

The woman sucked in a breath, squeezed her eyes shut, holding the arm tightly against her ribs, her face wracked with pain.

Jade dragged the chair out with both hands and scrambled up, oblivious to the tiny contact.

Samara, however, had seen it. "Should you still be that painful?"

Mabel swallowed. "I haven't read the rules on fractures."

"Let me see." Samara sat down next to her, taking the casted arm very gently in her hands.

The tips of her fingers were mottled, grey, and when Sam touched them, they were cold.

"Can you wiggle them?"

"I could yesterday," said Aunt Mabel. Tiny beads of perspiration had sprung out along her silver hairline.

Samara didn't need her first-aid training to see that the hand was not healing as it should. Maybe the cast had been put on too tight; maybe the tissue beneath had swelled far more than expected. Maybe there was something else entirely going on. Whatever the cause, she needed medical care.

"Who's your doctor?" she asked. "That arm should be examined. As soon as I've got some juice in my phone, I'll call the office."

The fact that Mabel did not argue only increased Sam's anxiety. She ran to her room and plugged in her cell.

Logan's scent still lingered on the bedding. She'd call him too, as soon as she could. She had to let him know about the movers.

She wanted to tell him... what?

Now in the light of day, her conversation with Mabel seemed ridiculous. Surely Mabel hadn't suggested she and Logan were in love with each other? Sam couldn't think of a less likely romantic than her crusty hostess. But she could hardly ask, especially now that Mabel was feeling the full effect of her injury.

"Mama!"

As always, the word brought her crashing back to earth.

Samara dashed back to the dining room just in time to see the older woman slip sideways in her chair, gently, as if drifting off to sleep.

"Auntie M!" cried Jade.

Sam leaped forward just in time and immediately, Mabel returned to consciousness.

"I'm fine, I'm fine." She frowned in confusion.

Samara half-carried her over to the couch. "You're the farthest thing from fine. I'm calling an ambulance."

But her phone wasn't charged yet.

"No ambulance," said Mabel. "I won't be hauled out of here feet-first for all the world to see."

"Fine. I'm taking you to the ER myself."

"I believe that may be in order," conceded Mabel weakly. "Though I may need a shoulder to lean on."

Chapter Eleven

❦

S AM EDGED SLIGHTLY over the speed limit, her pulse pounding. All her other worries faded away into nothing.

Logan would look after the house. He'd deal with the movers.

Jade, seeming to understand the urgency of the situation, sat quietly in the back seat, sucking her thumb.

"I left a message for Eliza, but we should call Sage, too." She pushed her cell phone, now on the car charger, at Mabel. "She should know what's happening."

"No!" Mabel let the phone drop into the console between them. "Not Sage. This is none of her business. Eliza's bad enough."

Sam had no time to argue the point. She left the car in the drop-off zone, an anxious Bob hovering at the cracked window. Jade didn't make a peep about leaving her beloved friend, and in fact ran to get the wheelchair parked outside the ER doors.

As soon as they wheeled Aunt Mabel inside, a team of pastel-clad workers descended upon them, some of whom Sam recognized from the night before.

"We've got her now." A clerk pointed toward the front

desk. "We'll need you to fill out the paperwork."

Helplessly, she watched them shuttle Mabel through a whooshing door marked Critical Assessment Unit.

"Mama," said Jade, tugging at her sleeve. "I want Auntie M."

Jade began tapping her sides.

"It's okay, honey," said Sam, feeling her own stress ramp skyward. She rummaged around in her bag. Thank goodness, she had an extra pack of dog cards.

"Look, I found your dog pictures."

Jade took them and spread them out on the coffee table, temporarily mollified.

Sam took the opportunity to use the pay phone, just across the hall from the waiting room. Good thing she remembered his cell number. How did we ever communicate before cell phones, she wondered?

"Hi, you've reached Logan Stafford. Please leave a message."

Samara wanted to bang the tan-colored receiver against the wall. Voice mail would be the death of her.

"Hey, it's me." How did you greet a man who only last night ...well. No need to go there. "I had to take Aunt Mabel back to the ER. Her arm is really sore, though she's pretending it isn't. Eliza's out, I don't know where and Mabel wouldn't let me call an ambulance, even though she almost passed out. She wouldn't let me call Sage. So Jade and I are here, waiting. But that's not all. There's a problem with the-"

Beep.

"Argh!" She plugged in more coins and redialled the number.

"Me again," she said, watching Jade from the corner of her eye. "The movers messed up the dates. Instead of pushing it off a week, they bumped it up. They'll be here this afternoon with our furniture. I'm going to arrange for storage unless you can think of another way-"

Beep.

Why did everything have to happen at the same time? She pressed her forehead against the cool green concrete wall. Everything in her wanted to do something, go somewhere, talk to someone.

Talk to Logan.

But she couldn't leave Mabel.

Samara thought of the strong woman who'd shown her such kindness, despite her brusque ways. The woman who'd insisted that Logan was in love with her.

She hung up the phone and went back to the vinyl-and-chrome chairs, where Jade had found a package of crayons and was busy drawing a picture.

A brown-haired woman. A black-white-and brown dog with one ear up and one ear down. A tall woman with wrinkles and grey hair.

And a black-eyed chipmunk on the back of a smiling man with a heart bursting out of his chest.

"Mama?" Sam gathered her daughter into her lap, her throat too full to speak. "Where's Mr. S?"

ഇരു

LOGAN HAD BEEN at the house since before sunrise. Working alone, he'd managed to finish painting the baseboards and much of the trim on the lower level.

He straightened up and ran a hand over his face, realizing he hadn't shaved since yesterday morning. He went to the kitchen to start a fresh batch of coffee in the pot on the floor in the corner. Students would be arriving shortly and he needed to pull himself together.

He'd barely slept the night before. He left Bramble House

aching, not just with physical need, but with hope.

Sam had opened up to him last night, trusting him with her body but – and this was far more significant – with her child.

She'd have taken him back to her room. He knew it and had no idea how he'd managed to resist. Or why. Surely once they made love, she'd fall in love with him again.

Or, she'd back away entirely and he'd lose her forever.

The sound of water trickling and the rich aroma of dark roast broke into his thoughts.

He took his coffee and walked through Sam's beautiful new house. His kids had done a fantastic job, under tremendous time pressure.

Sam and Jade were going to love it here.

Wouldn't they?

He ran his hand up the banister, that small rough patch now smooth and glossy as the rest.

She'd come here seeking peace and quiet. A safe place to raise her daughter.

Sam hadn't been looking for him, she said. She certainly didn't want to confuse her daughter by bringing a new man into their life. But on some level, she must have known there was a chance he'd still be here. His family was still in the area, after all.

To be fair, he'd never intended to stay. They'd dreamed about the life they'd make after graduation. How they'd go to New York or San Francisco, maybe Paris.

Instead, Sam had ended up in New York, and he'd settled here.

He'd left briefly, after his divorce. But life has a way of circling around, reminding you of your roots and the people you loved. So he'd come home.

Sam didn't have roots. She didn't have people who loved her, family or friends she'd made over the years.

Perhaps she'd returned to Marietta because it was the closest thing she had to everything he took for granted. And instead of a soft, peaceful landing, she'd gotten a house that wasn't ready and a man she wasn't ready for.

They'd gotten so close last night. But here he was, the morning after, wondering if he'd pushed her too far, too fast.

Whatever ache he'd felt last night was nothing compared to the bleakness in his soul at the thought of her always being around, and never being his.

ℴ∛

"COME ON BACK," said a cheerful nurse in soft yellow scrubs. "Ms. Bramble says you're family."

"Oh, I'm-," Sam bit off her automatic protest. "Thank you."

"I remember you!" The nurse smiled widely at Jade. "You're a squirrel, if I recall correctly."

Sam squatted down for Jade to hop onto her back, expecting her to bury her head against her mother's shoulder immediately.

But Jade stood close beside Sam instead, clinging to the hem of her jacket.

"I'm a chipmunk!"

She refused to look directly at the nurse and she spoke softly, but there was a distinct note of defiance.

Samara knew better than to acknowledge Jade's comment, but inside, she was cheering. In so few days, her daughter had blossomed.

"But I'm invisible," continued Jade. "You can't see me."

"Well then, I hope I don't trip on you!" She grinned and gestured for Sam to follow her.

"Thank you." Samara flushed. She'd definitely met the nurse last night and she'd undoubtedly made a less-than-optimal impression.

But the nurse touched Sam lightly under the elbow. "You

were scared for your daughter last night. I get it. I'm a mother too."

Sam shook her head, wincing. "I don't like hospitals, but that's no excuse to be rude."

"Trust me," she answered with a laugh, "you didn't even register on the rude-o-meter."

They turned the corner into a bustling treatment area with narrow beds cordoned off from each other by curtains.

"To answer your question," said the nurse, growing serious, "you were right to bring Ms. Bramble in. The swelling had gotten to a point where her circulation was compromised. We're not sure what's going on yet, but she's in the right place. And she tells us that you're the one who pushed her to come in."

As they found Aunt Mabel's bed she patted Sam's arm again. "Good job, Samara. Here you go, then. Let me know if the squirrel needs anything while you're here."

"Chipmunk!" Jade glared at her.

"I don't know what's wrong with my memory." The nurse winked, then hustled away.

Chapter Twelve

ഇൗ

I T WAS WELL past lunchtime when the rumble of a large vehicle made Logan look up from his work. A-1 Movers.

A moving van!

He leaped to his feet and ran outside to meet them.

This couldn't be right! Between a generous plumber, his students, various friends, and about a dozen pizzas, they'd managed to get the house inspection-ready, but the kitchen cabinets needed some final touches, several rooms had unpainted window casings and trim, and the entire place still needed a final, deep cleaning.

He and Principal Stern had come to an agreement, thank goodness. The permission slips he'd received from all his students' parents ensured there were no liability issues and in fact, the principal had seemed relieved that Logan had made it work for everyone's benefit.

However, even if he got occupancy approval right now, the place wasn't move-in ready, at least not the way he'd intended.

He'd always imagined his first project to be exemplary, a prototype of what future projects would be.

Having his first project go to Samara only ramped it up. He

wanted to present her with nothing short of perfection.

"You taking delivery?" asked a heavy-set man wearing coveralls and a ball-cap. "Sam Davis?"

"Uh, it's Samara Davis and she's not here." He patted his pockets. Where had he left his cell phone?

"I'm on a tight schedule," said ball-cap, his attention caught by the tools and equipment littering the front porch.

"You're on the wrong schedule," said Logan, rummaging through a pile of jackets on the porch. "We weren't expecting delivery until next Wednesday."

There it was. He grabbed the well-worn denim button-down he'd put over his t-shirt this morning. His cell phone was right there, in the breast pocket. Two missed messages from an unknown number. He cussed under his breath and hit the button to retrieve his voicemail.

The mover blew out a loud, exasperated breath. "We made a special trip to get the trailer off the broken-down rig. You'd think people would be happy, but no, it's confusion and annoyance all around."

Logan didn't appreciate the way the man's attitude, and his barroom holler made hearing his messages impossible.

"When did you last speak to her?"

Ball-cap grimaced. "I don't talk direct to clients. I do what A-1 tells me. And I never talk to the same girl twice there. Last one I got sounded like she was ready to drop this truckload in the lake."

A second man, younger and athletic, stepped out of the truck, rubbing his hand over his eyes as if he'd been sleeping. "What's the plan, Walt?"

"Unless we hear from this Sam in ten minutes, we're unloading." He glanced at his watch. "We've got to be back on the road by three."

It was almost 2 pm now.

"Hold up there, cowboys," said Logan, putting a hand on the roll-up door at the back of the truck. "Until I say otherwise, you're sitting tight. Got it?"

Ball-cap Walt glowered, then fumbled a pack of cigarettes out of his pocket. "One smoke, then we start."

"You'll start when I tell you to start."

Logan turned his back, making shut-up motions. He hit the replay button and listened.

The messages were from Sam. She was at the hospital with Mabel again and her furniture was arriving early.

As he already knew.

She must be going out of her mind.

At the hospital again, alone. But at least this time, she didn't have to worry about Jade.

His chest constricted as he recalled her unintentional revelation about the circumstances surrounding her husband's death. No wonder she didn't like hospitals. No wonder she panicked so easily when it came to Jade.

But in fact, her messages hadn't sounded panicky. She and Jade were waiting, which meant they must both be okay.

But her request for storage had been given with a note of fatalism, as if she wasn't surprised that it had come to this.

That calm acceptance had been the last straw for him. She'd grown so much stronger since he'd known and loved her before, but her chronic expectation that people would let her down had only gotten worse, it seemed.

Thus far, he hadn't exactly helped, either. But that was about to change.

He clapped his hands, gathering the attention of the crowd of kids in front of him.

"Okay, guys," he said. "We've got a lot of work to do and not much time to do it in. You ready?"

Taking an entire class out for a job like this and calling it a field trip stretched the boundaries of acceptable teacher behavior, but if Principal Stern didn't like it, he could lump it.

A cheer erupted from the group in front of him. They were great kids.

"I've told the gentlemen from A-1 they'll be back on the road by four," he continued.

The conversation had been slightly less civil than that, but his students didn't need to know that. He gestured to the sky above, where ominously thick clouds were gathering. "Think we can get Ms. Davis's possessions safely inside before the rain hits?"

Whoop-whoop chorused the students.

"Let's go, then! Burgers and fries once the truck's empty," he added, to renewed shouts of joy.

It wouldn't be the staged perfection he'd hoped to present her with, but Sam would get her house. She would see that people cared, and that not everything ended in disaster.

And that she could count on him, after all.

His students hovered around the back of the truck, their arms open to receive boxes and smaller items. Walt and his tough-guy assistant began moving the heavier things inside – couch, table and chairs, Sam's disassembled king-size sleigh bed, Jade's twin princess bed, and the associated dressers and night tables.

Gradually, the truck emptied and the house filled. The echo disappeared and in its place was the sound of boisterous enthusiasm and teamwork.

Finally, with a honk and a wave, Walt pulled the A-1 moving van away from the curb and it was over. Samara's things were all inside, jumbled and disorganized, but there, safe and sound.

And, just in time. Logan stood at the door, watching the truck drive away. Just as they turned out of sight, a crack of thunder sounded and the skies opened above them. The soft golds of evening disappeared like a blown-out candle and the air grew cold. Lightning made the sheets of rain show up like a matrix against the shadowy neighborhood.

Logan checked his phone. No new messages. He tried her cell phone again but she didn't pick up. No service at Bramble House. Eliza's cell went to voice mail as well.

Were they all at the hospital? Still?

Then a thumping, bumping noise sounded from inside the house, followed almost immediately by shouts.

"Mr. S!" yelled Gabi. "Come quick. Josh just fell down the stairs!"

₮⃒℞

JADE HAD SPENT the ever-darkening afternoon playing with her cards, sorting them into different piles – terriers, hounds, white dogs, brown dogs, long tails, short tails – but her time limit was about to run out.

Sam checked the window for the millionth time, watching the rain beat sideways on the glass. She couldn't have ordered up a worse moving day if she'd tried.

It turned out that a clot had formed deep in Mabel's arm. They suspected she may have suffered a transient ischemic attack – a mild stroke – as well. The nurses had been great about bringing Sam any news. Mabel was still undergoing diagnostic tests, a lengthy process requiring permission and signatures at every turn, but even without that, Sam didn't want to leave. Other than Eliza, still missing in action, and Sage, who Mabel wouldn't let her contact, she didn't seem to have anyone else.

Sam couldn't help but feel disappointed that Logan hadn't shown up to check on them. He knew they were here.

Then again, she'd left her furniture debacle in his hands. And now with the storm, who knows what sort of disaster he was dealing with. He had more than enough trouble without having to worry about her. And it was her own fault for not charging her phone.

She just wanted to talk to him.

"Mama, I'm hungry. I want junk food."

They'd already been to the cafeteria twice but Jade needed more than fruit, cheese and yogurt. Jade had made her desires crystal clear: saturated fat and white death, i.e.: mac and cheese, followed by dye and sugar, i.e.: Jell-O.

"We're going home soon, honey," she responded. "We'll eat then."

But Jade had that unerring ability to recognize when she was being fed a line.

"You said that two times before, Mama." One hand began slapping lightly at her side. "I'm hungry now. Where's Auntie M? I don't want to be at the hospital anymore. I miss Bob."

Before Sam could respond, the doors into the ER whooshed open and a group of kids burst in. In the middle of the group was a red-faced boy who appeared to be arguing with the rest of them. Sam recognized them, at the same time they saw her.

"Hey Ms. D," called Gabi. "Here you are! Mr. S has been trying to find you."

"We were working at your place and Josh fell down the stairs," added Robbie.

"And I'm fine!" snapped Josh.

"Mr. S?" said Jade, perking up at the name. "Where is he?"

"He's parking the car, chipmunk." Gabi grinned at her.

The triage nurse called the kids into a room then and they followed her, all seeming to talk at once.

The door whooshed again and this time, it was Logan. When he saw Sam, his eyes widened. He ran to her and caught her up in his arms.

"Are you okay? How's Mabel? Oh Sam, I'm so sorry I

couldn't get here sooner. It's been chaos but your things are safe and dry."

He'd come. He'd taken care of everything. Just like she knew he would. She should never have doubted him.

Jade threw herself at his legs. He caught her and swooped her up onto his back. "Hey, chipmunk, what a day, huh?"

"They think Mabel threw a clot in her arm," said Sam. Tears filled her eyes. "Is Josh going to be okay?"

"He's fine," said Logan, touching her shoulder. "I have to take all precautions for school insurance purposes, that's all."

"Excuse me?" A clerk stuck her head out of the little window by the triage desk. "Are you with Josh Peterson? We need to do his paperwork."

Logan's face told her that all he wanted was to gather her into his arms. Instead, he hiked Jade up farther onto his back.

"Don't disappear, okay?"

"I won't."

"Good." For a moment he stood as if memorizing her, his warm blue-green gaze washing over her like a soft autumn sky. "That's good."

℘℘

THANK GOODNESS HE'D brought Principal Stern on side, thought Logan while he filled out the necessary forms, as Josh's teacher.

Jade clung silently to his shoulders and he patted her knee absently. They hadn't located Josh's parents yet, likely due to a power outage because of the weather.

Had there been a single telecommunication that had gone right today?

Was it Friday the 13th?

No. It was Thursday. The 18th.

September 18th.

Something twigged.

"I'll take that paperwork, if you're finished." The clerk paused. "Mr. S, is that you?"

He recognized her as a Marietta High grad from several years ago. Her name tag said Andi.

"Bad timing for Livingston, just before the big game," she said, running the end of her pen over the questions he'd answered. "Good for us though, am I right?"

A Livingston team member injured while working on a school project in Marietta... the optics weren't great. But hopefully it was nothing serious.

Outside, the electrical portion of the storm had played itself out, but the rain continued to fall. As soon as he reached Sam, he peeled Jade off his back.

"Mr. S, I'm hungry," said Jade, jumping from foot to foot. "I want macaroni and cheese and Jell-O."

Sam's expression was a painful sight. "I'll make you some proper food at Bramble House."

"I want macaroni and cheese and Jell-O!"

"Jade, that's enough." She tried to hold onto her daughter's arm, but the kid wriggled out of her grasp.

"Macaroni! Cheese! Jell-O!"

Logan recognized the escalation, the wild eyes, the tell-tale tics and repetition.

He caught her just as she was about to run, wrapped her up tightly in his arms and braced himself. She struggled and screamed, gathering the attention of anyone within earshot. Sam sat hunched, her face crimson, but she didn't object.

Within a minute or so, the episode ebbed, leaving Jade trembling and damp with sweat.

"Macaroni? Cheese?" she said in a hitching voice. "Jell-O?"

He stroked the child's ebony hair, smooth like her mother's.

His heart broke for her.

"Make you a deal, chipmunk." He laid his cheek against the top of her head. Then he covered her ears.

"Is frozen yogurt okay?" he whispered to Sam.

She nodded gratefully.

"Turkey sandwich, carrot sticks, frozen yogurt." Jade's stiff limbs eased.

"Will you sit beside me?" she asked.

"Sure. Do we have a deal?"

Jade sighed as if exhausted. "Okay."

She tucked her thumb into her mouth.

"Sit with your mom for a minute, okay, chipmunk?" He transferred Jade to Sam's lap. "Give me your keys. We need Bob."

As she handed over the fob, Sam grabbed his hand and kissed it.

೮೧೦೪

TO SAM'S RELIEF, Jade ate several carrot sticks and almost half a sandwich before she started head-bobbing. They'd moved to the casual seating adjacent to the cafeteria, where the dog would be allowed.

She heard a woof and looked up to see Logan striding down the wide corridor with Bob straining at her harness.

His long legs ate up the distance and he held the excited dog easily, laughing at her antics. Maybe it was the storm still raging outside, but it seemed to Sam that the whole solarium grew brighter, warmer, with his approach.

"Bob, Bob, Bob," called Jade blearily.

The dog threw herself at them, her tail thumping wildly. She pressed her head against Jade and groaned.

Logan slid onto the upholstered seat beside Sam. Raindrops

sparkled in his hair and his shirt was wet and molded to his shoulders.

"Now that," he said with a grin, "was a dog that needed to pee."

"She's such a good girl," said Sam, ruffling Bob's ears. "Thank you, Logan. I didn't even think to ask if she could come inside."

He shrugged. "That's the beauty of a small town; word's gotten around that she's a service dog, even if she doesn't have a vest."

Jade gave Bob a lick of her frozen yogurt. Sam pretended she didn't see.

"How's Josh?"

"Fine. His dad's with him, and his mom's on the way," said Logan. "Kid's going to have a nice bruise to show the girls, but nothing to affect his game. He'll get beat up far worse on the field, just watch."

Even though Sam hardly knew Josh Peterson, relief coursed through her at the news.

"Better safe than sorry though," continued Logan. "With Homecoming excitement ramping up, everyone's justifiably twitchy."

Logan had been distracted by her and Jade and Sam felt bad about that. He was up to his eyeballs in stress and work and obligations, much of which were due to her own overly-demanding inflexibility; she shouldn't keep him from where he really needed to be.

"You don't have to stay with us, Logan," she said.

He smiled, put his hand on her thigh, lightly, and ignored her.

"I talked to Mabel's nurse. They'll be keeping her for a few days while the clot-busters work, but they expect her to make a full recovery. She was already complaining about the tea, apparently. She's asleep now."

Sam dropped her head backward. "Thank heaven."

"Auntie M's sleeping?" mumbled Jade.

"Yes, she is." Logan gathered her onto his lap. "And you should be too. You've got a busy day ahead of you."

The movers!

She couldn't believe it had been the most important thing on her mind this morning.

"My furniture," she said. "What happened with it?"

"It's all fine. We got it in before the rain."

He said it so casually, as if it wasn't a big deal.

"Wait. You got it in where? In storage?"

"In the house."

"What?" She couldn't believe what she was hearing. "But it's not ready. How did you… when did you…?"

"A promise is a promise, Sam." Logan stood up, holding Jade's wobbling head gently against his shoulder. "I had to call in a few favors. Lucky for you, people like me."

"I want to see it!" Sam scrambled to her feet, nearly tripping on Bob, who responded with a yelp.

A slow smile spread over Logan's face. "It's a mess. You're tired. Maybe in the morning."

"Logan!" She punched him lightly in the arm. It was like punching concrete.

They hurried through the quiet corridors toward the parking lot.

"Here, take her, I'll bring the car around." Logan deposited Jade gently into her arms before dashing out into the rain.

Suddenly Sam's chest was so tight it felt like it might burst. She pressed her face into Jade's warm hair, her breath coming in short, sharp jerks.

She was thrilled and relieved and excited about seeing her house.

But that's not what had her in tears.

It was those little gestures, remembering the dog, carrying Jade, getting the car, that cracked her heart wide open.

Logan was with her, at her side, recognizing her needs and doing what he could to meet them, without being asked, with no expectations or fanfare.

Because that's what you did when you loved someone.

She sucked in a great gasp of air.

It was the Spider-Killing Factor.

ℰᘒ

IT WASN'T THE grand finale he'd hoped for, thought Logan, as he pulled Sam's car to a stop on Collier Avenue.

He saw her face as she stepped over the threshold, hands clasped in front of her mouth, and wondered if he'd made a huge mistake bringing her here tonight.

Bob trotted through the doorway, her ears perked. She ran from one piece of furniture to the other, sniffing and whining, her tail flapping like a flag.

At least the dog was happy.

"It's a mess, I know," he said, stepping around the couch. "We'll finish cleaning and get everything in the right place tomorrow. Inspector's coming then, too. But it's all here, Sam. I watched them unload and there's no damage."

She walked through as if dreaming, trailing her hand over things as she passed. She was sort of smiling, but she was sort of crying too. Maybe this was her worst nightmare.

In his arms, Jade twitched. It certainly wouldn't do the chipmunk any good to see such disorder. What had he been thinking?

"This is…" Sam shook her head, moving to the kitchen. "I can't believe it. Who did all this?"

"My crew, mostly," said Logan, wincing. The kitchen was the worst. "They each called a friend or two. Good kids, but not detail-oriented."

The table was piled high with boxes bearing labels such as **Bath Towels** and **Jade's Room** and **Winter Boots.** Who knows where the dishes and cutlery landed? Tools and trash littered the countertops. The new sink was covered with grime, the faucet set dull and smeared.

By the time she went upstairs, his heart was hammering in his chest. Sam pushed open the door to the master bedroom and stopped, stock still. Bob darted past her.

Instead of going in, she moved to Jade's room, her steps quickening. The canopy was up on the princess bed and the lamp was plugged in.

"Did you do this?" She gestured to the stuffed bear he'd nestled against the cushions. Her hands were at her mouth again and her voice sounded choked.

Logan nodded. Once the big items were in, he'd worked on these rooms himself. The rest of the house might be a mess, but at least this part would be clean and somewhat orderly.

Sam went back to her room and entered this time. She touched the bed frame and fingered the edge of the duvet.

"You made the beds. You put soap in the bathroom. You did all this. You found Jade's pajamas!"

She looked at him in wonder, her eyes shining. In that endless, wordless moment, gazing at each other, he felt something that could only be called synchronicity. Their timing finally clicked. The compass points of their individual lives overlapped, connected, slid into perfect union and snapped into place.

They were locked together like crosshairs on a target, no escaping the inevitable, each of them fighter plane and rebel at the same time.

He would never, ever let her go again. And he'd forever be

her captive.

"I probably put the sheets on all wrong," he said. But his spirits were soaring.

She went back to Jade's room, gesturing for him to follow.

"Put her down."

Logan laid the child gently on the bed. "Shouldn't we get her back to Bramble House?"

"Nope."

Quickly, Sam replaced Jade's rumpled street clothes with the Hello Kitty pajamas and tucked her under the covers.

"Up, Bob," she said.

The dog needed no further encouragement. She curled up tightly next to Jade, put her head on the girl's body and sighed deeply.

Sam took his hand and led him out of Jade's room, leaving the door open just a crack.

"You and I need to talk," she said.

"Those," he said, "are the most dreaded words a woman could say to a man."

She laughed and tugged him up against her.

"It's okay," she said, pulling his face down for a kiss, "because first, you're going to show me how that beautiful new shower works."

Her arms were around his neck and he could feel her breath tickling his ear.

"Then we're going to examine exactly how you put on the sheets."

Between each word, she planted soft kisses along his jawline. The throaty purr of her voice sent heat ripping through him.

"Then we're going to finish what we started last night."

ജ‌ᘓ

INSTANTLY, THE MOOD changed. As Sam tugged his shirt off, the air grew charged between them, heavy, like the moonlit sky outside her window that even after the storm remained raw and unsettled.

Logan leaned forward, but she put her hands on his chest.

"Let me look at you," she whispered.

She trailed her fingers across the hard planes of muscle and bone and sinew. This was not the body of a boy playing a pickup shirts-and-skins game after school in the park. This was a man, solid and real.

She let her fingers travel lower, to the top of his jeans.

"Sam," he muttered.

She lifted her gaze. His jaw was clenched; his eyes squeezed shut, as if he was in pain.

"Logan. I want this. Don't you?"

He laughed, a brief, strangled sound. "Since the second I saw you."

"Then kiss me."

For a moment he stood there, staring, as if he was fighting a battle with himself.

Then he swallowed, the Adam's apple bobbing in his lean, tawny throat. He lifted his hand to her jaw and cupped it, the tips of his fingers curling toward the back of her neck. Shock waves rippled down her spine.

He leaned closer slowly, keeping his eyes on hers, his gaze intense and focused. Then his lips were on hers and it was all touch and taste and pressure. She tightened her arms around his neck, clinging, grasping, unable to get him close enough or deep enough.

She felt suddenly desperate, more naked even than last night. This was a *don't-stop, never-let-go* kind of kiss.

A *my-life-depends-on-this* kind of kiss.

An *I-love-you, I-love-you, I-love-you* kind of kiss.

At least, it was for her. But was it the same for him? Was Mabel right? It was there in his actions, in everything he'd done for them, for her, since she'd returned. She wanted to believe it, but she was afraid.

"Sam," he whispered, his breath warm against her cheek. "Are you sure?"

Always so damn thoughtful, she thought.

He kissed her as if she was something rare and precious, a treasure just discovered by a man who wasn't certain of its existence, and who couldn't quite believe his good fortune now.

Time to make him a believer.

"Absolutely," she said, reaching for the button of his jeans. "But if you're not…"

He grinned then, grabbed her by the butt and lifted her against him. She wrapped her legs around his hips, biting back a shriek of laughter.

"Okay then," he said, walking them both toward the ensuite bathroom. "You mentioned something about inspecting the shower?"

He was snaking his hands up her shirt, undoing her bra, sliding his fingers down the waistband of her jeans, touching her everywhere, all at once, it seemed.

"I'm a tough critic," she said, gasping as he set her onto the cold marble countertop. The bathroom mirrors reflected their nakedness, his skin against hers, their limbs intertwining.

"I know." He reached into the shower and turned on the spray. "I'm not worried."

Chapter Thirteen

৪০০৪

THE SOUND OF knocking nudged at Logan's consciousness, but not enough to bring him fully awake. He shifted to his side, and immediately Sam adjusted her position, curling her back against him. He pulled her tight and let the sweet simmer of desire build again.

They'd made love twice more during the night and if he had his way, they'd stay in bed all day.

Knock, knock, knock.

"Logan?" called a voice.

His eyes flew open, just as he recognized the sound of a key turning in the lock.

He sprang to his feet.

"Wassa matter?" murmured Sam without moving.

"Someone's here," he said, yanking on his clothing.

From downstairs came the clatter of footsteps – definitely plural – and cheery voices.

"What?!" Sam sat up in bed, her hair adorably dishevelled, her face still flushed with sleep and lovemaking. "Who?"

"I'll find out."

ఞఌ

"Mama, you're pulling," complained Jade, as Samara brushed her hair.

"Sorry, sweetie, but we've got surprise guests downstairs."

Jade's face darkened. "Who is it?"

"Don't know yet. Let's go downstairs and find out."

She braced herself but Jade took her hand without complaint.

Sam tried not to resent the invasion downstairs. It was probably for the best anyway. If whoever it was hadn't stopped by, she and Logan would have stayed in bed and if they'd stayed in bed...

She shivered.

"Bob's hungry, Mama."

The dog wagged her tail hopefully.

Sam turned off the bathroom light, then glanced once more at the mirror, unable to resist the memory of Logan's body pressed against her. Watching in the reflection as water sluiced over his muscles, as he ran the bar of soap over her body, as he licked droplets off her breasts and trailed his tongue lower and lower.

"Mama!"

She jerked her head. What was wrong with her?

"Sorry, baby."

As they walked down the stairs, she forced herself to focus on the reality at hand. She had boxes to unpack, food to buy and – according to dust and smears visible in the bright morning sunshine – a lot of cleaning to do first.

Whatever happened later, well, there was no time to think about that now.

She followed the voices to the kitchen and pasted on a smile.

A crowd of faces turned to her. Or at least, it seemed like a crowd. Eliza was there, and Sage and Dawson, a couple of Logan's students and some other people she couldn't put names to.

Jade shrank back behind her legs.

"There they are!" Immediately Logan came forward. "Look, Sam, reinforcements have arrived. Eliza organized a cleaning party."

So she could see. They'd come equipped with brooms, mops, buckets, sponges, everything they could possibly need. They'd thought of everything.

Sam put a hand against her chest, overwhelmed and ashamed of her earlier resentment.

"I brought muffins, too," said Eliza. She stepped up quickly, her cheeks pink. "I'm so sorry about yesterday, Samara."

"You had your own worries," she managed. "This is incredible, Eliza! You didn't have to do this."

Sage frowned. "Wait. What worries, Eliza?"

Eliza's face got even redder. She was obviously twisted with guilt. "Oh, it's nothing. A mix-up at the bank, that's all. Thank goodness Samara was there to take Aunt Mabel to the hospital."

"Everything worked out," said Sam. "That's the main thing, right?"

Logan squeezed her shoulder, smiling. The compassion in those beautiful eyes and the easy grin felt like a landing pad, a safe place for her to come home to.

"Have some coffee before it gets cold," said Sage. "There are breakfast sandwiches on the table, too, for whoever wants.

She handed Sam a pretty beribboned box labeled Copper Mountain Chocolate.

"Because no one should ever have to clean house without chocolate," said Sage with a smile. "Don't open it now, though. It's not for sharing."

A groan rose from behind them.

"Don't worry." Sage revealed another box, this one without ribbons. "I brought seconds for the rest of you."

The groan turned to a cheer.

"Of course," Sage lowered her voice and winked, "I suppose you could share it with Logan. Later."

"Mama?" Jade tugged on her shirt, sparing Sam from answering Sage. "Bob wants to play outside with Savannah."

Jade pointed out the open door to where the girl was waving at them.

"Go ahead," said Sam. "There's a muffin here for Bob when she's ready."

Jade dashed off, the dog at her heels.

"Can I get you some breakfast?" Logan spoke quietly as people gathered supplies and dispersed to their various tasks. "I know I worked up quite an appetite last night."

He was pressed up against her, their sides touching. She could feel the solidness of his hip against hers, the warmth of his body, the welcome weight of his arm.

"I could eat," said Sam. "But I feel bad, all these people here, for me. Who has time to do something like this?"

She gestured to the bustling crew moving about the kitchen.

Suddenly Eliza was at her side again.

"Listen here, Samara Davis." A smile softened her words. "You're not used to accepting help. You're independent; I get that. But you're not in Manhattan anymore. You're in Marietta. We help each other out. You did it last night for Mabel. We're doing it now, for you. It's what we do. So can you just let us? Please?"

Sam laughed, in spite of herself.

"Okay," she answered helplessly. She stepped away from Logan and turned in a circle, her arms spread, encompassing the soon-to-be-friends, in her forever-home. Tears thickened her voice. "Thank you. Thank you, everyone."

"You're welcome." Eliza cleared her throat and turned away. "Dawson O'Dell, Sage told us how you clean bathrooms at home. You're not going to get away with that here."

❧❧

"WHERE ARE WE going?" Sam asked, laughing as Logan pulled her along by the hand.

He owed Eliza Bramble big-time, for organizing the whirlwind cleaning blitz that had just ended.

And then, Savannah O'Dell had begged her father to invite Jade to their house, which left Sam's evening open, perfect for the surprise Logan had in store for her.

"You'll see."

With his other hand, Logan patted his jacket pocket. His heart was thumping. He was as nervous as he had been that same day, sixteen years ago. Worse, in fact. They were adults now. The stakes were that much higher.

When they got to the high-school stadium, he led her to the bleachers.

"Our spot," said Samara.

Was he imagining it, or did she sound nervous too?

"Our spot," he agreed. "Only we'll stay topside tonight. We can watch the stars better."

"Good thinking. Grass stains don't have quite the appeal they once did anyway."

They sat down together, snug against each other. He wanted her closer.

She leaned back, resting her elbows on the tread behind them, a position that made her breasts jut out. In less than a week, he thought, her curves had gotten lusher. There was more color in her cheeks and the exhaustion lining her eyes had lifted.

"If you're planning on making a move," she said, a knowing smile on her lips, "you should know, I'm a good girl. Very good."

His throat went dry. Her voice had gone husky. If he didn't do this soon, he'd forget all about why he brought her here. There were things that needed to be said and it was now or never.

"Happy birthday, Samara." He pushed a card at her. He'd chosen a pretty card with flowers on the outside and blank inside, so he could write his own message.

She sat upright, the teasing expression gone. "Oh, Logan!"

"It's September 19, isn't it?" he said. "Happy birthday, sweetheart."

She nodded, taking the card as if in a daze.

"I never forgot, Sam. That day, I was a first-class tool, a selfish, immature kid who let you down."

She swallowed and he heard her throat click.

"I never meant things to end the way they did, Logan."

He touched a finger to her chin. Her eyes were shining.

"Open the card."

She obeyed, her fingers unsteady as she carefully unstuck the seal.

A drop of moisture trickled down his back.

She looked up and turned the card to face him, as if he was unaware of the contents.

Close your eyes, he'd written.

And with sweet simplicity and trust, she did.

It was as if his entire life leaped into rewind mode, as if the intervening years were gone and it was the two of them, innocent, certain of nothing but their love for each other, aching for a world where they could be together always.

He leaned in, cupped the back of her head gently, and kissed her.

Samara put her hand up, touching his neck, drawing him closer. Suddenly, their bodies were pressed together, his hands on her back, her arms linked behind him, their lips moving feverishly, their tongues tasting, feasting, remembering.

Then he pulled back and pressed his forehead against hers, breathing hard.

"There's something else," he said hoarsely.

Gently, he peeled her arms away from his neck. He took the box from his pocket and handed it to her, plus a second card that went with it. "Don't get excited. It's nothing much."

He saw the moment she noticed the discolored paper, the careful handwriting on the card, the yellowed tape. She jerked her head up.

"Keep going." Nerves made his voice crack.

She opened the faded card, warped with time.

True love stories never have endings.

Sam seemed to freeze. Then her hand went to her throat.

"Jonathan Livingston Seagull," she whispered.

"You remember," he said. They'd been so young. So very young. Drinking in the idealism and romantic fervor as only teenagers could, certain that no one had ever loved as they did, that theirs was the first and last of its kind.

Sam peeled away the yellowed tape and took off the wrapping. Inside was the little cardboard box, exactly as it had been that day, sixteen years ago, when he'd prepared it for her. His heart had been in his throat then, too.

"It's a little late." It was a lame joke, but he was desperate to break the silence.

Her hands were shaking so much she nearly dropped the lid. He could hear her breath, coming in quick short gasps.

She lifted the cheap gold-plated chain inside and held it up, so that the tiny faux sapphire pendant lay against her hand. For several endless moments, she just stared at it. Her chest rose and fell jerkily, and that tendon was jumping in her neck.

"I always felt bad I couldn't give it to you. It's just a cheap necklace but I thought it was hot stuff at the time. I probably should have thrown it out years ago but-"

Something hot splashed onto his hand.

"Logan," she said, putting a finger against his lips. "This is, without question, the best birthday present I've ever had. In my entire life."

Everything in him stopped, his heart, his breath, his brain, like a power outage. Then, it surged back, alarms going off, bells rushing, appliances clattering and whirring back to life.

"It is?"

The smile on her face was the most beautiful thing he'd ever seen. Pure, sincere, open and aimed one hundred per cent at him. And the tears glistening on her cheeks only made it more beautiful.

"It is. And I'm going to keep it forever. On one condition."

"Anything," he said. If, somehow, a miracle had occurred, helping her find her way back to him, he was never, ever going to let her go again.

"I'll keep this necklace forever," said Samara, "as long as Jade and I can keep you forever too."

His whoop of joy echoed across the empty field and the stars reflected their joy back down, multiplying it until it was infinite as space.

Then Logan grabbed her around the waist, dragged her onto his lap and kissed her senseless.

The End

About the Authors

After a short career as a feature writer and TV critic, **Kathleen O'Brien** turned to writing romance, and the job fit so well she never looked back. Now she's published more than forty titles, is a five-time finalist for the Romance Writers of America's RITA award, and holds an MFA in Writing Popular Fiction from Seton Hill University. She lives near Orlando with her former-journalist husband, just down the road from their two grown children and, of course, the ever-famous Mouse.

Check out Kathleen's website at KathleenObrienOnline.com

After twenty-five years of writing and submitting, **Dani Collins** won the 2013 Reviewer's Choice Award for Best First In Series from Romantic Times Book Reviews. Known mostly for her emotional, passionate Harlequin Presents, she has also published a hilarious romantic comedy, an epic medieval fantasy romance, and a pair of extremely erotic erotic romances. Dani writes anything, so long as it's romance.

Hometown Hero is Dani's debut with Tule, but look for a Christmas story late 2014 and other projects so secret that if she printed them here, this bio would have to explode after it was read.

Check out Dani's website at danicollins.com.

Eve Gaddy is the best-selling award-winning author of more than seventeen novels. Her books have won and been nominated for awards from Romantic Times, Golden Quill, Bookseller's Best, Holt Medallion, Texas Gold, Daphne Du Maurier and more. She was nominated for a Romantic Times Career Achievement Award for Innovative Series romance as well as winning the 2008 Romantic Times Career Achievement award for Series Storyteller of the year. Eve's books have sold over a million copies worldwide and been published in many foreign countries. Eve lives in East Texas with her husband of many years.

Check out Eve's website at evegaddy.net.

Award winning multi-published author **Terri Reed** discovered the wonderful world of fiction at an early age and declared she would one day write a book. Now she is fulfilling that dream writing full-time. Her romance and romantic suspense novels have appeared on Publisher's Weekly top 25, Nielsen's Bookscan top 100 and featured in USA Today, Christian Fiction Magazine and Romantic Times Magazine. Her books have finaled in Romance Writers of America's RITA contest, National Reader's Choice Award contest and three times in American Christian Fiction Writers The Carol Award contest. She resides in the Pacific Northwest with her college-sweetheart husband, two wonderful children, and an array of critters. When not writing, she enjoys spending time with her family and friends, gardening and playing tennis.

Check out Terri's website at terrireed.com.

Born under a Scorpio moon, raised in a little house on the prairie, **Roxanne Snopek** said "as you wish" to her Alpha Farm Boy and followed him to the mountain air and ocean breezes of British Columbia. There, while healing creatures great and small and raising three warrior-princesses, they found their real-life happily-ever-after. After also establishing a successful freelance and non-fiction career, Roxanne began writing what she most loved to read: romance. Her small-town stories quickly became fan favorites; print editions of her latest series were recently launched in France.

Check out Roxanne's website at roxannesnopek.ca.

Thank you for reading

Montana Homecoming!

If you enjoyed this book, you can find more from all our great authors at MontanaBornBooks.com, or from your favorite online retailer.

TULE
PUBLISHING